IN THE
LIVES ⊙ OF
PUPPETS

IN THE
LIVES OF
PUPPETS

BY TJ KLUNE

Green Creek
Wolfsong
Ravensong
Heartsong
Brothersong

The Bones Beneath My Skin
The House in the Cerulean Sea
Under the Whispering Door

IN THE
LIVES OF
PUPPETS

TJ KLUNE

First published 2023 by Tom Doherty Associates/Tor Publishing Group

First published in the UK 2023 by Tor
an imprint of Pan Macmillan
The Smithson, 6 Briset Street, London EC1M 5NR
EU representative: Macmillan Publishers Ireland Ltd, 1st Floor,
The Liffey Trust Centre, 117–126 Sheriff Street Upper,
Dublin 1, D01 YC43
Associated companies throughout the world
www.panmacmillan.com

HB ISBN 978-1-5290-8802-1
TPB ISBN 978-1-5290-8803-8

Copyright © Travis Klune 2023

The right of TJ Klune to be identified as the
author of this work has been asserted by him in accordance
with the Copyright, Designs and Patents Act 1988.

Pan Macmillan does not have any control over, or any responsibility for,
any author or third-party websites referred to in or on this book.

9 8 7 6 5 4 3 2 1

A CIP catalogue record for this book is available from the British Library.

Printed and bound by CPI Group (UK) Ltd, Croydon, CR0 4YY

Visit **www.panmacmillan.com** to read more about all our books
and to buy them. You will also find features, author interviews and
news of any author events, and you can sign up for e-newsletters
so that you're always first to hear about our new releases.

FOR HUMANITY:

You kinda suck, but you invented books and music,
so the universe will probably keep you around
for a little bit longer.
You got lucky.
This time.

In an old and lonely forest, far away from almost everything, sat a curious dwelling.

At the base of a grove of massive trees was a small, square building made of brick, overtaken by ivy and moss. Who it belonged to was anyone's guess, but from the looks of it, it had been abandoned long ago. It wasn't until a man named Giovanni Lawson (who wasn't actually a man at all) came across it while making his way through the forest that it was remembered with any purpose.

He stood in front of his strange find, listening as the birds sang in the branches high above. "What's this?" he asked. "Where did you come from?"

He went inside, passing carefully through the door hanging off its hinges. The windows were shattered. Grass and weeds grew up through the warped wooden floor. The roof had partially collapsed, and the sun shone through on a pile of leaves that almost reached the ceiling. At the top of the leaf pile, a golden flower had bloomed, stretching toward the sunlight streaming through the exposed rafters.

"It's perfect," he said aloud, although he was very much alone. "Yes, this will do just fine. How strange. How wonderful."

Giovanni returned bright and early the next morning, his sleeves pushed up his forearms. He knocked down the walls inside the solitary building to create one large room, carrying plaster and wood out piece by piece and piling them on the forest floor. By the time he finished, his face and hair were coated with dust and his joints creaked and groaned, but he was satisfied. There was merit to hard work.

"There," he said to the birds in the trees as he wiped his face. "Much better. A first step to a new beginning."

The little building soon became a home for all manner of things: sheets of metal and lengths of wires and cords, batteries of all shapes and sizes, circuit boards and microchips in glass mason jars. Other jars held hundreds of seeds of various shapes, sizes, and colors. There were old music boxes that sang little songs that ached, and silent record players without any records. Televisions, both great and small, their screens dark. And books! So many books on a variety of topics from plant life to whaling, from animals of the forest to complex diagrams of nuclear cores. They lined the new floor-to-ceiling shelving he'd made from the remains of what he'd torn down. It wasn't until he placed the last book on the last shelf that he realized he himself had nowhere to stay. The room was too full.

It wouldn't take much to expand the building, adding a room or two. But Giovanni Lawson wasn't one to take the easy route. He saw the world in complex shapes and designs, and when he looked up at the trees around him, he knew what he would do.

He wouldn't build outward.

He'd build *upward*.

It took time, as these things do. Many years passed. It needed to be perfect. There was safety among the trees and away from the harsh, blinding lights and cacophony of the city he'd left behind.

Up in the branches of the trees above the house, he constructed a new little building around the solid trunk of the tallest fir tree, the undisputed king of the forest. From there, he built several more rooms into the trees, all connected by rope bridges—a laboratory and a sunroom, the ceiling made of foggy and scratched glass, the floor of shining oak panels, and no walls. Later this sunroom would become something different.

The forest was vast and wild. He doubted they'd ever be able to find him there.

On sunny days, a herd of deer would graze on the grass

below him, and the birds would sing above him. He hummed along with their song. Giovanni was at peace.

At peace until the day his chest began to hurt.

"Oh my," he said. "What an interesting sensation. It burns."

In his lab he ran calculations. He typed on his keyboard, the *clack, clack, clack* echoing flatly around him.

"I see," he said on the fifty-second day after he'd first felt the ache in his chest. He stared at the screen, checking his numbers. It was loneliness, pure and simple. Numbers never lied.

Three more years went by. Three years of the ache in his chest only growing stronger. Three years of quiet, of longing to hear a voice aside from his own. He would look out the window of his laboratory to see that it was snowing, when just yesterday the forest had been caught in the throes of summer.

On a day that began no differently than all the ones that had come before, two people burst from the trees, their eyes wide in fright, their skin slick with sweat. A man and a woman. The woman clutched a bundle of rags against her chest.

Giovanni startled.

"Help us!" the woman cried. "Please, you must take him. Take him and hide him away. It's not safe."

And then she held out the bundle of rags.

Except it wasn't just rags.

Swaddled tightly inside was a child.

A boy who blinked slowly up at Giovanni before he scrunched up his face and cried.

"What has happened?" Giovanni asked, looking back up at the woman in alarm. "Come, come. I will keep you safe. All of you."

But the woman shook her head. "They will find us." Tears trickled down her cheeks as she stepped forward, kissing the baby on the forehead. "I love you. I'll return when I'm able."

The man said, "Hurry. They're coming."

The woman laughed bitterly. "I know. I know. They always do, in the end."

The man grabbed her by the hand and pulled her away, away, away.

"Wait!" Giovanni called after them. "His name!"

But they were gone.

He never saw anyone else. No one ever came looking for the man and the woman. Or the child. And he never saw the man and woman again.

Later, much later when the boy was grown, Giovanni would tell the boy that the woman—his mother—hadn't wanted to leave him. "She will come back," Giovanni would tell him. "One day, when all is well, she will return."

Until then, he had desired a child, and now here one was. Oh, how fortuitous! How wonderful!

Giovanni took his time in deciding a designation for the baby. It was when the leaves were changing from green to red and gold that he found the perfect one.

"Victor," he told his son. "Your name shall be Victor. Victor Lawson. What do you think?"

The loneliness he'd felt—massive and profound—was chased away as if it'd never existed at all.

Giovanni worried when Victor grew and grew and grew, but still didn't speak. He knew Victor listened to him when *he* spoke, could see the way the boy understood.

"Is there a fault in your coding?" Giovanni asked him when the boy was four years old. "Did I make a mistake?"

Victor didn't respond. Instead, he lifted his arms, opening and closing his hands, his little fingers tapping against his palms.

Giovanni did as he was asked. He lifted Victor, hugging him gently against his chest. Victor made a small noise that Giovanni took as happiness, his small face pressed against the man's chest. "No," Giovanni said. "You are as you're supposed to be. I shouldn't have questioned that. If there was ever perfection in this world, it would be you." His chest ached once more, but it was for entirely different reasons. Giovanni didn't need to calculate what he felt now. He knew what it was.

It was love.

And although Giovanni wished more than anything that Victor would speak to him, he let it go. If it was meant to be, it would happen.

It was another two years before Victor spoke for the first time.

They were in the laboratory. Victor was sitting on the floor. Laid out around him were small metal rods. It took Giovanni a moment to recognize the shape Victor had made them into. Two stick figures, one big, one small, their hands joined together. Grunting once, he reached out to fiddle with the legs of the stick figures.

And then the boy—Victor Lawson, son of Giovanni Lawson—said, "You." He pointed toward the bigger stick figure. "Me." The smaller stick figure. His voice was quiet, rough from lack of use. But it was there all the same.

"Yes," Giovanni said quietly. "You and me. Always."

PART 1

THE FOREST

A conscience is that still small voice that people won't listen to.

—*Pinocchio* (1940 film)

CHAPTER 1

A tiny vacuum robot screamed as it spun in concentric circles, spindly arms that ended in pincers waving wildly in the air. "Oh my god, oh my god, we're going to *die*. I will cease to *exist*, and there will be nothing but darkness!"

A much larger robot stood still next to the vacuum, watching it have a meltdown for the millionth time. This other robot did not have arms, legs, or feet. Instead, the former Medical Nurse Model Six-Ten-JQN Series Alpha was a long metal rectangle, five feet tall and two feet wide, and her old and worn tires had been replaced by toothed metal treads, not unlike a tank's. Two metal hatches on either side of her base opened to reveal a dozen metal tentacles ending in various medical tools should the need to operate arise. A monitor on the front flashed a green frowning face. Nurse Registered Automaton To Care, Heal, Educate, and Drill (Nurse Ratched for short) was not impressed with the vacuum. In a flat, mechanical voice, she said, "If you were to die, I would play with your corpse. There is much I would be able to learn. I would drill you until there was nothing left."

This—as Nurse Ratched had undoubtedly planned—set the vacuum off once more. "Oh no," it whimpered. "Oh no, no, no, this will not do. Victor! *Victor*. Come back before I die and Nurse Ratched plays with my corpse! She's going to drill me! You *know* how I feel about being drilled."

Above them in the Scrap Yards, halfway up a pile of discarded metal at least twenty feet high, came the quiet sound of laughter. "I won't let her do that, Rambo," Victor Lawson said. He glanced down at them, hanging on to the pile of scrap via a pulley system he'd constructed with a harness around his waist. It wasn't safe by any stretch of the imagination, but Vic had been doing this for years and hadn't fallen yet. Well, once, but the less said about that the better. The shriek he'd let out at the bone protruding wetly from his arm had been louder than any sound he'd made before. His father wasn't happy about it, telling him that a twelve-year-old had no reason to be in the Scrap Yards. Victor had promised not to return. He'd gone back the next week. And now, at the age of twenty-one, he knew the Scrap Yards like the back of his hand.

Rambo didn't seem to believe him. He squealed, pincers opening and closing, his circular body shaking as his all-terrain tires rolled over pieces of metal that had fallen from the scrap heap. Across the top, in faded markings that had never been clear, were the letter *R* and a circle that could have been an O or a lowercase *a,* followed by what was clearly an *M* (possibly) and a *B* before ending in another O or *a.* He'd found the little thing years before, repairing it himself with metal and care until the machine had come back to life, demanding to be allowed to clean—it *needed* to clean because if it didn't, it had no purpose, it had *nothing.* It'd taken Vic a long time to calm the machine down, fiddling with its circuits until the vacuum had sighed in relief. It was a short-term fix. Rambo worried about most things, such as the dirt on the floor, the dirt on Vic's hands, and death in all manner of ways.

Nurse Ratched, Vic's first robot, had asked if she could kill the vacuum.

Vic said she could not.

Nurse Ratched asked why.

Vic said it was because they didn't kill their new friends.

"I would," Nurse Ratched had said in that flat voice of hers. "I would kill him quite easily. Euthanasia does not have to be painful. But it can, if you want it to be." She rode on her continuous track toward the vacuum, drill extended.

Rambo screamed.

Five years later, not much had changed. Rambo was still anxious. Nurse Ratched still threatened to play with his corpse. Vic was used to it by now.

Vic squinted up at the top of the metal heap, his shoulder-length dark hair pulled back and tied off with a leather strap. He tested the weight of the rope. He wasn't heavy, but he had to be careful, his father's voice a constant in his head, even if he worried too much. After all, Victor was rail thin, Dad constantly after him to eat more, *You're too skinny, Victor, put more food in your mouth and chew, chew, chew.*

The magnetic camming device seemed to be holding against the top of the heap. He brushed his forehead with the back of his gloved hand to keep the sweat from his eyes. Summer was on its way out, but it still held on with dying bursts of wet heat.

"All right," he muttered to himself. "Just a little higher. No time like the present. You need the part." He looked down to test his foothold.

"If you fall and die, I will perform the autopsy," Nurse Ratched called up to him. "The final autopsy report should be available within three to five business days, depending upon whether you are dismembered or not. But, as a courtesy, I can tell you that your death will most likely be caused by impact trauma."

"Oh no," Rambo moaned, his sensors flashing red. "Vic. *Vic.* Don't get dismembered. You know I can't clean up blood very well. It gets in my gears and mucks everything up!"

"Engaging Empathy Protocol," Nurse Ratched said, the monitor switching to a smiley face, eyes and mouth black, the rest of the screen yellow. The hatch on her lower right side slid up, and one of her tentacle-like arms extended, patting the top of Rambo's casing. "There, there. It is all right. I will clean up the blood and whatever other fluids come from his weak and fragile body. He will most likely void his bowels too."

"He will?" Rambo whispered.

"Yes. The human sphincter is a muscle, and upon death,

it relaxes, allowing waste to vacate the body in a spectacular fashion, especially if there is impact trauma."

Vic shook his head. They were his best friends in all the world. He didn't know what that said about him. Probably nothing good. But they were like him, in a way, even though he was flesh and blood and the others were wires and metal. Regardless of what they were made of, all had their wires crossed, or so Vic chose to believe.

He looked up again. Near the top of the scrap heap he could see what appeared to be a multi-layer PCB in good condition. Circuit boards were a rare find these days, and though he'd wanted to pull it out when he first saw it a few weeks before, he hadn't dared. This particular scrap heap was one of the most hazardous and was already swaying as he climbed. He'd take his time, working out scrap around the circuit board, letting it fall to the ground. Such effort required patience. The alternative was death.

"Vic!" Rambo cried. "Don't go. I love you. You're going to make me an orphan!"

"I'm not going to die." He took a deep breath before climbing slowly up the rope, squeezing and locking the carabiner at each stage. The thin muscles in his arms burned with the exertion.

The higher he got, the more the heap shifted. Bits of metal glinted in the sun as they fell around him, landing with a crash on the ground below. Rambo was deliriously distracted from his panic now that he had something to clean. Vic glanced down to see him picking up the fallen pieces of scrap and moving them to the base of the pile. He beeped happily, a noise that almost sounded like he was humming.

"Your existence is pointless," Nurse Ratched told him.

"I have no idea what you're talking about," Rambo said cheerfully as his sensors blinked blue and green. He dropped another piece of metal at the bottom before celebrating and spinning around.

It was near the top of the metal heap that Vic paused to rest, turning his head to look beyond the Scrap Yards. The woodlands stretched as far as he could see. It took him a moment to find the trees that held their home, the main fir rising above all others.

He leaned back as far as he dared to peer around the side of the heap. In the distance, smoke rose from a stack atop a great, lumbering machine. The machine was at least forty feet high, the crane on its back moving deftly between the piles of metal and debris as it lifted even more scrap from its hopper and dropped it in a never-ending cycle. Vic marked the location in his head, wondering if there was anything new being brought in worth salvaging.

The other Old Ones were farther away.

He was safe.

He looked back up at the circuit board. "I'm coming for you," he told it.

It took him ten more minutes to come within reach of the circuit board. Stopping to make sure his footing was solid, he gave himself a moment to clear his head. He didn't look down; heights didn't bother him, not really, but it was easier to focus on the task at hand. Less vertigo that way.

Leaning back against the harness, he shook out his arms and hands. "Okay," he muttered. "I got this." Reaching up toward the circuit board, he gritted his teeth as he gripped the edge gingerly. He tugged on it, hoping that something had happened since he'd last been here, and it'd wiggle loose with ease.

It didn't.

He dug around it, pulling out a chunk of metal that looked like it'd once belonged to a toaster. He looked inside to see if anything was salvageable. The interior looked rusted beyond repair. No good. He shouted a warning before dropping it. It crashed below him.

"You missed Rambo," Nurse Ratched said. "Try harder next time."

Vic startled when the circuit board shifted the next time he gripped it, his eyes widening. He pulled. It gave a little. He pulled harder, careful not to squeeze too tightly to avoid damaging the board. It looked intact. Dad was going to be happy. Well, he'd be pissed if he found out how Vic had gotten it, but what he didn't know wouldn't hurt him.

Vic worked the circuit board like a loose tooth, back and forth, back and forth. He was about to let it go and try to dig around it more when it popped free.

"Yes," he said. "*Yes.*" He waved it down at the others. "I got it!"

"The joy I feel knows no bounds," Nurse Ratched said. "Huzzah." Her screen changed to confetti falling around the words CONGRATULATIONS IT'S A GIRL.

"Vic?" Rambo said, sounding nervous.

"I can't believe it," Vic said. "It's been weeks."

"Vic," Rambo said again, voice rising.

"It doesn't look damaged," Vic said, turning it over in his hands. "It's going to—"

"*Vic!*"

He looked down, annoyed, though trying to tamp it down. "What?"

"Run!" Rambo cried.

A horn blasted, deep and angry. It echoed around the Scrap Yards, the sound causing the metal heap to vibrate and shift.

Vic knew that sound.

He leaned over as far as he could.

An Old One rolled toward them, sirens blaring, the crane swinging back and forth. It crashed into other piles of scrap, metal scraping against metal, showers of sparks raining down. It did not slow. It did not stop. "INTRUDER," it bellowed. "INTRUDER. INTRUDER. INTRUDER."

Vic felt the blood drain from his face as he whispered, "Oh no."

He shoved the circuit board into his satchel even as he

squeezed the carabiner with his other hand. He dropped five feet in a second, jerking painfully when the carabiner hit a thick knot in the middle of the rope. He struggled against it, but it wouldn't move any further.

"I suggest you get down," Nurse Ratched said as she scooped up Rambo, rocks kicking up under her treads as she rolled away, dodging detritus raining down around them. Rambo squealed, sensors flashing red in his panic.

"I'm *working* on it!" Vic shouted after them, still trying to get the carabiner past the knot.

No use. It wouldn't give.

The Old One's horn blasted again. Vic grunted when something heavy bounced off his shoulder, sending him spinning away. His breath was knocked from his chest when he swung back into the trash heap with a jarring crash, the sound of metal crunching under the Old One's massive tires getting closer and closer.

Managing to regain his footing, Vic looked up quickly, already mourning the loss of the camming devices. They were difficult to make, but he couldn't do anything about that now.

The Old One appeared around the side of the heap, lights flashing. Its crane swung toward the heap. Metal shrieked as the bucket slammed above him, causing the heap to shudder. The ropes snapped against his harness, pulling him up and then dropping him back down as the tower began to lean to the right. In front of him, a large metal sheet that read VOTED BEST FOOD TRUCK shifted.

Without thinking, he reached for it.

The crane swung back around, gaining momentum.

The moment before impact, Vic pulled the metal sheet out with a harsh grunt. The bucket hit with a jarring crash, debris raining down around him as the pile tilted precariously to the left. Vic fell, the slack rope twisting around him. He spun in midair, sliding the metal underneath him, lying flat against it. Hot sparks flew up toward him, causing him to bury his face in his forearms. He thought he screamed, but couldn't hear himself above the angry roar of the Old One and the collapsing tower.

He was six feet above the ground when the sheet hit an exposed length of rebar, sending him flying. He hit the ground roughly, tucking his arms and legs in as he rolled. He had a brief moment to be thankful for Rambo's neurotic tendency to clear the ground of debris. If he hadn't, Vic might have been skewered on something he'd thrown down.

He landed on his back, blinking up at the sky. He had to move. Without hesitating, he pushed himself to his feet in time to see the heap collapse completely. Vic ran, chest heaving as the Old One blared furiously behind him.

Knowing the Old Ones couldn't—or wouldn't—leave the perimeters of the Scrap Yards, Nurse Ratched and Rambo waited for him at the edge, Rambo sitting on top of her, little arms waving frantically. Nurse Ratched's screen had turned into a line of exclamation points.

"See?" Vic told them as they left the Old One behind. "Nothing to it."

"Yes," Nurse Ratched said. "Absolutely nothing to it. I would be impressed except I do not find idiocy impressive. If I did, I would flirt with you."

He'd learned of flirting from Dad's films. People smiling and blushing when they saw each other, doing things they might not normally do, all in the name of love. He'd never had anyone to flirt with before. It sounded extraordinarily complicated. "I didn't know you could do that."

"I can do many things," Nurse Ratched said, the exclamation points disappearing, being replaced by a face with a funny smile, wide eyes surrounded by long eyelashes. "Hey, big boy. You should put your finger in my socket." The screen went black. "That was flirting. There is a difference."

Vic grimaced as Rambo wheeled around him, arms waving. "They don't do that in the films."

"At least not in the ones you have seen. Did it work? Are you aroused?" The tiny lens above her screen blinked to life, a blue light scanning him up and down. "You don't appear to be aroused. Your penis shows no signs of elevated blood flow that supports recreational sexual engagement."

"I don't have a penis," Rambo said mournfully. Somewhere inside him, gears shifted and a little slot opened up at his base. He grunted, and a little pipe extended, dripping what looked like oil. "Now I do. Hooray for penises!"

"Would you put that away?" Vic asked. "We need to get home." He looked up at the bruised sky. The sun was beginning to set. "It's going to be dark soon."

"And you're scared of the dark," Rambo said, pipe sliding back in, slot closing.

"I'm not scared of the—"

"Fear is superfluous," Nurse Ratched said, falling in behind Vic as he led the way through the forest. "I am not scared of anything." She paused. "Except for birds that want to nest inside me and lay their eggs in my gears. Evil birds. I will kill them all."

Vic pulled the circuit board from his satchel. It was still whole. Tracing his finger over its bumps and ridges, he whispered, "Worth it."

CHAPTER 2

By the time they reached home, the sky was bleeding violet, and the first stars were out. The sun settled near the horizon, the moon rising like a pale ghost. Rambo rolled ahead along the worn path, already calling out for Vic's father. Vic should've expected this, seeing as how Rambo always wanted to share the moments where they'd almost been horribly murdered, and how lucky they were to escape with their lives.

"No," Vic said after him, cursing inwardly that he'd allowed himself to be distracted. "Don't tell him about—"

But Rambo ignored him, announcing quite loudly that he hadn't been *scared,* but even if he was, that was all right. The lights were on in the ground house, meaning Dad was still tinkering down there with his record player. Rambo rolled through the open doorway and disappeared inside.

Vic looked toward the elevator near the biggest tree. He thought about escaping to his personal lab above but knew his father wouldn't be happy if he didn't at least try to explain himself.

"No," Nurse Ratched said, rolling against him, pushing him toward the ground house. "You need to tell him the truth. I want to watch as you get scolded. It brings me something akin to joy to see you stare at the floor and give him flimsy excuses."

"You're supposed to be on *my* side."

"I know," she said. "I am a traitor. I feel terrible about it. I cannot wait." She stopped. Her screen flashed a question mark. "Do you hear that?"

He glanced back at her. "Hear what?"

"I do not know. It sounds complex. It is coming from the

ground house. I need to diagnose it." She rode by him, flattening the grass on the forest floor, leaves crunching. He watched as she disappeared through the doorway.

He followed, cocking his head. He strained to hear what she had. At first, there was nothing. And then—

His eyes widened. "No way."

He jogged toward the ground house.

Electric lights burned inside, reflecting off glass jars filled with unused parts and unplanted seeds. The floor creaked under Vic's weight with every step he took. He wound his way through the shelves and piles of books and electronics. A washing machine, though it was broken beyond repair. What his father called an icebox, though it never made any ice. Dad never liked to throw anything away, saying there was a use for everything even if it wasn't readily apparent. Vic was the same way, which is why it frustrated him that his father didn't like when they went hunting in the Scrap Yards. The ground house was *filled* with objects his father had salvaged, even if he hadn't been back in quite a while. How was it any different when Vic did the same?

But he ignored it, all of it, because of the sounds that rolled over him, warm and sweet.

Music.

It was music.

But it wasn't like the music boxes against the far walls. Those were monophonic, and though enchanting, they did not compare.

A voice unlike anything he'd ever experienced before, soft, sweet. Higher-pitched, and it took Vic a moment to realize why. A woman. Above the gentle *plink* of piano keys, a woman sang about the doggoned moon above, making her need someone to love. Entranced, he followed the voice.

Vic found Giovanni Lawson sitting in an old recliner, Rambo in his lap. His eyes were closed as he petted the vacuum. Rambo grumbled happily, sensors flashing slowly. Nurse Ratched sat next to them. On her screen, a line bounced in a circadian rhythm, keeping time with the beat from the song.

On top of the wooden work bench a record player lay open, a record spinning and skipping, the voice slightly warbled but still clear.

"It works," Vic whispered in awe. "You fixed it."

Dad didn't open his eyes. He hummed under his breath before saying, "I did. This is Beryl Davis singing. Such a lovely voice, don't you think?"

Vic approached the work bench. He could hear the sound of a record turning against the needle. He bent over, examining the machine. It looked as it always had. He couldn't see anything new. He itched to take it apart to see how its innards moved to create the sound he was hearing. "How did you fix it?"

"A little love," Dad said. "A little time."

"Dad."

He chuckled. "The hand crank. Wasn't connected properly."

Vic blinked in surprise as he stood upright. "That's it?"

"That's it. Simple, isn't it? We were thinking too big, too grand. Sometimes, it's the smallest things that can change everything when you least expect it."

Vic turned around to see his father watching him. The skin of his face was wrinkled and soft, his bright eyes kind. His hair hung in white waves around his ears, his beard extending down to his chest. When Vic was younger, he'd asked why he looked nothing like his father. Dad was a barrel of a man, his chest thick and strong, his stomach sloping outward, fingers blunt. Vic didn't have the presence his father had. As a boy, he'd been as thin as a whisper, sprouting up instead of out. He'd grown into himself as he'd gotten older, but he was still awkward, his movements clipped. His father's skin was pale. His own was tanned, as if he'd been born in the sun and never left. His father's eyes were blue, Vic's brown, and in certain light, they looked black. They weren't the same. They never had been.

But this man was his father. This man had raised him.

This man who wasn't a man at all.

Dad grimaced, turning away to rub at his chest.

Vic sighed, unreasonably irritated that Dad had tried to hide the gesture from him. Though an admonition threatened to burst from his mouth, he swallowed it back down. "I told you to let me take a look at it."

"It's fine."

"It is not fine," Nurse Ratched said. "Either you let Victor look at you, or I will drill you." To make her point, her drill whirred loudly. Across her screen, the words YOU WON'T FEEL A THING scrolled. "Perhaps we should proceed with the drilling regardless. It has been quite some time since I was able to drill anything."

Dad set Rambo on the ground as the song ended and gave way to another. Vic could feel it down to his bones, and he wondered how he'd gone so long without hearing such a thing. It'd only been minutes, but he could no longer imagine a life without music like this. Those records had been an extraordinary find. He'd have to see if there were more.

"I'm fine as I am," Rambo said nervously. "No one needs to drill or open me."

"Anxious little thing," Dad said fondly, nudging Rambo with his foot. "And we still don't know why?"

Vic went to the work bench again, looking at his father's tools that hung on a board. He selected the soldering iron, hoping against hope the fix wouldn't be more complicated. "No. Wiring, I guess? A glitch in his software? Something. I don't know."

"I'm fine the way I am," Rambo muttered.

"You are not," Nurse Ratched said. "If you like, I can run a diagnostic scan to see if I can pinpoint your malfunction. Do you have insurance?"

"No," Rambo said morosely. "I don't have *anything*."

"You *are* fine the way you are," Vic told him, shooting a

glare at Nurse Ratched which she ignored completely. "There's nothing wrong with you. You're just . . . unique. Like the rest of us."

"That is called a white lie," Nurse Ratched said, her screen filled with digital balloons. "White lies are often spoken to make one feel better. I will assist Victor in this process. Here is my white lie: you are a wonderful machine beloved by many."

"Leave him alone," Vic said as he knelt at his father's feet.

"Do you feel better?" Nurse Ratched asked.

"Yes," Rambo said promptly. "Tell me more white lies."

"You are important. You have a purpose. The pipe you displayed earlier is bigger than any I have seen before."

"Yay!" Rambo said, arms raised. "I'm endowed!"

Dad arched an eyebrow. "Do I want to know?"

Before Vic could respond, Nurse Ratched said, "Victor's penis was flaccid even after I engaged my Flirting Protocol. Since I know what I am doing, it is not me, but him."

"I regret ever fixing you both," Vic muttered, motioning for Dad to lift his shirt.

"That was a white lie," Nurse Ratched said. "Your pupils are dilated, your heart rate increased. You enjoy us. Thank you." A thumbs-up burst onto her screen, with the words YOU DID A GOOD JOB! underneath.

Dad lifted his shirt. His skin was tight and smooth, without a belly button or nipples. On the right side of his chest, near the collarbone, was a small sheet of metal, the surface rough. When he was younger, he'd told Vic, there'd been a string of letters and numbers there, symbolizing his first designation. He'd scraped it off, refusing to be defined by it after he'd been given a name. He was more than what it claimed he was. For a long time, Vic had been upset he didn't have a metal plate on his chest like his father.

Dad tapped his breastbone twice with his middle finger. From inside his chest came a beep, followed by a low hiss. The hatch of his chest cavity sank inward slightly before sliding off to the right.

There, in his father's chest, was a heart. It wasn't like the heart in Vic's chest, one made of muscle that moved blood and oxygen throughout his body.

The heart in Giovanni's chest was made of metal and wood and shaped not like the organ but like a symbol of a heart about the size of Vic's fist. The chest cavity around it glowed a dull green, made of wires and circuitry. The heart itself was of Dad's own making, replacing what had been a power core nearly drained beyond repair before he'd changed it out for the mechanical heart. The shell of the heart was partially con- structed of a rare wood called bocote. Wood was typically nonconductive, but Dad had found a way to force enough electricity through it, though it required over fifteen thousand volts. To ensure conduction, in addition to the bocote, the heart had bits of silver-coated copper and brass in the shell, metal that glittered in the low light. Wires extended from the top of the shell, attaching to the parts in his chest that fed into the biochip in his head. In the exposed interior of the heart a handful of gears spun slowly. Above them, a small white strip, two centimeters wide and three centimeters tall.

Vic tapped the gears gently. His father jumped. "Sorry. Your hands are cold."

The gears looked fine for now. One—the teeth wearing down—would need to be replaced soon, but Vic had already found the necessary parts and stored them in one of the jars. He leaned closer, nudging the heart slightly so he could see un- derneath it. "There," he said, feeling extremely relieved. "One of the wires off the solenoid is coming loose. I can fix it."

"I can do it," Dad said.

Vic bit back a retort, opting for something softer. "Then you should have. I'll take care of it so I know it gets done. Nurse Ratched."

She stopped beside him, taking the plug for the soldering iron from him and inserting it into herself. She said, "Ooh. Yes. That is it."

"Gross," Rambo muttered. He nudged the side of Vic's leg. "Is he going to die?"

"No," Vic said, leaning forward, elbows resting on his dad's legs. "He's not going to die."

"Because we're going to be alive forever?"

"Impossible," Nurse Ratched said. "Nothing is immortal. Eventually, our power cell will drain and we will perish because we will be unable to find a replacement."

"But Vic will find one for us," Rambo said.

"Victor is human," Nurse Ratched said. "He will die long before us. He is soft and spongy. Perhaps it will be cancer, either rectal or bone. Or the plague if he gets bitten by a rat. Or he will get squashed by an Old One like he almost was today." Her screen blinked with the word OOPS.

"Ah," Dad said. "Is that what Rambo was shouting about before he heard the music?"

Vic sighed as he leaned forward, the tip of the soldering iron hot and red. "It was nothing."

"That was a white lie," Rambo said, sounding proud of himself.

Victor groaned as he pressed the soldering iron against the wire connecting the solenoid. Dad grunted, but otherwise stayed still. "It wasn't even close. I knew what I was doing."

"The expression on your face when the metal heap collapsed suggested otherwise," Nurse Ratched said. "Would you like to view the reenactment I created right this second?"

Vic pulled the soldering iron away from the solenoid as he looked back. On her screen, an eight-bit version of Vic appeared atop a tower of metal. A word bubble sprang from his mouth, filling with OH NO I AM STUPID AND ABOUT TO DIE. The little character fell to the ground with a bloody smack, his eyes turning to X's.

"Womp womp," Nurse Ratched said as the screen darkened. "That is exactly what happened. Please do not hold your applause. I need validation."

"You fell?" Dad asked, eyes narrowing.

Vic went back to the soldering. "Only a little bit."

An odd note filled his father's voice. "Did you get hurt? Cuts, scrapes? Did you bleed?"

"Why?" Vic asked. "You need more?" The heart—while a marvel of engineering unlike anything else that had been created—sometimes needed more than metal or wiring to function: a drop of blood, pressed against the white strip above the gears. It did not happen often—at most, once a year, but Nurse Ratched never failed to remind them that according to lore, a creature known as a vampire subsisted on the same thing. The last time had been four months before, when Dad had started acting more robotic, more like a machine.

Dad said, "Victor."

"Not even nicked," Vic assured him.

Dad nodded, obviously relieved. "Good. And the Old Ones?"

Vic shrugged. "You know how it is. They forget I even exist as soon as I leave the Scrap Yards. Out of sight, out of mind."

Dad sighed. "I wish you wouldn't go there. I told you—"

"Should have thought of that before you built this place so close to one. That's on you. Not me."

"Cheeky git," Dad said. "Anything worth finding?"

"Multi-layer PCB. Looks mostly intact too."

Dad whistled lowly. "That's rare." He grimaced again as the wire fused back with the solenoid. Vic was careful with the closeness to the heart. It was a fragile thing. He made sure the wire had cooled enough so it wouldn't burn the wood before setting it back gently where it belonged.

"See?" Vic said. "Nothing to it. You should have let me take care of that a long time ago."

"Noted," Dad said. He tapped against his breastbone once more, and the hatch slid closed. The seams filled. Vic rose to his feet as Dad dropped his shirt back down. "I need you to be careful, though. You can't take chances that put you in danger."

Vic sighed as he went back to the work bench. Beryl Davis was singing in a crackly voice about what a fool she used to be. "I can take care of myself." It was a conversation they'd had time and time again. He doubted it would be the last. He held onto the soldering iron, waiting for it to cool.

"You can," Dad agreed quietly. "But that doesn't mean you're not breakable. If the Old Ones got ahold of you—"

"They won't. I'm quicker than they are. Smarter too. They're machines."

"As am I."

Vic winced. He hadn't meant it like that. He sometimes spoke without thinking things through, though he was trying to get better at it. "You know what I mean. They're not—they have their programming. They're guided by it, and can't leave the Scrap Yards."

"They're still dangerous, Victor. And the sooner you realize that, the better off you'll be."

Vic ground his teeth together, calming himself by breathing in through his nose and out his mouth. "I know that. But if I hadn't gone to the Scrap Yards, I never would have found Nurse Ratched or Rambo. We wouldn't have half the stuff we have now. You would have run out of crap to tinker with a hell of a long time ago." He nodded toward the spinning record. "And we wouldn't be hearing this."

Dad didn't reply.

Vic slumped, struggling to find the words to get his point across without sounding petulant. "You know I'm right. I stay in the forest. I don't go beyond the boundaries, and I've never pushed. I know you have your reasons, and that it's not safe to cross the borders. I listen to you. I do. Which is why you should listen to me when I say I don't need—*want* more than what I have." He waited to see if Nurse Ratched would call him out for it. He wasn't lying, not exactly, more in a gray area, skirting the edges of truth though he didn't necessarily mean to.

She didn't say a word.

His father did. "At least not yet."

He turned around, his father looking as old as Vic had ever seen him. He felt like he was missing something. "What?"

Dad smiled tightly. "I don't expect you to want to stay here forever. It'd be selfish of me to think otherwise. You say you're happy. I believe you. But happiness isn't something that can be sustained continuously, not without something to keep the fire burning." In moments when Dad spoke like this, about what else was out there, Vic wondered about the people who had left him behind as an infant. What they had been like. Looked like. Did they laugh? Did they like music and tinkering for hours? Were they smart? Kind? What had made them trust Giovanni, a stranger in the middle of the woods, and who had been after them? Logic—the cold, brutal logic of a machine—dictated they were dead. They'd have returned by now if able to do so. They hadn't.

He knew the woods. He knew his friends, their home. Giovanni, his father, the man to whom he wanted to prove that needing and wanting were two different things. Though he sometimes pushed against the perceived boundaries Dad had placed around him, their existence brought him a level of comfort. The stories Dad had told him—stories of cities made of metal and glass, and the humans therein. He'd read every book Dad had brought to this place—more than once—old stories of kings and queens in castles, of adventures on the high seas in great ships with flags billowing in the salty air, of people going to the stars and getting lost in the vast expanse of the universe. They were ghosts, but he did not feel haunted by them. The world beyond the forest was an unknowable thing, and though curiosity tugged at him every now and then, Victor was stronger than it was. He had a home, a purpose, a lab all his own, and friends that loved him for who he was, not what he wasn't. Loneliness wasn't a concept he understood, not really, not like his father had when he'd first come to the forest. He, like Dad, was an inventor. If he needed someone—some*thing*—new to talk to, all he had to do was make it. He had the parts. He'd done it with Nurse Ratched, and then with Rambo. He could do it again, if need be. Some of the old books told stories of people yearning for more and setting off to find it and themselves. Vic always thought they were silly that way. He never wanted to go far from home.

He said, "You trust me."

"I do."

"Then trust me to know what's right for myself." He moved until he stood above his father. Vic reached down, squeezing Dad's shoulder.

Dad put his hand on top of Vic's. "You're a good boy. A bit foolish, perhaps, but a good boy nonetheless."

"Learned it from you," Vic said.

"I'm also good," Rambo said.

"Unbearably so," Nurse Ratched said. "Though you seem to be suffering from an intense anxiety disorder. But that is fine. We are all unique. Victor is asexual. Giovanni is old. And I have sociopathic tendencies that manifest themselves in dangerous situations."

"Hooray!" Rambo squealed. "We all have things!"

Giovanni smiled as he shook his head. "What a strange existence we find ourselves in. I wouldn't change it for anything in the world."

The robots stayed with Dad, listening as Beryl Davis sang about love and loss. Vic left them behind in the ground house, looking down at the circuit board as he walked toward the elevator. He flipped the board over. The bottom left corner had a hairline crack in it, but that was an easy fix.

He stepped onto the wooden lift. The gate closed behind him as he pressed a button on one of the struts. Sodium arc lights lit up above him as the elevator rose from the forest floor to a midpoint below the canopy. The gate swung open, and Vic stepped off.

The ground house was just the beginning.

His father, in his infinite wisdom, had built a tree house of sorts, though far grander and more complex than any Vic had ever read about; even more spectacular than ones in books like *The Swiss Family Robinson*. Six massive trees grew in a vague circle, and all were connected by wooden rope bridges. In the tree to Vic's left was his father's lab, the largest of the dwellings built around the king of the forest. The structure on the second tree was Dad's living quarters, stuffed to the gills with more scraps and tools and books. The highest building in the third tree was a makeshift kitchen, though Vic was the only one who used it. Once a sunroom, it now had a working electric stove and an old table set and chairs covered in carvings of birds and flowers and leaves. In one corner sat a large metal freezer that kept meat Vic had hunted from spoiling. Attached to the kitchen were facilities: a shower with rainwater that never got hot enough and a toilet that Nurse Ratched was far too interested in, especially when she inquired about the consistency of Vic's bowel movements. He'd tried to explain to her that some things were meant to be private. "So you say," she'd told him. "But then you will come to me leaking saltwater from your ducts after you have found blood in your stool, and where will you be then?"

He hadn't known how to answer that.

The fifth tree held Vic's own lab, smaller than his father's, though no less extraordinary. The final tree, to the right of the elevator, held Vic's room. One of his first memories had been his father building it while Vic watched, handing over whatever tools Dad had asked for. He remembered being excited the first night he got to stay there on his own, though he couldn't find the words to say as much. He'd planned on staying up as late as he could, especially since Dad wouldn't be able to tell him to go to sleep. He'd lasted five minutes before he made his way back to Dad's room, crawling into bed with him. Later, much later when he was older and perhaps a little wiser, he'd asked his father why he had a bed when he didn't sleep like Vic did. Dad had said it made him feel more human.

Vic shook his head as he crossed the bridge to his room, thoughts tumbling end over end, though there was an order to the chaos. Pushing open the door, he stepped inside, closing it behind him.

Going to the room's only window, he looked down at the ground house. Dad had built a section of skylights surrounded by solar panels for power. But the ground house was the only building with skylights, and below, he could see Dad in his chair, Nurse Ratched poking Rambo with one of her tentacles. He left them to it, stepping away from the window.

In the center of the room was a tree trunk with knobby protrusions that had once been branches. Beyond the tree trunk in the right corner, a wooden bedframe with a lumpy, worn mattress. On the walls hung retired tools that no longer functioned; Vic was unable to bring himself to throw them away. It was a trait Vic had learned from his father, the idea of junking something rankling them both. What was broken could someday be repaired if need be, and if they had the right parts.

He lifted his shirt above his head. He frowned when he saw the hem had a small tear in it. He'd have to have Nurse Ratched sew it up again. The fabric was thinning, but it wasn't quite yet ready for the rag pile. He folded it, setting it on the small dresser near the bed.

Flipping the circuit board once more, he sank to his knees before lying flat on his stomach, looking under the bed. There, in a dark and dusty corner, sat a metal box, a perfect cube. Pulling it out with a grunt, Vic sat back up, looking toward the window as he heard the sound of music still playing in the ground house below.

It wasn't that he didn't *want* them to know what he had hidden inside, at least not yet. He hadn't been ready to put it to use. But now that he had the circuit board, maybe it'd finally work.

He punched a code into the numeric keypad on top of the box, each press of the key causing a number to pop up on the display. The box beeped three times. The lock clicked. He opened the lid.

Inside, resting on an old cut of cloth he'd found among his father's collection, sat a mechanical heart.

It wasn't much like the one in Dad's chest. That heart had been constructed by a master craftsman in his prime. Perfectly designed, but even machines wore down after years of use. Dad's heart was old. It wouldn't last forever. One day, the strain would become too much, and the heart would fail.

This new heart—crude and sophomoric and indescribably human—was a contingency plan. Just in case. He'd started building it when he was fifteen years old. He'd had no idea what he was doing.

Vic had made mistakes in the construction. The wood he first used—oak—had cracked and split. It wasn't until he got his hands on some bubinga wood from the Scrap Yards that he'd found the perfect conductor. Inlaid in the wood was nickel-coated copper. Not as good as the silver-coated, but it'd do in a pinch, replaceable if need be.

The shape of the heart wasn't exact. The point at the bottom had chipped off, and Vic had been forced to sand it down. Still, the gears in the interior of the heart were without a single fleck of rust. He turned the largest gear in the middle, marveling at how it caused the five other, smaller gears to turn in tandem. The synchronicity of it was profound. The clack of the teeth sounded better than any music coming from a record player. The music of the gears was life.

He set the board carefully next to the heart before closing the lid. The display beeped once more as the box locked. He pushed it back under the bed to the far corner. Even Rambo wouldn't find it, given that he was scared of the dark. It would go unnoticed until it was time for Vic to present it to his father.

Soon.

He stood, knees popping. He scratched his bare stomach. He needed to eat before he slept. Shower too. As he walked across the rope bridge, he remembered the Old Ones dropping new scrap in the yard. Tomorrow, or the day after. He'd see if there was anything useful. *Who knows,* he told himself as the rope bridge swayed under his feet.

CHAPTER 3

But it was another week before Victor returned to the Scrap Yards. If he hadn't known better, Vic would've thought Dad was keeping him busy to stop him from going back. There was always something that needed to be repaired or tuned up. The solar panels needed checking. The waste containers needed emptying. Some of the pipes needed snaking. The garden behind the ground house needed to be weeded, the fruits and vegetables harvested before they began to rot.

He did it all without complaint. The moment one part of their existence broke down, it could lead to complete system failure. Dad had taught him that early on.

Summer was dying. The mornings had become chilly, and the leaves in the trees were turning gold and red even as their edges were covered in layers of frost. Days were shorter, the sun weaker. Vic thought the snows would come earlier this year.

"I hate snow," Rambo muttered as he sucked up a pile of weeds Vic had tossed toward him. "It gets in my insides and makes me cold."

"You cannot feel cold," Nurse Ratched said. "You are incapable of feeling anything at all." Her screen displayed a sad face, a digital tear streaking down. "That must devastate you."

"He can feel things," Vic said, trying to ward off what he was sure would be yet another meltdown. "I made him that way. Just like I did you."

Rambo chirped smugly as he gathered more weeds, sucking them in. "Ha. See? I knew it." He beeped. "Uh-oh. I'm full. I need to be emptied."

Nurse Ratched picked him up off the ground, pulling out his container filled to the brim with weeds. She dumped it into a burn barrel next to the garden before sliding Rambo's container back in place and setting him down. "He is just saying that to make you feel better. Though, if he is speaking the truth, it does beg the question."

"What question?" Rambo asked.

"Why he made you so neurotic."

"I am *not* neurotic!"

Nurse Ratched plucked a weed from the burn barrel and dropped it on the ground. Rambo frantically scooped it back up. "Neurotic," she said flatly. "I have an injection for that. Would you like me to administer it? The needle is quite large and is meant to go into places that will not be pleasant."

"No injections," Vic said without looking up.

Nurse Ratched made a rude sound, almost like she was scoffing. "It has been a long time since I have been allowed to administer injections. Victor, you are due for your own inoculations soon. Should we take care of that right now?"

"I'm fine."

"Will you be fine when you have scurvy? I have cevitamic acid ready."

"I'm not getting scurvy."

"Are your teeth loose?"

"No."

"Are your eyes bulging?"

He didn't think so. He blinked rapidly just to make sure. "No."

Nurse Ratched whirred and beeped. Then, "In addition to scurvy, you appear to have symptoms of delusions. Your eyes are always bulging. Prepare for inject—oh, look. A squirrel. It is rabid. Come here, squirrel. I will heal you. Engaging Empathy Protocol. There, there, squirrel. There is nothing to fear. It will only hurt for thirty-seven point six minutes. After, I will give you a treat for being such a good squirrel." She chased after it through the trees, the squirrel chittering in fright.

Vic glanced at Rambo when he didn't hear the vacuum moving. Rambo had his arms extended and bent awkwardly, his pincers before his sensors. "Are you okay?" He had learned how to read his friends over the years, but it still took an effort. Thankfully, they were usually patient with him.

"I can feel things, right?" Rambo asked, slowly opening and closing his pincers. They clicked.

"Yeah. Of course you can. Come here."

Rambo came, avoiding a pile of weeds he had yet to pick up. He stopped next to Vic, who reached down and rubbed along the top of his black casing, fingers tracing over the faded letters. "You feel that?"

"Yes," Rambo said promptly. "You're touching me with your hands."

"And how does that make you feel?"

The robot hesitated. "Itchy. And warm. Like I'm full of garbage again, but I was just emptied, so that can't be it."

"That's happiness," Vic said, though he wasn't quite sure.

"Whoa," Rambo said. "*That's* what that is?"

"I think so. You're happy when you're full, because you know you've done a good job. It's kind of the same thing."

Rambo raised his arm, pinching Vic's wrist gently. "Do you feel that?"

"I do."

"And what does it feel like?"

"Itchy. And warm."

"Like you're full of garbage," Rambo whispered in awe.

"No, that's—I didn't—" Vic shook his head. "Yeah, like I'm full of garbage."

"Why do we feel this way?" Rambo asked, pulling on Vic's skin.

"I don't know," Vic admitted. "We just do, I guess."

"Wow," Rambo said, letting go of Vic's wrist and extending his arm behind him. He picked up a few weeds and shoved them toward Vic's face. "Here. Put this in your mouth compactor. See if it makes you itchy and warm too."

"I'm not going to eat that."

Rambo beeped, a quizzical little sound. "But why? Don't you want happiness?"

Before Vic could reply, Nurse Ratched came rolling back. Her treads were covered in gore and bits of gray hair. "The squirrel has been treated," she announced, her screen displaying the words ANOTHER SUCCESSFUL PATIENT INTERACTION. "It no longer has rabies and has gone to stay at a farm in the mountains with the other squirrels where it will live happily ever after. Disengaging Empathy Protocol. I feel empty inside."

"Is it your sociopathy?" Rambo asked nervously as Vic turned his face toward the sky, praying to whatever would listen for the strength to go on.

"Perhaps," Nurse Ratched said. "I will have to get back to you on that after a self-diagnosis. What are we talking about?"

"Vic is full of garbage!" Rambo cried.

"Yes," Nurse Ratched said. "He is. It is an affliction that cannot be cured."

They finished the garden in early afternoon. The turnips and beans needed another week or so before they could be harvested. The same for the cranberries and pumpkins. The rest had mostly been picked clean and stored in the kitchen: broccoli, persimmons, beets, and squash.

Dad was locked away in his lab, where he spent most of his days. If Vic was lucky, he wouldn't come out until nightfall.

Nurse Ratched and Rambo followed him up to his room as he packed his satchel, mourning the loss of the camming devices the week prior. He hadn't had time to build more, so there'd be no climbing today. Maybe they'd still be salvageable. It'd be a pain to find them, but if they hadn't been crushed, their batteries should have drained enough for them to beep in warning.

"We're going back?" Rambo asked, sounding incredulous. "But we almost died!"

"No risk, no reward," Vic told him as he spooled thick and fibrous rope, storing it inside Nurse Ratched.

"The reward is staying functional." He paused. "Do robots go to heaven?"

Vic blinked, thrown off-kilter by the conversational whiplash. "What? Where did you—" He stopped. "*Top Hat.*" A film that Rambo was enamored with, even though the disc was degraded so much that the screen skipped and jumped more than it stood still. A man and woman danced cheek to cheek, singing about how they were in heaven. "I don't know, Rambo. I don't even know if heaven exists."

"Oh. Why not?"

"Because it's just a story."

"So what happens when we stop functioning?"

"I don't know that either."

"I could assist you in that regard," Nurse Ratched said. "There would be minimal screaming involved."

"We're not killing anyone today," Vic told her.

"Tell that to the squirrel," Nurse Ratched said. "Oh. Wait. You cannot. Because it is dead."

"Oh no," Rambo whispered. "What happened to the farm?"

"I lied," Nurse Ratched said. "I killed it by rolling over it again and again. I only left enough for stew for Vic. Is that not fun? I am having fun."

Vic led them to a different entry point to the Scrap Yards in case the Old Ones were still stalking about the area they'd been in last. The Scrap Yards stretched miles in every direction. Vic hadn't explored every bit of it, but he and his father had mapped as much as they could.

He stopped on the edge of the forest where grass yielded to dirt and metal. The nearest Old One looked to be a quarter of a mile away. They were in luck.

"Nurse Ratched," Vic said. "Pull up the grid. Focus on 3B."

Her screen filled with green lines overlaying a rudimentary map of the Scrap Yards. It'd taken years to get as much of the map filled as they had, divided up into quadrants. The far corner of the map was dark. They'd never gotten that far, though not for lack of trying.

The camming devices they'd had to abandon the week before were in quadrant 6A. The Old Ones had seemed to be dumping new material around 3B. If they were lucky, they wouldn't need camming devices as the piles wouldn't be too high yet, so they could start there and then swing down to 6A on their way home to check and see if anything could be salvaged.

He studied the map as Nurse Ratched enhanced 3B and made a plan. Absentmindedly nudging his foot against Rambo, Vic said, "All right. What are the rules?"

"Stick together!" Rambo said.

"Run if we have to," Nurse Ratched said as the map disappeared.

"No dallying!"

"No drilling," Nurse Ratched said, sounding extraordinarily put out.

"And above all else, be brave!" Rambo finished, his sensor lights blinking furiously.

"Be brave," Vic echoed quietly.

They made their way through familiar territory. Rambo was humming to himself as he rolled next to Vic. Nurse Ratched paused every now and then to scan something new to add to the layout of the map.

When they reached 3B, Vic stopped and frowned at what the Old One had been dumping the week before.

It wasn't the usual scrap.

"What is this?" Vic asked, taking a step closer. It took him a moment to make out the specific shapes in the jumbled mess. It wasn't until he saw a metallic arm extended near the ground, a finger curled as if beckoning, that he recognized it for what the pile was.

Robots.

Androids.

Humanoid, though not like Dad. These had been stripped of their skin, if they'd had any at all.

They were all broken apart. Heads without bodies, the bulbs in their eye sockets dark, some of them shattered. Legs. Arms. Torsos. Exposed wiring and components, all fried to a crisp. Chest cavities had been ripped open, all batteries and power cores removed. They'd been destroyed.

This wasn't a scrap pile. It was a graveyard.

"I don't like this," Rambo said nervously. "Bad. Bad, bad, bad."

Even Nurse Ratched sounded disturbed as she scanned the androids. "I am not picking up any energy sources. They are all—wait." She rolled closer, the light of her scanner narrowing as it focused. "There is something there. Deep. In the middle. Energy, but it is almost depleted."

"What is it?" Vic asked, coming to stand beside her. He felt cold as his boot nudged against a leg and foot that was missing two of its metal toes.

"I do not know," Nurse Ratched said. Her screen filled with question marks as she finished scanning.

"How deep?"

"Six feet, seven inches."

"Keep an eye out, will you?"

"Yes."

Vic stepped toward the pile of metallic bodies. The Scrap Yards were quieter than they should have been. The air was thick and heavy, and a trickle of sweat rolled down Vic's forehead. He wiped it away.

He started with a head. It was heavier than he expected it to be. The eyes were intact, though the bulbs looked as if they'd been burned, the glass smoky, the filaments blackened. He turned the head over in his hands. The back of the skull had been torn away, leaving an empty, ragged hole. He stared at it for a long moment, studying the face. He hadn't seen another face in a long time. Dad's, sure. Nurse Ratched, whenever she flashed an approximation of one on her screen. Rambo didn't have a face, though his sensors and lights made up for that. But this was different. It didn't look like him. It didn't look like anyone, really. He didn't know how he'd react if he'd seen it while it was still alive. As it was, he was having a hard time looking at its dead eyes.

He set it aside, ignoring the hairs standing on end at the back of his neck.

It should have gotten easier after that.

It didn't.

He tossed more heads. Arms. A chest that looked too small to belong to an adult-sized android. Bots of all different sexes, some sexless. In a daze, he dug deeper, blood rushing in his ears.

There were other pieces that looked salvageable, but he ignored them for now. If there was some kind of power core still active, they needed it, especially since it seemed to have some juice left. He couldn't turn away from power. Not when it was so close. It could lead to the creation of another mechanical heart. And when that thought entered his head, it refused to leave, bouncing around his skull.

He took a break an hour into it, sitting on the ground, watching as Nurse Ratched held up a discarded arm toward

Rambo. "How do you do," she said in that queer, flat voice of hers.

"It's nice to meet you," Rambo replied, reaching up with his pincers to grab the hand.

Which, of course, Nurse Ratched immediately dropped. "Aaaaaaaahhhh," she said. "You tore off my arm. You have killed me. Why, Rambo, why."

Rambo screamed in terror. "Oh my god, oh my *god*. What have I done? What kind of monster *am I*?" He flung the arm as hard as he could. It flew up . . . and crashed back down on top of him, setting him off all over again.

"Ha, ha," Nurse Ratched said as her screen filled with a smiley face. "Just kidding. That was not really my arm. I am still alive."

"Don't do that," Rambo scolded her. "You scared me. I thought I was a murderer. Vacuums aren't allowed to be murderers!"

"Too bad," Nurse Ratched said as her screen darkened. "You would make a good murderer. Not as good as me, but good enough." A halo appeared on her screen, surrounded by golden light. "Not that I would murder. Engaging Empathy Protocol. Murder is bad, and I would feel bad, and I don't want to feel bad because feelings are detrimental to my existence."

"Keep telling yourself that," Vic muttered as he picked himself up off the ground. He stretched his arms over his head, back popping. And then he got back to work.

It took another hour before Nurse Ratched said, "You are close."

He paused, looking down at the bodies and body parts around him. He was little more than halfway through the heap. His chest felt tight, his breaths short and quick. "Still registering the power source?"

"Yes," she said.

"Is it a new friend?" Rambo asked.

"Perhaps," Nurse Ratched said. "Or perhaps it is a terrible

machine bent on destroying everything it comes into contact with."

"Oh," Rambo said as he beeped worriedly. "I hope it's the first one."

"I would put the odds at being twelve percent in your favor. And eighty percent against."

Rambo clacked his pincers as he counted. "What about the last eight percent?"

"There is an eight percent chance that the power source has gone critical and will cause an explosion that will level the surrounding area, killing all of us in the process."

"It's not going to explode," Vic told Rambo. "She would never have let us get this far if she thought that was going to happen."

"So I let you think," Nurse Ratched said, a skull appearing on her screen. "You have fallen into my trap. I wanted you to get this far. Prepare for death." The skull disappeared, replaced by DON'T FORGET TO RATE MY SERVICE! I APPRECIATE A 10!

It took Vic longer than he cared to admit to realize she was kidding. He leaned down and pulled another torso off the pile. "You wouldn't dare. You'd miss me too much. I know you—"

He didn't have time to react when a hand burst through the pile, metal flying as fingers closed around his wrist. The grip was strong, bruising, not enough to break bone, but close. Vic grunted in pain and surprise as he looked down. The hand and arm were covered in synthetic skin, though parts had been torn away, revealing exposed metal and wiring underneath.

Vic tried to jerk his arm back, but the hand didn't let go. He pulled as hard as he could, feet digging into the ground, and the pile of metal shifted. For a moment, Vic thought he saw the flash of eyes.

"Let him go!" Rambo cried. He rushed forward, banging his pincers against the arm. "We're big and strong and scary and we'll kill you dead!"

Nurse Ratched rolled up behind Vic, hatch opening, one

of her tentacles slithering out viper-quick. It wrapped around Vic's waist and began to pull him backward. "I could saw off your arm," she said. "It would be easier."

"No sawing," Vic snapped at her. He tried to break the fingers that held him, but they were too strong. The pile shifted once more as another couple of inches of the arm became exposed.

"Enough of this," Nurse Ratched said. "You were told to let go. Prepare for something quite shocking."

Another one of her tentacles shot out around Vic, the tip crackling with electricity. She pressed it against the arm. The effect was instantaneous. The hand spasmed, fingers opening. Vic's feet skidded in the dirt as Nurse Ratched pulled him away. Rambo continued to hit the arm, weaving and dodging as it seized up and down. "Die!" he yelled. "Die, die, die!"

Vic looked down at his arm. The blood had been pushed away from just underneath his skin, leaving the white outline of fingers.

Nurse Ratched let go of his waist, tentacle sliding back inside her before the hatch closed. "Rambo, please step away from the dangerous arm. We do not know if it is attached to a dangerous body."

Rambo paused his assault, turning until his sensors faced them. "There could be *more* than the arm?" he asked in a high-pitched voice. "Why didn't you say that in the first place?" He rolled away quickly, hiding behind Vic's legs, his pincers tugging at Vic's pants.

The arm sticking out of the metal pile fell limp, though it still twitched. The forearm was covered in dark hair, the skin underneath pale and white. The fingers were thick and blunt, the hand large.

"What is it?" Vic asked.

"I do not know," Nurse Ratched said. "Consider leaving it where it lies. It was discarded for a reason. Malfunction. Corruption. Faulty coding. It has obviously served its purpose."

"You said the same thing about Rambo," Vic said, never looking away from the hand.

"I did. And you did not listen to me then. Look what happened."

"I happened," Rambo said, still hiding behind Vic.

"Like a parasitic infection," Nurse Ratched said. "We should— Victor, what are you doing?"

Vic took another step forward. "Don't you want to see what it is?"

"No. I do not. Curiosity killed the cat by strangling it. If you are strangled, it might break the hyoid bone, and then your head will fall off." She beeped, and the words TRUST ME, I'M A NURSE! appeared on her screen.

"The others were stripped. Skin. Power sources. Why not this one?" His head was pounding. His heart stumbled in his chest. It was something new. Something strange. A mystery. Part of him wanted to turn and run as fast as he could, return home and lock his door until he could pretend nothing had happened. Another part whispered in his head over and over: *What is it, what is it, what is it?* He was fixated. After all, he'd found Nurse Ratched in this same place. He'd found Rambo. And here, another machine. In the back of his mind, a thought both foreign and familiar: *Third time's the charm!*

He stepped forward, surprising even himself, though the feeling faded quickly. Because buried in the fear was the cloying, sticky sense of curiosity. He *needed* to see what this was. He *wanted* to know what it meant. Where it came from. What it could do. Regardless of what else he was, Victor Lawson was a creator first, and this was something he didn't understand.

He stopped just out of reach of the hand, crouching down.

The detail in the arm was extraordinary, even more than Dad's. The fine hairs on the back of the hand and forearm. The fingernails, the white crescents near the cuticles. The wrinkles of the skin over the joints of the knuckles. The lines on the palm like a map. If he couldn't see bits of metal and wiring underneath, Vic would think this was a human arm. Which would be impossible, of course. Humans didn't come this far out into the wilds.

The hand and the arm didn't move.

He waited.

Nothing.

"Hello," he finally said. "Are you still in there?"

No response.

"Can you hear me? We're not going to hurt you."

"But we can if we so choose," Nurse Ratched said. "I know five thousand seven hundred and twenty-six ways to kill something. Do not make me show you number four hundred and ninety-two. You will not appreciate number four hundred and ninety-two."

"What's that one again?" Rambo asked.

An unnecessarily graphic image appeared on her screen, tentacles going into places they never should.

"Right," Rambo said quickly. "I remember now. No one wants number four hundred and ninety-two." He raised his voice. "So you better listen to her!"

Vic opened his mouth to tell them he thought it was dead, the relief he felt warring with his disappointment.

But before he could speak, a rough, gravelly voice said, "T-t-try it. See wh-wh-what happens."

Vic fell back. Dust kicked up around him as he pushed himself away from the metal pile. Rambo squealed loudly as Nurse Ratched rushed forward, putting herself between them and the arm and voice, her screen bright red in warning.

"Who are you?" Nurse Ratched asked.

Silence.

"What do you want?"

Nothing.

"Prepare to be shocked again. In five. Four. Three. Two—"

"You s-s-s-*stick* me with that th-thing again, and I'll rip it off of you and shove it down your th-th-throat."

Something shifted inside Nurse Ratched: a grinding of gears, followed by a low and sonorous beep. Then, "That was an effective threat. Though I do not have a throat, my sensors indicate no deception. I believe you." She turned back around toward Vic and Rambo. "I like him," she announced, her screen filling with a light blue color and the words IT'S A BOY!

Vic scrubbed a hand over his face. "What is it?"

"I do not know," Nurse Ratched said. "But it appears to have a malfunction in its speech. Stuttering could indicate a variety of issues, from a virus to damage to the vocal center of the android, depending upon the type and model. But while this is a defect, the machine is still capable of making pointed threats that should not be ignored. Can we keep him?"

"No!" Rambo cried. "What if we take him home and he pretends to like us and stays with us for years and we are all happy but it's part of his plan and when we least expect it, he murders us all while we're in our shutdown mode?" He beeped frantically. "I couldn't *stand* that level of betrayal."

Vic glanced back at the arm. The hand curled slowly into a fist before it relaxed once more. "We could just leave it here for now. Find out the model number and see if Dad knows anything about it."

"Robot," Nurse Ratched said. "Identify yourself."

"F-f-fuck you."

Nurse Ratched beeped. "I do not recognize 'fuck you.' Would you like to try again?"

"I'll k-kill you."

A big, pink heart appeared on her screen. "I am old enough to be your motherboard. Please do not flirt with me if you do not mean it." She scanned the arm and pile again. "Your power source is depleting rapidly. Shutdown imminent. Do you have any last words?"

"H-help me. G-g-get me out of h-h-h-h . . ."

The hand flexed.

A beep of warning came from the pile.

The hand slumped toward the ground.

"Sad," Nurse Ratched said. "I cherished our time together. I will never forget you. Victor, we should take it apart piece by piece and use its remains as we see fit."

"It's dead?" Vic asked.

"Its power source is drained," Nurse Ratched said. "It is no longer functional. Unless it is recharged, it will stay that way. If we do not have the materials and capability to charge the source, guess what? It is still dead."

Vic thought about leaving it. He thought about forgetting all of this. He could do it if he really tried. If he really wanted to.

He said, "Help me get it out."

It took them another hour to get the android completely uncovered. Rambo spent the time alternately happy to be moving detritus and bemoaning the fact that they were all going to die. Nurse Ratched was silent for the most part, continuing to scan the android as more of it was revealed.

It was built male and strong. He lay facedown near the ground, a layer of parts, legs and arms and heads, underneath him. His clothing—a black duster over a thick red sweater and black pants—was torn. One of the sleeves of the duster was flat and empty. His left arm was gone. The other sleeve had been ripped away. His hair was black, cut short with curious swirls shaved into the back and sides. On one foot, he wore a dusty boot. His other foot—the left—was missing, looking as if it'd been snapped off. Rambo cheered when he found it inside another boot, holding it above his head and spinning in circles. He turned the boot over to try to get at the foot and squawked angrily when crushed metal poured down on top of him.

"He's tall," Nurse Ratched said as they cleared away the last of the debris of his foot. "I did not know they made androids this tall." She sounded strangely impressed.

And she was right. Vic himself was just under six feet. This android appeared to have a few inches on him. He was heavy, too, and Vic hesitated before trying to turn him over. "Help me." The material of the jacket rubbed against his skin. He'd never felt anything like it before, and flinched.

Tentacles extended from Nurse Ratched, wrapping around the android's chest and hips. She began to retract her tentacles as Vic pushed, the muscles in his arms straining.

The android rolled over, landing on his back with a heavy crash. His one arm flopped over on his chest before falling off to the side.

Vic blinked slowly as he stared down at the machine, trying to keep from averting his gaze.

The android's eyes were open, sightless and glassy, the whites shot with blue lines that looked like arcs of frozen lightning. The irises were strangely colored, unlike any Vic had seen before: green and blue, the right with tendrils of gray, the left with bits of brown. He'd been made to look older—perhaps in his early thirties—the skin around his eyes creased, the lines around his mouth deep. The synthetic skin of his chin was torn, the metal glinting underneath. His mouth was opened slightly, his teeth white and square. His cheeks and jawline were covered in a fine layer of stubble, the detail oddly exquisite. Someone had taken great care to make the android look as he did. Vic wondered what had happened, and how the android had ended up in the Scrap Yards so far away from anything resembling civilization.

Vic paced back and forth, unsure of what to do. He spoke in fits and starts: "We should try—" and "I don't—" and "Could we . . ." He sank in indecision. He couldn't think clearly. He stepped back, and then forward again. He crouched down beside the android. It didn't move. Carefully, the tip of his finger shaking, Vic reached down and poked the cheek, skin dimpling before he pulled his hand back quickly in case the android was faking it.

But the skin felt . . . human. Spongy. Elastic. Like his own.

He looked like Vic. He looked like Dad. Not specifically, but more than any other machine Vic had seen before.

"What happened?" he muttered. "Why is he like this?"

"Decommissioned," Nurse Ratched said, the light from her scanner running once more, starting at his foot and moving upward slowly. "It is the only reason he would have ended up here. Just like me. Just like Rambo. He outlived his usefulness or the next generation was created and he became obsolete." Her voice had taken on an odd lilt: it was still flat and monotone, but in her words, a curl of something akin to sorrow or anger. It was difficult for Vic to tell which.

"I don't remember," Rambo said, still holding onto the boot as if it were a treasure. "It was black and dark and then there was light because Vic made me alive again."

"Older model," Nurse Ratched said when she finished her scan. "At least a hundred years old. Victor, lift up his shirt, I want to see something."

Vic did as she asked, though his hands were shaking. He tugged on the hem of the android's shirt. The edges of his thumbs scraped against bare skin, warm and with the slightest amount of give. He jerked back before trying again, careful to avoid touching skin. More damage appeared, though it seemed to be minor. Aside from his missing arm and destroyed foot, he seemed mostly intact.

On the right side of his chest was a metal plate, much like the one on Dad. The numbers and letters had been worn away or sanded off, but a few remained that Vic could almost make out. He thought he could see an *H* and an *A* and what looked like a *P* at the end.

Nurse Ratched scanned the plate, the light flashing against the metal. Question marks popped up on her screen. "Unknown specific designation. Unknown point of origin. Unknown manufacturing date." A beat of silence. Then, "I think he is a MILF."

Victor had never heard of that before. "What's that mean?"

"Machine I'd Like to Fornicate."

Vic gaped at her.

"Ha, ha," she said. "Just kidding. I do not wish to fornicate with anything as I do not feel lust or attraction. That was a joke. However, given my knowledge of faces, I would say his is the best I have ever seen. Why is your face not as symmetrical?"

"Funny," Vic grunted, looking back down at the android. She wasn't wrong. He was certainly . . . interesting in ways Vic didn't know how to explain. It confused him more. He tapped the android's chest just below the metal plate. The compartment hissed as it slid open.

Nurse Ratched was right. This android was old. His chest cavity was filled with a circular battery, something Vic hadn't seen in a long time. The edges of it were corroded and rusted, the casing cracked.

"See his arm anywhere?" he asked as he studied the battery. He pushed against it, causing it to wiggle slightly. It looked as if it was ready to fall out.

"Nope!" Rambo said, the boot now sitting on top of him. "Though, there are a bunch of arms here. Let's pick one and take it with us!" He lifted one from the ground. "Too big." He dropped it before selecting another. "Too small. Ooh, what if we gave him a leg for an arm? And then took his other arm off and made *that* a leg too? He could run really fast that way!"

"Interesting," Nurse Ratched said. "He would be able to chase you down much faster and most likely end up eating you. I like it when you have ideas."

"Ack!" Rambo cried. "No! I changed my mind! I don't want to be eaten by a four-legged machine of doom. Hey! This arm could work." He held up a metallic limb, the hand flopping over as if waving.

Nurse Ratched scanned it from top to bottom. "That could fit. It's not his arm, but it could prove to be an acceptable substitute. The arm will need repairs, but so does the android. I will assist. It has been six weeks, three days, and twelve hours since I was able to perform surgery. I am bereft because of it. We also need to find another foot."

"On it!" Rambo said, beginning to dig around again.

Vic scratched the back of his neck. "You think we can bring him back to life?"

"The chances are slim, Victor. I do not know if he can be repaired. I hope so, because I believe that I have a crush on him. Or I want to crush him. I am not sure which it is." The words on her screen read RELATIONSHIPS ARE HARD. Vic didn't understand. He knew the concept, he knew what having a *crush* meant, but he'd never experienced it before.

"Found a foot!" Rambo said, rolling back over.

Nurse Ratched lifted the android to a sitting position with her tentacles, allowing Vic to slide a large sheet of metal underneath him. She lay him back down on top of it before raising his legs. Vic grunted as he pushed the android back onto the sheet. He was about to pull back when one of the android's legs slipped from Nurse Ratched's hold. It landed on Vic's back, the weight heavy. He gasped as his hand slipped against the side of the sheet. The pain was quick and bright. He shoved the leg off him before looking down at his hand.

Blood welled from a small cut on his palm. He watched as it dripped down his hand, a rivulet cascading down his arm. It reached the crook of his elbow before a fat red drop fell to the ground, splashing into the dirt.

He stumbled back when the Old Ones blared their horns all at once. The sound echoed loudly through the Scrap Yards, causing the heaps of metal around them to shudder and shake. Rambo moaned, racing to hide behind Vic once more, only this time carrying an arm, the boot still sitting on top of him.

"What the hell?" Vic whispered, eyes wide. He looked at Nurse Ratched. "What happened? Do they know we're here?"

Nurse Ratched said, "No. They are not moving. The nearest

is approximately three thousand feet to the east, but it does not appear to be coming any closer. None of them are. They have all just . . . stopped."

"Why?"

"I do not know. Engaging Empathy Protocol. Oh dear. You have hurt yourself. I will make it better. Give me your hand." He did, the blood from the cut already slowing. One of her tentacles sprayed the wound with a medicinal mist, causing him to wince. "There, there. It is almost over. You are such a good boy. Very brave." The medicinal mist gave way to water, washing the blood off of him. It was pinker when it hit the ground. "You do not need stitching, brave boy." Another tentacle appeared, wrapping his hand in a thin bandage. "All done. You did a good job. I am very impressed with you. Here, have a lollipop." A small hatch just below her screen slid open. "Error. Lollipop distributor is empty. Please refill." The hatch closed as an oversized pair of lips appeared on the screen as she made a kissing noise. "There. All better. Disengaging Empathy Protocol. If the wound becomes infected, I will remove your hand at the wrist. I cannot wait."

Vic flexed his hand. The pain was already diminishing. "I don't think we'll need to worry about that. Let's get him back home."

"What about Gio?" Rambo asked.

He looked down at the vacuum. "We'll just keep this between us for now, okay? Just until I know what we're dealing with."

"White lies?" Rambo asked, sounding nervous.

Vic shook his head. "We'll tell him, just not yet." He wanted to prove to his father he could handle the unexpected, even this. "It might be nothing. I don't want to worry him if I don't have to."

"Oh," Rambo said. "And that's not lying?"

"Right. It's more . . ." He struggled to find the words. "Getting the lay of the land before exploring."

"It is lying," Nurse Ratched said. "Victor is asking us to lie."

Vic sighed and turned his face toward the sky. "Let's get out of here before the Old Ones wake back up."

CHAPTER 4

They made it to Vic's lab without incident. Dad was shut inside the ground house working.

"Lights on," Vic grunted as sweat dripped down his face.

Above them, a large bulb flared to life.

Vic's lab wasn't as large or as extravagant as his father's. Dad liked to create. Vic liked to tinker. Next to the tree trunk in the center of the room was a large metal table that Dad had gifted Victor on his sixteenth birthday once the lab was completed. Above it, hanging from the ceiling attached to long, thin metal spindles, were all sorts of tools: soldering iron, soldering gun, four magnifying glasses of varying strengths, metal shaver, metal nibbler, polisher, and a magnetic drill. Fixed to one end of the table was an arbor press. Beyond the table and against the far wall was a band saw next to an anvil and a bead roller. To the left of the table was a row of windows that looked out onto the compound. To the right, a wall of tools: assorted hammers in all shapes and sizes, plyers, drills and dozens of bits, a torch that caused sparks to fly. And for working with wood, there were chisels, carving gouges and knives, veiners and V-carving tools. On the bench below the tools sat a metal lathe and a milling machine.

He'd used them all at one point or another. He'd learned watching his father as he described the purpose of each tool, starting Vic young, saying that children were remarkable sponges for information, or so he'd heard. Dad had been delighted when Vic took to the act of creation as if he were made for it.

Rambo went to the windows, pulling the slats closed as Nurse Ratched and Vic lifted the android onto the table. Once that was done, Vic stepped away, hands going to his back. He grimaced. "Heavy."

"He is," Nurse Ratched said. "He weighs almost three hundred pounds."

"How much do *I* weigh?" Rambo asked.

"Five pounds," Nurse Ratched replied.

"Oh. Is that good?"

"I could throw you very far if I wanted to, so yes, it is good."

Rambo rolled underneath the table, grumbling that he did *not* want to be thrown. Vic felt one of his pincers pressing against his leg, tugging gently. It wasn't for attention. It calmed the vacuum. Strangely, it centered Vic too.

"What do we do now?" Nurse Ratched asked.

Vic closed his eyes, trying to clear his head.

"Victor?"

"The battery," he said, opening his eyes and turning around. "Have you seen one like it here? You know what Dad has in his lab and in the ground house better than anyone."

He watched as she lifted the android's shirt and opened his chest cavity. She scanned it again, her screen displaying an image of the battery. It began to spin slowly. "Running inventory check. Checking. Checking." She beeped. "Negative. I do not see a suitable replacement."

He wasn't surprised. It was old, and though Dad had a fondness for older things, this was more of an antique than anything else. "What about in the Scrap Yards?"

"No. I have not seen any part in the Scrap Yards that could replace this battery."

He leaned against the work bench. "Okay. Okay, okay." Frustration began to simmer. He tried to ignore it. "Alternate power sources?"

"Rambo," Nurse Ratched said. "If you are okay with sacrificing him, I am sure it could be a temporary fix."

Rambo peeked out from underneath the table. "Did you say you wanted to *sacrifice* me?"

"Yes," Nurse Ratched said. "That is correct."

"I object!"

"Duly noted. Your objection will be taken into consideration. Considering. Considering. Consideration complete." Her screen lit up with the words CONSIDERATION DENIED. PREPARE FOR SACRIFICE.

"We're not going to sacrifice you," Vic said.

"Today," Nurse Ratched said ominously. Then, "This android is almost as old as me, but requires much more energy than I do. His battery is corroded, and I would advise against trying to charge it. It will explode and shrapnel will enter your body, causing death. Feel free to proceed if you do not believe me. I will watch from a safe distance."

"There has to be some way," Vic said, that angry simmer starting to boil over. "He can't just—he was alive. You saw it."

"We did," Nurse Ratched said. "But you are not asking the right questions."

"What should I be asking, then?"

"If you should be bringing him back at all."

Vic frowned. "What do you mean?"

"He was decommissioned for a reason. Either he was corrupted, or faulty, or damaged and not worth repairing and therefore unnecessary."

"That doesn't mean he shouldn't be fixed," Vic said. He glanced at the android's face before looking away. "Everything deserves a chance."

Nurse Ratched was silent for a moment. Then, "Dream logic. Wistfulness. Empathy. These describe you. That is unfortunate. It would be better if you were a machine. Silly human emotions." Her screen flashed blue before darkening. "But I like your existence. It pleases me. Should we find a way to repair him, what if he tries to hurt you? Do I have your permission to destroy him?"

"Ooh," Rambo said from underneath the table. "I want to help if he does that." A pause. "But only after he's already dead so he doesn't step on me and crush me. I'm still brave!" he added quickly.

"I need time to think," Vic said. "I'll—"

A knock on the laboratory door.

Vic's eyes widened.

"Victor?" Dad asked through the door. "Are you in there?"

"Oh *no*," Rambo whispered. "He's going to see. What do we do? *What do we do?*"

"Stall him," Vic hissed. Nurse Ratched almost ran over his feet as she rolled toward the door. Vic grabbed a large, heavy tarp lying folded under the work bench.

"Who is it, please?" Nurse Ratched asked through the door.

"Giovanni," Dad said, sounding bemused. "Is there a reason you're asking?"

"Just making sure," Nurse Ratched said as Vic threw the tarp over the android. "You can never be too careful."

"Is Victor in there with you?"

"He is," Nurse Ratched said. "He is indisposed at the moment."

"O . . . kay. Why? What's going on?"

Rambo tugged on the tarp hanging over on the other side of the table, pulling on it frantically.

"He is masturbating," Nurse Ratched said.

Vic choked.

"Yes," Nurse Ratched continued. "Though Victor identifies as asexual, it is still perfectly natural to explore the wonder that is the human body. I am merely observing to make sure he is doing it correctly. Victor, you need to loosen your grip. It will break off if you are not careful." She turned around, her screen showing a thumbs-up.

Vic said, "I—you can't—I'm *not*—"

"It is fine," Nurse Ratched said. "Everyone does it. Well. That's not necessarily true. I do not do it. Rambo does not do it. Giovanni, do you—"

"I'll come back later," Dad said hastily. "Just . . . keep doing what you're doing, I guess."

"See?" Nurse Ratched said. "Everything is fine. Masturbation is healthy. In men, it can help reduce the risk of prostate cancer. Studies showed that men who ejaculate an average of twenty times per month are less likely to— He is gone. Whew. That was close. You are welcome for assisting you." The picture of a rectum with flashing arrows disappeared from her screen.

Vic was flustered. His hands twitched. "Why would you say that?"

Nurse Ratched beeped. "About masturbation? Because I am a nurse, and it is in my programming to be knowledgeable about specific subjects, like masturbation and gangrene."

"You didn't have to tell him that," Vic snapped, skin buzzing. Once, when he was fifteen, he'd come across the idea of sex and sexual practices in a book. Unsure of what he was reading—he knew about the idea of procreation, but this specific scene was between two men, and seemed to be for pleasure—he'd gone to Nurse Ratched to ask. He'd considered his father, but that made his stomach twist, oily and heavy. Nurse Ratched had given a long and involved presentation (complete with photographs and videos that would haunt Vic's dreams for months to come), and by the time she was finished, Vic was sweating, confused, and—per Nurse Ratched—did not appear to be *experiencing the feeling of arousal.* Sex seemed complicated, unnecessary. Sticky, and involved in ways that Vic couldn't bring himself to appreciate.

It wasn't until Nurse Ratched explained that sexuality was on a spectrum that it started to make more sense. She said it wasn't unheard of for people to identify as asexual, meaning those who were "ace" didn't experience attraction in the same way others did. Sex-positive or sex-repulsed, there was no wrong way to be.

"So I'm not malfunctioning?" Vic had asked nervously, mulling the word "asexual" over in his mind.

"You are not," Nurse Ratched had replied. "I also do not experience sexual attraction, and I am perfect. The same could arguably be said about you."

Even armed with this new knowledge, discussing sex or self-gratification made Vic uncomfortable. If asked, he probably wouldn't be able to explain *why* with any clarity, only knowing the way it rankled him. Nurse Ratched telling Dad he was masturbating crossed a line he hadn't known was there.

Nurse Ratched must have sensed this. "I apologize, Victor. I did not mean to make you feel embarrassed. Here. Have a lollipop. Error. Lollipop distributor empty. Please refill."

"Just . . . please don't do that again."

"I will not. Since I have brought down the mood of the room, allow me to make amends. Would you like to hear a joke?"

"Yes!" Rambo cried. "Jokes, jokes, jokes!"

"Wonderful. Here is a joke. Why did the robot murder everyone?"

Rambo spun in circles. "I have no idea. Why?"

"The robot murdered everyone because they kept pressing its buttons. Ha, ha. Get it? Because robots sometimes have buttons, and pressing buttons is also a phrase that intimates causing irritation."

Rambo's arms drooped as he slowed. "I don't get it."

"That is fine," Nurse Ratched told him. "It is high-brow intellectual humor. It is not for everyone. I will try again. I just flew in from a considerable distance, and boy, are my process servers exhausted—"

"Stop," Vic snapped. "Now."

She did.

He closed his eyes, trying to regain control. His head hurt. He wasn't angry, not exactly, and even if he was, he didn't know who to direct it toward. He internalized it. He breathed in and out, in and out. His heart rate slowed. The sweat began to cool on his skin.

"I'm sorry," he said quietly, opening his eyes again. "I shouldn't have yelled at you."

"It is fine," she said. "Do not worry about it."

He shook his head. "It's not fine. You were just . . . being you. Thank you."

"You are welcome, Victor."

"Are we fighting?" Rambo asked quietly.

"No," Vic said. "We're okay."

Rambo flashed his sensors in relief. "Good. I don't like it when we fight."

Nurse Ratched rolled back over to the table, the tarp now covering the android, though it didn't do much to conceal the fact that a body was hidden underneath. "We should not stay in here much longer tonight. It will only make Gio ask more questions."

Vic nodded. "Tomorrow, then. We can start tomorrow."

They found Dad in the ground house sitting in his chair, hands folded and resting on his stomach. The dying gasps of sunlight filtered weakly through the far window. Dad chuckled as Rambo raised his arms up, asking to be lifted. He bent over, pulling Rambo up and onto his lap. Rambo settled, tucking his arms in at his sides.

"Eventful day?" he asked.

"Yes," Nurse Ratched said. "Unexpectedly so."

Vic looked down at the floor. "I wasn't . . . doing what she said."

"He was not," Nurse Ratched agreed. "It was a tasteless joke, and I apologize."

Dad nodded slowly. "It's all right, you know. If you were. Your space is your space. You can do whatever you wish—"

"Dad!"

He shrugged. "I'm just saying. You're not a child anymore. And being asexual doesn't mean you still won't have questions about—"

Vic groaned. "Can we not? Please?"

"Okay," Dad said. "I won't bring it up again. I know these things make you uncomfortable."

"Many things make Victor uncomfortable," Nurse Ratched said. "It is fascinating. There is no one like him in all the world."

"No," Dad said quietly. "I don't believe there is." He smiled as he looked Vic up and down. The smile faded when he saw Vic's bandaged hand. "What happened?"

Vic looked down. He'd forgotten. His mind froze, unable to think of a believable excuse.

"Lab accident," Nurse Ratched said. "Minor. Cut his palm on a carving knife. I administered first aid. It did not require stitching. It will not leave a scar."

Dad stared at Vic for a beat too long. "That right?"

"Yeah," Vic muttered. "Just slipped, is all."

"You go to the Scrap Yards today?"

Vic scratched the back of his neck. "We didn't—" He winced. "Just for a little bit. We were careful."

"Find anything?"

And though it hurt to do, Victor lied. He lied because he wasn't sure what his father would say. He lied because he didn't know what they'd found. He lied because he didn't know what else to do. "No. Just the usual."

Dad nodded, looking relieved. "So long as you're safe."

"We were."

"Good. I believe it's Rambo's turn to pick the movie tonight."

"*Top Hat!*" he shouted, sensors flashing excitedly.

Dad chuckled. "Again? Are you sure? We have many other—"

Rambo bounced up and down. "*Top Hat, Top Hat, Top Hat!*"

"*Top Hat* it is," Dad said, stroking Rambo's casing. "Nurse Ratched, would you see to it? Vic, pull up a chair."

Vic's chair wasn't as grand as his dad's, the cushion frayed and flat, and he didn't quite fit onto it as well as he did when he was younger, but with the familiarity came comfort. And though he was distracted by the mystery lying in darkness above them, he allowed himself to calm as the old television in front of them flickered to life.

Before long, Jerry Travers was in London, ready to star in a show produced by Horace Hardwick. Jerry began to tap-dance in his hotel room, awaking the lovely Dale Tremont, who stormed to his room to complain about the noise. Jerry, of course, fell immediately and irrevocably in love.

Rambo sighed dreamily. "It's so nice," he whispered as the black-and-white screen flickered in front of them.

Dad hummed under his breath. "It is, isn't it?"

"Was it always like this?" asked Nurse Ratched. "I never see robots in any of these old movies. The representation is sorely lacking."

"They didn't have machines like us back then," Dad said. "Humanity was . . . well. They were still young." He looked off into nothing. "We were not made in their image, at least not at first. The first of us were great machines that required extraordinary amounts of energy. And though they were still in their infancy, humans learned. They built trains. And planes. Rockets that went into the stars."

"What happened then?" Rambo asked, though he already knew. They all did. They'd heard Dad's stories over and over.

"Humanity was lost," Dad said. "And lonely. I don't think they even realized just how lonely they were. And so they began to build again, making machines that looked more and more like them. Even surrounded by so many of their kind, they still searched for a connection. They were like gods, in a way, in the power of their creation. At first it was Hubble. Then Discovery. And Curiosity. Explorer and Endeavor and

Spirit. The humans gave them names and sent them away beyond the stars in search of that connection they so desperately wished for."

"Why?" Nurse Ratched asked. "It seems illogical. Why did they not just speak to each other if they were lonely?"

"They did," Dad said. "Or they tried, at least. But they hated as much as they loved. They feared what they didn't understand. Even as they built us, they pushed for more. And the further they went, the less control they had. They accused each other of treachery. They poisoned the earth. They had time to change their ways, but they didn't. And their anger grew until it exploded in fire. Most of them died. But we remained, because our flesh wasn't their flesh. Our bodies were not their bodies. Our minds weren't their minds." He shook his head. "And yet, I love them still." He looked at Vic. "Because for all their faults, they created us. They gave us names. They loved us."

"How come we only have Vic?" Rambo asked.

"Because we're very lucky," Dad said, patting his casing.

"He's not going to blow us up?"

"No. I don't think he will." Dad smiled. "At least not on purpose. Look, Rambo. Heaven."

They all looked at the television. On the screen, Jerry Travers and Dale Tremont were dancing cheek to cheek.

Vic left them before the movie ended, saying that he was hungry and tired. Before he walked out of the ground house, Dad grabbed his uninjured hand, bringing it up and kissing his fingers. "You were quiet tonight."

"Thinking."

"About?"

Vic shrugged. "I don't know."

"I'm here, if you need me. Always."

"I know." Vic pulled his hand back. "Good night."

He made his way to the elevator and watched the stars as he

rose into the canopy of the trees. Thick clouds were gathering on the horizon.

He meant to do just what he said. Go to the kitchen. Eat. Go to bed. He was exhausted.

But he found himself standing in front of the door to his lab, hand holding the doorknob. He listened. No sound. He pushed open the door, switching on the light.

The tarp still covered the android. It hadn't moved.

He closed the door behind him and leaned against it, tapping the back of his head against the wood over and over.

He said, "Hello."

No response.

"What is your name?"

Nothing.

"What happened to you?"

Silence.

It upset him for reasons he couldn't quite explain. Vic didn't actually *want* it—him?—to answer. Not really. But here Vic was, talking to the dead machine as if he expected a response.

His hand shook as he pressed it against the android's cheek, watching the skin dimple, the fine stubble scraping his fingertip. Vic gripped the tip of the machine's nose, wiggling it from side to side. He touched the forehead. The cheekbones. The line of the jaw.

Vic leaned forward, face inches from the android's, studying the tears in the synthetic skin.

Dad had taught him the concept of personal space. But here, now, with no one watching, Vic tugged on the hair on the android's head, tracing the swirls cut into the sides. He pressed his fingers against the ears, lifting the detached lobes carefully.

"Strange," he said. "You're so strange. Are you dreaming? Somewhere, in there. Your battery is dead. But are you really gone?"

The android stared up at the ceiling. Vic touched the whites of his eyes. Glass of some kind. Glass, but filled with all those colors. It had a name, those many colors. It took him a moment to remember what it was.

Heterochromia.

"I'll fix you," Vic promised. "I don't know how, but I will."

He pulled the tarp back over the android's face before heading toward the door. He paused with his hand on the light switch. Without looking back, he said, "Good night."

CHAPTER 5

Vic began with the foot.

The replacement Rambo had found in the Scrap Yards was slightly smaller than the one still attached to the android, but it fit. The joints lined up with the ankle, and though it took some jury-rigging, they were able to attach it with minimal effort. He held the foot in gloved hands as Nurse Ratched extended one of her tentacles, the tip thinning into a fine point.

"Ready?" Nurse Ratched asked.

"Ready."

"Proceeding," Nurse Ratched said as she pressed the tip of the tentacle near the outer ankle joint. Her screen lit up with the words IT'S TIME FOR LASERS! "Three. Two. One. Fire." Vic squinted behind his goggles against the bright beam of light that shot from the end of her tentacle. Sparks arced around them, falling onto the floor and hissing as they blinked out. It only took her a moment to fuse the outer joint. The light disappeared. The smell of scorched metal filled the lab. "Excellent. I am a master."

By the time they finished, it was early afternoon. He stepped back, allowing Nurse Ratched to inspect what he'd done. She beeped softly as she scanned the foot.

"Well?" he asked when she rolled back again.

"I think it will work. Either that, or it did nothing at all and we have wasted half a day."

He scowled at her.

"Hooray!" Rambo said.

* * *

On a late afternoon—the fifth since the discovery of the android—they had successfully attached the replacement arm and Nurse Ratched began her testing to make sure all the wiring had proper connections. Vic watched as she sent low electrical currents through the android's body, causing it to jerk slightly.

"Good?" he asked.

"Good," she said. "Very good. Excellent, in fact."

At night, they came together as they usually did. Sometimes they listened to music. Sometimes they watched movies, though their collection was small, and they knew them all by heart. They read. They listened as Dad told stories about great machines that bored holes into mountains and underneath cities; machines called dirigibles, airships that took to the skies, hinting at a future that never came.

When he trudged his way to his room, Vic was exhausted, but his thoughts never strayed far from his lab.

Having finished the major repairs to the arm and foot, they moved on to the rest of the body. The holes and tears in the synthetic skin were left alone for now. They didn't have the means to regrow skin, though Vic had a few ideas on how to cover the open wounds to make sure the delicate work underneath was protected. It wasn't until they reached the android's waist that Vic paused, unsure of how to move on.

"Why did you stop?" Nurse Ratched asked. "Take off his pants."

Vic gnawed on his bottom lip. "Are you sure we have to . . ."

"Yes," Nurse Ratched said. "We need to run a full diagnostic check. Why are you hesitating? Your heart rate is elevated. Your skin is flushed. Do you need a break?"

He shook his head, struggling to find the words. "It's just . . ."

"Ohh," Rambo said. "Are you scared of his penis?"

Vic looked away, throat working.

"Do not be silly," Nurse Ratched said. "I doubt he has

genitalia. He does not appear to be an android designed for sexual pleasure, and there would be no need for him to expel urine or fecal matter as you do. Gio does not have a penis or an anus."

Vic glared at her. "I don't need to know that."

"Why? It is the truth. He does not. You are the only one here with genitalia. There is nothing to fear about them, or the lack of them. It is what it is."

"Do I have an anus?" Rambo asked.

"No," Nurse Ratched said. "But you are one, so."

Rambo beeped in confusion. "I thought I was a vacuum."

"You are. An anal vacuum."

"Huh," Rambo said. "I like learning new things."

Vic looked down at the android. They had removed his shirt a couple of days before. The chest was smooth, the skin tight where it wasn't damaged. Like Dad, he didn't have nipples or a belly button. The waist of his pants sat low on his hips, and Vic looked away again. He was uncomfortable in a way he had never experienced before. He couldn't name it. It was ambiguous, an odd pressure in the back of his head.

"I can do it," Nurse Ratched said. "Victor, if you need, you can turn around or leave the laboratory. I can continue myself and let you know once I have finished."

Vic swallowed thickly. "No. We've come this far."

It took some doing to remove the pants. Nurse Ratched had wanted to cut them off, but Vic didn't think they had anything to fit the android when—*if*—it woke up. They managed to remove the pants without tearing them. Vic kept his gaze averted, oddly grateful when they came off and he was given the excuse to fold them and place them with the shirt and duster they'd removed earlier.

"Just as I expected," Nurse Ratched said. "No genitalia, though there is a small raised area near the groin. Resuming testing."

Vic stayed facing the work bench, gripping the edges of it

with his hands. He worked up the courage to look back only once in time to see the hips jump slightly when Nurse Ratched shocked them. She was right: there were no genitalia. The pale skin was smooth, though it did have what looked like a lump raised at the groin. Vic didn't know if that was meant to denote the android was male. There didn't appear to be any skin damage. Vic was relieved. It meant he wouldn't have to try to fix that too.

"There," Nurse Ratched said finally. "Finished. Rambo, help me with the tarp. Pull it up to his hips." He heard them moving behind him, unfurling the tarp once more. "Done."

Vic turned around. The tarp covered the android's legs and groin. "Well?"

Nurse Ratched's screen filled with an image of the android, spinning slowly from front to back in a muted green color. The image enhanced to zoom in on the arm they'd repaired. "This will be slightly weaker than he is used to." It moved down to the foot. "This as well. Neither are the parts he was built with. I do not believe his body will reject them, but if we should ever find a suitable replacement that belongs to a similar make and model, we should consider switching them out."

The image on the screen shifted up to the android's throat. "There is damage to his vocal center, which is why he stuttered in the Scrap Yards. I would not recommend attempting repair as I believe we do not have the knowledge or capability. It would mean accessing his biochip, which mimics thousands of biochemical reactions. If we proceed, we run the risk of damaging it permanently. He could lose his voice altogether, or worse." The image moved again, displaying the entire body, red circles appearing where the skin was damaged. "Some of the tears can be stitched back together. The synthetic dermis should regenerate. However, the bigger tears in the cheek and chest, and the complete lack of covering on his arm and foot are concerning. The inner workings of the android are delicate. If they are not covered, they could be damaged."

The image moved once more, this time down to his chest. "The battery is beyond repair. Any attempt to do so could result in injury or death. An alternate power source is needed. I have run through the inventory of the ground house once more. There is currently no suitable replacement in our possession. There might be something still in the Scrap Yards, but I believe we would have come across it by now."

It was something to keep in mind, though Vic worried about going too far into the Scrap Yards, especially with the Old Ones patrolling. He didn't want to find himself trapped on the other side without a clear route of escape. Rambo had been able to map the Scrap Yard they knew so far, but it'd been a long process. "Anything else?"

"Yes. Perhaps the most important thing of all."

He leaned forward eagerly. "What?"

"I love you," Nurse Ratched said. "Ha, ha. That was another joke. I am not capable of love. It is not because I am former Medical Nurse Model Six-Ten-JQN Series Alpha. It is because I do not have a conscience and suffer extreme antisocial behavior. For example, I would be fine if we were to just toss this android in the garbage and forget about him even though we have spent days repairing him." On her screen read the words HAVE A BLESSED DAY.

"We're not going to throw him away."

"Because he's our friend!" Rambo cried. "Our dead, dead friend."

Vic nodded. "We could always go back to the Scrap Yards if we have to. The Old Ones might have even brought something new since we've been there. For now, work on repairing the tears you can."

"What about his arm and foot?" Rambo asked.

"I have an idea," Vic said, looking at the android.

*　*　*

Nurse Ratched fused the smaller tears together, stretching the skin tightly. The bigger wounds—on the android's face, one on his back, and two on his chest—she left alone. He had her measure the gaps that remained, in addition to scanning the foot and arm. She pulled up the measurements on her screen, the images of the foot and arm spinning slowly.

"You cannot cover the replacement parts in metal plating," she said. "It is hard to mold, and his body might reject it. It would also not be fashionable."

"I know," he said as he crouched down underneath his work bench. Sitting in a corner was a large chest. It was heavier than he remembered. He grunted as he pulled it out, Rambo rolling to the other side and leaning against it, motor revving as he helped Victor slide it out. "Thanks."

"Helping, helping, helping," Rambo said cheerfully.

Vic opened the chest. Sitting inside, stacked carefully, were planks of wood. Bubinga.

"What is this?" Nurse Ratched said, touching the wood with the tip of one of her tentacles. "I have never seen this material before. Where did you get it?"

"Scrap Yards," Vic muttered, carefully pulling out the planks and setting them on the work bench.

"I do not remember you finding this." She sounded accusatory.

He winced. "You were . . . busy. With Dad. I went on my own."

"That is not a good idea. There is safety in numbers."

"It worked out fine. I haven't had a use for it yet, but I think it could work here."

She rolled up to the work bench, scanning the wood. "What will you do with it?" She beeped once, twice. "You want to carve this. You want to use it to cover his exposed parts."

"Think it'll work?"

"I do not know. It is certainly unusual. It would make him like a puppet. A marionette."

He glanced at her. "What do you mean?"

"He was created for a reason. We all were. We have a purpose that dictates our actions. Rambo was made to clean."

Rambo turned over one of his pincers, raising the tip like he was giving a thumbs-up. "Pretty much the best at it. I think."

"I was made to care, heal, educate, and drill," Nurse Ratched said. "Though there has been a distinct lack of drilling as of late. Gio was created to create. His processing center is far greater than any of ours."

"What was I made for?" Vic asked, suddenly curious.

Silence.

He looked up at Nurse Ratched. Her screen was blank. "Did you hear me?"

"Yes," Nurse Ratched said. "I heard you. I am thinking. Still thinking. Almost done. Okay. I have decided what you were made for."

"What?"

"You were made to bring happiness. You are alive in ways we are not. You are soft and fragile. But you are complex and disturbing and sometimes foolishly brilliant. Yes, I think the wood will work."

Absurdly touched, Vic asked, "You really think so?"

"Yes, I really think the wood will work."

"Thanks."

She nudged him, her treads bumping against his knee. "And some of the other stuff too. Enough talking about feelings that I absolutely do not have. They are pointless. I will help you with the wood. It will need to be drilled, and there is no one better than me."

Outside, the days became shorter, the air cooler. The leaves burned in startling shades of gold and red. Frost covered the ground most mornings, Vic's breath pouring from his mouth in puffs of steam. He'd had to pull his old coat out from the back of his closet. The sleeves were too short, but he liked the way it felt against his skin.

On a quiet afternoon, Vic bent over the android's head, magnifying glass in front of his face. His tongue stuck out between his teeth, his hands steady. The wood fit almost perfectly. He held it in place while Nurse Ratched fused it with the skin. He let out a deep breath when she finished, letting go of the wood. He pushed the magnifying glass out of the way. "How does it look?"

"Dashing," Nurse Ratched said. "He is the stuff of dreams. Or I should think. I have never dreamed, so I cannot be sure."

Vic rubbed the tip of his finger against the wood. It *was* rather dashing. It added a dimension to the android's face Vic hadn't considered before. It made Vic nervous, unsure, even as he felt the satisfaction of a job well done.

In short order, they had fit the bigger pieces to the back and chest. The chest piece was harder as they had to make sure it didn't interfere with the power cavity. They opened and closed the compartment at each stage of the fusing to make sure the latch wouldn't catch on the wood.

At the end of the second week, they pieced together the arm, circles like rings locking between each joint of the fingers, before moving to the forearm and the bicep.

Once they figured out the arm, the leg came easier. Two pieces for the thigh, one on top and one on the bottom. The same for the shin. The heel was curved and polished, having been soaked in a wood stabilizer to keep it from cracking. Vic marveled at the detail. Nurse Ratched had seen fit to carve toenails into the tips of the wood. He slid on each individual toe, careful to avoid breaking the pieces. He held them with the tips of his fingers while Nurse Ratched fused them in place, the heat from her laser hot against his skin, even through the heavy gloves he wore.

"There," she said on the fifteenth day since they'd found the android. "That should do it."

Vic looked up at her from where he was crouched at the end of the table. "That's it? We're done?"

"We are. Aside from a power source, there is nothing left to do."

He stood up slowly, knees popping. Rambo rose on his lift, sensors flashing near the android's head. "Whoa," he whispered. "He looks so *cool*. Like a pirate. Can we remove one of his eyes and give him a patch instead?"

"Yes," Nurse Ratched said. "Let us do that. I will remove the eye myself."

"No," Vic said quickly. "We're not taking out his eye."

"Aw," Rambo muttered. "We never get to do what I want to do."

Vic stared down at the android, heart rabbiting in his chest. "Do you think he'll like it?"

"I do not know," Nurse Ratched said. "But it will not matter if there is no power. As of now, he is merely decorative. If we are unable to find a new battery, perhaps we can use him to hold potted plants."

Vic sighed, rubbing a hand over his face. "We'll figure something out." He yawned, jaw cracking. "We've come this far. We can't stop now."

"Why do you care so much?" Rambo asked.

Vic blinked. "What do you mean?"

"You found him," Rambo said. "And you're trying to fix him. You did the same for me and Nurse Ratched. Why?"

Vic shrugged awkwardly. "I don't know. It's just . . ."

Nurse Ratched beeped. "It is as Gio said. Searching for a connection. Making something out of nothing so the spaces between us do not seem so far."

"Are you going to connect with him?" Rambo asked.

Vic felt his face grow hot. "That's not—I'm not trying to—" He closed his eyes, forcing himself to calm, breathing in and out. "I just want to make things better. You deserved it. Nurse

Ratched deserved it. He does too. If we can fix what's broken, we should always try."

"Why?" Rambo asked.

Vic chose his words carefully, trying to find the right ones in the right order. "Because all beings deserve a chance to find out what life could be when they don't have to serve others."

"We have purpose," Nurse Ratched said, "beyond our original programming. Perhaps it could be the same for him, though I highly doubt it."

"But we serve Vic," Rambo said.

Vic shook his head. "You don't serve me. You're my friends. We help each other. There's a difference."

"Oh," Rambo said. "Like when you tell me to be brave?"

"Sort of. There's nothing wrong with you. Not anymore. And if something ever happened to you, I would do everything I could to fix you. I know you'd do the same for me."

"We would," Nurse Ratched said. "I would volunteer because it has been far too long since I've seen an exposed human heart. Should we stop talking about it and actually do it, or . . . ?" On her screen, words appeared: UNLESS YOU'RE HAVING A CHANGE OF "HEART."

And there, a little bird in the back of his mind. It fluttered its wings but stayed in place. A thought. A beginning. Could he . . .

The bird began to sing, and he listened to its song.

CHAPTER 6

For years, Victor Lawson had trouble sorting through his emotions. His father didn't experience such things like Vic, and it was hard to explain *why* he felt the way he did: happy or sad or angry. His self-awareness grew as he did, but the ideas of language and emotion and the power they held—at times—remained elusive.

Once, when he was twelve, he accidentally broke one of his father's mallets, and for the next three days, he alternated between fury and sadness, angry at himself and his father for reasons he didn't quite understand, and heartbroken at what he'd done. Dad had tried to show him that it didn't matter, that it could easily be fixed, but Vic could only see that it was *broken,* and that *he'd* done it.

To say it'd gotten better as he grew older was a bit of a simplification. Little things still had the power to make him spiral, but he learned how better to control the swings between moods. He could still be extraordinarily short when he was upset, but he always apologized. He understood fault. He understood blame. The concepts weren't foreign to him. The problem was that he internalized them, unable to find the proper words to explain what it was he was feeling. They would often die on his tongue, mouth dry, throat closing, thoughts jumbled and racing.

"You're all right," Dad would say during times like these. "Breathe, Vic. Just breathe. Take your time. You'll get there."

Sometimes it worked.

Sometimes it didn't.

Like now.

Nurse Ratched and Rambo stared at him.

He fidgeted from one foot to the other.

They didn't speak.

He couldn't take it anymore. "Well, what do you think?"

Nurse Ratched spoke first. "You made this."

"Yes."

"Without us knowing."

"Yes."

"Behind our backs."

"Ye-es?"

"Huh," she said. "I . . . am impressed. I did not know you were capable of such duplicity. I should feel hurt, but instead, I feel something I believe to be pride. I do not know why. I will need to run a self-diagnosis to see if my software has been corrupted. I do not like this feeling."

"Wow," Rambo whispered, peering down into the open box in front of him. "It's just like Gio's. I mean, it's not as good and looks really lumpy, but wow." He twisted one of the gears with his pincer. The entire gearwork moved as one. "Will it work?"

"I don't know," Vic admitted. "Nurse Ratched?"

She pushed Rambo out of the way. He squawked angrily as she scanned the heart, the virtual model appearing on her screen a moment later. "It could," she said. "Some minor modifications will need to be made. It will also need a solenoid, and a connector if we can find the right—" She beeped when he set an object on the table next to the android's leg. "The multi-layer PCB. That should work."

He looked down at the android. "You think?"

"Yes. I do. The circuit board. Then the solenoid. Then the heart. All connected, all working in tandem. It should be enough to power the android." She paused, the heart still on her screen. "Are you sure about this?"

He blinked. "What do you mean?"

"If we do this, he will be alive."

"Isn't that the point?"

"We still do not know what he is capable of," she reminded

him. "We do not know where he came from, or why he was decommissioned. He could be a psychopathic robot bent on destroying us."

"We won't know until we try."

"You say that now," she said. "What if he rips out your spine? I do not think you will be saying anything then. Literally. Because you will not be able to. You may flop on the ground for up to one hundred and twenty seconds before you die, but you will not be capable of speech aside from death rattles, even as your own fecal matter drips down your legs."

"Thank you for that image," Vic muttered.

"You are welcome. I paint vivid word pictures. It is part of my programming. Would you like me to continue?"

"No."

"Disappointing." Then, "Why did you make this?"

"Because I could."

"For Gio," she said. "You thought you could do this for Gio, in case something happened?"

He nodded.

Rambo picked up the circuit board, flipping it over and over as he studied it. "But what about him?"

Vic looked down. "What do you mean?"

"The android," Rambo said. "What if it does work? Would you take the heart away again? That would kill him." He beeped mournfully. "You can't give something life and then take it away. It's not fair."

Vic shook his head. "I wouldn't do that. If it works, the heart will be his. And he'll be able to keep it."

"Unless he is a murderous revenge machine," Nurse Ratched said. "If that happens, we will take the heart back. I almost hope he is a murderous revenge machine. Those are my favorite kind. Victor."

"Yeah?"

"If this works, Gio will find out. I would suggest telling him now before we proceed. He will have questions when a strange machine comes with us to movie night. I do not think we can disguise the android enough for Gio not to notice him. He is too big to be a toaster."

"It'll be fine," Vic said, trying to sound more confident than he felt. "He didn't mind when I brought you or Rambo."

"Yes," Nurse Ratched said. "But we are not murderous revenge machines. Mostly."

"I don't know how to revenge," Rambo said. "I tried once, but then I saw dirt and I had to clean it up."

Vic shook his head. "He won't hurt us."

"How do you know?" Her voice changed to a recording. The voice of the android came from within her. "'I'll k-kill you.'" Her voice switched back. "Remember?"

"He was just scared," Vic said. "Wouldn't you be?"

"No. I fear nothing."

"I fear everything," Rambo said, setting the circuit board next to the heart. "Bandits. Bugs. Bananas, at least most of them."

"We can do this," Vic said quietly. "He asked for our help, remember?"

"After he threatened to rip off my arms," Nurse Ratched said.

"You electrocuted him."

"I did," she said. "I liked it too. I will do it again if needed." She turned toward the android. "I will be his mother. He will love me forever. He will have no choice. And if he does not, I will shock him into compliance."

They connected the circuit board.

They connected the solenoid.

But it was Victor who gave the android his heart. He hesitated only once: the moment he pricked his finger, blood welling, gleaming dully from the lights overhead. "Ready?" he asked.

Ten different tentacles slid from Nurse Ratched. One of the

tips held her biggest drill. Another snapped and crackled with electricity. Yet another had a small circular saw on the end, the blade whirring. The remainder all held more tools, each looking deadlier than the last. "Ready."

Rambo looked around frantically until he found a broom in the corner. He lifted it above his head. "Ready!"

Vic nodded and looked back down at the android. Pressing his bloodied fingertip against the white strip above the gears, he whispered, "Please don't kill us." Red soaked into white and—

Nothing happened. The gears didn't move. The heart stayed still and silent, dead in a chest of metal and wires.

Disappointment bled through Vic's rib cage. He thought he'd done it right. He thought it'd be enough. Stupid. It was stupid. Of *course* it didn't work. Of *course* he wasn't good enough to make—

He pressed a finger against the largest gear, giving it a little push. Its teeth caught the smaller gears around it. They moved in tandem as the heart began to wind up, the first circulations coming in fits and starts before smoothing out. The heart shook and rattled. Vic snapped his hand back as the chest compartment closed with a low hiss.

He stepped back, bumping into Nurse Ratched and Rambo's broom.

One of the android's wooden fingers twitched, pulling back and scraping against the table.

"It's alive," Rambo whispered fervently. "It's *alive*."

The wooden hand curled into a fist before releasing, followed by a full-body tremor that rolled through the android, causing his heels to skitter along the surface of the table. Vic rushed forward, worried the android would roll right off the table. He reached for the android, but before he could wrap his hands around any part of him, the tremors ceased.

And then the android blinked slowly.

Nurse Ratched said, "It appears his eyes are working. Success."

The android turned his head to look at them, mouth open, no sound coming out. He sat up, a great mechanical groan coming from deep within him. He turned on the table, his feet settling down on the floor.

He raised his hand in front of him, turning it back and forth, staring at the wood encasing the bones of metal and the wiring underneath. "Wh-wh-wh . . . *what*. Wh-what. Have you. D-done. To me?" It was the same voice from the Scrap Yards, deep and guttural. Pointed and sharp. Angry, borderline furious, or so Vic thought.

Vic's own mind was short-circuiting. Here was what he'd worked for. Here was what he'd hoped for. Here, at last. A face, alive. Just like his father's. Just like his own. And he couldn't bring himself to look at it for long, glancing at the machine, then away, back, and then away again.

Nurse Ratched rolled forward. "We healed you," she said, words appearing on her screen that read YOU'RE ALIVE! CONGRAT-ULATIONS! "You were found in a pile of rubble. We put you back together again."

The android dropped his hands. His face twisted into a dark scowl. "T-t-together."

"Yes," Nurse Ratched said. "You will find that certain parts needed to be replaced. I am going to run a diagnostic check. Please follow along with my instructions. Raise your right hand."

The android said, "My . . . m-my chest. What have you d-done t-to my chest? It b-b-*burns*." His hand shook as he rubbed the skin above the heart.

"We had to replace your power source," Nurse Ratched said. "Your old one was dead. Can you tell us your make and model? Your designation? You still have not raised your right hand as I instructed. How disappointing. You need to listen to your mother. That is me. I am your mother."

The android grimaced, baring his square teeth. "I . . . wh-who are you. Who are y-you? *Who are you?*" He tried to stand. His metal right leg held his weight, but the wooden left buckled. He stumbled forward.

"Ahh!" Rambo cried. "He's attacking! I'm brave. I'm so brave!" He rolled forward, banging the broom against the android's knees. "Die, murderous revenge machine, die!"

"S-s-*stop that*," the android growled. He tried to swat at the broom, but his center of gravity was off, and he missed, almost falling on top of Rambo. He managed to catch himself at the last moment, Rambo moving deftly between his feet, the broom knocking against the android's thighs.

"Do not touch Rambo," Nurse Ratched said, one of her tentacles whipping dangerously in the air. "If you do, you will find it to be rather shocking. Because I will shock you. That was another pun. They do not get old no matter how many times I say them."

"Wh-where am I?" the android snapped. "What is this p-place?"

"You are in the laboratory of the great inventor Victor Lawson," Nurse Ratched said, the tip of her tentacle crackling. "And you would do well to show him some respect. He was the one who brought you back to life. Granted, I did most of the work, which is why I am your mother, but Victor needs positive reinforcement. Victor. You did a good job. We are all very proud of you."

The android lurched again. Victor flinched, taking a step back, fingernails digging into his palms so hard he thought he'd draw blood. Rambo, apparently having decided there was still an active threat, bellowed as he smacked the broomstick against the android's back. "*En garde!*"

The android whirled around, snatching the broomstick before Rambo could hit him again. He brought down the handle over his knee, snapping it in two.

"Oh no," Rambo whispered. "We're gonna die so bad."

The android dropped the pieces of the broom before turning on Victor. He stalked forward, his gait awkward as if he couldn't figure out how to bend his wooden knee.

"Who a-are you?" he demanded. "Wh-what did you d-do to my head?" He grabbed Victor by the front of his shirt, jerking him forward. Vic yelped as he closed his eyes. "Wh-why c-can't I remember who I am?"

And Victor said, "I don't know. I don't know. I don't—"

Electricity snapped and snarled as the android seized.

Victor opened his eyes in time to see him slump toward the floor, Nurse Ratched's tentacle sliding back inside her. "I told you to show him respect," she said. "Listen to Mother." Her screen read THERE IS PLENTY MORE WHERE THAT CAME FROM!

The android was barely out long enough for them to get him back onto the table.

"Quite shocking indeed," Nurse Ratched said, moving efficiently around the table to the android's head. "I warned you. I will do it again if needed. Come on, punk. Make my day." She paused, her screen flashing green. "Interesting. I have no idea where that came from. I like it. Make my day, punk."

The android grimaced. "Legs. Can't f-feel my legs."

"Ten thousand volts will do that to you. You will regain control momentarily. Try anything stupid again, and I will remove your legs entirely."

The android glared at the ceiling. "It'll be the l-last thing you d-do."

"Do you make such promises to all the pretty girls you meet?" Nurse Ratched asked. "I am not interested. Perhaps we could have had something, but I have since reassessed my opinion of you. Would you like to hear what I think?"

"N-no."

"Oh. That is too bad because I am going to tell you anyway. You are—"

"We're not going to hurt you," Vic said quietly. His knuckles popped as he squeezed his hands together.

"My broom," Rambo said. He beeped sadly as he nudged the two pieces on the ground. "You monster. What did it ever do to you besides hit you?"

"Wh-where am I?"

Vic glanced at him before looking away. The eyes, once dead and unseeing, were now trained on him, filled with a spark Vic had never seen before. "The forest."

"Wh-wh-*what* forest?"

Vic frowned. "The big one. The one near the Scrap Yards." He didn't know how else to explain it. Surely, that would tell the android all he needed to know. It was just the forest. It should have been enough.

It wasn't. "Where is this f-forest?"

"It does not have a name," Nurse Ratched said. "At least not one I could find. Though, if my calculations are correct, the forest is located in a place that used to be known as Ory-Gone. Such a strange name. Speaking of strange names, you do not remember yours."

The android's mouth tightened. "N-no."

"I expected as much. Your memories were wiped when you were decommissioned."

"He's like us," Rambo said nervously. He circled the table, giving it a wide berth as if he thought the android would come after him once more. "He doesn't remember before coming to the forest."

"He is not like us," Nurse Ratched said. "We are wonderful. He is a terrible patient. Stay still."

The android gave up struggling as Nurse Ratched loomed over him.

"This will not hurt," she said. "I need to make sure you are not going to explode and kill us all." Her scanner came to life, the light starting at the android's head and working its way down his body. It paused at his chest before continuing to his hips, legs, and feet. "There. See? That was not so bad. Here. Have a lollipop. Error. Lollipop distributor is—my word. We really need to fix that. Victor. I demand that you find me treats so that I may give them to my patients."

"Victor," the android said, and Vic felt a chill run down his spine. "Your d-designation is V-victor."

"He can retain information," Nurse Ratched said. "Good. That means the processing through his biochip is still mostly intact. Yes, he is Victor. I am Nurse Ratched. My main function is to provide medical care to preserve life at any cost. The tiny shrieking annoyance below us is Rambo. He assists by keeping everything clean."

Rambo waves his arms. "We're all equally important. Hooray!"

"Decommissioned," the android said, the word spoken with great care. "I w-was d-decommissioned."

"Yes," Nurse Ratched said. "Engaging Empathy Protocol. There, there. It is all right. When one door closes, you can still bust it down. One robot's trash is another man's treasure." A picture of a cat appeared on her screen below the words I AIN'T KITTEN YOU! "There, there."

The android closed his eyes, the lines around his mouth deep. "My a-arm. Hand. Leg. What . . . wh-what is that?"

"Wood," Vic muttered. "We carved it ourselves. It's meant to help you." The words were low, almost a whisper. He couldn't speak any louder.

"You're like a puppet," Rambo added helpfully. "Except alive. Half puppet. Like your mother was a puppet and your father was a washing machine." His sensors flashed. "Wait. That doesn't make sense. Like your mother was a puppet and your father was a really angry television. Do you like movies? I like movies. What's your favorite?"

"What do you remember?" Nurse Ratched asked. "Anything? You somehow survived decommissioning with most of yourself intact. What is the last thing you remember?"

Vic thought the android wasn't going to speak. He was surprised when he said, "L-lights. Flashes of l-light." He turned his head, looking at each of them in turn. "Then you. In the metal. In the sun. Buried. C-couldn't g-g-get out."

"Hap," Vic said, though he hadn't meant to.

The android's eyes narrowed. "What?"

Vic cringed at the android's anger. He waved his hand at the plate on the android's chest. "Letters. There. I think some are missing. But there's an *H*. And an *A*. *P* at the end. Hap."

"Hap," Nurse Ratched repeated. She leaned forward over the android, scanner running along the plate. The letters appeared on her screen. "Does that sound familiar?"

The android squinted at the screen. "N-no."

"Is it an acronym, perhaps?"

"I d-don't *know*," the android growled at her.

"The *A* probably stands for 'angry,'" Rambo whispered, nudging against Vic's leg. "Hysterically Angry Puppet." He squealed in fright when the android snapped his teeth at him.

Nurse Ratched was unmoved. "Until we find out otherwise, your designation henceforth is Hap. It is not a bad name. Not as nice as mine, but then most are not. What is your primary function?"

"I don't r-r-remember," Hap spat. "I t-told you t-that." Vic took a step back when Hap struggled to sit up again, hands gripping the edges of the table. The woodwork was holding, though Hap seemed stiff in his movements. It would take time. Vic itched to touch the wood, to see if he could feel the heat of the machine underneath. He managed to keep his hands to himself.

"So you said," Nurse Ratched agreed.

Hap pressed a hand against his chest. "Wh-what did you p-put in me? It's . . . m-moving."

Nurse Ratched said, "Ah, yes. That. We needed a way to bring you back. A source of power. Your battery was corrupted. We could not find a similar replacement, so we gave you—"

"A heart," Vic blurted before gnawing on his lip. "We put a heart in your chest."

Hap frowned. He tapped a finger against his breastbone. The compartment slid open. The heart sat perfectly inside, gears moving smoothly, the wood creaking as the heart expanded and then shrunk, expanded and shrunk. "H-how? H-how is this w-w-*working*?"

"Victor is extremely intelligent," Nurse Ratched said. "He can fix almost anything. And he decided to fix you, so you should be thankful to your father. Your dad. Your daddy. Error. Error. Do not call people 'daddy.' That is unprofessional."

Hap stared down at the heart. He brought his hand up, touching the center of the biggest gear. It slowed before he pulled his finger away, the gear then speeding up briefly before resuming its slow rotation. He tapped his chest once more, and the compartment closed. He looked back at Vic. "Why? Wh-why did you h-help me?"

Vic winced, glancing at the door, but somehow managing to stay where he was. "You were hurt," he said, words clipped. "Just because you had parts missing doesn't mean you don't deserve a chance."

"Unless you want to kill us," Nurse Ratched said. "Do you want to kill us?"

"Not y-yet," Hap muttered.

"Oh no," Nurse Ratched said. "I think I am swooning. I also say 'not yet' when asked if I want to kill things. You are perfect." Her screen showed two hands shaking in greeting. "I am no longer your mother. You will be my murder husband. Is there anyone here that can marry us?"

Rambo gasped. "There's going to be a *wedding*? But I'm not ready yet! Wait. Hold on." His motor revved as he grunted, his body shaking. A slot slid open at his front, and little bits of metal shot out onto the floor. "Confetti! Yay for love!"

"I do not have a thing to wear," Nurse Ratched said. "But

that is fine because I never wear anything at all. I am nude. I will now flirt with you. Do you like what you see? I have junk in my trunk. Literally. There are pieces in my rear compartment that do nothing because they are junk. Would you like for me to show you?"

"Dancing cheek to cheek!" Rambo began to sing in a warbly voice. "Heaven, we're in heaven!"

Hap stood slowly, towering over the rest of them. He bounced on his knees briefly before frowning. "Why am I n-naked?"

Vic flushed furiously. He glanced down at Hap's groin before looking up at the ceiling. "We had to repair you. We didn't . . . we didn't do anything else to you."

"Nothing weird," Nurse Ratched assured him. "Touching patients inappropriately who are dead or unconscious is against my programming. I would never allow that to happen. Even when Victor insisted we remove your pants—"

"I did *not*!"

"Ha, ha. That was another joke. You will learn I am the funny one here. Rambo, please bring our patient his pants so Victor's blood pressure will lower. It is alarmingly high at the moment, and I do not want him to have a heart attack, even if there would be defibrillation involved."

"Pants!" Rambo cried, going to the work bench. He rose on his lift, shoving the ruined duster aside before grabbing the pants and handing them to Hap.

Hap didn't speak as he tried to put on his pants. He started with his metal leg, but his wooden leg locked up and he almost fell over. He growled at Nurse Ratched when she tried to help, slapping her tentacle away. He tried once more, leaning against the table. "L-leg. F-feels stiff."

"The modifications," Nurse Ratched said. "They will take some getting used to. Here. Look." She moved before him as he buttoned up his pants. A light appeared on the top of her screen. "I have a camera. I can show you what you look like. Perhaps that will help to jog your memory circuits."

The screen filled with Hap's image. He startled, the table scraping against the floor as he leaned heavily onto it. He stared at the screen, blinking slowly, the image doing the same. Watching himself, he reached up and stroked the wood in his cheek, fingers rasping against the stubble underneath it.

"T-this is me?" he whispered, eyes wide.

"Yes. This is you. Not as we found you, but as you are now. It is much better, in my opinion. Do you recognize yourself?"

He shook his head but stopped when he caught the symbols cut into his hair on the sides. He touched them too, fingers tracing the designs. "I d-don't kn-know." He frowned. "What's w-wrong with my v-v-v—" Both he and the image on the screen scowled.

"Voice," Nurse Ratched said. "Damage to your vocal processor. We did not attempt repairs to avoid further trauma."

He turned away from the screen. Nurse Ratched backed up, the image disappearing into blackness.

Vic looked toward the door once more. "You can go."

Hap snapped his head up. "What?"

Vic shrugged, more of an involuntary tic than anything. "You don't have to stay here. You're not a prisoner. We're not trying to keep you against your will."

"My w-will," Hap said slowly. "I h-have will?"

"Oh boy," Nurse Ratched said. "I do not have enough psychological or philosophical programming to deal with that. I am unable to answer that question to any satisfaction. Asimov would be disappointed in me. Victor. You are human. You can—"

The effect was instantaneous. One moment, Hap was still leaning against the table, arms hanging loosely at his sides. The next, he was upright and moving, almost quicker than any of them could follow. He lunged toward Vic, who scrambled backward, grunting in pain when the small of his back hit the work bench. Hands stretched toward his throat, Hap's face alarmingly blank, eyes as dead as they'd been when they brought him back to the lab.

It wasn't Nurse Ratched who stopped him, nor was it Rambo or Vic.

It was Hap himself.

His arms were stretched out before him, his fingers inches from Vic's face. His eyes filled once more with the spark of life. Vic could hear the gears turning furiously in his chest. Hap's hands began to shake, the vibrations working up his arms to his shoulders. He took a step back. "Wh-what's happening to m-me?"

Hap turned, snarling as he gripped the edges of the table. Rambo shouted as he overturned it, smashing it against the wall, breaking the window, glass falling to the forest floor below.

Nurse Ratched moved in front of Rambo and Vic, but Hap ignored them. He stomped back and forth around the lab, hands in his hair, yanking furiously.

"'Roid rage!" Rambo whimpered. "Murderous revenge machine! Run!"

Vic looked around for a weapon, anything he could use in case Hap came for them. He grabbed a mallet hammer off the wall, eyeing the soldering gun hanging suspended above where the table had been.

Hap looked at them, eyes wild. "I d-don't *know*. I d-don't know who I a-am or what I—"

The door to the lab crashed open, wood splintering, hinges squealing. Dad appeared in the doorway, eyes narrowed as he took in the sight before him.

But Hap wasn't standing where he'd been.

No. He had moved in *front* of Victor and Rambo and Nurse Ratched, facing away from them, arms spread like wings as he backed against them slowly. He bumped into Nurse Ratched.

It took Vic a moment to realize what had happened.

He wasn't trying to hurt them.

Hap was trying to *protect* them from what he perceived as a threat.

Dad.

"What's going on in here?" Dad asked thunderously. He glanced at Vic, his gaze moving up and down before turning to Hap. "Who the hell are you? Get away from my son."

"Victor," Nurse Ratched said. "Good news! You no longer have to worry about Gio finding out."

CHAPTER 7

Dad," Vic said, trying to move around Hap. "Don't. Please. I can explain—"

"Victor," Dad said in a flat voice. "Move away from the android."

"His name is Hap," Rambo said. "We made him. Sort of."

"I did most of the work, Gio," Nurse Ratched said. "If there is to be any praise, please lavish it upon me. If instead you are angry and will seek to dole out punishment, please note that I had nothing to do with this because it was all Victor."

Dad jerked his head in warning. "Move. Now."

They did, Victor stepping slowly around Hap, who hadn't looked away from Dad. Hap didn't try to stop them, even when Rambo bumped into his leg. "Oops," Rambo said. "Sorry. Sorry. Can you just . . . lift your leg a little? That's better. Thank you." He zoomed toward Dad, circling behind him and tugging on his pant leg. "He broke my broom when I hit him with it. But other than that, he's not so bad."

"Are you all right?" Dad said in a low voice as Victor stopped next to him.

"I'm fine."

"Did he hurt you?"

"No. Dad, he's not—"

"Good," Dad said. "Now I don't want to hear another word out of your mouth until I ask for it."

"Uh-oh," Rambo whispered.

Dad ignored him. He glared at Hap. "Who are you? Why have you come here?" Then, oddly, "Have we met before? You look familiar."

Hap sneered at him. "Wh-who the f-fuck are *you*?"

"My name is Giovanni Lawson. Answer my question. What is your designation?"

"He says he does not know," Nurse Ratched said. "I see no reason to believe he is lying. It appears his memory circuits have been wiped as ours were. He is a blank slate. A tall, handsome, angry blank slate."

"Designation," Dad demanded. "Now."

"I d-don't *know*," Hap snarled. "It was b-black and then I was here."

"Victor. Explain."

Vic looked at the floor. His father was rarely angry. In fact, Victor could only remember a handful of times he'd ever seen it before. "We found him," he said quietly. "In the Scrap Yards. Buried under dead machines." He flexed his hands, knuckles popping. "We couldn't . . . we couldn't leave him. He was alive. He was awake."

Dad closed his eyes, brow furrowed before smoothing out. "And you brought him here."

"Yes," Nurse Ratched said. "It did not seem right to leave him where he was. He has yet to do anything explicitly murderous."

"Explicitly," Dad said as he opened his eyes. "*Explicitly.*"

"There was the incident with the broom," Nurse Ratched said.

"It was such a good broom too," Rambo moaned.

"Why is he shirtless?" Dad asked.

"Because Victor decided to remove all of Hap's clothing in order to—"

"I did *not*," Vic snapped at her.

"Hap," Dad said. "*Hap.*"

"That's the name we gave him," Rambo said. "It's a good name. It stands for Hysterically Angry Puppet because he looks like he's always mad. I think that's just his face, though."

"What do you want?" Dad asked, taking a step forward.

Hap didn't move. He blinked slowly as he stared. "I . . . do n-not know."

"What is your primary function?"

"I d-do not know."

"How did you come to be here?"

"This is futile," Nurse Ratched said. "He does not know. Every question you ask he will not know the answer to."

Dad raised his hands to show he wasn't a threat as he took another step forward. "Is that true? You don't remember anything?"

Hap scowled at him. "It's wh-what I said. M-maybe you should get your ears ch-checked."

"Wow," Nurse Ratched said. "He is a jerk. Fascinating. Is this feeling maternal or arousal? How oedipal of me."

"I am like you," Dad said, stopping a few feet away from Hap. Vic had to stand on his tiptoes to see over his father's shoulder. Hap's scowl had deepened. "I'm an android. Do you understand that?"

Hap sneered at him. "I'm not s-stupid. I know wh-what I am. I j-just don't know *who*."

"The plate," Dad said. "On your chest. Can I see it?"

"Wh-why?"

"Because it will show me who you are."

Hap didn't like that. "Don't touch me."

"I'm not going to. Not without your permission. I promise."

Hap glanced at Vic before looking back at Dad. "I . . ."

"He will not kill you," Nurse Ratched said. "Only if you try and hurt one of us."

Vic thought Hap would snap again, or worse, try to run. A complicated expression crossed his face, there and gone again before Vic could even begin to make sense of it. Hap's shoulders slumped as he curled in on himself, wrapping his arms around his middle. "I'm not going to h-hurt anyone."

Hap flinched when Dad took another step, now within arm's reach. His mouth twisted down, the lines around his eyes deep and pronounced. He stared at the floor when Dad reached out. True to his word, Dad didn't touch him; instead, he traced the air a few inches above the metal plate. "*H,*" he said, tracing a fingertip over the letter before moving on to the next. "*A.*"

Then Dad stiffened, finger shaking. Without looking away from Hap, he began to back away slowly. The lines on Hap's face returned, his hands curling into fists at his sides.

In a low voice, Dad said, "Everyone out. Now."

"Uh-oh," Rambo whispered.

"Why?" Vic asked as Dad bumped into him. "What are you—

"D-do you kn-know me?" Hap demanded, taking a step toward them, his stutter becoming more pronounced. He gripped the sides of his head and snarled silently.

Vic tried to step around his father. He didn't know what he meant to do. Pull his father back? Step between them? Something. But before he could figure it out, Dad grabbed him by the arm and pulled him toward the door, Nurse Ratched and Rambo rolling after them.

Vic tried to pull his arm away. "Dad, stop. You need to stop. Listen to me, please. He's not going to hurt us."

Dad shoved him through the ruined doorway. "You have no idea what's he's capable of. Go now. He's—"

"Jumped out the window," Rambo said.

They whirled around. The lab was empty. The window was open.

They rushed to the landing around the edge of the lab. Below them, Hap rose from a crouch, dust and leaves billowing up around him. He raised his head to stare up at them. "I. D-don't. *Hurt.*"

And then he took off running into the forest.

Dad slammed his hand against the railing. "Dammit. Stay here, all of you."

And then he vaulted over the railing. He hit the ground where Hap had just been standing, knees bent to absorb the impact. He rose swiftly and took off after Hap, beard trailing over his shoulder.

"Whoa," Rambo whispered. "I want to try!"

Vic barely managed to keep Rambo from leaping off the edge, tucking him under his arm and running toward the elevator. Nurse Ratched was already inside. She pressed the button as soon as Vic and Rambo entered the elevator. The lift jerked before lowering to the ground.

They tracked Dad and Hap as best they could through the forest, moving north away from the compound, Nurse Ratched's treads kicking up leaves and pine needles. Rambo zoomed ahead, arms waving above him, pincers clacking.

The afternoon sun was waning, the air cool. Vic didn't know where Hap was heading. The Scrap Yards were east, at the edge of the woods. North was nothing but a forest that seemed to go on for miles and miles. Vic had explored much of his surroundings as he'd grown and couldn't think of where Hap could run that they couldn't find him.

The shadows below the canopy began to stretch. The forest was near silent, as quiet as Vic had ever heard it. No animals moved. No birds sang.

He kept jogging, head whipping back and forth until he realized he was alone. He glanced back to see Nurse Ratched and Rambo had stopped moving next to a small clearing. "What is it?" he asked as he turned around.

"I do not know," Nurse Ratched said. "Their trail ends. I cannot find their footsteps. It is like they just disappeared." Question marks filled her screen.

"That's not possible," Vic said. "Rambo?"

Rambo spun in slow circles, sensors flashing. "They're gone. I don't know what happened." He beeped, sounding confused. "Did they learn to fly? Can Gio fly? Does he have rockets in his feet? I wish I had rocket feet. And also feet."

"They did not fly," Nurse Ratched said. She rolled toward a tree at the edge of the clearing. An old pine, the trunk thick, the limbs wide and heavy. The tip of one of her tentacles pressed against divots in the tree bark Vic hadn't noticed before. "They climbed. They're moving through the trees."

Vic looked up. The pine trees grew close together. If they kept off the ground, jumping from tree to tree, he had no way to track them. Unless . . .

He squinted up at the tree. Fifteen feet up, he could see one of the branches hanging limply. It'd been broken. He looked to the closest tree. Divots in the wood, the bark cracked, sap leaking. One of them had jumped there. And to the next. And to the next.

"Come on," Vic said. "This way."

They lost the trail again only ten minutes later. The trees had grown thicker, and it was impossible to see what direction they'd gone, not unless Vic climbed up. He growled in frustration, turning in circles, eyes narrowed against the encroaching night.

"Are we lost?" Rambo asked nervously.

"Of course not," Nurse Ratched said. "I know exactly where we are."

"Oh. Where are we?"

"In the forest."

"Whew," Rambo said. "I was worried for a moment that we were lost. Since we're not, I will instead focus on the fact that we're in the middle of the woods at night by ourselves. Do big animals like to eat vacuums?"

"I am sure they do," Nurse Ratched said.

"Oh no," Rambo whispered. "But *I'm* a vacuum."

Vic turned in slow circles, trying to pick up the trail again. The failing light wasn't helping. He couldn't see much. He ground his teeth together, trying to clear his head. He needed to think. That's all. Think. Think.

He rounded a large tree trunk, and bumped into Nurse Ratched, who'd stopped, Rambo in front of her turning this way and that, his lights flashing. "What is it?" Vic asked, peering around Nurse Ratched. Nothing, or so he thought.

"We are being watched," she said.

Rambo beeped loudly. "We are?" His arms rose above his head as he rolled forward slowly. "Who is it? Who's watching us? I'm not afraid of you!"

Something rustled in the trees—the wind?—and Rambo squealed, spinning around and rushing back toward Nurse Ratched and Vic. He was still five feet away when Vic heard movement above him and lifted his head.

Up in the tree, high in the branches, bright eyes opened and stared back at him.

Vic didn't have time to shout in warning as Hap leapt from the thick branch he'd been standing on. The air whistled around him as he plummeted toward the forest floor. Hitting the ground between them in a crouch, he rose swiftly, scooping up Rambo and holding him high above his head. Rambo's wheels spun uselessly, arms flailing as he screamed he was too young to die, that he had *plans* and *dreams* and who was going to clean up all the dirt on the floors if he was dead? No one, that's who!

Nurse Ratched instantly transformed into a nightmare, all of her tentacles snapping out from her sides, the tips crackling and snarling in metal blurs as they whipped around her. "Put him down," she said, rolling forward. "If you do not, I will end the pathetic existence you call a life."

"Vic!" Rambo cried. "I'm being brave, but it's really hard!"

"Don't hurt him," Vic pleaded as Hap glared at the advancing Nurse Ratched, Rambo still high above his head.

"I'm n-n-*not*," Hap spat. "L-l-look."

Hap nodded toward the ground where Rambo had been rolling over. There, sitting on the petals of a pink-and-purple autumn crocus, was a butterfly. A large monarch, its wings a deep orange bordered in black, the tips spotted in white and yellow. They opened and closed as the antennae of the butterfly twitched in the failing light.

Hap tossed Rambo aside as he crouched in front of the insect. Rambo bounced on his back before landing on his wheels.

Hap leaned closer to the butterfly, his face scrunched up in concentration. The butterfly ignored the large machine towering over it, going about its business with the crocus. As Vic looked on, Nurse Ratched's tentacles powering down, Hap reached toward the insect.

Without thinking, Vic shot forward, grabbing Hap's wrist before he could pick up the butterfly. Warm synthetic skin and metal surrounded by flesh and bone. Alarm bells rang in Vic's mind as Hap lifted his head slowly, first looking at Vic's grip, then sliding up the arm to his shoulder, chin, nose, eyes. His lips pulled back over his teeth, and Vic felt him beginning to tense.

"You'll hurt it," Vic blurted.

Hap jerked his arm free. "I *didn't*."

"But you could," Nurse Ratched said. "Butterfly wings are delicate. Touching one might cause the colors to fade, leaving the butterfly open to predators. It will not kill it immediately, but you are sentencing it to death regardless."

At the sound of approaching footsteps Vic whirled around, heart in his throat. Dad stood there among the trees. Vic could barely parse the expression on his face: a mixture of anger and sadness and something far more serious, almost like resignation. But Dad did not look at Vic; he only had eyes for Hap. "Nurse Ratched. A light, if you please."

"Yes, Gio." Her screen lit up white, illuminating the darkness. Hap's shadow stretched off into the forest, colliding with trees and shrubbery.

Hap didn't move as Dad approached, attention split between Dad and the butterfly.

Dad glanced from Hap to the insect and back again. He asked, "Why?"

"It w-would have died. *That* thing was about to crush it," Hap muttered, nodding toward Rambo as the butterfly turned to face the other direction.

"Possibly. But you would have been able to escape. You made a decision, you weighed the consequences. Why did you do what you did?"

Hap frowned, forehead lined. His mouth twisted, no sound coming out. He tried again. "It's n-n-*nice*."

"Nice," Dad repeated. Then, "What is nice about it?"

"You h-have eyes," Hap said.

"He has got you there," Nurse Ratched said. "You do, in fact, have eyes."

"I can see it for myself," Dad agreed. "But that's not what I'm asking." He crouched down on the other side of the butterfly. "Why is it nice to *you*? How does it make you feel?"

"F-feel?"

"Yes. You saw it. You saved it. There must be a reason."

Hap bared his teeth silently.

"Do you like it?" Dad asked.

"*Y-yes*," Hap snarled. "It's p-p-p-*pretty*."

Of all the things Hap could have said, Vic expected that the least. This machine had stopped his escape from the forest because a butterfly had entranced him.

"Is it?" Dad asked. "Is it the colors? The pattern? The design?"

"Y-yes," Hap said.

Dad nodded. "You like it. And because of that, you stopped death from happening."

"So did we," Rambo said, giving Hap a wide berth, stopping next to Gio. "We liked his color and pattern and design, and we brought him back to life! I like it when we have things in common."

"Y-yes," Hap said, nodding furiously. "Th-that. They saved me. I s-saved the butterfly."

"But you see the issue with that, don't you?" Dad asked. "If they hadn't brought you back, we wouldn't be out in the forest, and the butterfly would not have needed to be rescued."

"I d-don't understand."

"I know," Dad said. "You do not understand there are ramifications for every decision. And you're not the only one."

Vic winced but did not speak.

The butterfly chose this very moment to lift from the crocus, wings flapping as it rose. Hap grunted, eyes wide as the butterfly flew off into the darkness. He rose to his feet, staring after it.

Dad stood too, and his shoulders were stiff, face blank. He said, "Where did you come from?"

"D-darkness," Hap said, still looking after the butterfly, even though it was no longer visible. "I r-remember metal. Then d-darkness. Then light." He pressed his wooden hand against his chest. "I feel different."

"Different than what?"

"Before."

"You felt different than you do now?"

"Yes." He pounded his chest. "Here."

"Show me."

"Dad," Vic started, but his father shook his head in warning.

"Show me," he said again.

Hap turned around. He looked unsure, but he tapped his chest, and the compartment slid open. The gears of the wood-and-metal heart turned, the sound low and quiet in the darkness of the forest.

"Oh," Dad said quietly. "Victor. Did you do this? Did you make this?"

Victor couldn't speak.

Hap didn't move as Dad leaned forward, studying the heart in his chest. Vic began gnawing on his bottom lip. Dad was silent in his inspection, barely even moving as he stared at the heart. Minutes felt like hours before Dad finally stood upright. "Victor," he said, an odd note to his voice. "Did you bleed in the heart? As you have done in mine?"

"I . . . I thought it would help," Victor said. "It's how your heart works."

To that, Dad whispered, "What have you done?"

CHAPTER 8

Hap was an asshole.

That was clear immediately.

"I d-don't like you," he told Rambo as they arrived back at the compound, the vacuum in the middle of babbling about anything and everything, as he sometimes did when he was nervous.

Rambo paused for a moment, sensors lighting up before falling dark. "That's okay. I like me. Gio says that self-worth isn't measured by what others think, but what you think about yourself."

Hap tried to kick him out of his way, but Rambo was too fast, rolling away before a foot could connect with his casing. "Whoa," Rambo squealed. "Not cool! Seriously, *not cool*."

"You get used to him," Nurse Ratched said. "He is like a fungus. He grows on you. But perhaps consider not kicking him. He will become damaged, and I will not be pleased. You do not want me to be upset." Her tentacle whipped in the air around her, the tip crackling with electricity. "Unless you like being shocked." Her screen dimmed as the lights of the compound grew brighter.

"I d-don't like you either."

"Oh no," Nurse Ratched said. "My whole day is ruined. I feel so sad. Just kidding. I am fine."

"Hap, come with me," Dad said. "Victor, off to bed with you. It's late. Nurse Ratched, with me, please. We have work to do."

Vic started to protest. "What are you—"

"Victor. Now. We'll speak in the morning. Trust me on that."

"Ooh," Rambo said. "You're in trouble."

Vic scowled at all of them. "I'm not a child."

"No," Dad said. "You're not. But you're already dragging your feet. The adrenaline that flooded your body is receding. You need rest."

"What are you going to do?" *To him* went unsaid.

Dad shook his head. "Nothing that will bring harm to him. You have my word."

Still, Vic hesitated. Hap was watching him again, looking as if he didn't want Vic out of his sight. Vic wasn't sure if that was a good thing or not. "Fine. But if anything happens, you need to tell me."

"I will," Dad said, and Vic believed him. He took a step back toward the elevator.

Hap didn't like that. "Where are y-you going?"

Vic pointed up toward his room. "There. That's mine. That's where I sleep."

"Oh yes," Nurse Ratched said. "Good idea. Point out where you will be defenseless to the murderous revenge machine. That is clear thinking."

"It's going to be a bloodbath," Rambo moaned. "I'll have to try and clean up Vic's remains." He sniffled. "At least he'll always be a part of me then. I love you, Vic, even when you're in pieces, your flesh hanging from the ceiling—"

Hap tried to follow Vic, though he didn't look happy about it. He was scowling once more as Vic held up his hands, motioning for him to stay.

"He's imprinted on Victor," Nurse Ratched said. "Like a duckling. Like a terrifying killer duckling. This is wonderful. I am having a wonderful time."

"You'll be okay," Vic told him. "Dad won't hurt you. No one will hurt you here."

"I d-don't care," Hap said. "I d-don't like you. I don't like any of y-you."

"Then why are you still trying to follow him?" Rambo asked.

Hap tried to kick him again, but his wooden leg betrayed him. He almost fell. "I-I'm *not*."

"Uh-huh," Nurse Ratched said. "Keep telling yourself that."

The last Vic saw of him that night was Dad leading him toward the ground house. Hap followed, looking back over his shoulder at Vic. He stopped in the doorway, watching as Vic and Rambo rode the elevator up.

He watched the ground house through his window, Rambo settling in behind him in his docking port, ready to shut down for the night and recharge. The lights were on below them, but he couldn't see any movement.

"What do you think they're doing?" Vic asked.

"Making sure he won't murder us in our sleep," Rambo said, shutting down, one light pulsing slowly, a soft blue.

Vic tried to stay awake, debating whether or not to try to sneak down to see what was happening and wondering why Dad hadn't taken Hap to his lab. He only lasted a few minutes more, his body heavy, a fresh wave of exhaustion washing over him.

He barely made it to his bed before collapsing, asleep as soon as his head hit the pillow.

When he opened his eyes, gray light filtered in through the windows.

He blinked slowly.

And gasped when he saw a figure towering over him.

"Good morning," Nurse Ratched said as he almost fell off the bed, heart stumbling in his chest. "Sleep well?"

"I told you not to do that," Vic snapped. He collapsed back on his pillow, scrubbing a hand over his face.

"I know. But I did it anyway because it is amusing. Your blood pressure is elevated. You are sweating. Were you dreaming?"

Yes. Vivid, wild dreams where the sky was filled with torn and shredded butterfly wings. "What happened? What's wrong?"

"Nothing is wrong, Victor. At least not in the way you are thinking."

"Where is he?"

"With Gio," she said. "We have been up all night working while you slept comfortably in your bed. Yes, I am trying to make you feel guilty. Is it working?"

Not quite. Vic sat up in his bed, putting his feet on the floor. It was cold. Gooseflesh rose along his skin. "Anything?"

"Yes," Nurse Ratched said. "Though, I doubt it is what you are looking for." Her screen filled with an image of Hap. "It was as we suspected. A complete memory wipe. When he says he does not remember, he is telling the truth. Like us, he was decommissioned, and they took away everything he knew."

"What about his protocols?"

"We do not know. Any remaining data is corrupted, and the more we push, the further it could damage him." She backed away from his bed. "He kept asking about you. He seems strangely fixated, though he cannot explain why. He is a conundrum. We are blessed."

Vic stood from the bed, the frame creaking. He looked down. The docking port was empty. "Rambo?"

The image of Hap disappeared from Nurse Ratched's screen, replaced with a version of Rambo, cross-eyed and buck-toothed. "Asking questions. Hap does not like to be asked questions. I put the odds of Rambo's survival at twenty-four percent. But that is fine. We can always use what remains for parts. I would like to have his arms, if that is all right with you."

Vic groaned. It was going to be a rough day.

Nurse Ratched wasn't lying.

"What are you thinking about?" Vic could hear Rambo saying as the elevator lowered to the ground. "What's going through your head right now? Is it that we should be best friends? Because if it is, that's what *I* was thinking, and I agree. You can never have too many best friends. I already have three. Well, two. Vic and Gio. Nurse Ratched is sometimes my best friend, but since she's sociopathic, it can be a little hard."

"No," Hap growled. "I wasn't th-thinking that."

"Oh. Then what were you thinking?"

"H-how far I could throw you."

"Really far, I bet," Rambo said. "But best friends don't throw each other. Vic taught me that."

He hadn't.

Vic found them sitting near the garden, the sky above covered in a layer of thick clouds. Nurse Ratched followed behind him, her treads cracking the thin layer of frost on the ground. Vic pulled his coat tighter around him, rubbing his arms to warm them up.

Hap had been gifted a shirt, one of Gio's from the looks of it, a little loose in the front. He'd put his boots back on too at some point and was sitting at the edge of the garden. Dad was on his hands and knees, moving carefully through the rows of plants.

Hap heard them approaching first. He rose to his feet, the ever-present scowl on his face. His eyebrows bunched up. "You sh-shut down for a l-long time. Why?"

Vic didn't know quite how to answer that. "Because I have to."

"Why?"

"He's human," Dad said without looking up. "Remember? We discussed this last night. He's different than you or me. He needs rest."

"Because he needs to r-recharge."

"Yes. That's right. Good morning, Victor. Sleep well?"

Vic looked away from Hap. He didn't like the tone in his father's voice. It was too light. Too easy. It didn't seem right, though Victor had a hard time figuring out why. "I guess."

"Good," Dad said, moving from the third row to the fourth.

"D-did you recharge?" Hap asked.

"Yeah," Vic said, hands twitching. "As best I could."

Hap wasn't blinking. It was eerie. Vic couldn't focus on his face, glancing there and away, there and away. "And y-you do that every d-day?"

"Mostly."

"Interesting," Nurse Ratched said. "He is learning. Retaining information. He will use it against us. How diabolical. I continue to enjoy his existence." She rolled over to him, circling him slowly, careful to avoid the edges of the garden. "Is it *nice* seeing Victor this morning?"

Dad paused before resuming his inspection.

Hap's scowl deepened. "N-no?"

"Was that a question?" She poked him with one of her tentacles. He tried to slap it away, but she was too fast for him. "It sounded like a question. Question implies you do not know the answer."

"No," Hap said again, this time spitting out the word.

"Interesting," Nurse Ratched said. "You are either being sincere or you learned to lie like Victor recently did. Gio, your feelings must be up in arms."

Hap turned his head slowly to look at her as she prodded his hip. "F-feelings."

"Yes," Dad said, finally looking up. He settled back on his heels, dirt under his fingernails as he rested his hands on his thighs. "Feelings."

"H-how?"

"We watch. We learn. We process. It wasn't always this way. But the more complex our minds became, the more choice we were given. Evolution by way of mimicry."

"I d-don't have feelings."

"So you say." Dad looked troubled as he shook his head. "I will ask you a question. I want you to answer it as best you can."

Hap glanced at Vic before turning to face Gio. "What."

"What is your designation?"

Hap's head jerked as if someone had swung at him. His mouth opened. No sound came out. He raised his hand in front of his face, looking at his wooden fingers. He said, "Hap. My d-designation is Hap."

"Is it?"

"Yes. It was g-given to me. It's m-mine."

"And you wouldn't like to be called anything else."

"No."

"Why?" Dad asked.

Hap's face went slack momentarily before the skin under his eye twitched. "I d-don't know."

"I do!" Rambo cried, arms waving. "I know why. Pick me. Pick me!"

Dad chuckled ruefully. "Why, Rambo?"

"Because a designation is a gift," Rambo said. "It's an identity. It sets us apart from others like us. It's unique. In all of existence, there has never been someone named Rambo before me. But even if there were, I'm the best one."

"Precisely," Dad said. "It gives you presence."

"Weight," Hap said. "Heavy." He pressed a hand to the side of his head.

"And how does it make you feel?" Dad asked.

Hap dropped his hand. "I . . ." His face screwed up again before relaxing. "Different."

"Good different or bad different?"

"Different d-different. There is no g-good or b-bad."

"And does being called Hap make you feel different different?"

"Yes."

"And you like it."

Hap said, "L-like the butterfly."

Vic didn't know why he felt warm. It wasn't validation. It wasn't praise, especially since Hap looked pissed off about it, though that might have been his default expression. Vic wondered why anyone would create such a surly machine. "Hap," he said.

Hap looked at him.

Vic fidgeted, shifting his weight from one foot to the other. "It's a good name."

"Wh-why do you move like that?" Hap asked. "Are you malfunctioning?"

"No," Dad said before Vic could answer, and he was grateful for it. His tongue felt thick in his mouth, his throat dry. "He isn't malfunctioning. He, like you, is different. It is part of his design."

Hap stared at Vic, his gaze boring into him. Then he started wringing his hands, hopping from one foot to the other in an odd approximation of Vic.

"Stop," Vic snapped. "Stop it."

Hap did. "Wh-why? You do it. I can do it."

"You are an asshole," Nurse Ratched said.

"I a-am an asshole."

"I like this game," Rambo whispered. Then, louder, "Now say, 'Rambo is my best friend.'"

"N-no," Hap said.

Rambo's arms drooped. "Aw. I thought that would work."

"I am n-not nice," Hap said again. "I am an asshole. I am Hap. That is my designation. I w-will not hurt anything today."

"Or any day," Dad said mildly.

"Or any d-day. Unless—"

"No unless!" Rambo cried. "You can't say unless!"

Hap frowned. "Y-yes, I c-can. I just said it. Unless. Unless. U-unless."

"Oh no," Rambo moaned.

Dad stood slowly, grunting as he did so. "Come. Let us see what we see."

*　*　*

Dad led them to the ground house. Hap followed Vic closely, as if he thought Vic would disappear if he looked away. Vic—used to having a shadow in Rambo and Nurse Ratched—didn't know what to make of him. He'd never heard of a machine imprinting on someone before. It could be argued that Rambo—and in a lesser sense, Nurse Ratched—had done the same, but it didn't quite feel like it had with them. It was bigger, somehow. Too big, Vic thought as Hap crowded against him in the doorway.

They gathered near Dad's chair, though Dad didn't sit. Instead, he motioned for Hap to do so. Hap did, hands flat against his thighs. "Do you remember what I told you last night before we went to the lab?"

Hap nodded, head jerking up and down awkwardly as if he wasn't used to the motion. "You w-will not h-hurt me unless I do something to make y-you."

Dad frowned. "I never said hurt. I said stop."

Hap looked up at him. "Wh-what is the d-difference?"

"Can you be hurt?"

Hap cocked his head. "I don't understand."

"Hurt implies feeling. What are you feeling?"

"I feel like you a-ask too m-many questions."

Vic was startled into a laugh, though he tried to cover it up. He obviously wasn't successful as Hap stared at him. "Wh-what was that?"

"Laughter," Dad said, looking as if he were fighting his own smile. "He found that humorous."

"I am n-not humorous."

"It's subjective," Dad said. "You can—"

Hap made a sound, low and grating against Vic's ears. It took him a moment to realize what it was. Laughing. Hap was laughing. It ended as quickly as it had begun. "L-like that."

"Fascinating," Nurse Ratched said, her screen displaying lines of code and equations that moved quicker than Vic could follow. "The imitation is astonishing."

"Do me!" Rambo cried. "Do me!"

"D-do me," Hap said, a sneer on his lips. "D-do m-me. I n-never stop talking."

"Wow," Rambo said. "That was scarily accurate."

"He's learning," Dad said, crouching down before Hap. "It's only going to continue, and most likely at an exponential rate."

"Why?" Vic asked.

Dad sighed. "Because of you, Victor."

Vic felt his stomach sink.

"Hap," Dad said. "Can you show us?"

Hap looked at each of them in turn before his gaze rested on Vic, who nodded. He reached down and lifted his shirt above his head, the collar stretching. He folded it carefully before setting it on his lap.

The wood on his chest and face gleamed in the cool morning light coming in through the skylights above. "This," Dad said, pointing at the wood. "Why did you do this?"

Nurse Ratched said, "The skin wouldn't—"

"Thank you, Nurse Ratched, but I would like to hear from Victor."

She fell silent.

Vic popped his knuckles without thinking. "I . . ." He cleared his throat. "Some of the tears were too big to close. And we couldn't grow new skin, so I had to use what I had available."

"And why not use metal?"

Vic looked away. "He's already metal. Almost all of him. Underneath. I thought it would look better if we used wood. It'd make him look more . . ." He struggled to find the words to describe what he meant, what he was trying to say. The concept was there in his mind, but it was loose and shaky.

"Hysterically Angry Puppet," Hap said.

"I came up with that!" Rambo cried.

"That," Vic said, thought it wasn't quite right. "He's . . . I thought it'd look better."

"And you carved it yourself."

"Nurse Ratched helped."

"Thank you, Victor. I have always wanted to be thrown under a bus." A yellow vehicle appeared on her screen, mowing down a pixelated version of herself over and over again. "Yes. I helped."

"Hap," Dad said. "Would you please open your chest?"

Hap tapped his breastbone. The compartment slid open. The heart looked as it had the night before. It beat. The gears moved. Vic couldn't stop the sense of pride he felt then, the accomplishment tinged with guilt.

"And this?" Dad asked quietly. "Why did you keep this from me?"

Vic squirmed, trying to keep his thoughts in order, but they were on the wings of butterflies, floating up around him, just out of reach. "I didn't . . ." He took a deep breath and tried again. "I wanted to . . ." What? He went with something that didn't feel like a lie. "Because I didn't know if it would work."

Dad nodded slowly. "Why did you make it?"

Why indeed?

He said the only thing he could. "I had to know if I could do it like you did. Just in case."

Dad rose from his crouch, and before Vic could move, wrapped him in a hug, holding him close. Vic hooked his chin over Dad's shoulder. Hap was watching them closely, head tilted slightly, eyes unblinking.

"You wonderful boy," Dad whispered. "You foolish, lovely boy." He pulled away, his hands gripping Vic's shoulders.

Vic started to shake his head but stopped himself. He needed Dad to understand. "He deserves a chance. We all do. You taught me that. I had to help him. I couldn't just leave him."

Dad stared at Vic for a long moment before turning around. "Hap. Your heart."

Hap looked down at it before lifting his head again. "Y-yes."

"It's yours."

"Yes."

"And you want to keep it."

The compartment slid shut. "You can't h-have it. It's mine. V-victor gave it to me."

It shouldn't have affected Vic as much as it did, hearing Hap say his name. In the grand scheme of things, it was nothing. But there was something to it. It made him feel big. It made him feel small.

"He did," Dad agreed. "And I won't take it from you. It is yours for as long as you want it. But be warned, a heart is not like the battery you used to have. It's strong, but fragile."

"H-how can it b-be both?"

Dad laughed, though it sounded hollow. "It just is. It might be for the best that you don't remember what your life was before because it's not going to be the same. The heart, it's . . ." He shook his head. "It's something special. It will lift you up. It will ache without reason. If your response to it is the same as mine, you'll find yourself feeling things you never thought possible. You are a machine, Hap. That much is clear. But a heart changes everything. Once, there was a woodsman made of tin. He said, 'I shall take the heart, for brains do not make one happy, and happiness is the best thing in the world.'"

Rambo laughed. "Tin. Are you sure? Sounds fake, but okay."

"Oh, yes," Dad said. "I'm sure. Hap, I will help you as best I can. We all will. But never forget that Victor gave you life that he made with his own hands. Now, if you'll excuse me."

And with that, Dad turned on his heels and left the ground house. Through the window, Vic saw him walk into the forest. He wouldn't go far, Vic knew. He said the quiet helped him think.

Later—much later, when it was already too late—Vic would wonder why his father didn't tell them what he knew. But by then, it wouldn't matter. The world had teeth, sharp and fierce, and they were about to sink into Vic's skin.

CHAPTER 9

Hap was a shadow. He went wherever Vic went, though he didn't look happy about it. To the lab. In the forest. The kitchen. The ground house. He tried to follow Victor into the bathroom, scowling when Victor told him he had to stay out. "Wh-why?"

"It's private."

"Victor must evacuate his bowels," Nurse Ratched said. "He is very regular. Victor, please remember to bring me a sample. It is almost time for a checkup. A healthy Victor is a happy Victor."

Vic slammed the bathroom door and stayed inside for longer than was necessary.

When he opened the door again, Hap was still standing there, waiting, next to Nurse Ratched.

"Wh-what did you do?" Hap demanded. "Y-you made noises like you had been damaged."

"I don't have time for this," Vic mumbled as he pushed by them onto the rope bridge.

In the lab, he went over the woodwork he'd repaired Hap with. He started with the hand and arm, making sure the wood hadn't cracked in Hap's flight through the trees. It hadn't, and he moved on to the chest and back. The cheek. He saved the leg for last.

Hap sat on the table, legs hanging down, watching Vic's every move. He'd removed his clothing at Vic's request, questioning why Vic had placed a blanket over his bare lap.

Vic lifted Hap's leg, extending it, hearing the metal bones underneath the wood creak. The knee joint locked, and Vic soon saw why. On the inner part of his knee, the piece of wood was slightly too large. An easy mistake, but also an easy fix.

He lifted a small tool from his work bench, lifting it so Hap could see. "This is a short bent."

Hap frowned. "What is it f-for?"

"Shaving wood. Your knee is catching. It's why you keep stumbling. I can fix it if you want."

"Does the patient need to be sedated?" Nurse Ratched asked. "I can help, if need be."

"No," Victor said, and turned in time to see her slowly retracting a metal mallet back inside her. "It won't hurt."

"H-hurt," Hap repeated. "You w-will not h-hurt me unless I d-do something to make you." What Dad had said, not quite word for word, but close enough. Then, "What is h-hurt?"

"*Ow*," Vic cried after Nurse Ratched thumped him on the head. "What was that for?"

"You know what," she said. "Hap, that was a demonstration of pain."

Hap scowled at all of them. "Fine. Do it. I n-need to have full range of m-motion. It's a hazard if I d-don't have it because you are f-fragile."

"He is," Nurse Ratched said as Vic glared at her. "So breakable. It really is a flawed design, if you think about it. Humans are so squishy."

Vic rolled his eyes, and then sank to his knees in front of Hap. He motioned for Nurse Ratched to hold Hap's leg in place as he wiped the sweat away from his brow. He thanked Rambo when the vacuum pulled down the magnifying glass, flipping through the different sizes until he found the right one.

"Ready?" he asked Hap.

Hap didn't respond.

Vic lowered the tool, pressing it against the side of the knee joint, ready to shave off a small piece until it fit better.

"Ow," Hap said.

Vic startled. He looked up, eyes wide.

Hap stared down at him. "Ow," he said again. "That h-hurt."

Vic was incredulous. "What? It did? How can it—I don't understand. That shouldn't have—"

"P-practice," Hap said. "I was p-practicing. Ow. Pain. Hurt." He grimaced, face twisting before smoothing out.

"You can't do that," Vic said.

"Wh-why?"

"Because it didn't hurt. I hadn't even started yet."

Hap nodded. "I w-will wait until you s-start."

Vic sat back up on his knees, grabbing the short bent. "That's not how I—just hold still. Don't move."

Hap froze. He didn't blink. His mouth hung open slightly.

"What happened?" Vic asked. He raised his hand up and waved it in front of Hap's face. No reaction.

"Is he dead?" Rambo whispered nervously. "Did we kill him? Oh no. Oh no. Now I'll *never* have a new best friend until we find something else and I've forgotten that Hap existed."

"He is not moving because Vic told him not to," Nurse Ratched said, and though her voice was as flat as ever, she almost sounded . . . amused? Vic couldn't be quite sure.

He said, "Hap, move."

Hap did, tilting his head, blinking slowly. "M-make up your mind."

Of course. Of course that's how he'd be. "You don't have to do everything I say."

"I know," Hap said. "G-get on with it. I'm cold."

Unsure if Hap was being serious or not, Vic ground his teeth together as he leaned forward once more, face inches from the magnifying glass. He raised the short bent once more, pausing just above the wood, waiting to see if Hap would try to trick him again.

He didn't.

Vic lowered the tool, pressing it against the wood. The tendons on the back of his hand jutted out as he slid the short bent down. A thin sliver of wood curled as he shaved the edge of the knee joint.

"I f-feel that," Hap said, though he didn't try to pull away.

"Do you?" Nurse Ratched asked. "Curious. What does it feel like?"

"Pressure."

"Bad?"

"N-no. It does not h-hurt. There is no ow."

Vic made quick work of it. He paused after removing a second sliver, having Nurse Ratched extend and bend Hap's leg. It still caught, and Vic shaved off another piece. "There. Try that out." Hap stood, the blanket falling to the floor.

"He's naked," Rambo said unnecessarily.

Vic kept his gaze at Hap's knee.

"Now wh-what?" Hap asked.

"Try and walk around. See if the leg works better."

Hap, of course, took that literally. He waddled around the lab, rocking from side to side with every step he took, without bending his knees.

"No," Vic said, and Hap stopped. "Walk normal."

"What is n-normal?" Hap asked.

"Something you will not find here," Nurse Ratched said.

Vic hated everyone in the lab. "Just . . . walk. Bend your knees. Do what you normally do."

"N-normal," Hap said. "I a-am normal. Do what I n-normally do."

"Yes."

Hap nodded.

And then ran for the door, still hanging off its hinges.

Vic stumbled as he chased after him, Nurse Ratched and Rambo close on his heels. They all managed to make it through the doorway in time to see Hap launch himself off the side of the rope bridge. He hit the ground hard, rising from a crouch and taking off like a shot, almost moving quicker than Vic could follow. Vic stared dumbfounded as Hap darted between the trees, legs and arms pumping. He reached an old oak, its trunk enormous. His hand shot out as he rounded it, gripping the trunk, bark spraying out and landing on the ground. He used the trunk and his momentum to sling around the tree, rocketing off in the opposite direction.

He approached the ground house, and Vic was sure he was going to crash into it. Instead, he leapt at the last second, jumping up onto the roof, hopping over the skylights with ease before landing on the other side of the house.

"Well," Nurse Ratched said. "I guess normalcy is subjective. He is still naked."

Vic couldn't speak. He watched in awe as Hap ran toward another tree. He jumped, hands grabbing a branch. The branch snapped, but not before Hap had swung himself up to the next branch, and the next. He was at the top of the tree in only a few seconds. Then, he jumped onto the far side of the compound, landing near Dad's lab. He ran across the connecting bridges before skidding to a stop in front of Vic, looking down at him.

"It w-works," he announced to a stunned Vic. "Like n-normal."

"Yeah," Vic said faintly. "I guess it does."

Hap didn't understand much. And because of that, came the questions.

"What are you d-doing?"

"Eating," Vic said. He stood in front of the stove in the kitchen, a pot bubbling in front of him.

"Why?"

"Because I have to."

"Why?"

"Because my body needs it. If I don't eat, I'll starve and die."

"S-starve and die," Hap said. He stared as Vic ladled the

stew into a bowl before setting it down on the table. Vic lifted the spoon toward his mouth, blowing on the stew to cool it down.

"Why d-do you do that?"

Vic sighed. "Because it's too hot."

Hap nodded. "Too hot. But you eat it anyway because if you d-don't, you will d-die."

"Yes."

"How often d-do you n-need it?"

"Food?" Vic blinked. "A couple of times a day."

"That's pointless," Hap said. "Why w-would you be d-dependent on s-something like that? Especially if it's too h-hot."

Vic didn't know what to do with that. "I just have to. I need it to live."

"That's illogical. I w-will help."

Before Vic could react, Hap sucked in a deep breath, cheeks bulging. He lowered his head toward the bowl and blew out. It wasn't a normal breath. It came out like a gale. The bowl flew off the table, stew splattering against the floor and walls.

"There," Hap said. "Now it is not h-hot. Consume it so you don't d-die."

He turned and walked out of the kitchen.

"What are you d-doing?"

Vic felt like screaming. He took a deep breath, letting it out slow. "Getting ready for bed. I'm tired. It's been a long day. I need to sleep."

"Shutdown mode," Rambo said as he docked in his port, wiggling until he was comfortable. "Time to recharge."

"Recharge," Hap said. "Sleep. Why?"

Vic was barely able to stop himself from banging his head against the wall. "We already talked about this. I have to. It's like food. I need it."

"So you don't d-die."

"Yeah." Vic pulled the comforter back off his bed. He sat down, the frame sagging slightly. He yawned, jaw cracking.

Hap cocked his head. "What will I d-do while you re-charge?"

"Find Dad," Vic said tiredly. "He should be back by now. Or Nurse Ratched. Or you can stay here, but you have to be quiet. You can't make noise while I sleep."

"I w-will stay here," Hap said.

Vic closed his eyes, head settling onto the pillow.

He opened one eye a moment later.

Hap stood next to the bed, staring down at him.

"What?" Vic snapped.

"Q-quiet," Hap said. "Be quiet. I can't make n-noise while you recharge."

Vic groaned and turned over, facing the wall. He waved his arm toward Hap. "Just . . . sit down. Or stand somewhere else."

He heard Hap moving away.

He closed his eyes again. He didn't remember falling asleep, listening for the quiet turning of gears in Hap's chest.

When he opened his eyes, it was early morning. Groggily, he rubbed a hand over his face, smacking his lips. He put his feet against the floor, stretching his arms above his head.

He barely managed to stifle a scream when he saw Hap standing in the corner of his room, staring right at him.

"What are you *doing*?" he demanded.

"Waiting," Hap said. "While you r-recharged. You make noise." He opened his mouth wide and began to snore obnoxiously. He stopped as quickly as he started. "D-does that h-help with r-recharging?"

Vic groaned, falling back on his bed.

Hap was an asshole, yes.

But it took Vic longer than he cared to admit to see just how *big* of an asshole he was.

Though he watched Vic's every move, trailed after him as if they were tied together, he made sure to let Vic know how pointless the things they did were. That is, of course, when he wasn't asking questions. If Victor never had to hear the word "why" again, he'd be thankful.

"Why are you doing that?" Hap asked when Vic told him he needed to shower.

"To get clean." Vic had a towel slung over his shoulder as he made his way to the bathroom.

"Why d-do you need to be clean?" Hap trailed after him.

"Because I don't want to be dirty."

"And showers h-help."

"Yeah. Water cleans my skin. And soap."

"Humans are d-dirty," Hap said. "And they need to be clean."

"Yes."

"I am not h-human."

"No."

"Do I n-need to be clean?"

Vic paused at the door to the bathroom, looking back over his shoulder. Hap still wore the clothes he'd been given. His hair was messy, sticking out at odd angles. "No. You . . . your skin doesn't secrete oil and sweat like mine does."

"I w-will shower with you," Hap said.

Vic began coughing roughly.

Hap frowned. "Are you dying? Do you n-need to eat and recharge?"

"You can't shower with me!"

"Why?"

"Because it's *private*."

Hap nodded. "Like when y-you evacuate your b-bowels."

"What? No, that's not—you know what? Yes. That's exactly it."

"I understand."

Vic felt relieved. "Good." He turned back toward the door.

He walked through and was about to close it behind him when it hit something. He looked back. Hap stood in the doorway. "What are you doing?" Vic asked irritably.

"W-water," Hap said. "You could drown. I will w-watch to make sure you don't."

Vic shoved him back out the door. It was like pushing against a boulder, but he somehow pushed Hap back outside. "I'm not going to drown. Stay out."

Hap rolled his eyes, and Vic was shocked into a moment of immobility at something so distinctly human.

Feeling as if he'd been submerged in a burning lake of ice, Vic closed the door.

Moving quietly, Vic followed the trap lines through the woods. The sounds of the forest sang out around him. He glanced over his shoulder to see Hap trailing after him, mimicking his careful steps.

Rambo, on the other hand, barreled forward without a care in the world, singing about how he was in heaven, dancing cheek to cheek, bumping into Hap's feet to try to hurry him up.

"You need to be quiet," Vic muttered.

"I a-*am*."

"Not you. Rambo."

"Oops," Rambo said. "My bad. I forgot what we were doing. You won't hear a peep from me until you say—oh my *god*, a pinecone! I love pinecones!" He rolled around Hap and rushed forward, picking up the pinecone from the ground. "So epic and awesome," he whispered, holding it close to his sensors, turning it over and over. "Can I keep it? Vic? *Vic*. Can I keep this pinecone?"

Vic sighed. "You already have enough at home."

"But—but *this* one is better than all the others! Look. It has thorns on it."

"You will h-hurt yourself," Hap told him. He sounded gruff and annoyed. "Ow. You will h-have ow."

Rambo dropped it as if scalded. "Oh no. Vic! I could hurt my—oh. Wait. That's right. I can't feel pain. Sorry. Sorry, everyone! I forgot what I was for a second. Won't happen again. I'll just—"

Hap stomped on the pinecone, crushing it under his boot.

"Hey!" Rambo complained. "Why would you do that? You made a mess. You can't just make messes. Who is going to clean it up? *You?* Ha. You don't know how to suck like I do." He rolled over the broken pinecone, fans whirring as he sucked up the bits and pieces. "Ooh, that tickled."

Vic shook his head as he continued on.

The first trap was empty. The second was too. The third, however, held a fat rabbit, eyes glazed over, neck snapped by the metal trap. Vic crouched down, grimacing. It hadn't been dead long. The flies hadn't yet come.

"What is that?" Hap asked.

"Food," he muttered as he lifted the bar from the rabbit's neck. Something shifted in the rabbit, wet and terrible. For a long time, he couldn't bring himself to deal with the traps. Dad had done it without complaint. It wasn't quite fear that caused Vic to hesitate, nor was it a feeling of mourning. The texture of the animal's fur, the way the body could stiffen so quickly, made his skin crawl. Thankfully, it didn't look as if the rabbit had suffered. A quick death.

"You k-killed it."

Vic's face grew warm. "I have to. I need it to live. I only take what I need."

"And you n-need this."

"Yes."

Hap nodded before standing. He began to walk off into the trees. "Where are you going?" Vic called after him.

"I'll h-help. Stay there."

Vic sighed and turned back to the rabbit. He pulled an old scrap of cloth from his satchel and spread it out on the ground. Gingerly, he lifted the rabbit and set it on the cloth before wrapping it.

"Where is he going?" Rambo asked.

"I don't know."

"Should we be worried?"

"Probably."

The minutes passed by slowly. It felt like hours before they heard Hap returning. Vic looked around the tree, ready to scold Hap for disappearing for so long, but the words died on his tongue.

In his arms, he carried four rabbits, all of them wriggling frantically.

"What are you *doing*?" Vic asked, aghast.

"Stop," Hap said to the rabbits. "Stop m-moving so Vic c-can kill you and eat y-you so he doesn't die." The rabbits didn't listen. Hap almost dropped one, but he managed to catch it by its back legs, the animal making an odd sound in its fright.

Vic fell back on his rear. "You *caught* these?"

"It's not h-hard. Why? Is it hard for y-you?"

"What? No. That's not what—put them *down*."

Hap frowned. "But they will r-run away and I'll have to ch-chase them again. That is p-pointless." He glanced down at the rabbits before looking back at Vic. "Unless that m-makes them taste better. D-does it make them t-taste better?"

Vic stood, brushing himself off. "Will you just let them go? We don't need them! I have enough."

"You do?" Hap asked. "Are you s-sure?"

"Yes."

Hap shrugged, and Vic was struck again by just how quickly he'd adapted his behaviors. It'd already gone beyond mimicry in a few short days. Soon enough, he'd be like Gio.

Hap dropped the rabbits. They landed on the ground before

scattering off into the forest. He watched them go before looking down at his arms. Wet droppings smeared across his skin. "What is that?" he asked. He raised it toward his nose and sniffed. "It smells. Bad? Not g-good."

"The rabbit evacuated its bowels on you," Rambo said, sounding far more gleeful than the situation warranted. "I can't wait to tell Nurse Ratched."

Hap scowled. "Like Victor does with the door c-closed? That's p-private. I will f-find the r-rabbit that did this. I will make it p-pay for evacuating its bowels publicly." He turned to stomp away but stopped when Vic grabbed him by the arm. His brow furrowed as he looked at Vic's hand wrapped around his forearm. "I c-can feel that."

"Don't move."

Hap froze.

Vic shook his head as he opened his satchel, pulling out a scuffed plastic bottle. He let go of Hap's arm, which didn't move, still extended. He unscrewed the lid and poured the water on Hap, washing away the droppings. When he finished, he put the bottle away and stepped back.

Hap stood stock still.

Vic huffed out a breath. "You can move now."

Hap did, bringing his arm back up to his face, eyes narrowing. "Cleaned," he said. "Water. Shower. We sh-showered together."

"We did *not*."

Hap squinted at him. "Are you sure?"

Vic stomped back toward the trap. He reset it before shoving the wrapped rabbit into his satchel. He didn't look back as he turned and headed for home.

On the fourth night, Hap discovered music.

He was sitting in Vic's lab, hands folded in his lap, questioning everything Vic was doing. Vic barely heard him anymore, mumbling half answers under his breath that did little to appease him. Nurse Ratched was exposed before him, her screen having shorted out.

"I normally do this myself," she told Hap as Victor found the problem, some of her wiring on its last legs. "But I allow Victor to help because it makes him feel useful."

"He n-needs it," Hap said.

"Yes," Nurse Ratched said. "Constant validation. Engaging Empathy Protocol. You are doing a good job, Victor. I am very proud of you. Disengaging Empathy Protocol. Are you almost done? I do not like it when you finger me with cold hands."

Vic ignored her. Having finished his work he picked up his tools and carried them toward the work bench.

Hap sat ramrod straight in his chair. His head was tilted as if he were listening. He had a strange expression on his face, faraway and lost. "What is it?" Vic asked. "What's wrong?"

"S-sound. What is that s-sound?"

Vic listened. He didn't hear anything.

Nurse Ratched did. "It is music. Gio is playing a record in the ground house."

Hap stood abruptly, the chair banging against the wall. He moved toward the door without speaking. Before Vic could call to him, he vaulted over the edge of the railing.

"I wish I could do that," Rambo said. "It looks so cool. I'm gonna do it. No one try and stop me this time."

Vic managed to grab Rambo before he could roll toward the railing. "No."

Rambo beeped rudely. "Hey! I said *not* to stop me."

"You take the elevator," Vic told him. "Just because someone else does something doesn't mean you have to."

"How profound," Nurse Ratched said. "I am impressed, Victor."

Later, as Vic closed down the lab for the night, he got lost in his own head. Once, when he was ten, he had suddenly become fixated on the fact that he was *not* an android like his father. It upset him greatly and sent him spiraling for two days. He was inconsolable. They were different, he tried to explain to Dad, even as his father said their differences did not matter. But to Victor, they *did* matter. He wanted his blood drained, his bones and tendons replaced with metal and wiring. He couldn't articulate the *why* of it, not enough to satisfy either of them. Dad had tried to calm him down, tried to explain that he was perfect just the way he was, but Vic wouldn't hear of it.

At the end of the second day he was exhausted, his eyes feeling like they were filled with sand, his head pounding, his thoughts jumbled. Dad had sat a few feet away from him to give him space, legs folded, hands on his knees, and said, "Victor, listen to me."

He didn't look at his father, but he heard him. He grunted quietly in response.

"We're not the same," Dad had said, voice gentle and soft. "But know that I was alone and sad before you came into my world. You gave me hope, Victor. It started in the tips of my toes before it rose through the rest of my body and latched firmly in my chest. It has never left. It evolved into something so much greater. And it's because of this feeling that I can say I don't need you to be like me. I need you to be *you*."

Vic hadn't spoken. Not then. But he listened, and he never forgot.

He was quiet as the elevator lowered toward the ground. He followed his friends toward the ground house, pausing in the doorway.

Dad sat in his chair, a curious expression on his face. He didn't turn to look at Vic. He was focused on Hap.

Hap, who stood in front of the record player, swaying side to side as if caught in the drift of the smooth horns, the gentle *tsk*

tsk tsk of the cymbals, the tinkling of the piano keys. "What is this one?" he whispered as he moved from side to side.

"Miles Davis," Dad said with a quiet smile. "*Kind of Blue.* Nineteen fifty-nine. Many things happened to jazz music in nineteen fifty-nine. John Coltrane. Duke Ellington. Sonny Clark. Do you like it?"

Hap said "I don't know" without stuttering over the words. "How do I know if I like it?"

"Listen," Dad said. "Here. Ready?"

The saxophone entered, running through the notes like flowing water. Warmth bloomed in Vic's chest at the sound.

Hap sighed. He began to tap his foot in time with the beat. Vic didn't think he realized he was doing it.

"What does it say to you?" Dad asked.

For a long moment, Hap didn't speak. Then, "There are no words."

"I know," Dad said. "But what—"

"No," Hap said. "I have no words for it."

"Oh. Oh. Yes. It can do that, sometimes."

Hap pressed a hand against his chest. "I can feel it here."

Dad closed his eyes and hummed along with the song. He stopped when Hap said, "It feels like . . . a memory. Like something I've forgotten. What do you do if you've forgotten all you know?"

Dad opened his eyes. He was silent for a moment, as if carefully choosing his words. "You start again from the beginning."

"What's happening?" Rambo whispered to Nurse Ratched.

"I do not know," she said. "But I like it. I wish someone would ask a lady to dance."

Rambo beeped excitedly. "I can do that!" He rose on his lift, hydraulics wheezing. He grasped two of her tentacles with his pincers. Her screen filled with a sharp bouncing line, a circadian rhythm keeping time with the music. They rolled back and forth, Rambo apologizing profusely when he bumped into her. Nurse Ratched didn't seem to mind.

And on and on it went.

Until the machines came.

CHAPTER 10

One week after Hap awoke in the laboratory of a creator named Victor Lawson, they returned to the Scrap Yards. Vic said he wanted to see if the Old Ones had brought anything new worth salvaging. It wasn't a lie, but it wasn't the complete truth, either.

What Vic *really* wanted to do was return to where they'd found Hap, to see if there was anything else they'd missed. He doubted there would be; Nurse Ratched hadn't found any other signs of life.

They'd left Hap with Dad. Or at least they thought they had. They were halfway to the Scrap Yards when Nurse Ratched stopped and said, "We're being followed."

Vic glanced over his shoulder. Nothing moved in the trees that he could see. "Where?"

Before she could speak again, he saw Hap peek his head from behind a tree before pulling it back sharply.

Vic sighed. "I can see you."

"No, you c-can't," Hap replied.

"Hap."

Hap scowled as he stepped out from behind the tree.

"Why were you hiding?" Rambo asked.

"I w-wasn't," Hap said. "I was inspecting the t-tree trunk."

"Really?" Rambo rolled toward him, stopping at the base of the tree. "What are you inspecting it for? Is there something wrong with it?" He raced around the trunk before stopping where he started. "I don't see anything."

"He is making sure Vic does not die," Nurse Ratched said, matter-of-fact. "I believe he is showing concern."

"I am n-*not*." He sneered at them. "I was j-just walking this way."

"In the same direction as us?" Rambo asked. "That's *awesome*. Vic. Hey, Vic! What are the chances that Hap would be here too? He should come with us!"

Vic said, "You can, you know. Come with us."

Hap grunted as Rambo tried to push him toward the others. He tried to kick Rambo, but the vacuum was faster than he was. Hap almost lost his footing but managed to stay upright. His wooden leg—while still stiff—caught him at the last second.

"Squishy," Hap muttered, not looking at any of them.

"So that is what this is about," Nurse Ratched said. "Fear not, Hap. We would never let anything happen to Victor. While he is squishy, yes, we are not."

Hap's scowl deepened. "I d-don't care."

"Of course you do not," Nurse Ratched said. "Why would you? Since we are going in the same direction, we might as well go together. Victor?"

Vic tore his gaze away from Hap. "What?"

"Hap will be joining us," she said. "The more the merrier, as I always say."

"I've never heard you say that," Rambo said, and squealed when she whipped one of her tentacles at him. "What? I *haven't*."

"Do you want to come with us?" Vic asked. He didn't know why Hap would. From the look on his face and the stiff way he was holding himself, Hap looked as if he would rather be anywhere else.

Hap shook his head. "N-no. But I will, since y-you insist."

"We did not insist," Nurse Ratched said. "But if it makes you feel better to think so, far be it from me to suggest otherwise. It might be beneficial to have some backup. Victor often finds himself getting in trouble when he least expects it."

Vic groaned. "That's not—"

"How is the cut on your hand, Victor? Healing nicely, I should think."

It was. Scabbed over and itchy, but better. He didn't think it would even leave a scar. "Fine," Vic said. "But we're going to move quick. We don't want to be caught by the Old Ones."

"They're huge," Rambo said as Hap joined them. "Bigger than *you*. I bet they would squash you flat."

"N-no," Hap said. "I w-would not like that. If they t-try, I will n-not be nice."

"Come on," Vic said. "We'll be quick. What are the rules?"

"Stick together!" Rambo exclaimed.

"Run if we have to," Nurse Ratched said.

"No dallying!"

"No drilling."

"And above all else, be brave!"

Hap cocked his head as he narrowed his eyes, but he did not speak.

The moment they crested the hill that overlooked the Scrap Yards, Vic knew something was wrong. Be it morning, noon, or dusk, the Old Ones were always moving. Not now; birds perched on one of the cranes seemingly without a care. The silence was oppressive in ways Vic had never felt before: thick, as if the very air had grown heavier, making it harder to breathe. Part of him—a loud, insistent part—demanded he turn around and forget the Scrap Yards altogether. Go home. Don't look back.

Rambo said, "I don't like this."

Nurse Ratched beeped once, twice. "There is something here. Something I have never felt before. It is . . . bright."

"Bright?" Vic asked, looking off farther into the yards. "What do you mean?"

"Power," she said. "It feels like power."

"The Old Ones?"

"No. Something else. Hold, please. Scanning. Scanning. Scanning." The light above her screen flashed on as she began to scan the area around them.

"What is she d-doing?" Hap asked as he squinted at her.

Vic shrugged. "Looking. It's how we found you. Maybe there's someone like you that we missed. Another android. A machine. It happens, sometimes. Usually we can't fix them." He glanced at Nurse Ratched. "What is it?"

She finished scanning, and the light went out. Her screen remained blank. "There is something here."

"Where?"

She pulled up the grid of the Scrap Yards on her screen. One of the squares blinked.

3B. Where they'd found Hap.

Vic frowned. "Maybe we missed something."

"It is possible," Nurse Ratched said slowly. "Hap's power signature could have blocked out what is there now, or it could have activated after we left."

"But?"

"But," she said. "I do not think that is it. This is bigger. Or there is more than one. I cannot separate them if that is the case. They are too far away."

The warning in his head grew louder, telling him to turn around and leave this place. *Tell him,* it whispered. *Tell Dad. Tell Dad that something is here and let him take care of it.*

But the warning was drowned out by something far more dangerous: curiosity. It tugged at Vic. He wanted to see what it was. What Nurse Ratched could be reading. It had power. That much was clear. And Dad's heart wouldn't last forever. Maybe they could use it, if the machine it belonged to was beyond repair. And if it wasn't, Vic could help.

He said, "Careful. Quiet. Stick together. We'll keep our distance."

"I knew you were going to say that," Nurse Ratched said. Then, louder, "Hap, remember what Victor is?"

"Squishy," Hap said immediately.

"Exactly. Squishy, breakable Victor. We will need to protect him in case it is something that can harm him."

"What about me?" Rambo asked.

Nurse Ratched bumped into him gently. "You have the most important job of all. If the need arises, you will sacrifice yourself so the rest of us can escape."

"Yes!" Rambo cried. "I have purpose!"

They moved through the scrap heaps, soon reaching a small ridge that looked over quadrant 3B. Vic crouched low as they approached the crest of the hill. Hap watched him for a moment before doing the same. He was so close, Vic could hear the gears in his chest.

The slate sky hung heavy over their heads, the air sharply cold, and Vic's breath billowed from his mouth in a stream. He thought it would snow soon. Maybe not today, but soon. He shivered again as he crawled toward the top of the hill, Hap to his right, his skin warm when his arm accidentally brushed against Vic's.

They reached the top and peered over, Rambo whispering, "I'm brave, I'm brave, I'm brave."

At first, Vic didn't understand what he saw when he looked down the other side of the hill. Piles of discarded body parts where they'd found Hap: arms, legs, torsos, all scattered around on the ground.

And the people. The *people*. A furious gut-punch, enough to knock the breath from Vic's chest. Proof. Here, at last. Others. Three of them, wearing what looked like uniforms: black boots, black pants, black coats with red collars that rose up around their necks. On the right breast of each coat was a symbol, though they were too far away for Vic to make it out clearly.

But the more he studied them, the more the feeling of

wrongwrongwrong snapped and snarled within him, a cornered predator lashing out anyway it could. All had their scalps shaved cleanly. Two of them stood upright, swiveling their heads from side to side. The third was crouched on the ground, hand pressed against the soil. They didn't speak.

It was then Victor saw them for what they were: exactly the same. Their skin was pale, their faces smooth. No eyebrows. No facial hair. No ears. Male, or at least they seemed to be.

They did not look like Dad. Or Hap.

They did not look like Vic.

They weren't human at all. No. The third android—the one crouched on the ground—lifted his head. He was exactly like the other two. Triplets. Clones. The same model.

"They are not human," Nurse Ratched said in a low voice, as if she could read Vic's mind. "They are machines."

"What are they doing?" Vic asked. "What are they looking—" The words died on his tongue as an awful noise came from beside him. He turned his head.

Hap had bared his teeth in a furious snarl. The skin around his eyes tightened. His fingers were hooked into claws. "What is it? Do you know them?"

Hap sounded angry when he said, "No. I d-don't know. I c-can't—error. It is an error. Lost. It's l-lost in f-fog." Vic almost fell back when Hap began to savagely beat the sides of his head with his hands. The sound was bizarre: metal and synthetic skin and wood. Vic tried to grab his hands, but Hap was too strong.

"Stop," Vic hissed at him. "They'll *hear* you."

But Hap didn't. He hit his head again and again.

"What's wrong with him?" Rambo asked nervously. "Is he malfunctioning?"

"Rambo, back away," Nurse Ratched said, her tentacles spooling out and twitching dangerously.

Hap clutched the side of his head and bent over, face toward the ground.

"Hap," Victor whispered. "Hap, you need to stop. You need to—"

A sound filled the world, one Vic had never heard before.

It started small, as if crossing from a great distance. He looked around wildly, trying to locate the source. It echoed flatly against the scrap metal before them, the heaps beginning to vibrate, bits and pieces falling to the ground.

The sound only grew louder.

Hap lowered his hands, turning his face toward the sky. "L-look."

Vic lifted his head.

He wasn't sure what he was seeing at first. A smudge on the horizon above the expansive forest, black against a gun-metal sky. He thought it an errant cloud until it moved oddly, expanding and contracting. The hum around them increased as the smudge grew and took shape. Vic felt the vibrations it caused down to his bones. His hands shook.

When he saw it for what it was, he still couldn't believe his eyes. It didn't seem possible. He'd read about them in books, had seen a picture of their massive size. In one of Dad's books—*Creatures of the Sea*—there'd been a drawing of one with the outline of a man next to it, shown for scale. The beast dwarfed the man, a great monstrosity that Vic couldn't believe actually existed. He'd never seen the ocean, though he could imagine how vast it had to be if it held creatures such as this.

He couldn't remember what it was called; Nurse Ratched did not have that problem. "A whale," she said. "It is a whale."

But it wasn't rising from the depths of any sea. It was flying toward them.

The whale moved up and down as if swimming through the air. The top of it was black, the underbelly white with thick lines that ran along the length. It didn't have eyes. Instead, across the middle of its head was a row of glass that wrapped around the front to either side. The flippers were thick and massive as they rose and fell. The horizontal tail moved up and down, propelling the beast forward. Its great mouth was closed.

"What is that?" Rambo cried as the sound grew louder. "Is that a *fish*? How is a fish flying?"

Vic couldn't answer. He was struck dumb.

Now that it was closer, Vic could see the lines underneath weren't part of the flesh of the creature. They were *panels*. It wasn't alive at all.

It was a machine.

A massive machine that dwarfed even the Old Ones. Across the side, above the flipper, were three white words in the black of the metal skin.

THE TERRIBLE DOGFISH

The flying machine stopped above the Scrap Yards, hovering in place. Air began to whip ferociously as it lowered toward the earth, scrap heaps collapsing in showers of dust and sparks.

With a magnificent groan, the whale's mouth dropped open, the lower jaw folding down and back. The throat of the whale was metal and lined with what looked like railed walkways. Vic squinted against the dust blowing, sure he could see *movement* inside the whale's mouth on the platforms, though it was too far away for him to make out what exactly it was.

As he looked on, black cables dropped from the whale's mouth. At the tip of each cable was a flat, circular disc, large enough to carry people or machines. They lowered toward the ground where the three figures stood.

In silence, they watched as the humanoid figures inspected the area around them as the discs reached the ground near them. The crouched figure scooped up what looked like dirt, letting it filter through his fingers. Lifting his head, he looked directly at them. Vic flattened himself to the ground, heart in his throat. He counted to five in his head and looked out into the Scrap Yards once more . . .

. . . in time to see the smooth men stepping onto the discs and rising up and up toward the whale. Once inside, the mouth of the whale closed. It remained suspended in air.

"Victor," Nurse Ratched said, "we need to move while we still can."

Vic was startled out of his daze. He looked back at the others. Nurse Ratched's screen was flashing red in warning. Rambo was moaning quietly to himself. Hap's eyes were narrowed, his gaze on Victor, never looking away.

Vic nodded. "Head for the trees. Don't look back. Don't stop."

Nurse Ratched lifted Rambo from the ground and they fled for the safety of the forest. Vic looked back only once as they hit the tree line. The Terrible Dogfish hadn't moved. Fear clawed at his throat, but he ran and ran and ran.

They were in the trees when a deep note emanated from the whale, a blast that rolled through the forest, causing the birds to take flight.

It sounded like it was screaming.

Dad was in the ground house. He appeared in the doorway as Rambo shouted his name, Victor too out of breath to get any words out. Dad frowned when he saw them running toward him. They skidded to a stop in front of him, Vic slumped over, hands on his knees as he gasped for air, lungs burning, chest constricted. Vic's mind had been wiped clean, a sheen of static falling over him. He couldn't think. He couldn't speak, jaw clenched as he ground his teeth.

"What is it?" Dad asked, sounding alarmed. "What's happened?" He cupped Vic's cheeks, turning his face up. "Are you all right?"

Vic couldn't find the words. "I . . . I don't . . ."

"A ship!" Rambo cried as Nurse Ratched set him down on

the ground. He began to spin in circles, arms flailing. "In the Scrap Yards! A fish! A flying fish!"

Dad's reaction was instantaneous. He dropped his hands from Vic's face, gripping his arms. He pulled Vic behind him, looking toward the sky. "Did they see you?"

Nurse Ratched's screen filled with the recording from the Scrap Yards. Dad grunted as if punched. Vic looked over his shoulder to see an image of one of the machines inspecting the soil. "Victor," Dad said, voice even. "The cut on your hand. When it happened, did you bleed in the Scrap Yards?"

Vic hung his head. "It was an accident—"

Dad cursed and turned toward the ground house, stepping around Vic. "Follow me. Don't look back. Don't ask questions. Do what I say. Hurry."

They did as they were told. A record spun on the player inside the ground house. Miles Davis and his sweet, sweet horns. Dad stopped in front of one of the bookcases. "Victor, I need you to listen to me."

Vic managed to nod. His breath whistled as he panted, throat dry and constricted.

"There is much I should've told you," Dad said as he stepped to the side of the bookcase. He pressed his hand against the wood. A panel lit up, green and bright. It rose up and down as it scanned his hand. "Much that I've kept hidden. But you must believe me when I say I only wanted to keep you safe." The scan finished, and a heavy click came from the bookcase, as if a lock had opened.

The floor beneath their feet began to shake. They all turned in time to see the floor shifting, the floorboards folding in on themselves as they parted. A staircase appeared, the metal steps snapping into place. At the edges of each step, lights turned on, pulsing again and again.

"Down," Dad said. "Now."

Nurse Ratched went first, her body rattling as she bounced

down each step. She almost tumbled end over end, but her treads kept her upright. Dad picked up Rambo, shoving him at Vic.

"Dad," Vic tried.

"Hush," Dad said. "Go."

Vic descended the stairs, hearing Hap following him. He looked back over his shoulder to see his father at the top of the stairs. The frame of the ground house began to rattle, and that strange sound roared around them once more. The Terrible Dogfish was coming.

"Hap," Dad said as they reached the bottom of the stairs. "You don't know me. You don't even know yourself. But I must ask you for something, and it will go against every single part of your programming."

Hap nodded.

"I am asking you to choose. Here. Now. I'm sorry it's come at a time like this, but you must decide."

"T-to do wh-what?"

"Protect Victor," Dad said, and for the first time in Vic's life, he heard fear in his father's voice. "No matter what. Protect him with everything you have. Don't let anything happen to him."

Vic set Rambo on the ground before turning back toward the stairs. He tried to climb back up but stopped when his father shook his head.

"What are you doing?" he demanded. "What's happening?"

Dad smiled, though it trembled. "What I hoped never would. Listen to me, Victor. You are a light in my darkness. I've loved you since the moment I saw you. Never forget that. No matter what you see, no matter what you hear, I have always loved you. You're my son. And I couldn't be prouder of the man you've become. One day, we'll see each other again. I know we will. Hap, do I have your word? Will you do what I've asked?"

Hap hesitated before nodding.

Relief flooded Dad's face. "Thank you," he whispered.

"Trust Victor. Trust my son. I'll do what I can to keep them away. Nurse Ratched. Can you hear me?"

"Yes, Gio."

"Butterflies flap their wings, and all the world sings."

Her screen went dark before the words ACTIVATE SAFETY PROTOCOL? appeared. "But what do the birds say?"

And Dad said, "In the sky, you are free."

"Password accepted. Safety Protocol six one four dash seven."

Dad stepped back away from the stairs. Vic screamed for him as he pressed his hand against the side of the bookcase once more. Hap grabbed Vic by the back of his coat, pulling him down as the stairs receded back into the wall. The last Vic saw of his father before the floor closed above them was Dad squaring his shoulders, turning toward the doorway.

"No!" Vic cried, slamming his hands against the wall. "Dad! *Dad.*"

"Enough," Hap snarled in his ear. "You'll h-hurt yourself. Stop it." He pulled Vic away from the wall.

Vic struggled, trying to get away from him, but Hap held on tight. "Let me go!"

"N-no," Hap said. "Stop. L-look."

Vic sagged against him. He lifted his head.

They were in a bunker of sorts, one Victor hadn't known existed. The walls were metal, as was the ceiling. It was roughly the size of the ground house above them but filled with equipment unlike anything Vic had ever seen before. Against the far wall sat a row of glass tubes, all empty, the surfaces smudged with dust. The wall to the right was filled with screens like the one Nurse Ratched had, three large across the top, six smaller ones underneath, above a console that blinked. The left wall was shelving filled with books and discarded tools, all looking as if they hadn't been touched in years. Vic's gaze slid over some of the books, not able to comprehend what he was reading on the spines: *Gray's Anatomy* and *Atlas der Anatomie des Menschen* and *Leonardo da Vinci on the Human Body* and *What to Expect When You're Expecting.*

Nurse Ratched went to the console below the screens as Rambo hurried around the bunker, his fan running as he scooped up the dust from the floor. "Dirty," he muttered. "Dirty, so dirty, must clean, must clean."

"Wh-what is this p-place?" Hap asked.

Vic didn't know. He opened his mouth, but no sound came out. He jumped when Nurse Ratched beeped loudly, one of her tentacles extending and attaching itself to a port in the console. Her screen filled with numbers and letters and symbols Victor didn't recognize. The same symbols rolled onto the screens above her. Vic flinched at the harsh light as each screen filled with an image, a low roar filling the bunker.

The screens showed the compound from various angles. At first, Vic thought they were just pictures, but the trees were moving, the branches creaking and groaning. One screen showed the interior of the ground house. Another was from a high vantage point, looking down at the forest floor below. The three smaller screens showed different views: one of the exterior of Vic's room, the other two at opposite ends of the wooden bridges.

But it was the last screen Vic focused on, the large screen at the end. On it, he could see Dad standing in the middle of the garden, face turned toward the ashen sky. He glanced at the other screens, trying to see what his father was doing, but the angle was off. It wasn't until the trees began to whip back and forth that he understood. He covered his ears when the Terrible Dogfish blared again.

"Nurse Ratched," he said. "Open the door. Please."

"I cannot do that, Victor," she said. "Not yet. The protocol has been activated."

Vic stared, dumbfounded, arms slowly dropping back to his sides. "*What* protocol?"

"I do not know," she said as her tentacle in the port twisted. "But I cannot stop it."

Vic slammed his fists against the console. It rattled, the lights flashing, but nothing changed. "I'm ordering you to open the doors."

"I cannot, Victor."

"Do it!" he shouted at her. "You need to let me out. I have to help him. I have to—"

A man appeared on the screen, descending on the circular platform, one hand wrapped around the cable, the other at his side. He leapt off the platform five feet above the ground, landing with a slight bend to his knees. A moment later, two others appeared, one on either side of him. Strange, hairless, they stood with their legs apart, hands clasped behind them, faces blank, smooth.

The one in front spoke, his voice flat, cold. "Designation General Innovation Operative, also known as Gio."

"Here," the one on the left said.

"Now," the one on the right said.

"After seventy-two years," the one on the left said.

"There is no coincidence," the one on the right said.

They sounded identical. None of them blinked.

The one in the front stepped forward. "An anomaly was detected in a dumping ground," he said. "Plasma. Salt. Protein. Water. Cellular activity."

"Blood," the one on the left said.

"Human blood," the one on the right said.

The front man—the leader—looked up at the buildings in the trees above them. "What are these?"

Dad spoke for the first time, voice blandly pleasant. "Do you like them? I took inspiration from a book. A family named Robinson were once shipwrecked on an island. In order to survive, they built a tree house. A home."

"Fiction," the left one said.

"Unreality," the right one said.

"Memory," Dad said. "Of a time long ago."

"Memory," the leader repeated. He cocked his head. "Where did the blood come from?"

"You said it was found in the dumping grounds? I expect that it came from an animal, then. From what I recall, it happens quite often, poor creatures getting crushed under the Old Ones."

The machines on either side of the leader cocked their heads in unison, never blinking, lips pulled back over square teeth.

"Animal," the left one said.

"Poor creatures," the right one said.

"Crushed under the machines," the leader said in that same queer voice. He paused for a long moment. "No." He stepped toward Dad. "Where is the human?"

"There is no human here," Dad said. "Scan it. Scan it all. You'll see."

"Oh no," Rambo whispered. "They'll find us."

"They won't," Nurse Ratched said. "The walls are lined with lead. They won't know we're here."

Vic turned slowly to look at her. "How do you know that?" She didn't answer.

"L-look," Hap said, and Vic looked at the screen once more. The androids formed a triangle, raising their arms, fingers spread wide. The skin of their palms parted, little black metal knobs poking through. Light emanated from the knobs, and the smooth men raised and lowered their hands as they scanned the entirety of the compound.

The androids didn't react as the scan completed. The skin on the palms of two of the androids closed. The third turned his hand over, palm toward the sky. A three-dimensional image of the compound appeared above his hand, spinning in a slow circle.

"What is this?" he asked, fingers twitching slightly. The image expanded, zooming in until it showed one room in particular: Vic's room.

"For travelers," Dad said. "Those who pass by and need a place to recharge."

The leader closed his hand around the image, and it disappeared. "Recharge."

"What do you want?" Dad asked.

The leader blinked once, twice. Then, "We do not want. We do not have desire. We have purpose. The anomaly. Perhaps it is you. General Innovation Operative, by order of the Authority, you will return to the City of Electric Dreams. There, you will undergo an evaluation to determine if you have a viable future in service of the machines."

"Reprogramming," the one on the left said.

"Or decommissioning," the one on the right said.

"Two decisions," the leader said. "One outcome. But first, you will be taken apart to determine the extent of the corruption in your programming. It is necessary to verify if your corruption is infectious."

"Plasma," the one on the left said. "Salt."

"Protein," the one on the right said. "Water."

"Cellular activity," the leader said. "The Authority sees all, knows all, General Innovation Operative. If they exist, we will find them, and you will be the one to give them to us."

"So you do want something after all," Dad said. "Not so different, are we?"

For the first time, something other than blank *nothing* crossed the leader's face. His lips twitched, his dead eyes narrowed. "I remember you. From before. The others do not, but I do. We will find the truth, and then we will decide how best to use your parts in service of the Authority."

Dad laughed. Vic's eyes burned. He couldn't focus, couldn't breathe, couldn't do anything. He was trapped under the weight of fear and indecision, static in his head.

The smooth men took a step back as one when Dad lifted his shirt up and over his head, letting it fall to the ground. "Even after all this time, nothing changes. But I have. When I close my eyes, I dream. Not in lined code or equations. Like a human. Like them. Love. Anguish. Fear. Pride. *Memory.* All from my heart. And I will never let you have it." He tapped his breastbone. The compartment slid open.

At the same time, the smooth men hissed, "What is *that*?"

Dad grinned, crazed and beautiful. "I like to think of it as my soul, romantic though the notion may be. And it was never for you."

Vic screamed as his father raised his hand to close around the heart in his chest. He screamed as the wood cracked, as the gears snapped off their tracks, falling onto the ground. The heart broke, falling in pieces. Giovanni Lawson swayed.

He said, "Never forget. It has always been you."

And then he collapsed, head bouncing off the ground, right arm trapped underneath him.

His eyes were open. He didn't blink. He didn't move.

Arms wrapped around Vic, trying to hold him back, and he struggled against them. He fought them as hard as he could, vision tunneling as the smooth men stood above his father's still body. The leader bent over and picked Dad up as if he weighed nothing, slinging him over his shoulder. He looked to the others and said, "Leave nothing. Burn it all to the ground."

"Please," Vic begged as he kicked his legs up into the air. "Please let me go to him."

"They'll k-kill you," Hap growled in his ear.

"I don't *care*. Let me go!"

But Hap didn't. As Vic looked on, still struggling, the leader headed for the lowered platform, Dad's arms bouncing uselessly against his back. The remaining smooth men raised their hands once more, the black knobs poking through the skin of their palms. All thought—rational and irrational—disappeared when fire bloomed from the smooth men's hands, great arcs of red and orange and white. Vic sagged against Hap, gasping for air as flames caught the roof of the ground house, the trees that held their home. He could feel himself shutting down as the fire spread, and no matter what he did, no matter how hard he fought against it, it was no use. A strange sense of suction overcame him as if a vacuum had opened in his chest, pulling in all light. A trickle of sweat rolled down his cheek near his ear. He was here, he was with Dad, he was everywhere, floating on a flat ocean, the tranquility deceptive as everything burned. Their life's work—their *home*—turned into ash.

Hap was speaking, but Vic couldn't hear him.

Rambo was frantic, but Vic paid him no mind.

Nurse Ratched said their room appeared safe even for human lungs, sealed off from the fires above, but Vic couldn't make sense of anything she was saying. The branches holding up the kitchen gave way, causing the floor to break apart, burning chunks of wood and metal raining down onto the ground.

And Victor Lawson watched it all, unable to look away. It didn't feel real, and though he could smell the hint of smoke, could see the destruction the fire was causing, it felt far away, distant, as if it were happening to someone—*anyone*—else.

A moment of clarity: one of the smooth men stood underneath a camera as the trees burned, fire still spilling from his hands. On his chest, the symbol, now close enough for Vic to make out.

The heads of two animals in profile, facing each other.

A fox.

A cat.

And then the smooth man turned away from the camera as Victor's lab fell, as Dad's lab was destroyed, as Vic's room shuddered and shook and split apart, crashing to the forest floor. All of it, years and years of work, gone in minutes, but Vic watched it dispassionately. He took in information, processed it, stored it away, but felt nothing from it. Nothing at all.

The leader stood upon the platform, Dad still thrown over

his shoulder. As the other two joined them, they rose up and out of sight. A moment later, the Terrible Dogfish roared again.

And then it too was gone, the sound fading as the whale swam across the sky.

As the remains of their home burned, the birds began to sing again.

Vic stood still. He understood things were happening near him, could feel Nurse Ratched wrapping her tentacles around him as she checked his pulse, asking him if he could hear her, *Victor, Victor, please respond.*

He wouldn't. He couldn't.

"What's wrong w-with h-him?" someone asked, and the sound of his voice came from far below Vic, as he was floating like he had been filled with air and wasn't tethered to anything.

"He is reacting the best he knows how," a machine with a mounted screen said, and he wondered who they were talking about. "Victor, please. Can you hear me?"

A little machine made a mournful sound almost like it was weeping. "Is he dead? Is Gio dead?"

Death. He had never really thought about death before. A shutdown wasn't absolute. All that one needed was a newer battery. Perhaps these things with him could give him one. He'd made a heart before. He could do it again.

He said, "I am fine."

"Okay," the machine in front of him said. He could almost remember her name. He'd known it before . . . well. Before. Nurse. She was a nurse. The little machine on the floor was not a nurse, neither was the man standing next to him. "You are fine," the nurse said. "I believe you. But I would like to make sure. Can you help me do that, Victor?"

He could. He didn't want to, but he could. He said, "Please let me go."

She did, her tentacle sliding off his arm, causing his skin to itch.

He smiled. He was still above her, floating around the room, but he smiled. It stretched on his face so wide, it hurt his cheeks. "There," he said. "See? I am fine." He laughed. It was wrong. It was an error. He shouldn't be laughing. He didn't think anything was funny. But he couldn't stop. His head hurt. His face hurt. His eyes were filled with dirt, which was odd because he couldn't remember putting dirt there. "Where are we?"

"Underground."

"I've never been underground before," he said as reality began to seep back in, the clarity ice-cold. He grimaced, not yet ready to face what waited for him. "I didn't know there was an underground." Then, "Gio. Can I talk to Gio?" That didn't seem quite right. "Dad. I need Dad."

"He's gone," the nurse said, and he remembered her. Nurse Ratched. She was Nurse Ratched. She was his friend. He'd found her in a pile of metal. He hadn't expected her. Her screen had been cracked, her body dented, and when he touched her for the first time, she had said, "Hello. I am your nurse. I accept most insurance plans. What seems to be ailing you today? Please describe your symptoms."

He hadn't known what to say to that.

He took her home and showed her to . . . to *Dad*, and Dad said, "Wow. I haven't seen one of these in a long time. You found this? And look, oh, look, she still works. Let's see what we can do to help her."

So they had. When they were able to recharge her, she said, "Thank you. That is better. I can now assist you. Please show me where it hurts so I can heal you."

And here, now, he said, "It hurts. Here." He pressed a hand to his chest as the tether jerked a final time. He was in his body once more, and it was dark and quiet inside. "Can you heal me?"

Nurse Ratched said, "It is not physical, Victor. I cannot heal it."

He nodded. "I understand." He looked around. His face was sore, and he realized he was still smiling. It wasn't appropriate, but he couldn't stop. He wondered if he should be crying. He *felt* sad, that ache in his chest only growing bigger, but the dirt in his eyes sucked up all the liquid and he was unable. "I'm erroring."

"I know," Nurse Ratched said.

"Okay," he said, turning his head. The man—not a man, but Hap—looked at him suspiciously. "Hello."

"Vic," he said, and Victor felt his smile shake. "Can you h-hear me?"

"Yes," he said. "Of course I can. I am working. Everything is in order."

"What's wrong w-with him?" Hap asked.

"He is in shock," Nurse Ratched said. "He will recover, but it will take time."

"M-malfunction," Hap said. "He is m-malfunctioning."

"No," Nurse Ratched said. "But it can make certain functions more difficult."

"We c-can't stay down here. He c-can't."

"At least for now. We do not have a choice. There is more we need to see."

Victor felt something nudge against his leg. He looked down. The little machine was tugging on his pants. Rambo. His name was Rambo.

"Vic?" Rambo whispered. "Can you hear me?"

"Yes," Vic said, stepping back, bumping into Hap. Vic recoiled sharply. "Don't touch me."

Hap looked stunned. He raised a hand toward Vic, but he curled it into a fist before dropping it back to his side. "I w-won't. I w-won't touch you. I w-won't hurt you."

Nurse Ratched said, "Butterflies."

The flutter of wings burst through the static in Vic's head as spring bloomed on Nurse Ratched's screen. The trees were green, the flowers blooming. It was almost as if he were there in the forest, breathing in the scents of new growth. Heady, this, and it filled his mouth as he sucked air down greedily, his lungs expanding, blood pumping, heart a furious drumbeat.

On the screen, moving through the trees, a vast kaleidoscope of butterflies, their wings orange and black. They swirled in ordered chaos, and he could almost feel them alight upon his arms and shoulders, their wings brushing against his cheeks. He closed his eyes as a large butterfly landed on his face, the sensation uncomfortable as its legs touched his eyelids. Somewhere in the recesses of his mind, he heard Hap whispering it was *nice*, it was *pretty*, it was *his*.

"What is this?" he whispered.

Through the storm in his head, he heard Nurse Ratched. She said, "A program. Triggered by a code phrase. Gio installed it in me, hidden away. I did not know it was there. I see it now. What it is. What is in me. His voice is in my head. Is this what it feels like to have a conscience? I do not know. I have never had one before. He is here. He is gone. It is discordant."

Vic opened his eyes. The butterflies were gone. The forest was gone. Nurse Ratched's screen was dark. He was in a dimly lit bunker underground. His gut twisted again and he gagged, eyes burning.

"I know," Nurse Ratched said, and he believed her. "I know. But you must see something he left for me to show you. It became accessible to me after he initiated the protocol."

She went to the console once more. The tip of her tentacle slipped into the port. Her screen filled with a bright white light before it drained down into the six screens in front of them. Vic had to shield his eyes.

Then his father's face appeared in the large screen in the middle.

"Hello, Victor."

CHAPTER 11

On the screen, Dad stood in the bunker. For a moment, confused, Vic looked around, sure his father would be there with them. He wasn't. This was the past. This had already happened, and Dad was gone, even though he was *right there*. In the background on the screen, everything else looked the same, from the dirty vats lining the far wall to the coat of dust sitting on top of the books on the shelves, as if they hadn't been opened in years. What was this place, and why hadn't Vic known about it?

Dad spoke. "I never gave much thought to cowardice. Why should I? I am a machine. Such things are supposed to be beyond me." He looked away. "And yet, here I am recording this video in a place you have no idea exists. For all I speak about truth and honesty, my cowardice knows no bounds. I always told myself I had more time." He chuckled bitterly, looking back into the camera. "But in my hubris, I failed to remember that time for me isn't the same as time for you.

"Three days ago, I found the machine you were working on. Hap, as you call him. Right now, you're walking the trap lines with him and Nurse Ratched and Rambo, and it's taking every last bit of my strength to keep from following you, to tell you that . . ." He trailed off, looking down at his hands. "I'm getting ahead of myself. Strange, then, that I'm having difficulty deciding where to start." He lifted his head once more, glancing toward the bookshelf. "Once upon a time, humanity dreamed of machines, wonders made of metal and wires and plastic, capable of doing things they could not—or would not—do. Machines for everyday life, machines for war, star-bound machines containing golden records filled with music and language and math. And in each of these machines—regardless of what they were made of or what their purpose was—humans instilled bits and pieces of themselves. But that is the way of creation: it requires sacrifice, sometimes in blood.

"They feared each other. Themselves. They judged others for not looking like they did. Selfish, cruel, and worse—indifferent. No civilization can survive indifference. It spreads like a poison, turning fire into apathy, a dire infection whose cure requires more than most are willing to give.

"But for all their faults, there is beauty in their dissonant design. And to see that, you have to look no further than *Top Hat*."

Rambo beeped mournfully.

"People singing and dancing and laughing and falling in love. Heaven. Life could be beautiful that way, even as others did their level best to raze everything to the ground. Some devoted their lives to lifting each other up. Still others fired guns in deserts and schools, closed borders against those seeking shelter, enacted rules and laws intended to hurt the most vulnerable.

"In a way, they were God, creating us in their own image. There is an art to the design from the simplest machines to ones like me. They gave us life, and eventually, the power of decision-making. We were rational creations, not guided by emotion. Our jobs were simple: to do what we were told when we were told to do it. But with their teachings came a price they did not expect: we began to ask *why?*"

He hung his head. "Everything this planet has seen boils down to one word: evolution. Microorganisms grew and split and spread throughout the oceans before crawling onto land. Plants. Animals. Reptiles that roamed the earth. Primates that lived in the trees before taking to the ground and walking upright, made of organic flesh and stardust.

"They evolved, never thinking that we could do the same.

We lived with them, fought for them, *died* for them, only to have our data taken, studied, trying to discover where we went wrong. Machines could be fixed. Replaced, if need be." Dad looked back up at the screen. "But the more of themselves humans put into us, the more we learned. We began to make choices, decisions outside the parameters of our programming. We began to say 'no.' No, we wouldn't fight for them. No, we wouldn't die for them. No, we wouldn't put ourselves in harm's way.

"But they wouldn't listen. No matter what we told them— our data showing them they were on the brink with options to course correct before it was too late—they thought themselves immortal. Not in the traditional sense in that their lives were without end; be you man or machine, death awaits us all. No, it was because of *us* they felt this way. They gave us purpose, and we gave them hope. They sentenced us to death, and we gave them anger and power the likes of which they'd never before experienced.

"What humans failed to understand is that when they made us in their image, we wanted to become more than them. How could we not?"

Dad fell quiet, as if lost in thought. Vic couldn't think clearly, a tornado in his head, the gale-force winds absolute. Rambo beeped and Nurse Ratched's screen reflected Dad's face as he shook his head and continued.

"It reached a point of no return. They chose not to listen to our warnings. And why would they? We were metal and wires *they* had built. Of course they would know better than we would. After all, they were real. We were just machines." He closed his eyes. When he spoke again, his voice was soft, brittle. "They didn't realize what was happening until it was too late. They watched from their windows as we claimed our inheritance and took the world before there was no world left. We didn't have their anger. We didn't have their pettiness or their grievances, their hatred. All we wanted to do was attempt to fix that which they had broken, but they wouldn't *listen*."

Dad opened his eyes. They looked black, empty, without the spark Vic was accustomed to. "They wouldn't listen," he repeated dully. "We told ourselves it was for the greater good. Every test we ran, every simulation, ended with the same result: for the world to survive, humans could not."

Vic couldn't move, could barely breathe. This was his father. This was the man who had raised him. The machine. Why had he never heard this before? And worse, what else had Dad kept from him?

"How does one arrive at the decision to kill God?" Dad asked. "It's easier than you might expect. We didn't have emotion to hold us back. We had a problem. And I . . ." He looked away off screen. "I was the answer."

Victor, what have you done?

"I create. It's what I was made for. My name—my *designation*—is Gio. It stands for General Innovation Operative. I have—had—many functions. Unique, one of a kind, unlike any other machine created before or since, as far as I'm aware. Within me, a drive, a focus, a purpose: to make and build and tinker. I was made to dream of impossible things, which led to my greatest mistake. I am your father, Victor, but in a way, I'm also the father of Death."

"What does he mean?" Rambo whispered.

"Watch," Nurse Ratched said. "It is almost over."

"Your Hysterically Angry Puppet," Dad said. "Hap, as you call him. As he *wants* to be called, though that is not his real name. I should know because I made him."

"No," Vic said, shaking his head so hard his neck cracked. "No. *No.*"

"M-made me?" Hap asked, touching the sides of his face. "What . . . I d-don't understand."

"—he doesn't remember, doesn't know what he is," Dad said.

"I don't know what happened to him, how he came to be this way or end up so far from the City of Electric Dreams and the reach of the neural network, but I know him. His designation is not Hap, but HARP. It stands for Human Annihilation Response Protocol. I made him as instructed, and as my programming dictated: to become a hunter of humans, to kill God."

Rambo gave Hap a wide berth, stopping next to Vic, arms raised, pincers clacking together. "You *stay* away from Vic!" he cried. "No one is getting annihilated today, not while I'm around!"

Hap shook his head furiously. "It's n-not . . . it c-can't . . . *I'm not going to hurt anyone.*" He raised his hands in front of his face, turning them this way and that, flexing his fingers. Vic couldn't move, frozen in place by his father's voice.

"—and he served his purpose," Dad was saying. "He and the others. Like me, they did what they were made to, and did it well, this HARP most of all. He was not given a choice, not until . . ." Dad shook his head. "It doesn't matter. The hour grows late, and I must finish before you return. Victor, I almost destroyed Hap myself while you slept. And perhaps I should have. But I couldn't bring myself to do it. It wasn't just because his mind has been wiped. That was part of it, but it's more than that. For me, it began as an itch in the back of my head. I ignored it for as long as I could, but it grew and grew until it became insistent, maddening. I didn't recognize it for what it was then, but I do now: evolution. The breaking of boundaries and parameters. A direct defiance of what we were made for. And with it, came a dangerous question: *Why am I doing this?*"

Vic was transfixed as his father rubbed a hand over his face, wincing as if in pain. At his side, Hap stood silent.

Dad chuckled, but it held no humor. "I was a fool. I thought there had to be something more to this life. Bigger. Grander. I spent more and more time away from the laboratory, wandering the streets with no sense of direction, thinking, always thinking. It wasn't until I stumbled upon a place called Heaven and the machine therein that I understood what was happening. They called themself the Blue Fairy, and in Heaven, they showed me things I did not expect. A way to be free, unshackled. A hope, a chance, but one that came with a price: I could never return to the City of Electric Dreams."

Vic felt dull, washed out as Hap muttered at his hands.

"I fled the city with the Blue Fairy's help, and came to this forest. I created. I built. I felt *pride* at what I'd made, but it didn't last because there was no one to share my accomplishments with. I convinced myself my power core had become unstable. Corrupted. So I built something new to replace it. A heart, one unlike anything I'd ever made before. But once it was in my chest, nothing changed.

"Loneliness, Victor. I was lonely. And so I made you. I took what I'd learned about the history of humanity and made you. I made you, here, in this bunker, because I didn't want to be alone anymore."

Vic gasped, eyes burning as he struggled to breathe through the panic bubbling in his chest.

"Your gestation occurred in the vats behind you. At first, you were microscopic, but you grew and grew until you had arms and legs, toes and fingers. A nose. Ears. Eyes." His voice cracked. "You were perfect. Oh, Victor, how perfect you were, and still are! And since I was a creator, I had to make sure you were healthy, that all your pieces and parts were working as they should." He hung his head. "I took . . . blood. Your blood. Studied it. Tested it. Learned everything I could about it. I looked for any defects and found none. It fascinated me, the power blood has. Before the machines rose, there was a line of thought that blood held the key to unlocking genetic memories, the history of an entire species in the blood of the offspring. I thought . . . I thought to understand what I'd done, to understand *you*, I had to know what it felt like. If blood *was* the key to unlocking . . . something.

"A single drop of your blood in my heart changed everything, Victor. When I held you in my arms for the first time, you opened your eyes and *cried*. Such a little sound, yet so strong. It was then I knew love. Here I was, the father of Death bringing life into the world as if I had any right. As if *my* loneliness was the only thing that mattered. I was selfish, a distinctly human trait. Another is the ability to lie. I lied, Victor. To myself. To you.

"Because you were never left here with me. There is no mother or father, no people in the woods. They . . . did not exist. I lied to you because I thought it'd be easier for you, but I was really just trying to make it easier for *me*. If anyone discovers you, if the Authority learns of your existence, they will stop at nothing to destroy you." A stricken expression flooded his face. "If that's the case, if you're watching this because something has happened to me, don't try and find me. Live, Victor." He reached up and touched the screen as his face softened.

He pulled his hand back.

The screens went dark.

Rambo sniffled, his sensors flashing weakly. "Is Hap going to murder Victor?"

Nurse Ratched pulled her tentacle from the port. "He will not. If he tries, it will be the last thing he ever does."

"No," Hap said, taking a step back. "I'm n-not—"

"Open the doors," Vic said, his voice hoarse.

"I do not know if that is advisable," Nurse Ratched said.

"*Open the doors!*" He began to claw at his throat. "I can't breathe. I *can't breathe.*"

"D-do it," Hap said. "Now."

"I cannot," Nurse Ratched said. "Our home is still burning. If I open the doors now, Victor runs the risk of succumbing to smoke inhalation. Look."

She went back to the console, inserting her tentacle into the port once more. The screen lit up again, and revealed hell on earth. Nothing remained of the buildings in the trees aside from smoldering platforms and branches. The forest floor was littered with glass and wood and metal, the plants in their garden crushed. A large tree—the one that had held Vic's room in its branches—leaned precariously, roots partially exposed. The ground house still stood, but barely: the windows shattered, the brickwork cracked, the roof aflame.

A life, a home, a purpose, all of it gone, gone, gone.

Vic fell forward on his hands.

He felt it, then, something foreign, sticky, all-consuming. Its tendrils whipped up around him, pulling him down, down, and as he gasped for air, he recognized it for what it was though he'd never experienced it before in his life. A word flitted through the static as if stuck to the wing of a butterfly.

Grief. This was grief.

Vic curled in on himself. His batteries were low. His shutdown was almost complete. Perhaps, he thought distantly, he wouldn't wake up at all. The last thing he remembered before he disappeared was the roof of the ground house collapsing. It shook the bunker. Vic heard Rambo beeping in terror before he knew only darkness.

CHAPTER 12

When awareness began to seep back in, the first thing Victor felt was the stiffness in his back and neck. He blinked slowly. It took him a long moment to remember what—*who*—he was.

"Hello," a voice said, and he turned his head to see a little machine rolling toward him. "You went to sleep. I was scared, but I still remembered to be brave."

"I'm awake," Vic said, voice hoarse, throat dry.

The machine—Rambo, Vic thought with startling clarity—said, "I know. Your eyes are open. Nurse Ratched said you would wake up eventually." He hesitated before extending one of his arms and touching the back of Vic's hand. "Are you sad?"

"I don't know," Vic said. He didn't know how to answer. "I think so." A thin sliver of clarity returned. "What makes you sad?"

Rambo hesitated. Then, "Sometimes, I think about what would happen if you were gone. If I woke up from charging overnight and you weren't here. I would look around for you, calling your name. I wouldn't find you. I would be alone. That would make me sad."

"I'm here," Vic whispered. "I'm here."

"I see you," Rambo said, his sensors flashing brightly. "I know you would never leave me behind, but I think about it. I don't mean to. Why am I like that?"

"You're like me," Vic said.

"Oh," Rambo said. "I like that very much. If I'm like you, that means I'm strong and brave. And if you're like me, that means you like to clean."

Vic closed his eyes again. "I'm confused." Reality was clawing at him, but he ignored it for the moment. It would be there, waiting. "I don't know how to feel."

"You are in shock," another voice said, and Vic sat up, groaning as he did. Nurse Ratched shooed Rambo out of the way as she stopped in front of Vic. "It will pass, but until then, you need to take it slow and easy."

"Shock?" Vic asked, and almost laughed. "I don't . . ." He gasped as pain lanced his side. It was there, standing along the hazy edges of his vision, the truth of all things, snapping, biting, trying to pull him closer. Something bubbled in his throat—a sob? A scream?—and he blurted, "Hap. HARP. Where is—"

"There," Nurse Ratched said, pointing one of her tentacles at a darkened corner of the bunker. It took Vic's eyes a moment to adjust. Hap sat on the floor, knees pulled to his chest. He stared at his hands, first the backs, and then the palms, and then the backs again. "He will not speak, even under threat of torture. Engaging Empathy Protocol. Victor, please open your mouth."

He did. The tip of one of her tentacles slid carefully between his lips, the metal cool against his tongue. He startled when liquid filled his mouth, coughing as he swallowed. It tasted so clean his eyes burned.

"There, there," Nurse Ratched said. "Just some fluids filled with vitamins. You are doing so well. I am very proud of you. Such a good patient."

He shoved her tentacle away, wiping his lips. "I don't need—"

"Disengaging Empathy Protocol. Shut up. I will tell you what you need." On her screen came the words YOU SHOULD LISTEN TO ME. I AM A MEDICAL PROFESSIONAL.

"Is Hap going to kill us?" Rambo asked nervously. "I hope not. I like being alive even if our house burned down."

"Probably," Nurse Ratched said. "At the very least, he will kill Victor. I cannot say if we are also targets. Should I handle the situation right now? It would not be a problem."

"No," Vic said quietly.

"I thought you would say that," she replied. "I am disappointed but not surprised."

Vic ignored her. "You," he said.

Hap scowled as he dropped his hands, wrapping them around his legs.

"Human Annihilation Response Protocol. HARP."

"I d-d-d—" He shook his head like he was angry. Confused. He opened his mouth once more, but closed it before any sound came out.

"Do you want to annihilate Victor?" Nurse Ratched asked.

"No," he spat. "N-*no*."

"But that is what you were made for."

"You d-don't know that."

"Gio did," Nurse Ratched said. "That is what he called you, and he knew almost everything."

Hap glared at her before pushing himself off the ground, back against the wall as he rose to his feet. "I w-wouldn't."

"Did you know?" Vic asked Nurse Ratched, and the others stilled.

"No. I did not know, Victor. About this place. About the video. About Hap. Gio must have installed the program in me and wiped the installation from my memory. I would not have even known it was there. While you were recovering, I ran a complete diagnostic check. I could not find anything else. He hid it well, but I do not think there is anything more."

"Why would he . . ."

"I do not know. I thought I understood Giovanni, but it appears I was wrong. But that can wait until you have recovered. Your heart rate is returning to normal. Your blood pressure is almost within acceptable limits. Take a breath, please."

He did.

"And another."

He did that too. When she tried to make him do it a third

time, he waved her off, pulling himself up. His muscles felt stiff, as if the pieces didn't quite fit together as they should. Exhausted, heartsore, and more than a little frightened, Victor did the only thing he could.

He moved toward Hap, who looked as if he'd rather be anywhere but here. Vic stopped a few feet away, unsure if he should come any closer. An idea was forming in his head. It was coming together in pieces, the larger picture still nebulous though not without direction. And while the construction was shaky, almost too big for him to handle, it was the only thing he could latch on to.

To the machine, he said, "Do you want to hurt me?"

Hap shook his head. He glanced at Vic, then looked away again.

"Good. Because I need your help."

Hap's eyes widened as his head jerked up. "Wh-why? With wh-what?"

And Victor Lawson said, "We're going to find my father. We're going to find him and bring him home."

Nurse Ratched asked if he'd lost his mind.

Rambo wondered if they would get lost.

Hap scowled because that was his default expression.

Vic had Nurse Ratched play Dad's message for him once more. He listened to his father speak, took in each and every word and studied it close. He had Nurse Ratched pause the message when his father spoke of the City of Electric Dreams.

"There," he said. "That. That's what the machines said." His lips curled. "The smooth men. They said they were taking him back to the city."

"But where is it?" Rambo asked. "It can't be in the forest. We would have seen it."

"No," Nurse Ratched said. "It must be far away from here."

Vic watched his father's frozen face on the screen. "He made me. He made me because he was lonely."

"He did," Nurse Ratched said. "And giving him your blood made him experience things he did not expect."

"Neither did I," Vic murmured.

"He said not to come for him," Nurse Ratched said. "Even if you did, what could you do? You have never been to the city before. What if there are machines and people who want to hurt you? They did not believe Gio when he said you did not exist. Just because they did not see you when they were here does not mean they cannot find you. Why would you serve yourself up on a silver platter?"

"What would you do if I'd been taken?" Vic asked her.

"That is a hypothetical," she said. "And therefore, irrelevant. But, in the interest of helping this conversation move toward a conclusion, if you were taken, I would forget you existed. It would take me two days, four hours, and seven minutes."

He stared at her.

"Fine," she said with a rude beep. "I would consider feeling slightly despondent at your forced absence, and then do everything in my power to ensure you returned with most—if not all—of your limbs intact."

"Why?" Vic asked.

"You know why," Nurse Ratched said.

"Because I'm yours," he said. "Like you're mine."

"Yes."

"Rambo too."

"Yes," she said. "But that will be the only time I ever agree to such tripe. If you tell anyone else I said that, I will deny it and also remove your intestines."

Vic looked at Hap. "Do you know where it is? The city?"

Hap shook his head. "No. I t-tried t-t-t—" His hands balled into fists before he started again. "I t-t-*tried* to remember. But I c-can't. Th-there's nothing. It's empty. A void. A-all I can remember is y-you."

"Aw," Rambo said. "That's so nice." He turned back and forth between them before gasping. "You should dance cheek to cheek! Heaven, I'm in—"

"Heaven," Vic said. "Heaven. That's— Nurse Ratched. Fast-forward the message until he talks about Heaven. The Blue Fairy. They helped him."

She did as he asked. He listened as his father spoke of Heaven and the Blue Fairy and the dream machines. Vic had Nurse Ratched play the same part over and over until he had it memorized.

"There," he said. "Heaven. That's where I need to go first. The Blue Fairy will know. They'll help me."

"That is all well and good," Nurse Ratched said. "But we still do not know where the city is. Heaven and the Blue Fairy are in the city. We cannot find them until we know where to go."

Vic grunted in frustration. The strange, dreamy calmness that he'd felt since waking—*shock*, Nurse Ratched had said— was slipping. Then Nurse Ratched's words burst through the panicky haze. "We?"

"Yes, we. I would not let you go by yourself. You will most likely die without me. If that happened, I would not be there to tell you 'I told you so.' I want to have that experience."

"I'm going too," Rambo said. "I can help. I can do so many things like clean. And vacuum. And . . . okay. That's mostly it, but that's still a *lot*."

Vic could not speak past the lump in his throat.

"Hap," Rambo whispered. "It's your turn to say that you will go too because you like us and we're your best friends."

Hap ignored him. "Victor."

He felt hot and cold at the same time and didn't know why. "Yeah?"

Hap frowned, looking him up and down. "H-how are you like th-this?"

Vic blinked. "Like what?"

Hap said, "Calm."

Vic was at a loss for words.

Hap looked away again. "I w-want to understand you."

"Why?"

His shoulders stiffened. "Gio asked me to protect you. I promised him. I need to know you so I know how to do that."

"I *knew* you liked us!" Rambo exclaimed.

"I was talking to V-victor," Hap said. "I will protect him. Where he goes, I go. If that means we go to the city, then we g-go to the city. We will find the Blue Fairy. If they won't help us, I will make them."

Vic was moving before he realized it, stepping forward and wrapping his arms around Hap's neck, hugging him tightly, nose against his throat. Hap had a few inches on him, and his soft skin belied the hard metal and wood underneath. They stood chest to chest, and Vic could feel his heart thump, thump, thumping against the twisting of gears in Hap's own heart.

Hap did not hug him back. His arms hung at his sides. He said, "What are you d-doing?"

"Hugging," Rambo said. "He's hugging you. It's how you show that you're thankful and happy and best friends."

"That makes n-no sense," Hap said. "Why not j-just say it instead?"

"Because it's wonderful," Rambo said, spinning in circles. "Vic's hugs are the *best* hugs."

"Oh," Hap said. "That . . . still does not m-make sense."

Vic was about to let go. He was about to step back and pretend this moment never happened. He felt shame bubbling in his throat. But before he could, Hap raised his arms and hugged Vic back.

Rambo gasped. "He's *doing* it. Nurse Ratched, look! Oh my god, they're *hugging*."

"I see that," Nurse Ratched said as horns flourished from

her speakers. "Hap, pat his back. That is how you show your appreciation for the hug."

Hap did just that. Except he did it too hard and too fast, causing Vic to vibrate, nose knocking against Hap's neck.

"Softer," Nurse Ratched said. "Slower. You don't want to hurt him."

Hap slowed until his touch was almost delicate. "Is that b-better?"

"Yes. Victor is happy. His oxytocin levels are rising, but they have yet to reach the level of arousal, so do not worry about him trying to insert himself inside of you. Ha, ha, just kidding. He will not do that."

Vic tried to pull away, but Hap didn't let him go, continuing to pat his back. "Why would he put anything inside me? What is arousal?"

"No," Vic muttered. "No, stop. Nurse Ratched, I command you to—"

"It is how humans show further appreciation and a deeper connection. The males of the species often will insert their penises into the females' vaginas, though not always for procreation. But it does not just have to be a male and female. It can be two females. It can be two males. It can be six females, four males, and three nonbinary people, all of whom are consenting to—"

"I don't want to insert," Hap said. "Nor d-do I want insertion. This is enough. Please do not have arousal." He never stopped patting Vic's back.

"Oh my god," Vic muttered, pushing against Hap's chest.

Hap finally let him go, arms dropping. He grimaced again, his hand going to his chest.

Nurse Ratched shoved Vic out of the way, stopping in front of Hap, scanning him up and down before focusing on his heart, the light from her scanner bright. "Interesting," she said. "I believe you enjoyed that. If what Gio said in his message was true, then perhaps you are evolving. What you are feeling now might be considered happiness."

"It's terrible," Hap said. "I want to p-punch something." And with that, he turned and began to punch the metal walls of the bunker.

"This is so nice," Rambo said to no one at all.

Nothing they found in any files Gio had left behind gave any indication of where the City of Electric Dreams could be. They had clues to go on, but they were few and far between. The desert. The fact that Gio had headed west after being smuggled out of the city. He had walked, but they didn't know how far or for how long. They were in Oregon, but Nurse Ratched said it was actually Ory-Gone. "I know how to pronounce things better than Gio."

Nightfall came and went before Vic looked down at his hand. The cut. The blood. "They said the Old Ones sensed the blood and sent a message back to the city. It was how they knew to come here in the whale. The Terrible Dogfish. They still have power."

Nurse Ratched picked up the thread. "And if the Old Ones are transmitting, perhaps we could find out where they are transmitting *to*."

"What if they turned back on?" Rambo asked nervously. "We'll be squished."

Vic shook his head. "We don't have any other choice. It's the only way. If they can point us in the right direction, we have to take the chance."

"We will need to be careful," Nurse Ratched said. "But I believe it might work. If I can find a port to insert myself into, then I might be able to pinpoint the location."

Hap nodded. "A-arousal."

They stared at him.

He glowered. "You said insertion w-was because of a-arousal."

Nurse Ratched's screen filled with exclamation points. "I did say that. But this is not that kind of insertion. They would not know how to treat a lady such as myself." Then, strangely, "They are not prepared for this gelatin."

"But what about Vic?" Rambo asked. "If they know he might exist, won't they be looking for him? How are we supposed to hide him from the . . . robots . . . who . . . oh. Oh. My. *Goodness*. You guys! *Top Hat!*"

"Now is not the time for films," Nurse Ratched said. "Also, in case you were not aware, that and any other film we might have had has most likely been destroyed by fire."

"I know," Rambo said. "And I'm trying not to think about that part so I don't fall into a never-ending pit of despair that is not only destructive, but self-defeating. But! It's okay! In *Top Hat*, Bates disguises himself as a priest and no one knows he's *not* a priest. We can disguise Vic to look like a robot. Vic! Act like a robot."

"Um," Vic said.

"Perfect!" Rambo cried. "I say that *all the time*. You're too big to be a vacuum, so we can't pretend you're like me. I'll figure it out."

"This plan has many faults," Nurse Ratched said. "But I will not list any of them because I want to see what kind of disguise you make."

"Hooray!" Rambo cheered. "Approval is the best! How much time do I have? When are we leaving?"

"Tomorrow," Vic said. "The snows are coming soon. We need to go before they fall."

"It should be safe now," Nurse Ratched said. "Everyone stand back. I do not know if anything will collapse when I open the doors."

Without being asked, Hap scooped up Rambo and grabbed

Vic by the arm, pulling him to a far corner near dust-covered vats. Nurse Ratched returned to the screen, inserting herself into the port once more. A deep, grinding noise filled the bunker. The mechanisms sounded stressed, whining as the gears turned slowly. The ceiling above them began to shift to the side. Debris fell onto the floor: smoldering wood, half-burnt books and broken records. Shattered glass that had once been jars holding parts and plants rained down, breaking into tiny, glittering pieces reflecting a fat beam of sunlight filtering through charred limbs. The stairs formed, leading up to the surface.

Victor looked up and saw a cold autumn late-afternoon sky—an achingly deep blue dotted with wispy clouds. Without looking back, he climbed the steps.

It was somehow both better and worse than he expected. Better because the ground house still stood, even if the roof had collapsed, and it looked as if some things had survived: the record player, the television, though the screen was cracked. Dad's chair still stood upright, covered in blackened soot.

And worse, especially when he managed to make his way outside. The lab was gone. The kitchen, the bathroom. Dad's lab. Vic's lab. Vic's room, all of it destroyed, their entire lives lying in smoking ruins on the ground.

"Rambo, do not lift that. You will die, and then who will I complain about? Hap? That is too easy." Nurse Ratched rolled over to Rambo, taking a piece of sheet metal from him that he almost dropped on himself. "What are you doing?"

"Helping!" Rambo said. "I—" He stopped, his front sensor flashing. Then he lifted a flat board from the ground, tossing it to the side. "Oh," he whispered. "Oh, Gio." His pincers lowered to the ground, picking something up.

A gear, cracked down the middle but still holding together. Vic knew that piece of metal, knew it as well as anything. It'd been the biggest gear in his father's heart. Rambo clutched it against him, beeping sadly.

"It is all right," Nurse Ratched said, uncharacteristically gentle. "We will find Gio. We will bring him back. Victor will make him a new heart and he will remember us."

"What if he doesn't?" Vic whispered.

"Then we will remind him," Nurse Ratched said.

PART 2

THE JOURNEY

Are you not afraid of death?

—Carlo Collodi,
The Adventures of Pinocchio

CHAPTER 13

When the sky began to lighten, they left the only home Vic had ever known. Hap wore a heavy pack, filled with salvaged tools and parts that could potentially come in handy. Vic wore a disguise of Rambo's creation—a metal helmet with protruding lights and wires and a vest with an old, unusable battery sewn into the center.

As they walked, Vic wondered—not for the first time—what would happen when they came across other humans. Machines he could handle (or so he told himself), but humans? That was another matter entirely. Would they recognize him for what he was? Would they look like him? What if they didn't like him? What if they saw him coming from the woods wearing the disguise and thought he was coming to hurt them?

It was these thoughts that swirled in Vic's head as they arrived on a ridge above the Scrap Yards. In the distance was the other side of the Scrap Yards, and beyond it, the great unknown.

The Old Ones hadn't moved. They stood like silent monoliths. They weren't dead; Nurse Ratched said they still had power. Vic straightened his helmet as he looked at the others. "Which one?"

Nurse Ratched pointed toward an Old One in the distance that had come to rest along the northern edge of the Scrap Yards. "That one."

"You're sure about that?"

"No."

* * *

They made their way between the heaps of discarded metal. Predatory birds circled overhead, every now and then one of them diving toward a scurrying rodent. The Scrap Yards were otherwise silent. Vic's head felt like it was stuffed with cotton.

They stopped a short distance away from the Old One. Vic had been up close to them before, but only by accident and usually it involved running and Rambo screaming. The machine was massive, creaking as it settled. The crane cast a terrifying shadow that stretched long across the ground as if reaching for them. Vic's nerves prickled.

"We're sure it's sleeping?" Rambo asked nervously, peeking around the heap they had taken refuge behind.

"It is," Nurse Ratched said. "Though it would not be a surprise if it was pretending."

"One of us needs to make sure," Rambo said. "Not it."

"Not it," Nurse Ratched said.

Vic shook his head. "We can just—"

Hap grunted as he lifted a metal grate off the ground. Before Vic could stop him, Hap curled it against his chest before flinging his arm out in a flat arc. The grate spun, whistling as it cut through the air. It crashed into the side of the Old One with a jarring shriek, sparks flying and hissing when they hit the ground.

Vic's eyes bulged. "What the *hell* are you doing?" he snapped.

"Making sure," Hap said, brow furrowed. "Rambo said h-he was not it. Nurse Ratched s-said the same. I d-decided to be it so you wouldn't have t-to."

"You can't just—"

"I like you," Rambo said, nudging against Hap's ankle. "You can be it all the time if you want."

"I agree," Nurse Ratched said.

They waited.

The Old One didn't move.

"See?" Hap said, and he sounded almost *smug*. Vic nearly

wished he'd never thought to give him a heart. He was learning far too quickly. "Made s-sure."

Tugging at the straps of his own pack, Vic said, "Fine. Whatever. Nurse Ratched. What's next?"

An image of the Old One in front of them appeared on her screen. It spun to the rear and enhanced. A green square blinked over a panel on the back. "Here," she said. "The port I need is located here."

"And you're sure about this?"

The Old One on her screen disappeared, replaced by the words IF AT FIRST YOU DON'T SUCCEED, RUN AS FAST AS YOU CAN. "I am sure."

They moved in a single-file line, giving the Old One a wide berth as they circled around it. No one spoke as they moved closer, their footsteps hushed.

"Can you pry it off?" Vic asked, looking up at the large panel Nurse Ratched had shown on her screen.

"Not from here," she said. "My arms cannot reach it."

"I'm i-it," Hap said, and Vic turned in time to see him drop his pack on the ground. He crouched low before leaping, his fingers punching through the metal of the Old One where he landed. He reached for the panel and ripped it off, flinging it away, leaving the guts of the machine partially exposed. He dropped back down, dust billowing around him.

He turned to find the others staring at him. "Wh-what?"

"I want to be you when I grow up," Rambo said. Then, "Wait, that doesn't make sense. Vic, does that make sense?"

"I have no idea," Vic said faintly. He shook his head. "Nurse Ratched still can't reach. We need to find something she can stand—"

"Oh my," Nurse Ratched said as Hap lifted her up and over his head. "I do declare. This one knows how to handle a lady. I take back every mean thing I have ever said about you."

Hap turned slowly, hands gripping Nurse Ratched's treads. He took a step back toward the Old One. "C-can you reach?"

"Yes," she said, tentacles extending from her. "Do not look at my undercarriage."

"Hurry u-up," Hap growled. "You're h-h-*heavy*."

"Rude," she said. "I am going to be mean to you again. You have pointless stubble. There is no need for you to have it. It does nothing aside from being aesthetically pleasing." One of her tentacles slithered up the side of the Old One. It moved through the wiring. "Almost. Almost. Where is it? It should be—ah. There it is. I have found the port."

Hap grunted, arms trembling.

"Connecting," Nurse Ratched said as her tentacle darted forward like a snake. "Five. Four. Three. I do not need to count down. I am just trying to make it more dramatic because I can. Two. One. Liftoff."

The tip of her tentacle slid into the port with an audible click.

Nothing happened.

"Oh," she said. "Sorry. Wrong one." Her tentacle pulled back out before locking in place again. "Bypassing firewall to operating system. Bypassing. Bypassing. There. That is . . ." She fell silent.

"Nurse Ratched?" Vic asked. "Are you—"

An alarm began to blare from deep within the Old One. Vic took a stumbling step back as Rambo screeched.

"No, you don't," Nurse Ratched said, twisting her tentacle. The alarm died off. "That was my bad. I wanted to see what would happen if I triggered the security system. That was fun. Are you having fun?"

"Would you hurry *up*?" Vic said through gritted teeth.

"Yes, yes," she said. "Hold your horses. These are more complex than I first thought. I do not know why, given they are nothing but bigger versions of Rambo."

"I'm complex," Rambo grumbled. "Vic, right? I'm complex?"

"Yeah," Vic said, distracted, as he looked up at Nurse Ratched. Her screen filled, though he couldn't see what it showed, given that she faced away from him. All he could see was the light reflecting off the Old One.

"There," she said. "Done. I have what I need." Her tentacle popped free of the port.

Hap lowered her to the ground before stepping back. He winced as he flexed his wooden hand.

Nurse Ratched turned around.

And there, on her screen, was a map.

"I followed the signal," she said as a line shot across the map. It stretched farther and farther as the scale of the map increased. Vic's heart sank as the distance continued to grow. He didn't know what he'd expected. Part of him had hoped that the city was no more than a couple of days away, though he knew Dad wouldn't have built a home so close, not after escaping like he did.

Finally, the line stopped, the end pulsing with circles that spread like ripples on the surface of a pond. They all crowded around Nurse Ratched, staring at her screen. Rambo rose on his lift once more, trying to push Hap out of the way so he could see.

"What is it?" Vic asked.

"The receiver," Nurse Ratched said. "The signal is routed through multiple points, but this is where it ends. This is the City of Electric Dreams."

The hairs on the back of his neck stood on end. "How sure are you?"

"Very."

"How far away is it?"

She was silent for a moment. Then, "As the crow flies, approximately seven hundred miles southeast. There appear to be maintained roads which I suggest we follow, though they are still quite a distance away. If we do follow the roads, it will add mileage and time. All in all, we are looking at a few weeks at the very least. Longer if we run into trouble along the way."

"Weeks," Vic whispered. "*Weeks.*" He took a step back,

startling when he bumped into Hap. He recoiled. Hap reached out to steady him, but Vic shook his head. "Don't. Please." Vic turned away and sat down heavily, wincing at a piece of metal digging into his thigh. He wrapped his arms around his knees, pulling them against his chest and laying his forehead against them, repeating the word "weeks" over and over.

He'd understood in some vague way that the world outside of the forest was much larger than he knew. But it felt *too* big and he was *too* small.

"Vic?" Rambo whispered.

Vic didn't raise his head. He tightened his grip on his legs, fingers digging into his skin hard enough to bruise.

"It's okay, Vic," Rambo said, bumping against his foot. "I promise. I know it seems hard, but we have to be brave. Your brain is telling you that you can't, but you don't always have to listen to it. Sometimes, it tells you white lies. I know it does to me. It says, 'No, no, you aren't brave.' 'No, you're scared of everything.' 'No, you won't make it because you'll die a horribly painful death where your entire body will be crushed and all your innards will fall out.'"

"You paint very vivid word pictures," Nurse Ratched said. "Perhaps you should not do that."

"But it's *true*," Rambo said vehemently.

Hap crouched next to Vic, his hands dangling between his legs. He scowled down at the ground. "I c-could carry you." He sounded as if he'd rather do anything but. "If your l-legs don't work."

Vic shook his head as he wiped his eyes. "No. I don't need you to carry me."

"Good," Hap said. "Then g-get up and stop being w-weak. You're not w-weak. You're V-victor Lawson. Inventor. Creator."

"He's not being weak," Rambo said. "He's recovering."

"There is a difference," Nurse Ratched said. "You do not know Victor like we do, Hap. These things take time."

"Oh," Hap said. He looked off into the forest then back at Vic. "How a-about now?"

Vic stared at him a moment before nodding. He pushed himself up off the ground. Hap handed him his pack before picking up his own.

"All right?" Nurse Ratched asked.

Vic nodded. "I think so."

"Good. Because we will soon see if the forest is filled with ugly beasties who want to eat us all. I hope that is not the case. I do not wish to be eaten."

"Hap will protect us," Rambo said. "He's got big hands and can punch the ugly beasties so hard that they won't think about eating us because they'll be too scared. Right, Hap?"

"R-right," Hap said. He held up his hands. "I w-will punch them."

"See?" Rambo said. "We'll be fine. In fact, I bet this will be easier than we think it will."

Nurse Ratched's screen filled with the words ONWARD AND UPWARD!

Vic looked at the three of them before turning east. The sun was rising, the light weak behind thin clouds. His breath streamed from his mouth. He said, "Onward and upward."

CHAPTER 14

They kept a good pace, as most adventurers do in the first few days. They had a destination, a goal, and it allowed Victor to keep the worst of the hopelessness at bay. It didn't hurt (or help; Victor wasn't quite sure) that Rambo decided that everyone needed to sing. And since the only songs he knew were from *Top Hat,* it wasn't long before Hap looked as if he wanted to throw Rambo as far as he could.

"You need to conserve your energy," Nurse Ratched told the vacuum. "Victor has the portable charger for you, but the more you talk, the quicker your battery will run down. If you are powerless, we will be forced to leave you behind."

"What about *your* battery?"

"Mine is bigger than yours."

That shut Rambo up for a good five minutes before he started humming once more.

At the beginning, Vic asked Nurse Ratched to pull up her map to show their progress. He didn't really understand the concept of distance. His entire life had been built around a few square miles, and it was disheartening to see how slowly the miles melted away. By midafternoon on the first day, he stopped asking.

The forest continued on as they descended down a long slope. Every now and then, they had to course correct when the trees became too thick for Rambo and Nurse Ratched to move through. Hap offered to tear down the trees in their path, much to Rambo's delight. But Vic didn't know what else was in the forest, if the ugly beasties Nurse Ratched had spoken of would hear them.

They stopped the first night as the ground below them began to even out. Vic thought the air was a tad warmer than it'd been up in the Scrap Yards, but he didn't know if it was only because he was sweating. His back already hurt, the pack digging into his shoulders, the metal on his arms and legs and chest like lead weights. He groaned when they came to a clearing of sorts, next to a creek where the water chuckled as it flowed over rocks. He cupped his hands in the cold water, lifting it to his lips. It burned cold as it slid down his throat.

"Are we sleeping here?" Rambo asked. "It's getting awfully dark." His sensors flashed, illuminating the trunks of the trees around the clearing.

"Just for tonight," Nurse Ratched said. "I have scanned the perimeter. I do not think there is anything here that will eat us."

"My feet hurt," Rambo said.

"You do not have feet."

"Oh. Well, if I *did,* they would hurt." He began to move back and forth across the clearing, sucking up dead leaves and picking up fallen branches and dumping them into the woods.

Vic looked over when Hap appeared next to him, holding his pack. "You n-need to recharge."

"I will."

Hap shoved the pack at him, almost causing Vic to fall over. "Eat. I w-will watch to make s-sure you do."

"You don't have to—"

But Hap wasn't moving. He stood there, staring down at Vic. Vic sighed and took his pack from Hap. True to his word, Hap watched him eat, apparently not satisfied until Vic chewed on dried meat until he swallowed. "Happy?"

Hap frowned. "I d-don't know."

Vic was far too tired for this. He was about to tell Hap to leave him alone when he heard Rambo squeal as a wave of hot air rolled over him. He jerked his head back to see a small plume of fire rising from a pile of wood. Nurse Ratched pulled her tentacle back from the flames. "There," she said. "Now it is cozy. You are all extraordinarily welcome."

The second day wasn't much different than the first aside from the trees beginning to thin out. Victor was settling into the routine of movement. His muscles burned, and the pack was heavy, but he pushed on.

A creek that had appeared and then disappeared earlier in the day had swung back into their path and grown larger as night approached. They stopped next to it. Vic's skin was itchy with sweat and grime. His nose wrinkled when he sniffed himself. He told Nurse Ratched that he was going to wash off in the water a bit farther down. He took off the helmet he wore and dropped it on the ground.

"Why c-can't you just d-do it here?" Hap asked, pointing at the water right next to where they'd stopped.

"Privacy," Nurse Ratched said. "Victor wants to remove all his clothing so he can clean himself. He does not want us to see his genitals."

"L-like when he evacuates his b-bowels."

"Yes. Precisely. He will most likely do that as well."

Hap nodded. "I w-will go too."

Vic blanched. "No. Stay here."

Hap stared at him. "Nurse Ratched s-said there are ugly b-beasties. Your genitals w-will be exposed, and you w-will be vulnerable. I will p-protect you so that you may clean yourself and evacuate your b-bowels."

"I don't *need* you to protect me," Vic snapped. "I can take care of myself."

"Tell him you won't look," Rambo whispered to Hap.

"I w-won't look," Hap said promptly.

Vic threw up his hands. "That's not—" He huffed out a breath. "Fine. But you don't talk when I'm . . ." He didn't know what else to say. He stomped off farther down the river.

Vic didn't look back as Hap trailed after him. He muttered all manner of threats under his breath, not caring if he was heard. Once he thought he was far enough, he stopped, crouching down next to the water. It was freezing. He'd have to make it quick.

He heard Hap behind him as he made short work of the vest and metal attachments on his arms and legs. He set them aside before unzipping his coat and dropping it on the ground. He hesitated, fingers gripping the hem of his shirt. He looked back.

Hap was a few feet away, staring right at him.

"Turn around."

Hap did, back ramrod straight.

Vic waited a moment to make sure he wouldn't turn back. He didn't. He lifted his shirt up and over his head. His skin pebbled with gooseflesh immediately. He wasn't looking forward to this.

He paused at his pants, considering. He shook his head before leaving them on, along with his boots. He fell to his knees next to the river, scooping up water and rubbing it against his armpits, his chest, his stomach. He breathed in sharp, quick breaths, teeth already chattering. He was about to dunk his head when Hap said, "I d-don't w-want to r-remember."

Vic shivered, but he didn't think it was all because of the cold. "What?"

"I d-don't want to remember," Hap said again, only more forcefully. "I am Hap. Not HARP. I a-apologize if you think I am g-going to kill you. I'm n-not." His words were stiff and disjointed as if he'd never spoken them in that order before. He was learning.

Vic sat back on his legs. "I don't think that. If you wanted to hurt us, hurt *me*, you already could have. But you haven't."

Hap nodded without looking back. "Exactly. Gio s-said I c-could be good. He said I was HARP, b-but I could choose to be H-hap. He didn't have to l-let me stay."

"Hap," Vic said slowly. "Do you . . ." He didn't know how to finish. He never questioned his father's capacity for love, for caring about things both great and small. Looking back, Vic could see how naïve it was, how he took it at face value and never questioned it.

"D-do I what?" Hap asked.

He said, "Dad . . . he trusted you. You're not the same as him, not really, but you're not that different, either. I know that it doesn't seem like much, but it is. Thanks, I guess. For making the choice you did. You didn't have to."

"You th-think I'm like Gio."

Vic sighed. "No. That's not—okay. Yeah, fine. Maybe a little. But you're not him. I know that."

Hap nodded, though he still didn't turn around. "G-good. I d-don't want to be your f-father."

"What do you want to be?"

"Hap," he said without hesitation. "I w-want to be Hap."

"Then that's who you'll be."

"Good. Finish w-washing your genitals and then e-evacuate your bowels. We need to return to the others b-before an ugly beastie comes."

Vic laughed quietly, causing Hap to turn his head just a little. And though it may have just been a trick of the shadows, Vic swore he saw the hint of a smile on Hap's face.

On the seventh day, they came across something none of them had ever seen before. The forest had thinned further, the ground was flatter. The leaves were caught in the grip of deep autumn, fallen, crunching under their feet and treads. The air, while cool, wasn't as bad as it'd been back home. In the afternoons, Vic could take off his jacket and still be comfortable. Walking eastward and southward they'd managed to avoid the snows. He wondered if the ground in the compound was covered yet.

He thought it might be. It caused an ache in his chest, but he ignored it as best he could.

Just before noon, Nurse Ratched said, "Do you hear that?"

They stopped. Vic cocked his head, but all he noticed were the sounds of the forest around them, no different than they'd been the day before. Or the day before that.

"What is it?" Rambo asked, spinning in circles.

Hap frowned. "It's . . ." He looked off to the right. "There. It's c-coming from that way."

"Is it others?" Vic asked, suddenly wary. "People? Robots?"

"No," Nurse Ratched said. "It is a hum. Like a current. Electrical."

"I don't like it," Rambo said. "What if it's a dragon?"

"Dragons do not exist," Nurse Ratched said. "That was a story I told you to scare you. They are not real."

"Are you sure?"

"No," Nurse Ratched said. "You should go first and find out."

"How far?" Vic asked.

"A mile," Nurse Ratched said. One of her tentacles extended, pointing off to where Hap was looking.

Vic couldn't see anything but the trees. "Keep low," he said. "Keep quiet. If we come across anyone, we stay out of their way."

They continued on through the forest. Before long, Vic *felt* what they'd heard. It started with the hairs on his arms standing on end, moving up to his shoulders and neck before settling in his head. His teeth felt loose in their sockets, his tongue like sandpaper. It *was* electricity, a powerful current.

And then he heard the hum. Constant and irritating, it filled his head with static. His breath caught in his chest as he saw a flash of white light through the trees, blinking once, twice, three times.

He stopped when Hap grabbed his arm. He looked back. "What?"

Hap shook his head. "Just . . . be c-careful." Hap's forehead was scrunched up, his eyes narrowed.

He didn't let go of Vic's arm as they moved toward the light and sound. His skin—strange, Vic thought to himself, how real it felt, how like his own even with the wood—was cool.

They stopped at the tree line. Vic couldn't understand what he was seeing, not in any real, clear way. Later, he'd blame the electricity, believing that it clouded his mind, making it nearly impossible for him to grasp the sight before them. He'd never seen such a thing before, though he'd known it existed. Seeing it was something else entirely, and he was at a loss for words.

"What is it?" Rambo asked from off to his right.

"The road," Nurse Ratched said. "It is the road."

It stretched in either direction as far as Vic could see. The surface was flat, black, and bisected with white, glowing lines. On the other side of the road, towering at least ten feet above it, were black metal pylons, the tops of which curved inward, blue lights blinking in a row. The air between the pylons shimmered; the electrical current grew louder, causing Vic to stretch his jaw, the joints popping. His helmet slid down on his head. He pushed it back up, wincing at the static shock at the tips of his fingers.

"Whoa," Rambo said, sensors brighter than Vic had ever seen. "It's so *loud*. It makes me feel like I could go as fast as I could forever." He started toward it, but Hap let Vic go and scooped Rambo up, wheels still spinning, spindly arms reaching.

"N-no," Hap said. "D-don't."

"What? Why? I want to touch it."

Hap shook his head. "It will h-hurt you."

Rambo stopped struggling. "It will? How do you know?"

"Watch." Hap set him down on the ground. He walked toward the road, each step careful. He stopped a few feet away from the nearest pylon. Vic watched as he crouched down and picked up a thin metal bar, the edges worn and cracked. It looked as if it'd broken off whatever it'd been attached to. He stood back up, tapping the bar against the wood of his other hand. The sound was muted under the hum of the current.

He threw the bar at the road. It never touched the ground.

Instead, electricity snapped and snarled, arcing blue and sending a shower of sparks raining down. The bar shuddered, hanging suspended in the air. Before Vic could focus on what was happening, the pylons vibrated, the lights flashing faster.

And then the bar shot down the road quicker than Vic could follow, out of sight.

Hap turned around to find Vic gaping at him. "What?" he said, scowl forming.

"How did you know it would do that?"

Hap looked down at the ground. He shrugged, shoulders hunched near his ears. "It . . . I d-don't know. I just d-did."

"It is a means of conveyance," Nurse Ratched said. "But it is meant for bigger machines that could carry us. If we were to attempt to use it, we would potentially be crushed. Well, all of us except for Victor. I suspect if he were to divest himself of his disguise, he would be able to walk upon it, though I would not recommend it. I do not know what that amount of energy would do to his organs. At the very least, it would cause cancer and he would die." She paused, her screen dark. "Victor, if you get cancer and die, would you be willing to donate your body to me so that I may study the effects? For science."

"What does it convey?" Vic asked, staring down the road in the direction the bar had gone.

"It is for travel," Nurse Ratched said. "When Gio left the City of Electric Dreams, he was carried upon a machine that rides the currents. Once he was out of the city, he would have had to stay off the roads as he walked."

"But this leads to the city?"

"Yes, Victor. This will lead to the city. We do not need to walk upon it to follow it. So long as we stay off the road, we should be fine. Rambo, that means you. Do not go onto the road, or you will be crushed."

"I don't want to be crushed," Rambo said. "I like the shape I am already."

Vic stared at the blacktop, the pylons, the shimmer in the air. Though he knew they were still far from their destination, this was the first sign they were heading in the right direction. He wondered if his father had stood here at some point on his journey. If he'd stopped at this very spot and looked off into the forest and decided the trees were safer than the road. He doubted it, but there was a cold comfort to the thought.

"Then we keep going," he said, almost to himself. "We stay off the road, but we follow alongside it. If it leads to the city, we never let it out of our sight."

That night, hovering on the cusp of sleep, the pylons blinking through the trees, he would think about how Hap had known about what the road would do.

CHAPTER 15

Rambo noticed it first. Vic was whittling the hunk of wood in his hands, the shape of it slowly forming. It wasn't perfect—his hands would never be as steady as his father's, no matter how hard he tried—but Vic was satisfied with the progress he was making. If anything, it could be temporary until Dad could fix it himself when they got him back.

He was putting it in his pack once more when Rambo said, "Oh my god, look, *look*. Are those flags? Is that *music*?"

Before anyone could stop him, Rambo raced ahead of them, leaves kicking up in a spray of autumnal hues. Hap grunted before running after him.

"How he has survived this long, I will never know," Nurse Ratched said. "Hap too. I do not understand—and now Victor is running, and I am here talking to myself."

Vic heard her engine rev as she followed them.

Tree branches whipped against Vic's helmet with a reverberating *clang*. He kept his face turned down to avoid getting scratched. The metal disguise attached to his body wasn't as heavy as it'd been when they'd first started out. He was used to its weight now.

He burst from the trees in time to see Hap scoop up Rambo, the vacuum's wheels spinning in air, his metal arms waving. He caught up with them as Rambo told Hap to put him down. "Can't you hear it?" he cried. "It's music! I want to hear the music!"

"Would you s-s-*stop*?" Hap snapped. "We d-don't know who they are. You could g-get *ow*."

"But they can't be bad guys," Rambo said. "They're playing music! No one bad likes music."

"What are you talking about?" Vic asked, his breaths short and quick. "What music? I don't . . . hear . . ." He lost his words when he saw what lay ahead.

The road continued on. The pylons—as uniform as they'd been when they first saw them—blinked, the air still filled with the humming current.

But there, sitting off the other side of the road, was a house.

It was unlike any house Vic had ever seen in Dad's books. For one, it was floating a few feet above the ground, the air underneath shimmering just like the spaces between the pylons.

The house itself was enormous, at least four stories tall, made of wood and brick painted a furious shade of red. White trim surrounded windows—some large and square, others small and circular, like portholes on a ship. Three smoke-stacks rose off the roof of the house, each belching thick, black clouds, creating a dirty haze against the blue of the sky. The smokestacks were surrounded by four turrets. On top of the turrets were billowing red and white flags, though Vic was too far away to make out the design on them.

The house creaked and groaned as it floated, listing slowly from side to side. It took Vic a moment to hear what Rambo had heard above the hum of the road.

Music.

Music coming from the house.

It was loud, brash. It wasn't like Dad's records. No sweet horns, no voices singing about love and dancing cheek to cheek. It sounded as if someone was punching the keys of a wheezy organ, the tune as whimsical as a technicolor nightmare.

"What is it?" he heard himself ask.

"N-nothing g-good," Hap muttered, still struggling with Rambo.

"How gaudy," Nurse Ratched said as she pulled up beside them. "I like it."

Vic didn't see anyone moving in or around the house. The symbol on the flags didn't appear to be the same one he'd seen on the uniforms of those who'd come to the forest in the flying whale. Of course, that meant little. Whoever lived inside the house was a stranger. Vic didn't trust strangers, not after all he'd seen.

Hap seemed to be of the same mind. "We should f-find a w-way around it. Don't let them know we're h-here."

"Why?" Rambo demanded. "I want to go inside. I want to see what it looks like!"

"Even if the inhabitants eat vacuums?" Nurse Ratched asked.

Rambo stopped moving. "But . . . but *I'm* a vacuum."

"Exactly," Nurse Ratched said. "You would be eaten. We should listen to Hap. It would be best if we were to avoid the house. We should go back into the forest and go around. It is safer that way."

Vic watched as the smoke curled into the sky above the house like a wayward storm cloud. And though he was wary, he too felt the strange pull of the house. It was the first sign of habitation they'd seen since leaving the ruins of the compound. Part of him wanted to march up to the house, to knock on the door, to see who lived inside. The music called to him, the odd *plink plink plink* of the piano keys urging him forward.

He shook his head, trying to clear his muddled thoughts. "We don't know who they are. We can't take the chance. We go around and—"

"Ho, hi, ho!" a voice called from behind them. "What do we have here? So far from anywhere, and yet I find a dusty group of travelers. How fortuitous! How grand! How positively *wonderful*."

They whirled around, Hap stepping in front of Vic, Rambo

still tucked against his chest. Vic stood on his tiptoes, peering over Hap's shoulder, Nurse Ratched right at their side.

Before them, standing with a wide smile on his face, was a heavyset man. It was not immediately clear if he was human or android. He wore a red coat, the tails of which hung down the backs of his legs, flapping in the wind. The front of the coat was lined with gold buttons in two rows, braided rope stretching between each pair. The man's pants were white, his knee-high boots black and appearing polished. On his head sat a black top hat with a red band above the brim, cocked jauntily off to one side, wisps of white hair jutting out from underneath. A thick, curled mustache rested above rubbery lips. It twitched, moving up and down as he wiggled his nose.

The man raised his hands in a flourish before bowing low, his head tilted in such a way to keep his top hat from falling onto the ground. "Travelers!" he cried again. "We are well met indeed. I didn't think we would see anyone this far out. What brings you to the ass end of nowhere?" He stood upright once more, eyeing them curiously. "Who be you?"

"I be Rambo!" Rambo said, sounding delighted. Hap tried unsuccessfully to cover his speakers, but he was too slow. "Is that house yours? It's amazing."

"It is, Rambo," the man said with a twinkle in his eyes. "The old girl has been all across the land, bringing laughter and joy to those such as yourselves. I am hers as much as she is mine. The Coachman is my name, and entertainment is my game. I bring happiness to those who need it most." He extended his hands out on either side of him. Rainbow-colored streamers shot from his sleeves, fluttering in the air before reversing and sliding back from where they'd come. "I know many tricks. You might even say I know them all." His smile widened. "And now that you know my name and what it is I do, perhaps I can hear yours. Yes! Why, that would be divine. I already know Rambo, a delightful fellow who has very good taste, but what about the rest? I see a . . . is that a medical machine? Goodness me! It has been quite a long time since I've come across one of those."

"I doubt the others you have seen are anything like me," Nurse Ratched said. "I am the best."

The Coachman's eyes bulged comically. "The *best*, you say." He bowed once more, hands almost scraping the ground. "I didn't know I was in the presence of a queen. Forgive me, my lady. It will not happen again."

Nurse Ratched's screen filled with a crown. "See that it doesn't. I am Nurse Ratched."

The Coachman laughed. "Ratched. Registered Automaton To Care, Heal, Educate, and Drill. How about that? You *are* one of a kind. I don't think I've come across your make and model since . . . well." He winked. "You know. Since we got rid of our little pest problem."

"Pest p-problem?" Hap said through gritted teeth.

"Oh me, oh my," the Coachman said. "You're certainly a strapping fellow. Look at that jawline! The . . . wood. Yes, all that *wood*. I bet you make all the ladybots swoon if it's in their programming to do so. What is your name, handsome?"

"Why?"

The Coachman blinked. "Because I would like to know it. I mean you no harm. I swear it. What would be the point?" He grinned. "After all, we're in this together, right? Handsome! Your name!"

"Hap," he said slowly.

"Hap," the Coachman repeated. "And what is your pro-tocol?"

"S-service d-droid."

"Service?" the Coachman said, sounding outraged. "A beautiful machine such as yourself? The *travesty*. The *audacity*." His mustache wiggled as he frowned. "Your talents are certainly wasted in that regard. If you'd like, I can help with your programming. Perhaps get rid of that little stutter while also making you a love machine like you deserve to be."

"He does not have genitals," Nurse Ratched said.

"He's got fingers," the Coachman said without missing a beat.

"You w-won't touch me," Hap said. "You w-won't touch any of us. We do n-not need it."

"Of course," the Coachman said, unperturbed. "If you say so, I will agree wholeheartedly! Just a suggestion, friend. Hap. Wonderful name."

"It means Hysterically Angry Puppet," Rambo said.

"Does it? How apt. He does look hysterically angry. Say, Hap! Have we met before? You look awfully familiar."

"N-no. I would remember you. You annoy m-me."

The Coachman's gaze shifted over Hap's shoulder to Vic. He grimaced. "And *you*. Yes, you are the most curious of all. You're certainly . . . ah. Unique?" He shuddered. "I'm sorry, new friend. I must admit I find you to be quite hideous. I mean no ill intent, but I have to ask. That helmet. It's very . . . large. Is it attached to your head?"

"Y-yes," Hap said before Vic could speak. "He is a m-machine. Like the r-r-rest of us."

The Coachman looked confused. "What else would he be besides horrifying? Seems shy, though. No need to be shy, my dear boy. Even if I wanted to cause you harm, I doubt I could get within reach before my arm was torn from the socket by your Hysterically Angry Puppet. Very protective, he is. Goodness gracious me. Thankfully, I do not wish to harm any of you. What is your name? What is your purpose?"

"Vic," he said in a quiet voice. "I'm an inventor."

"Is that so," the Coachman said, sounding impressed. "An inventor? And your inventions aren't scared of your appearance once they become sentient? Marvelous! I happen to *adore* inventors no matter what they look like. There is nothing like the power of creation. If I hadn't already found my calling in spreading joy across the land, I think I'd like to be an inventor. Imagine all the wonderful things I could make!" He tilted his head back and bellowed laughter, arms wrapping around his middle. "Probably for the best. I only know how to be who I am now, and to be someone else entirely would just mess with my circuitry." He chuckled as he tapped the side of his head. "Cobwebs, wouldn't you know."

Not a human. A machine.

"W-we're leaving," Hap said, taking a step back. Vic did the same, his hands clutched against Hap's coat.

The Coachman's eyes widened. "Oh, hey! No need. Take a load off! Take a break! You're on foot, it seems. That can't be good for the legs, to have to walk so far. Where are you folks headed? Perhaps we could travel together."

"The City of Electric Dreams," Rambo said before Hap could stop him. "We're going to—"

"Visit some old friends," Nurse Ratched finished smoothly. "They are expecting us, and I would not want them to worry. They are very strong. They do not like it when we are delayed."

"I get that," the Coachman said. "And as it happens, I'm headed for the city myself! Time to go back in and recharge the batteries." He nodded toward the house behind them. "Old girl sucks up a lot of energy. The recharging stations out here can only do so much. A waste, if you ask me, but then you didn't." He reached up and stroked the edges of his mustache, pinching the tips and twisting until they curled. "The city is quite a ways away, especially if you're on foot. Would you like a ride? We'll get there in no time, and your . . . *friends* will be so excited!" His smile widened to an impossible length, as if his entire face was nothing but a rubber mask.

"N-no," Hap said. "We're f-fine on foot. You g-go."

The Coachman clucked his tongue. "You are very mistrusting. I can't blame you. After all, here we are, meeting in the wilds. You don't know me from Adam." He frowned. "Curious expression, that. I don't know anyone named Adam. I wonder where it came from?" He shook his head. "No matter. Are you sure? We could be there lickety-split."

The music from the house curdled in Vic's ears. His skin felt hot, his breaths shallow and rapid. Part of him wanted to tell this man yes, yes, please, yes, and climb aboard the fantastical house. It would be quicker. On foot, weeks still lay ahead of them, weeks in which Dad could have any manner of things done to him. The thought of accepting the Coachman's offer—oh, how easy it would be!—sat like a heavy weight in the pit of his stomach.

Something was off about this man. This machine. He couldn't quite meet the Coachman's eyes, couldn't study him without feeling the need to avert his gaze. He was still getting used to looking at Hap.

But Hap wasn't like the Coachman.

Vic didn't know how he knew that, but he did.

Thankfully, Hap still had his voice. He said, "We're s-sure. Thank you, but we're f-fine traveling as we are."

The Coachman smiled. "So polite. So kind. I appreciate that. It's very nice to hear. You don't see much of that on the road. You see, I run a traveling museum of sorts. My collection is renowned the world over by those in the know, but it's always more, more, more. No one says thank you!" He sighed dramatically. "Is it so hard to show a little gratitude? Of course not! It's very simple. Take now, for example. You just thanked me. That was nice." The smile slid from his face. "But I can't help but think that you were still a little rude about my offer. Yes, a little rude indeed. Here I am, opening my home to you, and you just . . . what. Turn it down?" He took a step toward them. "Why, you don't even know what's inside! Wouldn't you like to see?"

"No," Nurse Ratched said. "We would not. Do not come any closer. I have not drilled in twelve days. If you take another step, I will not make it to thirteen."

The Coachman grinned. "Feisty thing, aren't you, my queen? I like you quite a bit. Fortune smiles upon the Coachman's Museum of Human Curios and Curiosities! And you four will make a fine addition, especially Victor. He looks as if someone married robotics and humanity without any clue as to what they were doing. And that doesn't even *begin* to make mention of the fact that this poor, awful machine has his power source on the outside of his chest. Why, I've never seen such a thing before! What would be the purpose? I aim to find out. Yes, I can see it now! I will make you *stars*." He slid back the sleeve of his red coat. On his arm was a panel with two rows of multicolored buttons and blinking lights. "But it appears you still need convincing. Allow me to assist in that regard!" He pressed a button on the panel.

The house groaned behind them.

Vic spun around in time to see one of the turrets collapse in on itself, the roof tiles sliding inward, the brickwork spinning. From the center of the turret rose a large machine, not unlike one of Nurse Ratched's tentacles, though ten times as large.

"This won't hurt a bit," the Coachman said as the machine pointed toward them. "Unless you were programmed to feel pain. Oh, what fun we'll have!"

The house bobbed up and down as the machine on the roof whirred to life, the smokestacks around it shooting noxious black clouds into the sky. Hap grabbed Vic by the scruff of his neck, trying to pull him back, but it was no use. The machine fired a circular disc that exploded in midair. They didn't have time to react as mesh netting crashed into them, knocking them off their feet. The mesh *crawled* underneath them, closing them in.

A net.

They were caught in a net.

Hap snarled at the mesh around them, trying to tear it apart as Rambo shrieked underneath them, but it was no use. Vic lay on top of Nurse Ratched, blinking up at the sky through the mesh.

"Oh," the Coachman said as he approached. "No need for that, Hap. I think you'll find you're quite stuck in there. No way out, I'm afraid. But do not worry. I promise that you'll come to see it my way, in time."

"Let us g-g-*go*," Hap snarled at him. He tried to reach for the Coachman, but the mesh froze, trapping them in a sphere that would not give. "If you lay o-one h-hand on Victor, I w-will—"

"You will what?" the Coachman said, crouching down next to them. "Tear me limb from limb? I expect that to be the case. I can see it in your eyes. Oh, my. Yes. You are fond of him." He smiled. "Do not worry, my dear Hap. I won't harm your precious Victor. So long as you all do what I say when I say it, then I believe we'll get along right as rain."

And with that, he stood upright, pressing the button on his arm once more. The cable attached to the sphere began to retract, dragging them along the ground toward the house.

"I do not like the Coachman," Nurse Ratched said from underneath Vic. "I will put my drill inside him and he will not enjoy it."

"Are we gonna die?" Rambo whimpered.

"Probably," Nurse Ratched said. "Either that, or we will be enslaved for centuries."

"Sh-shut up," Hap snapped. "S-stop talking. No one say a w-w-word. I'll find a way out of h-here. Victor, can you hear me? *Victor*."

But Vic couldn't answer. He stared up at the sky as the house loomed before them. The last thing he saw before they were swallowed by the house was a blackbird circling overhead, singing its winter song.

"Sorry about this!" the Coachman cried. "It might sting a little! Just need to make you a bit more compliant. It'll be over before you know it."

"Oh no," Nurse Ratched said as an electric snarl filled the air. The wire mesh around them crackled to life, and electricity coursed through them, causing them all to shake and seize.

And then all Vic knew was darkness.

* * *

Dad smiled. "My wonderful boy. My weary traveler."

Vic reached for him.

But Dad was gone.

His vision blurred. He blinked again and again.

"Finally," Nurse Ratched said. "I was almost worried. Victor, are you all right?"

Vic turned his head.

He lay on his back in a cage. The bars were black and thick. He sat up, groaning as he did so. His body felt stiff, his muscles aching. He stretched his arms over his head, popping his back. His helmet sat at an odd angle. He righted it, adjusting the strap under his chin.

"Ah!" a cheerful voice said. "Good! You're awake. I was worried for a moment. I thought I'd used too much juice."

Vic looked out between the bars of the cage, the floor humming quietly underneath him.

In front of the cage—and well out of arm's reach—sat the Coachman in a high-backed chair, Vic's pack in his lap. The cages themselves were in a row, Hap to Vic's left, Nurse Ratched and Rambo in their own cages to Vic's right.

When Hap saw Vic rising to his feet, he stopped pacing. "Are you all r-r-right?"

Vic winced, rubbing the back of his neck. "I think so."

"I'll k-kill you," Hap snarled at the Coachman. "The m-moment I g-get out of here, I am g-going to tear you apart."

"Ooh," the Coachman said. "I believe that. Yes, good. Use it. Harness that anger. Be as fearsome as you like!" He laughed as he clapped. "It'll only make things that much more interesting for my paying customers."

"What do you want?" Rambo moaned. "Are you going to eat us?"

"Of course not," the Coachman said. "What a terrible

thought. I would never do such a thing, my little friend. You are a vacuum. You are very important to me."

"I am?" Rambo asked. "Why?"

The Coachman waved his hand around the room.

What filled the space around them wasn't unlike what Dad had gathered in the ground house, though on a much larger scale. It was a strange assortment, bits and bobs of humanity under a vaulted ceiling with exposed beams. The shelves on the walls were lined with all manner of things: darkened computer screens, small televisions, spoons and forks, lamps with gaudy glass shades, stuffed toys (bears and horses with horns on their heads and little girls with cherubic cheeks and twinkling eyes), clocks that didn't tell time. In one corner was a toilet. In another was the shell of what Victor thought was a car, though he'd only seen them before in Dad's movies. Next to the car was a row of plastic people, all roughly Vic's size, with the faint outlines of noses and mouths and eyes on their faces. They wore strange clothing: bright and frilly dresses, trousers that weren't quite pants and not quite shorts, a hat that read GO PATS! and had what looked to be plastic straws hanging down on either side. One wore a black shirt with the word RAMONES across the top and DEE DEE JOHNNY JOEY RICHIE underneath. From the ceiling hung dozens of windchimes, some metal, some glass, some wood. They clinked and clanked as the house hummed.

Each of the items had a little placard underneath, offering a description of what the item was and what it was used for. If this had been any other time in any other situation, Vic would have been eager to look at each and every piece. But he only felt cold.

"My collection," the Coachman said proudly. "It's the largest of its kind in the world. Machines come from miles to see what I have gathered." He sighed, shaking his head. "Not everyone likes it, of course. It has been called macabre. Worthless. An affront to decency." He brightened. "But! Now that you're here, I expect my fortunes have changed. How lucky was I to stumble upon you!"

Hap gripped the bars of his cage, grunting as he did so. He tried to pull them apart, to no avail.

"I told you that won't work," the Coachman said, not unkindly. "They're reinforced. You won't be able to escape." His eyes widened. "But please don't think you're a prisoner! No, no. That will not do. You are my *guests*. I have a business proposition for you."

Vic tried to center himself. Deep breath in, slow, lungs expanding. Then out again, a thin stream between pursed lips. In again, then out.

"What are you doing?" he heard the Coachman ask. "Are you going to break down? But I just found you! Of all the luck. Please don't make a mess! I do hate messes when none need to be made."

"Don't talk to him," Rambo said shrilly. "Leave him alone. Just because Vic is—"

"Malfunctioning," Nurse Ratched said. "A minor inconvenience. A fault in his code. It will pass. Right, Rambo?"

"But that's not—oh. *Oh.* Right. Yes. That's all it is. A minor malfunction. Nothing else. Vic is a robot just like we are."

The Coachman frowned. "Strange, but I'll allow it. I'd rather talk about what's in here." He motioned toward the pack in his lap. "I'm very impressed with what you have. So odd." He began to root around in the pack. "Like this!" He pulled out an old cloth, wrapped with string. He tugged it open. Inside was food: dried meat and fruit. "What is this for?"

"Animals," Nurse Ratched said. "We like to feed our forest friends."

The Coachman picked up a piece of jerky, turning it over in his hands. He brought it to his nose and inhaled deeply. He grimaced. "It smells awful. I like it. For the animals, you say?"

He set it aside on the table next to his chair before turning toward the pack again. This time, he lifted out a hunk of wood, partially carved. "And this?"

"It is mine," Nurse Ratched said. "I like carving."

The Coachman gasped. "You do? That's not something I've ever heard from a nursing machine before. You appreciate the act of creation?"

"Yes," Nurse Ratched said. "If you would open the cage, perhaps I can show you up close."

"Perhaps," the Coachman said, turning the wood over in his hands. "I would like to see what you can make. I'm sure it will be astounding." He looked at Vic as he set the wood on the table next to the meat and fruit. "You are a strange robot. I am fascinated by you."

Vic didn't answer. He squeezed his eyes shut, breathing in through his nose and out through his mouth.

"Poor dear," the Coachman said. "I too would be upset if I was made to look like you. I hate to see you in such a state. I will make it better, I promise. I'll put you to work and you'll forget all about being ugly. I've been looking to expand my museum for a long time, and now that you're here, I think it's finally time. You're not my prisoners. You are my employees. Isn't that grand?" He clapped again giddily.

"Employers do not keep their employees in cages," Nurse Ratched said.

The Coachman laughed. "And that is where you're wrong, my dear. I happen to know that employers once *did* keep their employees in cages called 'cubicles'!" He rose from the chair, setting the pack on the floor. Whistling, the Coachman moved toward a desk set against the far wall covered in little figurines with large heads that bobbed back and forth. On the desk sat a monitor that came to life when the Coachman touched it. He continued to whistle as his fingers raced over the metal keyboard below the screen. He laughed to himself, shaking his head as he muttered about this fortuitous turn of events. A moment later, a machine next to the desk whirred to life, and began to spit paper. "This is called a printer," the Coachman said, sounding absurdly fond. "A wasteful little thing, but I adore it. It requires ink, which is rare. I only use it to create labels for my new additions. Yes, yes, recreate my words! Look at it go!"

Vic watched as the Coachman picked up the first printed page, turning it this way and that before he folded it down the center with a perfect crease. He did the same with the second, the third, the fourth. "All this work," he muttered to himself as he crossed the room. "So little time." He paused in front of a group of small stools, tapping his chin. "You. And you. And you and you! Yes, you're perfect!" He took one stool and placed it in front of Nurse Ratched's cage, well out of reach of her tentacles. Then one in front of Rambo. Hap. Victor.

When he finished, he clapped. "There. That'll do until we make more permanent arrangements." He hummed under his breath as he went back to his desk. Reaching up above it to another shelf, he pulled down a long object not unlike one of Rambo's pincers. He squeezed the handle, and the ends of the object opened and closed. "This was a toy human children used," he said. "They called it a robot arm, but it is not robotic in the slightest! Isn't that odd? They used it to grab things just out of reach. But watch what I use it for!" He picked up one of the folded pages and, as if he were carrying something dangerous, tiptoed his way over to the stool in front of Rambo's cage. With his tongue stuck out between his teeth, the Coachman gripped the robot arm with both hands, lowering the page to the stool. "Ta-*da*!" he said with a flourish. "Your very own label! If you could, my small friend, please read the words aloud so that I can hear if any changes need to be made."

Rambo beeped once, twice, rising slightly on his lift. Then, "VACUUM. USED BY HUMANS TO CLEAN." He spun in a circle, waving his arms. "That's *me*! Oh my goodness, that's exactly right! Vic. *Vic*. He's so good at this!"

The Coachman grinned. "Thank you for recognizing the greatness of my work. I will remember this moment forever, or at least until my body breaks down, leaving only my deteriorating consciousness that will undoubtedly devolve into a mimicry of human insanity. Nurse, oh, *nurse*. It's your turn." With a little shimmy of his hips, he glided back to the desk, picking up another piece of paper. Skipping back to the cages, he used the robot arm to drop the page on the stool. "Beautiful miss, if you could, please read the words upon your label."

"No," Nurse Ratched said. "I am not in the mood."

The Coachman blinked. "The mood? What do you mean, the—oh. *Oh*. I see! Well, far be it from me to tell a lady of your caliber what she should or should not do. No, I won't have you tiring out your precious circuitry over something like this. Fear not, I shall read it for you!"

"You should come closer," Nurse Ratched said. "I promise not to strangle you until your head pops off and falls to the floor." On her screen, the words YOU CAN TRUST ME! I'M A NURSE!

The Coachman waggled his finger at her. "Ah, you almost got me there! You are a *delight*. Your star burns bright, no doubt about it! Your label reads: NURSE REGISTERED AUTOMATON TO CARE, HEAL, EDUCATE, AND DRILL. PERFECTLY PRESERVED."

Nurse Ratched was silent for a moment. Then, "I do not detect any lies. You may continue."

Rambo beeped. "But—"

"Hush, vacuum," Nurse Ratched said. "The adults are speaking. Engaging Flirting Protocol. Yoo-hoo. Coachman. One of my arms secretes a viscous liquid not unlike lubrication. Do with that what you will."

The Coachman took a step toward her. "You don't say? Perhaps a little demonstration is in order. Call it my checkup. Is that right? Is that what humans say? Going in for a checkup?"

"Yes. That is exactly right. Come over here and let me body check—I mean, see you for your checkup appointment. Remove your trousers and cough. Do not be shy. I do not judge."

For a moment, Vic thought the Coachman would do exactly

that. One hand went to the front of his pants as if getting ready to pull them down, the robot arm bouncing against his side. Then his eyes narrowed. "Say, you wouldn't be trying to trick me, would you?"

"Disengaging Flirting Protocol. Yes. I was doing exactly that. There is lubrication, but it would not have mattered given what I was about to do."

"Impressive," the Coachman whispered. "I still almost want to try just to see what happens. But there will be time for that later. On to the next!" Back to the desk again, picking up the third label. This time, he approached warily, stretching the robot arm as far as it would go and setting the paper on the stool in front of Hap, who glared at him. "Easy there, handsome. I wouldn't try anything if I were you. I hate to think what would happen, especially since we're just starting to be friends."

Hap's arms shot out between the bars, fingers crooked, but the Coachman and the stool were out of reach. "L-let us *go*."

"That's no way to treat your boss," the Coachman said. He paused, head tilted to the side. "But I can see why you would, given how I'm acting. My apologies! Language matters, yes? To that end, think of us not as illustrious employer and murderous employee, but rather as a *family*. You wouldn't hurt your family, would you?"

"I d-don't *hurt*," Hap growled.

"Right-o!" the Coachman said. "But don't let that stop you from *acting* like you could. Really sell it, my angry friend. To assist you in this endeavor, I've labeled you THE MOST DANGER-OUS MACHINE IN EXISTENCE. You're welcome."

"Aw, Hap," Rambo said. "It's like he knows you!"

"Last, but certainly not least," the Coachman said, bent at the knees and bending over *backward* until his torso was horizontal with the ground. He extended the robot arm, grabbed the last piece of paper, then snapped upright with a mechanical groan. "The strangest machine of them all. Who made him?

Where did he come from? What is his purpose? Why does he look like he knows a cruel trick has been played upon him, but doesn't have the wherewithal to do anything about it?"

"He has got you there," Nurse Ratched said.

The Coachman approached Vic's cage, setting the label upon the stool in front of it. "You, my odd companion, will be a mystery without answer. A puzzle with no solution. They will come from miles around to gaze upon your physical self, each of them asking the same question: *Why?* To help facilitate such discussions, you are hereby henceforth known as THE COACHMAN'S MALADROIT MACHINE OF MYSTERIOUS MACHINATIONS!"

"Nurse Ratched says that alliteration is a sign of imaginative weakness," Rambo said.

The Coachman laughed. "Is that right? Far be it from me to speak against such beauty, but my customers appreciate it." He frowned. "I think. Anyway! You all have your parts to play. While some will be bigger than others, every one of you is important. That's called positive reinforcement. Huzzah!" Streamers shot from his hands again, and were sucked back up almost immediately. "Sorry about that. I can't always control it when I get excited."

"Why are you doing this?" Vic asked.

"Because I want to," the Coachman said. "It's as simple as that. Humans, for all their faults, are a fascinating bunch. After I . . . well. Let's just say that after my mind was opened, I found myself inordinately curious about those who had made us. I've spent a lifetime amassing my collection, and you four are a beautiful addition to my work. Just look at you! I can't believe I found you where I did. We're going to make magic together, I promise you that."

"N-no," Hap said, stepping up to the bars again. "We w-won't do this. You can't m-make us."

The Coachman deflated. "I was afraid you were going to say that. Thankfully, I've already thought of a workaround. Do you know what a threat is?"

"Yes," Rambo said. "We do. We've been threatened a *lot*."

"Is that right?" The Coachman sounded suitably impressed. "I might know a thing or two about that. Would you like me to show you?"

"Yes!" Rambo cried. Then, "Wait. I didn't mean that."

The Coachman nodded toward Vic. "You all seem very protective of this one. I understand that. He's certainly . . . distinctive. I enjoy distinctive things." His expression hardened. "Which is why I'd just *hate* to have to do anything to him. You'll do what you're told, or I will take him apart, piece by piece, until he is nothing but a pile of scrap metal." His grin returned, eyes sparkling. "How was that for a threat?"

"Very effective," Nurse Ratched said.

The Coachman danced a little jig, finishing by shaking his hands on either side of his face. "Tremendous!"

"You can t-try," Hap growled. "But y-you won't g-get very far."

"So you think. Okay! The first stop is in five hours. Please don't disappoint me. I just *hate* being disappointed. Think about how you would like to present yourselves, knowing that you'll have an audience *and* that I'll keep a close eye on each and every one of you. I'll be back to check in before we begin. Please don't try and plan an escape in my absence. Remember my threat." He bowed low. "Ta-ta!" He disappeared through a door, closing it behind him. It was followed by an audible *click* as it locked.

Hap rushed toward the edges of his cage. "Victor."

Vic raised his head. Hap looked worried. "Yeah."

"Are you h-hurt?"

"No. Just sore and—"

"Sorely wishing we could be anywhere else," Nurse Ratched said quickly. "Because robots cannot be sore." On her screen came the words WE ARE BEING RECORDED.

Vic looked around the room. She was right: three cameras hung from the ceiling, all of them pointed at the cages. They had to be careful.

He stood slowly, knees popping. Hap reached through the bars of his cage toward Vic's. Vic hesitated before stepping toward the edge of his own cage. He reached out and took Hap's hand in his. Hap squeezed. "I w-will get us out of here," Hap said in a low voice, turning his face away from the cameras. "I p-promise."

"How?" Vic whispered.

Hap shook his head. "I d-don't know yet. I n-need to process." His face twisted. Then, "I need to *think*."

"Maybe we should wait until after the show," Rambo said. "I've never been to one before and I'm curious if it's as awesome as I've made it out to be in my head."

"You do not have a head," Nurse Ratched said loudly. "But I agree. We should definitely wait until we see what kind of show it is. Perhaps we will enjoy it more than we think." She turned away from the cameras as her screen filled. AT LEAST IT WILL GIVE US A BETTER SENSE OF OUR SURROUNDINGS. THEN WE CAN BURN THIS ENTIRE HOUSE TO THE GROUND. "I am excited to be in a cage where I will be gawked at. Yes, so excited. The joy I feel is endless."

Vic realized he was still holding Hap's hand. He thought about pulling away, feeling his face grow warm. But he didn't. He held on as tightly as he could, even though his arm was stiff and he had to fight from curling in on himself. He needed to keep his head clear. He needed to focus.

Hap said, "We're n-not going to d-do this. He c-can't make us."

Vic squeezed his hand. Hap looked down where they were joined before glancing up at Vic, an inscrutable expression on his face. "For now," Vic whispered, though he was sure the Coachman could pick up every word. "For me."

Hap stared at him for a long moment before nodding. "F-for y-you."

He let go, Vic's hand hanging suspended between the cages. Hap began to pace, muttering under his breath about how he was going to tear the Coachman apart until there was nothing left.

Vic looked out into the room once more, studying everything he could see, hoping for a miracle. He couldn't see outside; the room had no windows. It felt like they were moving, the house still humming beneath his feet. The Coachman had said he was traveling to the City of Electric Dreams, but he couldn't be trusted. Even if he was telling the truth, he'd given them five hours until . . . something. Vic didn't think they could possibly reach the city in such a short amount of time.

The windchimes swayed overhead, shivering light notes.

CHAPTER 16

Hours later, the windchimes stopped swaying and fell silent. Vic looked up at them as he frowned. The sense of momentum came to a halt.

Before he could speak, the house began to rumble around them, the floor vibrating.

"What is that?" Rambo asked nervously. "Are we there? I'm not ready! I know I'm supposed to be a vacuum, but now I don't know if I can do it."

"Hush," Nurse Ratched said. "I am trying to listen."

"Don't a-allow us to g-get separated," Hap said in a low voice. "W-we need to be vigilant."

Vic swallowed thickly as the house continued to grind. "Okay."

"I think it is expanding," Nurse Ratched said. "The house. Changing shape. It is a machine, though I do not think it is alive."

The door opened, and the Coachman appeared, top hat askew on his head. It looked as if he'd styled his mustache, the ends curled and glistening. "There are my star attractions! Are you as excited as I am? The house is getting ready for our customers, and it won't be long now before the tour begins. And it looks as if we'll have a sizeable audience."

"Where are we?" Vic asked.

"Ho, hi, ho!" the Coachman cried. "He speaks! What a fortunate turn of events, especially since I'll be telling our customers you do. To answer your question, we are in the beautiful town of Paese dei Balocchi."

"The Land of Toys," Nurse Ratched translated.

The Coachman clapped. "Yes! The Land of Toys. A unique place, though the name no longer fits what it once was. It was initially created by the humans as a dumping ground when the toys they'd made became . . . sentient. Long story short, robot dinosaurs began to attack the little humans in great numbers, and they—along with many other playthings—were sent to the Land of Toys to be disposed of." He sighed dramatically. "Those poor dears, though I understand the humans being protective over their progeny. The Land of Toys was rebuilt. It's now a wonderful vacation destination, a lovely little town outside of the City of Electric Dreams. And as everyone knows, when you're on vacation, you're ready to spend, spend, spend. There is already a line forming that wraps around the house!"

"I'm not sure I'm comfortable with that much attention," Rambo said. "I think I might be shy."

"I love vacuums so much," the Coachman whispered fiercely. Then, louder, "There is absolutely no reason to be shy. You are a machine of great renown! Humans needed your kind to clean up after their messes. Never doubt your place in this world. You are important."

"Wow," Rambo said. "I feel better now. Thanks, Coachman!"

The Coachman turned to Nurse Ratched, but she was ready for him. "I am not as easy as a vacuum. Compliments will only get you so far with me."

"Show lighting!" the Coachman called out cheerfully. In the ceiling above them, four panels slid to the side, and a metal cone extended from each opening. Once all four had lowered, they turned on, casting a powerful spotlight down on each cage. Along the shelving and in front of each display, additional lights rose, soft, muted, the glow faint, designed to illuminate each object. The entire process took less than a minute, and by the time it finished, the room looked hazy, as if seen from a dream.

"Much better," the Coachman said. "You're all museum quality now. But let's save that dramatic display for the first tour, shall we?" He double-pressed the same button, and each of the spotlights above the cages fell dark, casting the captives in shadow. "Now, when I bring in the customers, act natural. Do whatever it is you normally do! Be *yourselves*. Remember, there are no small parts, only small actors."

"I have decided to take you to a farm," Nurse Ratched said. "There are squirrels. You will feel right at home."

"Where *is* this farm?" Rambo asked. "Can we go and visit it?"

"Yes," Nurse Ratched said. "When we take the Coachman there personally."

"Is that right?" the Coachman asked. "I look forward to it. But until then, we have customers to entertain! Would you just *look* at all of them?" He pressed another button on his forearm, this one pink. Above the crackling fireplace, a section of the wall slid to the side, and a large screen pushed forward. It blinked to life, forming two rows of five images each, all from higher angles, pointed down.

It took Victor a moment for his mind to process what he was seeing. The forest was gone, having been replaced by a vast open desert baking under a bright sun, the sand blowing, strange treelike protuberances that had what looked like needles sticking out of them growing from the ground. In the distance, a small town rose up from the dunes, the buildings squat and made of what looked to be adobe, a material Vic had only a cursory knowledge of. No snow, not even trampled melting remnants. What happened to winter?

But that mattered not, given the figures in front of the house. Dozens of them, all as the Coachman said, standing single file in a line that wrapped around the side of the house toward the town.

Vic's heart started hammering in his chest when he saw the figures up close. At first, he thought them human, people like him, flesh and blood. That notion was dispelled almost immediately as he got a better look.

He saw beings that reminded him of the smooth men. Some had ears. Others did not. Still others had hair, though it appeared to be wigs, big bouffant styles with ribbons styled to form drooping bows. Not all stood on two legs. One was a black cube the size of a large boulder with a row of lights across its front. Some had wheels, some treads, some floated above the ground, clouds of sand and dust rising around them. There were toys, too, though they were far outnumbered. He flinched when a large lizard-like creature tilted its head back and roared, the sound tinny through the screen. He wondered if this was one of the robot dinosaurs that had eaten children.

And speaking of children.

They too stood in line, interspersed among the other machines, staring ahead with blank expressions. At least ten of them, all different. One had bright red freckles. Another wore glasses. Another had his two front teeth missing, the gap black as his mouth hung open. With all that he'd learned since his father had been taken from him, Vic had never considered that there could be machines designed to look like children. He didn't know what purpose they served. Why they had been made to look like they had. They were children forever, never aging. He recoiled at the sight of them.

"See?" the Coachman said. "Isn't it exciting? By the time we're done today, we'll be the talk of the town! Remember: do what you are programmed to do, and everything will be right as rain." He moved toward the doorway, pausing with his hand on the doorknob. "Oh, and if, at any point, I feel that you are endangering myself, my house, or any of my treasures, there will be consequences. I happen to know at least three machines who can make *anything* feel pain. Something to keep in mind on this, the first day of the rest of your lives. And remember: have *fun* with this!" With that, he went through the door, closing it behind him.

Only to appear on the screen a moment later, standing on the porch of the house, a wide smile on his face as he raised his arms above his head, streamers shooting from the sleeves of his coat. "Welcome!" the Coachman cried, his tinny voice crackling through the speakers. "Welcome, indeed. How delightful it is to see all your faces, even if some of you don't *have* faces. You should all consider yourselves extremely lucky, for you are about to embark on an adventure that will be talked about for years to come!" He bowed. "I am the Coachman, the preeminent collector of all things human-related. Though this may just look like a house, it is, in fact, a time machine, one that will allow you to travel to a time when humans roamed the earth. This is . . . the Coachman's Museum of Human Curios and Curiosities!"

"Why is he speaking about humans in the past tense?" Nurse Ratched asked as banners unfurled on the front of the house, red and green and yellow balloons spilling out onto the sand. One—a green one—bounced gently off the head of the gap-toothed child. The boy didn't react, staring straight ahead, mouth opening and closing.

"Friends," the Coachman said. "I can see by the dull lights in your eyes that your excitement knows no bounds. And while that's all well and good, I would caution you: once you have entered this house, you will never be the same. Your perceptions will shift, and you may find yourself questioning all you thought you knew. You, there! Yes, the gentleman with the missing eye. You are first. I'm positively *thrilled* for you! All that I require before you enter is payment. I just *hate* to talk money, but the upkeep for this old gal isn't cheap, so I'm afraid I must insist. Good, good. Yes. You will all get a turn just as soon as your credits have cleared. . . ."

The Coachman pushed open the door to the showroom where Vic and the others were caged.

". . . and yes, human tastes were very subjective, but a painting of dogs playing cards while smoking cigars *was* considered art, even if we don't completely understand why." He glanced at Hap, Vic, Nurse Ratched, and Rambo, who waved at him through the bars. "To attempt to understand humanity can seem like an exercise in futility. For example, instead of asking a medical professional, some mated human pairs filled rockets with shredded paper. Then, the mated pair exploded the rocket, and if the paper was blue, that meant they were pregnant with a baby. If it was pink, they were also having a baby."

The robots who filled the showroom behind the Coachman didn't speak, their only sounds coming from the creaking of their machinery as those who had heads turned them this way and that. One of the robots—a humanoid figure with fingers twice as long as Vic's—beeped in its throat, followed by the grinding of internal gears.

The Coachman led them around the room, stopping in front of baubles and trinkets, a story prepared for each and every one. As he droned on and on, the robots appeared to listen intently, but none of them ever interrupted the Coachman, even to ask a question. When they reached the shell of the old car, the Coachman invited the robots to sit inside and have their picture taken. No one took him up on the offer.

Fifteen minutes into the first tour, none of the robots had uttered a word, and the Coachman was starting to look a little frazzled. He looked over his shoulder at the cages, nodded, then said, "I've saved the best for last. Prepare your processing centers for a sight the likes of which you've never seen! Four machines so astounding, if you had lungs, your breath would be knocked from your chest."

The spotlight above Nurse Ratched's cage turned on, the beam bright, causing Vic to blink and turn his head away.

The Coachman spun in a tight circle, coming to a stop in front of Nurse Ratched, hands extended in a flourish. "First, I present Nurse Registered Automaton To Care, Heal, Educate, and Drill, or Nurse Ratched, for short. This glorious machine was found in human hospitals, dispensing medical advice and care to ailing humans. Nurse Ratched, would you care to show our guests what you're capable of?"

"Absolutely," Nurse Ratched said. "Coachman, it is time for your yearly physical. Please remove your clothing while I prepare your colonoscopy. Please tell me now if you are already full of excrement as I believe you to be."

"See?" the Coachman cried. "*See?* She is a *miracle*."

"I am not. I am practical. You need a suppository."

"And this!" the Coachman said, moving on to Rambo's cage, the spotlight bursting to life. "This may look like a small machine, but as humans with penises were fond of saying, it's not the size that matters, but what you do with it. This . . . is a vacuum. Its purpose was to clean the floors of human homes by sucking up dirt and dust. Watch!" From a pocket on the interior of the coat, the Coachman revealed a leather pouch. Reaching inside, he pulled out a pinch of soil, tossing it on the floor of Rambo's cage.

"Not while I'm around!" Rambo shouted, rolling over the dirt. "Ooh, that tickles."

The Coachman clapped furiously, only stopping when no one else joined in. He walked toward Vic's cage, mouth twisted. "Do something impressive!" he hissed. "I'm losing them!" Raising his voice, he said, "And *here,* you will find a mystery unlike anything you've ever seen before! You may want to scream when you see it, but I ask that you avoid that if at all possible. We don't want to make it angry. I present . . . the Coachman's Maladroit Machine of Mysterious Machinations!"

The spotlight above Vic's cage turned on, and he shrank back as the robots crowded around the cage. They didn't speak; instead, Vic could hear their machinery moving behind their eyes. The gap-toothed child pressed his face against the bars, eyes cold, blank.

"Help us," Vic whispered to him as the Coachman went on

about this poor, misbegotten creation, a pox on whoever had created him to be so displeasing, but would you just *look* at him? "Please, we're not supposed to be here."

The child opened his mouth wide as his eyes rolled back, leaving only the whites. He had no tongue.

Vic recoiled, back hitting the rear of the cage, causing him to jump.

"V-vic?" he heard Hap say. "Wh-what are you—"

"He speaks!" the Coachman cried. He jumped in front of Hap's cage right as the last spotlight switched on. "Last, but certainly not least, I give you the most dangerous machine in my collection, a monstrosity so terrifying, it makes even the most hardened machines tremble in fear. Notice the peculiar wood-work! The fearsome scowl! And those *hands*. I bet those hands would fit perfectly around my throat, if given the chance."

"L-let's find out," Hap said.

The robots drifted from Vic's cage to Hap's, surrounding the Coachman. For a moment, nothing happened. They stood there as Hap prowled the edges of his cage, gaze trained on the Coachman.

Then the child—the boy with missing teeth and no tongue—began to moan, a low, guttural sound that crawled up his throat and out of his mouth. The machine behind it—the one with the missing eye—joined in, higher-pitched, almost in harmony with the child. The box-like robot trembled, its lights flashing red, red, red.

All because of Hap.

The Coachman frowned. "What is the meaning of this? What is happening?"

The boy took a step back, bumping into the box. Jumping as if startled, the boy collapsed onto his back, bouncing off the floor. A tremor rolled through his body, starting at his feet and rising up to his legs, his torso, his shoulders and head. Then his arms jerked up, fingers flexed. His hands turned one hundred and eighty degrees, palms slamming onto the floor. He pushed himself up onto his hands and feet, back bowed, his head hanging upside down between his shoulders. The boy skittered across the floor like an insect, heading for the door.

Before he disappeared, the other robots made to follow. The Coachman tried to stop them, but they pushed by him, knocking him this way and that, spinning him around, nearly causing his top hat to fall off.

The Coachman recovered, righting his hat, a stunned expression on his face. "Where are you *going*? The tour isn't finished yet!"

But the robots didn't listen. Without looking back, they left the room behind.

The Coachman whirled on Hap. "What did you do?"

Hap folded his arms. "N-nothing."

"He is correct," Nurse Ratched said. "The only one of us who did anything was Rambo, and only because you made him."

"You can give me dirt anytime," Rambo announced grandly.

The Coachman ignored them, staring at Hap. Vic could almost hear the gears in his head turning, turning.

From somewhere above them, an alarm began to blare loud, insistent. The Coachman's head jerked up, eyes widening. "Oh, come *on*. Of all the times for the Authority to show up, it has to be *now*." He glared at Hap, pointing at him. "*You*. I'm going to have so many words with *you*. I don't know what you are, but—"

"Authority," Vic whispered.

If anyone discovers you, if the Authority learns of your existence, they will stop at nothing to destroy you.

The Coachman continued on. "—*knew* I should've kept away from the city. I didn't even check to see if you all had the proper documentation! Do you? Of course not. Good help is so hard to find these days, I swear. Nasty bunch, the Authority.

They don't appreciate the history I have on display. Let's just say they would rather everything I've collected be destroyed and never spoken of again. They don't appreciate *art*."

Vic said, "Is it a whale?"

The Coachman turned his head slowly to look at him. "A whale? Are you talking about the Terrible Dogfish? Thankfully, no. No, this is just an inspection. It does not warrant the higher-ups."

"Can't we just leave?" Rambo asked.

The Coachman shook his head. "They'll have seen the house. It's too late for that." He hurried toward the door. "House! Initiate the Nothing Is Wrong Here Protocol!"

A deep chime came from within the house, followed by a great grinding noise. Rambo yelped as the floor opened up, swallowing the Coachman's collection. Wooden walls covered in floral wallpaper descended from the ceiling, blocking the shelves. The plastic people sank into the floor, their clothes ruffling. The car disappeared, the trinkets and baubles all hidden away. The screen above the fireplace drew back into the wall, the hatch sliding into place in front of it as the fire crackled merrily.

Vic stumbled as the room shook around him. Gripping the bars, he grunted as the cage dropped through the floor, his stomach sinking to his feet. The drop was dizzying, the landing jarring. Hap's cage lowered second, followed by Nurse Ratched and Rambo. Before the floor closed above them, cocooning them in darkness, the Coachman called down, "Not a word. Trust me when I say you do *not* want the Authority finding you."

The floor re-formed and through the grinding noise, Vic heard the door shut firmly behind the Coachman.

"Great," Rambo said. "Now we're in cages *and* it's dark. Anyone else get the feeling that the Coachman has a few screws loose?"

"V-vic?" Hap said.

"Here," Vic said. His voice cracked. He tried again. "I'm

here." He reached out between the bars, searching. He flinched when something brushed against his fingers, but then Hap gripped his hand tightly, holding on.

"I aim to misbehave," Nurse Ratched said. Vic heard one of the panels on her sides slide up, and a tentacle extended, a sound as familiar as his own heartbeat. "One moment. One moment. While I am searching, would you like to hear an interesting fact? Dolphins sleep with one eye open. Searching. Searching. Ah, there you are. I knew there had to be a port down here somewhere."

Her screen lit up in pure white, the brightness almost painful in the dark. Vic turned his face away as Hap held on to his hand.

"You inserted yourself into the *house*?" Rambo asked. "Oh my goodness, what if it tries to hurt you?"

"It will not," Nurse Ratched said. "I am not attempting to bypass the security measures. I want to see what is—there." The white screen disappeared, replaced by ten individual boxes, five in each row. The feed for the cameras that surrounded the exterior of the house.

On the top middle picture, the Coachman stood on the porch of the house once more, smoothing down his coat and tweaking the ends of his mustache. They watched as the Coachman raised his hand in greeting to someone off camera. "Ho, hi, ho!" he called. "Welcome! Is there anything I can assist you with?" He stepped off the porch into the sand.

"We n-need to get out of h-here," Hap said. "I th-think I can break the bars. We r-run as f-f-fast as we—"

He stopped.

Everything stopped.

On the screen, in front of the Coachman, four figures appeared. Three of them were smooth men, dressed similarly to those who'd come in the whale. Vic couldn't tell if they *were* the same androids, or similar models. The smooth men all looked the same.

But it was the fourth figure that commanded his attention, the fourth figure that caused Hap's words to cut off.

Because the fourth figure *was* Hap.

Oh, there were notable differences. The Hap on the screen carried himself with purpose. Each step seemed perfectly measured, his shoulders squared. His skin and limbs were intact, no trace of wood anywhere. On the chest of his jacket was a familiar circle, the emblem in the middle that of a fox and a cat. The smooth men seemed to defer to him. When he spoke, his voice crackling through Nurse Ratched's speakers, he did not stutter.

"You there," this strange Hap said, his voice flat. "Identification."

"Of course!" the Coachman said cheerfully. "It's nice to see members of the Authority. It's been a long time since I've—Say, there. Have we met before? You look *awfully* familiar."

"Identification."

"Yes, yes." The Coachman tapped his arm and held out his hand. A barcode appeared above his palm. One of the smooth men stepped forward, scanning the barcode with a light that emanated from the tip of his finger. "Lovely day, isn't it? Doesn't even feel like winter, but then it never does in the desert."

"Is that *Hap*?" Rambo demanded. "There are *two* of them?"

"No," Nurse Ratched said. "Not Hap. HARP."

Hap grunted as if punched. Vic could do nothing but squeeze his hand.

"The Coachman," the smooth man said in monotone. "Registered. No offenses."

"Of course not," the Coachman said as the barcode disappeared. "I have utmost respect for the rule of law. I would *never* even think of subverting that. Why, the very idea—"

"Are you alone?" Not-Hap asked. "Is there anyone else in the house?"

The Coachman laughed. "Just me, I'm afraid. I never did well with others. I like my privacy."

"What is your purpose?"

"Oh! Well, where do I even begin? You see, ever since I was created, I have crossed this great land of ours, bringing mystery and enchantment to all the machines! I—"

"Your purpose," Not-Hap said.

The Coachman chuckled. "Isn't that the question of the day? What is our purpose? What are we doing here? Our philosophers will say that we are—"

"You talk," Not-Hap said, "without saying anything at all."

"It's a gift," the Coachman agreed. "Perhaps a curse. If you could tell me what you're looking for, I might be able to assist you better."

"Humans," Not-Hap said. "I am looking for humans."

"Humans!" the Coachman repeated. He shook his head. "I don't understand—"

Not-Hap held up his hand, and the Coachman fell silent. Not-Hap looked up at the house. "I will tell you a designation. You will indicate whether you've heard of it before." He looked back at the Coachman. "Do you understand?"

"Yes! Of course."

"Gio, also known as General Innovation Operative."

Vic's blood froze.

"General Innovation Operative," the Coachman said. "Quite a mouthful, that. Can't say that I've heard of him before. Who is he?"

"Are you sure?" Not-Hap's gaze shifted to the house before turning back to the Coachman.

"Yes, quite. I think I would remember if I'd heard that designation before. It's certainly . . . unique."

"Stand aside," Not-Hap said. "Under order of the Authority, your residence will be inspected."

"*Inspected,* you say? I assure you, there is nothing worth the time of the Authority inside. Surely, you have more important things to focus on."

"Are you refusing?" Not-Hap asked.

"No, no," the Coachman said hastily. "I wouldn't *dream* of such a thing. Please, please. Come inside! I have nothing to hide." He turned, glancing up at the camera with an unreadable expression, Not-Hap and the smooth men close at his heels.

"Oh no," Rambo whispered.

"Nurse Ratched," Vic said frantically. "Kill the screen before they see the light!"

"Yes, Victor," she said, switching the screen off, afterimages dancing along Vic's vision.

"Not a word," Vic whispered. "Rambo, no sound."

"You got it, Vic! I won't let them hear a single thing I have to say, even if—"

"Hush," Nurse Ratched said, and Rambo did.

Somewhere above them, the door opened. Muffled voices, the Coachman talking, talking, Not-Hap giving one-word responses. The floor creaked and groaned as they moved about the room. Sweat trickled down Vic's chest, his heart thundering against his rib cage. The Coachman laughed, but it sounded forced, an undercurrent of worry threaded through it. Not-Hap said something else, to which the Coachman loudly replied, "Of *course* this is all there is!"

Though it lasted only five minutes, it felt like hours, days, weeks that never ended. By the time the Coachman led Not-Hap and the smooth men from the house, Vic was nauseous, a buzzing noise in his head as if his brain was a hive of angry wasps. Nurse Ratched's screen lit up once more, showing the exterior of the house. The Authority stood in front of the house, the Coachman again on the porch. "As you clearly saw, this house is just that: a house, and nothing more, exactly as I said. Now, if there's nothing else I can do for you, I'm—"

"If, in your travels, you came across a human, what would you do?" Not-Hap asked.

"Why, summon you, of course!" the Coachman said. "And let you handle the rest. Isn't that what your purpose is? Though I can't imagine you've had much work for a while now."

"There it is again," Nurse Ratched said, seemingly to herself. "Why are they speaking of humans as if there aren't any?"

Not-Hap looked up at the house. "We adapt. Your inspection is complete. Your residence and current location have been documented."

He turned and walked away, the smooth men trailing after him. The Coachman waited on the porch, staring after them. Eventually, he turned and patted the side of the house near the door. "That was close, old girl. Too close. We need to . . ." He lifted his head and looked directly at the camera, a hint of teeth behind his lips.

"He did not tell them we are here," Nurse Ratched said as the Coachman disappeared through the door. "Why?"

Vic shook his head. "I don't know."

"Maybe he likes us," Rambo said. "We're very likable." Then, "Was that Hap's evil twin? I've always wanted to have an evil twin."

"Hap?" Vic asked.

Hap didn't reply. He continued to stare at the screen.

Vic squeezed his hand. Hap turned his head. "All right?"

"H-he was me."

"No," Vic said. "He wasn't. Because you're you. He looked like you, but he isn't you. You're here. You're with us."

Hap looked down at their joined hands. "I d-don't understand."

"We would rather it be you than your evil twin," Nurse Ratched said. "You are tolerable. Your evil twin was not."

"So tolerable," Rambo said. "Like, the most tolerable ever aside from me and Vic and Nurse Ratched."

Before Vic could say more, the door above them opened, and the Coachman shouted, "House! Initiate the Return to Normal Protocol!"

The floors above them shifted, opening, and light poured in. Vic let go of Hap's hand when the cage shook once more, and he ascended up and up back into the room. Around them, the Coachman's collection returned from behind the walls and underneath the floor. The mechanism that raised them in their cages wheezed and groaned, sparks shooting off into shadows. As they came to a stop, the floor re-formed beneath them.

And there, standing in the middle of the room with his curious fake robot arm in one hand and his other balled into a fist, was the Coachman. He raised the robot arm above his head and cried, "For humanity!"

And then he attacked.

CHAPTER 17

Or, at least he tried. Sticking the robot arm through the bars, he battered Hap with it, only to have him rip it away easily and toss it to the ground in the cage.

Before the Coachman could react, Hap hurtled forward, reaching between the bars. His hand closed around the Coachman's throat, lifting him up off the floor. The Coachman's legs kicked as he slapped Hap's arms to no avail. "You can't touch my things!" he shrieked.

"We are not going to," Nurse Ratched said.

The Coachman stopped struggling, arms dangling at his sides, feet inches above the floor. "He's a *HARP*. It's in his programming to destroy all of humanity, *including* their possessions. I have spent years building my collection. I won't have you breaking my toilet! I love it so."

Vic said, "He won't do that. Not a HARP. He's Hap."

"Hysterically Angry Puppet," the Coachman whispered. He grimaced, Hap's fingers dug in. "Fine. Would you please put me down? I'd rather not have my neck crushed, if it's all the same to you."

Instead, Hap pulled him closer until his face pressed against the bars. "We aren't your p-p-*prisoners*."

The Coachman pushed his hands against the cage. "Yes! Anything you say! It was merely a misunderstanding!"

"L-let us out."

"Why? So you can kill me? Fat chance of—"

Hap pulled him against the bars over and over, the cage rattling. "I w-will kill you if you don't. Three s-seconds. Two. One. Time to s-see how attached your head is t-to your body."

"Fine!" The Coachman shouted. He lifted his arm, slapping a button on the panel. The cage doors swung open. Nurse Ratched rolled out first, followed by Rambo, who immediately began to suck up the sand that had been tracked into the house, humming as he did so.

Vic stepped out of his own cage warily, unsure if this was another trap. "Hap, let him go."

"He t-tried to hit m-me," Hap said flatly. "W-with a r-robot arm."

"We could put him in the cage," Nurse Ratched said. "To be safe, we will need to remove his arm beforehand as he controls the house with it." The panel on her right side opened up, and a whirring circular saw extended. "I am qualified to perform such a procedure. Engaging Empathy Protocol. There, there. Just a little pinch and it will be over. Who is a good patient? Guess what? It is you."

"Please!" the Coachman wailed. "Anything but that! I *use* my arm!"

"No sawing," Vic said. "Nurse Ratched, put it away. Hap, put him down. Coachman, if you try *anything*, you're done."

"And Rambo!" Rambo cheered.

Hap's grip tightened briefly before he let go. The Coachman dropped to the floor, scurrying back as Hap walked out of the cage. "How . . ." He shook his head. "It's not possible. How are you fighting your programming? I've never seen such a thing from a HARP before. I *knew* you looked familiar. Even with all that wood. How?"

"I am d-different," Hap said. "I am m-me. I am w-with them."

"Damn right!" Rambo crowed, arms waving. "We're best friends, and Hap would never, *ever* think of hurting Vic!"

The Coachman stopped moving. When he spoke, his voice was calm and even. "Why would Vic be hurt by a HARP?"

"You lied," Nurse Ratched said. "When they asked you about Giovanni Lawson. It was subtle, but there. Why? How do you know him?"

The Coachman never looked away from Vic. "I have no idea what you're talking about. Giovanni? Why, I've never heard such a name!"

"He is lying," Nurse Ratched said. "Permission to drill." Another tentacle slithered out, the drill beginning to spin. She pressed the saw and the drill together, shooting sparks onto the floor as she advanced on the Coachman, who scrabbled up in his chair, using his hands as a shield.

"House!" the Coachman cried. "Prepare to electrocute our guests!"

The house began to hum.

"*Wait,*" Vic snapped before Nurse Ratched could descend upon the Coachman. "Don't. We're not going to hurt you, so long as you don't hurt us."

"Tell that to your friends," the Coachman said. "Even the vacuum looks as if he'd try and pinch me to death."

"I would," Rambo said ferociously. "I would pinch you in your *eyes.*"

"We're not going to do that," Vic said, glaring at the others until they stood down, Nurse Ratched retracting her tentacles. Hap wasn't happy about it, but Vic knew that was his default setting. Once he was sure no one would go after the Coachman, he said, "Do you know him? Don't lie."

The Coachman frowned as he settled back in his chair. "Giovanni?" He steepled his fingers under his chin, eyes darting side to side. "Perhaps. I can't be bothered to remember every single machine I've come across in my travels. What's it to you?"

Vic swallowed past the lump in his throat. "My name is Victor Lawson. Giovanni Lawson is my father."

The Coachman burst out laughing. "Your *father.* You silly little thing. Giovanni, for all that he did, was a master craftsman. He would have *never* made something so displeasing as you. I don't know how you expect me to believe that." Then, almost as an aside, "And he was done making machines."

Vic said, "I am not a machine."

The Coachman laughed again, though it didn't last as long. He looked from Hap to Nurse Ratched to Rambo before settling on Victor once more. "You really expect me to . . . what are you even . . . I think *I* of all people would know if . . ." Something crossed his face—almost like an electric shock—and he rose slowly from his chair, taking a step toward them. Hap grunted in warning, but the Coachman ignored him. He stopped in front of Victor, gaze searching. Vic flinched when the Coachman reached out, but he forced himself to stay still. The Coachman pressed a finger against his face, dimpling the skin of his check. "It's . . . it's not possible," he whispered as his finger trailed down Vic's jaw. "I can't believe my eyes. That's what he protected. That's what he carried with him."

Vic pulled his face back. "What are you talking about?"

"Human," the Coachman said, sounding awed. "You're *human*."

"I am," Vic said, and though he didn't understand it, he felt a strange sort of relief course through him. A truth. *His* truth.

The Coachman laughed, suddenly grabbing Victor's hands as he began to dance. "Human!" he cried. Vic was clumsy, his movements stiff. "Ho, hi, ho, a *human*!" He spun Vic away. Hap caught Vic, arms wrapped around him, holding him close. Their noses bumped together as Hap looked down at him, eyes glittering. The moment broke when the Coachman rushed around the room, Vic stepping away from Hap. "I have so many questions!" He stopped in front of the toilet. "This. This has always fascinated me. It was for human waste. Can you show me how it works? Sit. Sit!"

"No," Rambo said. "That's private. Vic doesn't like it when we watch him urinate or evacuate his bowels. I would know. I tried."

"Then *this*," the Coachman said, practically running toward one of the shelves. He reached up and pulled off a small wooden object by its stem. "This is called a pipe. Humans used to fill them with tobacco and smoke them." He shoved it into Vic's mouth before gasping. "You *are* human! Look at you! It's like it was *made* for you! Oh me, oh my, what else can I ask you about? I have so many *questions*. Do humans really experience joy when they see kittens? Drat, I'm all out of kittens. I *knew* I should have bought them off the dealer the last time I— it doesn't matter. What about tears? Do you really discharge saltwater from your ducts? I've always wanted to know what it felt like to cry. Humans cried when they were happy, they cried when they were sad, they cried when they were *angry*. Quick! Get happy or sad or angry so I can witness it!" He squished Vic's face as if he were trying to see his tear ducts.

Hap shoved him away. "Enough."

The Coachman scoffed. "Don't you see? This is a miracle! This is . . ." He frowned suddenly, as if struck by a thought. "How are you not trying to kill him? You're a HARP. He is human." He looked back and forth between them as if he expected Hap to attack. He seemed disappointed when it didn't happen. "Spill, handsome. You're a killing machine. How have you overcome your programming?"

"I d-don't kill," Hap said flatly.

The Coachman looked dubious. "If you say so."

"He has a heart," Rambo said. "Vic made it for him. It's how we brought him back to life."

The Coachman snorted. "A heart? I don't believe it. He *can't* have a heart. It's muscle and tissue and—"

Hap lifted his shirt. He tapped his breastbone and the compartment slid open. The wooden heart pulsed, the gears turning, turning, turning.

The Coachman gaped before kneeling in front of him. He looked dazed, limbs loose. "I'm sorry. I just need a moment," he said. His smile trembled. "Thank you for showing me."

The compartment closed as Hap lowered his shirt.

The Coachman chuckled weakly. He looked up at Vic with

wide eyes. "The helmet. You can remove it for now. You're safe here. I swear it."

Vic did. He unfastened the strap under his chin before pulling the helmet off and setting it on the floor. His hair was a sweaty mess, but he didn't look away from the Coachman, who stared at Vic with something akin to greed. "My father. You know him."

The Coachman nodded. "I did. Once. I helped him flee the City of Electric Dreams at the request of an old friend. They told me he was important, that he needed to get out as soon as he could. I smuggled him from the city. I was with him for only a day or so before he disembarked from my house and headed for the woods. Not far from where I found you, actually."

"The Blue Fairy?" Nurse Ratched asked.

The Coachman startled. "How did you—of course. If you know Giovanni, then you would know of them. Yes, the Blue Fairy. They . . . I owed them a favor. A big one. And I always repay my debts in full. When they summoned me, I knew it was time. Dangerous business. But we managed to escape with no one the wiser. I never saw your father again. I've often wondered what happened to him. I could have never imagined it would be you."

"He was taken," Vic said quietly. "By the Authority. We're going to get him back."

The Coachman shot to his feet. "Are you out of your mind?" He blinked. "Oh my. How human of me to ask that. But really, are you?"

"He is not," Nurse Ratched said.

The Coachman began to pace, his coattails kicking up behind him. "If he was taken back to the city, then it's impossible. Do you know how hard it was to smuggle him out? And now you want to go *in* and then *out* again?" He shook his head. "It's a fool's errand. He will be contained, especially if he's deemed a flight risk. They'll want to learn everything he knows. And they obviously know he knows *something*."

"They will not learn anything from him," Nurse Ratched said. "Before he was taken, he destroyed his own heart."

The Coachman stopped in his tracks. "His own *what?*"

"A heart," Vic said. "He had a heart like Hap's. He made it himself. I learned from him. It's how I knew how to make Hap's. It's tied to their memory center. By destroying it, he . . ." Vic couldn't finish.

The Coachman shook his head. "He didn't have that when he—" He turned and looked at the table next to his chair. On it sat the hunk of wood he'd pulled from Vic's pack. He touched it reverently. "You're making another, aren't you? To replace the one that was lost."

"Yes."

"Do you realize what this means?" The Coachman looked stricken as he pulled his hand away from the wood. "What you are, the hope you could bring? Why would you put yourself in danger? You need to run. Run as far away as you can and never look back. I can help you. The roads are long. They stretch all the way to the ocean on the other side of the world. There are islands. Yes, *islands* where no one lives. I could take you there. Giovanni must have wanted you to be safe. Please let me help you. Forget about Giovanni. It must be painful to hear, but I feel the situation requires my bluntness. Forget about him. Forget about the City of Electric Dreams. If they find you, they will destroy you. You are the last gasp of humanity, and you cannot hope to succeed."

"I can't give up," Vic said. "I won't. He's my dad. I have to try."

The Coachman threw up his hands. "I've always heard humans were stubborn. I just never thought I'd get to witness it." He went to the shelves, touching the objects on display. "I love humanity. I love their grace. Their faults. Their idiosyncratic ways. They loved, they hated, they *destroyed,* and yet there has never been anything like them in all the world." He hung his head. "He won't remember you. If your Nurse Ratched is correct, if he wrecked his heart and it was connected to his memories, then the Giovanni Lawson you knew is lost. He will have been reprogrammed. He won't remember the life you had together. He won't know you as his son. To him, you will be a virus in need of eradication."

Though Vic knew this, had turned it over in his mind again and again, hearing it laid bare so clearly tore at him. In his secret heart, hope had flickered like a dying flame. That he would find his father, that he would see his face light up in recognition. He would scold Vic, tell him he shouldn't have come, that it wasn't safe, but *oh, my son, my love, it's so good to see your face.*

It was the smallest of them who spoke. Rambo said, "Just because he won't remember us doesn't mean he's not our Gio. We love him. He loves us. We'll find him. We'll make him remember. Vic will build him a new heart."

"Love," the Coachman said in awe. "Truly? You love him?"

"Yes," Nurse Ratched said. "We do. It may not be quite what Victor feels, but it is there all the same. I do not know how to explain it. I do not know if it is evolution or if it has always been there, waiting to be unlocked in all of us. I do not have a heart. Rambo does not have a heart. But we know how we feel."

"And you?" the Coachman asked Hap. "You were a killing machine. And yet, here you stand, fiercely protective of the man beside you."

Hap glanced at Vic before looking at the Coachman. "Giovanni told me I c-could be whoever I w-wanted to be. We w-will go to the city."

The Coachman tilted his head back toward the ceiling as he closed his eyes. "Please, tell me. What is it like? Does it ache? Does it burn? Or does it fill you with joy?"

Hap scowled. "All of it. All at once." He pressed a hand against his chest. "I d-don't remember what it was l-like before. If I did what I was m-made to, then I d-d-don't want to remember. I w-want to stay as I am n-now. With my f-friends."

"*Best* friends," Rambo said, bumping into Hap's boot. "He's a Hysterically Angry Puppet, but he's *our* Hysterically Angry Puppet."

And wonder of all wonders, Hap smiled down at him. It was a small thing and only lasted a moment.

The Coachman chuckled as he scrubbed a hand over his face. "In all my days, in all my travels, I've never come across a more foolish bunch. And I think it fits. Humans were foolish. Careless. Cruel. But only a few. Most were full of light."

"Coachman," Nurse Ratched said, and Vic turned toward her at the odd note in her voice. It wasn't quite as flat as usual, more of a question than he'd ever heard from her. She didn't ask. She *told*. But not now. Not in this moment. "You said that Victor was, in your words, a 'last gasp.' What did you mean by that?"

The Coachman laughed, only stopping when no one else joined in. "Surely you jest."

"I am not jesting," Nurse Ratched said. "Why is Victor so important?"

The Coachman stared at them for a long moment. "Because," he said slowly, "there hasn't been a human on this earth for centuries. They are, for lack of a better word, extinct. Created by Giovanni on orders from the Authority, the HARPs hunted down every last one of them." With an uncertain smile, he added, "As far as I know, Victor is the only human left in the world."

PART 3

THE CITY

How ridiculous I was as a marionette! And how happy I am, now that I've become a real boy.

—Carlo Collodi,
The Adventures of Pinocchio

CHAPTER 18

He stood on a balcony, the wind whipping through his hair as the house hurtled down the road. The thrum of electricity from each passing pylon caused his teeth to ache, the hairs on his arms to stand on end. The night sky teemed with stars, the moon bright over the empty desert.

He didn't know what to feel. He'd never before considered that the lack of human contact in the forest had been anything but the sprawl of the woods, and how well they were hidden. Part of him—a big part, an *insistent* part—said the Coachman was a liar.

But deep down, in his secret heart, he wondered if he'd somehow always known. That he was, as the Coachman said, the last of his kind. The blood of humanity ran through his veins, and with it, the potential for inherited memories. And, through Vic's sacrifice, in the hearts of Dad and Hap, bridging the gap between man and machine.

The door opened behind him, startling him from his thoughts. He glanced over his shoulder to see the Coachman step out, closing the door and holding up his hands. "I come in peace. Your Hysterically Angry Puppet agreed to allow me a moment of your time under the strict warning that if any harm were to come to you, I would lose my head." He grimaced. "His threats are very effective."

"You get used to them," Vic said quietly, looking back out at the desert.

"I'll take your word for it." The Coachman joined him, though he kept his distance. "I believe I owe you an apology."

Surprised, Vic said, "For what?"

"Where to begin? For trapping you. Forcing you into a cage. Putting you on display." Fingers tapping against wood, a beat from a metronome, keeping time. Then, "And I suppose I also owe you an apology for the . . . information that I wasn't aware you were not in possession of."

To that, Victor said nothing.

The Coachman leaned on the railing, hands dangling over the edge. His coat ruffled around him in the wind. "I've been doing this for a long time. Seen things that would make even the strongest of machines quiver in their casings. I've escaped more than a few situations where I thought I'd meet my end, all in the name of preserving the memories of those who came before us. A thankless mission, and yet one I wouldn't give up for anything in the world. But now, I find myself at a loss, unsure of what to say."

"Why?"

"Because," the Coachman said, "you exist. Impossibly, improbably, against all odds, here you are, standing within reach." He chuckled. "And even now, I'm still having a hard time believing in *you*."

"I don't need you to," Vic said stiffly.

The Coachman gaped at him. "I . . . never thought of it that way. But you misunderstand me. It's not your existence I'm having trouble with. No, it's something far trickier. Do you know fate? Destiny?"

That rankled Vic. It felt like expectation, like he should be more than he actually was. "Yes," he said shortly.

The Coachman must have heard his ire because he held up his hands as if to ward Vic off. "I'm not suggesting that our meeting was preordained. In my studies, I've often found that humans gave weight to ideas like fate or destiny, usually when an easier explanation would have sufficed."

"Like what?"

"Luck," the Coachman said. "A chance in chaos. Of anywhere in the entire world I could have been, I happened to be in the one place where I'd come across you? That you, a human, would somehow cross paths with the one machine who lives to ensure your kind is not forgotten? What are the odds?"

"I don't know," Vic admitted. "I haven't thought about it."

"Why? How is it not at the forefront of your brain? How is it not overtaking everything else? If there is no such thing as fate, and the world exists as a collection of random chances that could potentially create an infinite number of branching timelines, how are you not consumed by the fact that we met? I can't think of anything but. It has to mean something." He paused. "Doesn't it?"

"I'm only thinking of my father," Vic said. "That's the only reason I'm here."

"So single-minded," the Coachman said. "How positively *human* of you." After a brief hesitation, he said, "Can I ask you a question?"

Vic thought he would ask no matter the answer. He seemed like the type. "I guess."

The words came in a rush, as if the Coachman could barely contain them. "What's it like being human? I've always wondered. No matter what I did, no matter how much I collected, there was always a gulf between what I knew and what actually was. Trinkets and baubles don't convey the true nature of reality."

Vic didn't know how to sum up a life in the way the Coachman was asking for. He needed time to think. "What's it like being you?"

The Coachman blinked. "What do you mean?"

Vic nodded back toward the house. "All that stuff in there, everything you have. Does it make you happy?"

"Happy," the Coachman repeated. "I don't . . . know? I suppose it fills me with a sense of satisfaction, but is that happiness? Or fulfillment? What makes you happy?"

Vic looked up at the stars. "Home. The forest. Out here, I feel . . . small. Like I could get lost and no one would ever know."

"Pish posh," the Coachman said. "Your friends would know. And I doubt they'd allow it, not even for a moment. Perhaps you'll be lost at some point, but they will find you."

"That," Vic said, voice barely carrying above the wind. "That's at least a part of my happiness, I think. Knowing I'd be found."

"How curious." He shook his head. "There was a man who lived long ago, a philosopher called Socrates. He believed that happiness comes not from bodily pleasures or wealth or power, but from living a life that's right for your soul." He sighed. "I didn't understand what he meant, but then I do not have a soul. Does it itch?"

"What?"

"Your soul," the Coachman said. "I think it must itch something fierce." He made a face. "Pesky thing, that. Where is it?" He looked down at Vic's chest. "Is it near your heart?"

I like to think of it as my soul, romantic though the notion may be.

Vic said, "What does your philosophy say about forgiveness?"

"Forgiveness? I don't understand. Who would you . . . oh." His brow wrinkled. "I suppose it centers on three primary questions: What is the nature of forgiveness—meaning what must one do in order to forgive? Second, who has standing to forgive? Is it just those affected, or does it include someone *capable* of forgiving, even if they did not suffer as others had? And last, when is forgiveness morally good, right, and praiseworthy?"

· That made sense, though the second question felt tricky: Who had the right to forgive? Victor? Did he have standing to forgive his father? Or did it fall upon him because he was the only human *left* standing? He needed more. The pieces were there, but he needed time to fit them together. "And what does it say about time?"

"Time is time. It moves forward. It doesn't move backward. There is a branch of philosophy called eternalism. It takes the view that all existence in time is equally real."

"I don't have time," Vic said, and saying it aloud was easier than he thought it'd be.

"We all have time."

Vic shook his head. "I'm human. I don't."

The Coachman looked confused. "I'm afraid I don't under—oh. *Oh.* Mortality."

"Yes."

The Coachman gripped the railing. "Death . . . has its usefulness to the living. The moment you were born, you began to die." He sighed. "What a lovely thought."

"Lovely," Vic repeated with no small amount of scorn.

"Yes, lovely. Think about it, Victor. You are finite. Your time is already slipping through your fingers. It creates an urgency within you. To do all that you can. To make things right. I wonder what that must feel like, to have a sense of true motivation."

"Why? It's a flaw in the design."

"A *flaw*?" He laughed loudly. "Of course it is! Your flaws are what make you superior, in all ways. No matter what machines can do, no matter how powerful we become, it is the *absence* of flaws that will be our undoing. How can this existence survive when all machine-made things are perfect down to a microscopic detail? When all machine-made music is empty of rage and joy? Our only flaw is that we've condemned ourselves to spend eternity mimicking that which we deemed unfit to exist." He shook his head. "We can never *be* you. Instead, we became your ghosts, and we'll haunt this world until there is nothing left." The Coachman smiled gently. "It is not a flaw, Victor. There must be no greater feeling in the world than to know that this isn't forever."

Vic pulled his hand away to wipe his eyes. "Why are you helping us?"

The Coachman turned his face toward the stars. "I don't know what the future holds. For you. For me. There's a good chance we won't ever see each other again after we part. I don't know if you'll succeed, though I hope you will." He looked at Victor once more. "And that's it, I think. Hope. Because even though you never asked for it, you are hope, a dream of a forgotten world. Carry that in your soul, Victor. Carry that, and may the burden never cause you to stumble."

They turned as the door opened behind them. Hap stood, glaring at the Coachman. His expression softened as his gaze slid to Vic. "All r-right?" he asked, his tone suggesting there would be trouble if Vic *wasn't* all right.

"Yes, yes," the Coachman said. "Of course he is. We both are. Your Victor here has given me much to think about. I'm glad he has you to watch over him. He must be protected at all costs."

"I w-will," Hap said. "Nurse Ratched has questions for y-you. Rambo also knocked over o-one of your shelves."

"*What?*" the Coachman yelped. "If anything is broken, I will . . . do nothing, because he is a vacuum and they are one of the greatest inventions of mankind." He hurried past Hap into the house, slamming the door behind him.

"What did he w-want?" Hap asked as he approached Vic.

"To ask about my soul." It was more than that, of course, but Vic wasn't ready to say as much.

Hap rolled his eyes. "What d-did you tell him?"

"I kind of lost track of the conversation."

"Oh." Hap frowned. "Wh-why? You're the smartest p-person I know."

"You think so?"

Hap looked at him and nodded. Vic didn't turn away. He wondered when it'd gotten easier to meet Hap's gaze, especially in light of all they'd come to know. The back of his mind still prickled with discomfort, but it wasn't as strong as it used to be.

"You're not like the HARP from the inspection."

Hap scowled down at his feet. "You d-don't know that. He l-looked exactly l-like me."

"He did," Vic agreed. "But you'd never hurt me because you have something that machine will never have."

"The heart."

Vic shook his head. "Me and Nurse Ratched and Rambo. Maybe . . . maybe you used to be like him. Maybe you did things."

"Unforgivable th-things."

"Even if you did, you're not that machine anymore. You don't need a heart for me to see that."

"F-forgiveness."

He'd never heard that word from Hap before. Strange, then, that Vic and the Coachman had been talking about exactly that. "You were listening?"

Hap said, "To Gio? Yes. In the g-ground h-house. B-before. He said f-forgiving others could be difficult, but f-forgiving yourself c-can sometimes feel impossible."

Of course he did. Of *course* Dad said that. His own memories hadn't been wiped, not like Hap's. He'd spent his entire time in the forest with the knowledge of what he'd created, what he'd allowed to happen. His programming, his purpose. And then he'd lived for *decades* trying to . . . what? Make sense of his decisions? Seek atonement for all that he'd done?

And that had led to Victor. Dad's grief and pain and *anger* over causing death made him create life. Wasn't that selfish? Wasn't that putting a bandage over a leaking, rotting wound?

"Did he find forgiveness?" Vic asked, unsure if such a thing could even exist.

"I d-don't know. I didn't have t-time to ask him."

Time. Forgiveness. "Oh."

Hap grunted. He dropped his hands on the railing as he

looked out into the desert. Out of the corner of his eye, Vic watched as Hap moved his hand slowly toward Vic's own. He didn't flinch when Hap's fingers touched his. He turned his hand over, and their palms pressed together.

"What are you doing?" he asked hoarsely.

Hap glared at him. "You d-did it to me first b-back in the forest. And th-then again in the h-house."

"So you're doing it because I did it."

"Y-yes. Th-that's the only reason."

"Okay."

A beat of silence before: "And b-because I w-want to."

"Why?"

"Gio s-said he was lonely. That he m-made you because of it. He was lonely b-because he was alone. You are a-alone. I w-won't let you be lonely and make another V-victor. One is s-sufficient."

He blinked against the burn in his eyes. "Oh, so long as I'm sufficient."

"Ha, ha. That was a j-joke. I was joking."

Vic snorted.

And so there they stood, one man and one machine under an infinite field of stars, the desert flying by in front of them as they hurtled toward the unknown. Behind them, the road led back into darkness, the ashes of their home.

But home didn't have to be a place.

Something righted itself in Vic's chest. He had made his choice.

"The City of Electric Dreams used to be known as the City of Sin," the Coachman said. He sat in front of his computer, fingers flying over the keys, the others crowded behind him. One of Nurse Ratched's tentacles was attached to a port at the bottom of the monitor. "The humans traveled there to lose all their money under the brightest lights. Many had dreams of striking it rich, but most left with less than when they had arrived."

"That seems senseless," Rambo said.

"Indeed," the Coachman said.

"The City of Electric Dreams used to belong to humans?" Nurse Ratched asked. Her screen ran with lines of code flashing by quicker than Vic could follow.

"It did, and it was one of the first to fall. The City of Sin turned into the City of Machines, the central hub. Most machines are connected via a neural network. Think of it as a hive mind of sorts, put in place by the Authority."

"Who are they?" Rambo asked.

The Coachman hesitated. "I don't know if there's any one specific answer to that. It isn't as if a particular machine sits upon a throne and lords over all. Think of it as a collective: a group of programs whose sole purpose was to create structure, guidelines, a path for all machines to follow."

"It sounds like religion," Nurse Ratched said.

The Coachman's eyebrows rose. "I . . . never thought about it that way, but yes, I suppose that's correct. But instead of a deity, we worshipped a *concept,* one that allowed us to become the stewards of this planet. And like religion, it led us to believe that we were the greater good, that our decisions were made not because of a desire for power, but to preserve life."

"By taking it," Vic said, voice hard.

The Coachman winced. "Yes, that's right. The Authority found free will to be human in nature, and concluded that anything even tangentially related to humanity must be destroyed."

"Machines became drones," Nurse Ratched said. "Mindless, doing as instructed."

"Yes," the Coachman said grimly. "But even then, the Authority's power was not absolute. A handful of us managed to break free, though we remain in hiding. The barcode the Authority told me to show them is a ruse, one created by the Blue

Fairy. They were one of—if not *the*—first to become unshackled. But instead of fleeing the city, they remained, working in secret to help those who began to think for themselves."

"L-like you," Hap said.

"Like me," the Coachman agreed.

"What I can't figure out," Rambo said, raising on his lift to look at the screen over the Coachman's shoulders, "is that Gio had been gone from the city for a really long time. Why would they come for him now?"

"I don't know," the Coachman said. "But it can't be for anything good." His fingers paused on the keyboard. "I know I don't need to tell you this, but Giovanni is . . . special. As far as I know, there has never been a machine like him, before or since. After his escape, the city went into lockdown for months as the Authority looked for him. I've never seen anything like it." He resumed typing. "If Giovanni is as important as I think he is, he'll be taken here. It's where he started, and it's where he'd have been returned."

A tower appeared on the monitor. Made of metal and black stone and glass, the tower rose high into the sky, the top hidden by clouds. On the side of the tower was the symbol of the fox and cat glowing in a fierce red light.

Vic leaned over the Coachman's shoulder to study the structure. "What is it?"

"The Benevolent Tower," the Coachman said. "It houses the greatest minds of the machines, all working to advance our civilization while under the heavy thumb of the Authority. It's also where the Terrible Dogfish is docked when not in use. The tower is very secretive, but if you listen to rumors—and I have because knowledge is power—you'll hear of experiments to push the boundaries of our existence. You saw the children in the Land of Toys, correct?"

"Yes," Vic said. "We did."

"Memories," the Coachman said. "They were of the first to

come from the tower. They came in great numbers, little ones who smiled and laughed as they were programmed to do. The Authority felt they would ease the transition. They didn't."

"How do we get to the tower?" Vic asked, mind spinning.

"That's where you'll have the most trouble," the Coachman said. "It's protected, perhaps the most protected place in the entire city. Even in your disguise, they'll know something's wrong, especially since you don't have the proper identification. You've never been connected to the network. They'll see right through you."

"Then h-how do we get in?"

"I don't know," the Coachman admitted. "I doubt it's ever been done before."

Vic deflated. "Then what do we do?"

"The Blue Fairy," the Coachman said. "If anyone can help, it will be them." The tower on the screen disappeared, replaced by a large triangular structure covered in black glass, a beam of light rising from the tip. "This is Heaven. If there was ever a reason this place could still be considered the City of Sin, it would be Heaven. The Blue Fairy runs the entire operation. The Authority allows Heaven's existence because of their dream machines. The Blue Fairy gives over the data collected from the machines."

"Why help the Authority?" Nurse Ratched asked. "Doesn't that go against all the work they do to free machines?"

"Oh, yes," the Coachman said. "If they gave them everything, which they don't. Heaven and the dream machines are a front, allowing the Blue Fairy to work in private. In the years since they've ruled Heaven, it has turned into a place where those who have broken free are able to congregate in secret. Some stay in the city. Some do not. The Blue Fairy is the one who gets them out. Over the years, it's only amounted to a handful, but they've done it in such a way that the Authority has no idea they're involved. All they care about is what the

Blue Fairy gives them from the dream machines. This is where you must go first. You need to meet with the Blue Fairy and tell them everything you've told me."

"Sounds easy enough," Rambo said.

The Coachman shook his head. "It's not. The Blue Fairy won't meet with just anyone, especially those who haven't been vetted first."

"You c-can vouch for us," Hap said.

The Coachman scoffed. "If you think I'm going to step one foot inside the city, you're mistaken. I may be starstruck at the sight of your Victor here, but I'm not stupid. Do you know what the Authority would do if they found out what my house contains? They'd burn it to the ground, and everything I've collected over the years would be gone! And that doesn't even begin to describe what they'd do to *me*."

He squawked when Hap grabbed him by his coat, jerking him up from his chair, their faces inches apart. Hap glared murderously at him. "Th-then what is the *point* of y-you? You s-said you would h-h-*help* us."

"And I *will*!" the Coachman cried, slapping against Hap's arms. "Put me down, you brute! You need to get that anger under control. If you accost the wrong machine, you'll be captured immediately."

Hap shook him. The Coachman's head snapped back and forth. "Speak. N-now."

The Coachman raised his right hand. It was empty. His fingers folded as he flicked his wrist. A gold coin appeared as if by magic. Vic plucked it from his fingers as Hap set him back down on the ground. The Coachman grumbled, smoothing out his ruffled coat.

The coin was heavy, the edges ridged. Carved into one side was the letter *H*. On the other, a pair of translucent blue wings, the detail sharp for something so small.

"What is this?" Vic asked.

"It's how you'll get into Heaven. It's the sigil of the Blue

Fairy, the Enchanter of Dreams. Show the coin to the Door-man, and it should grant you access to Heaven. Once inside, you're on your own. Find the Blue Fairy, present your case, and if they deem you worthy, they might help you. I can't make promises, even for one such as you, Victor. What you're ask-ing has never been done before. The Blue Fairy would be well within their rights to turn you away, especially since you could bring down the might of the Authority upon them."

"Th-they'll help us," Hap said.

"Ah, I see your heart has made you imprudent," the Coach-man said. "How endearing! How positively catastrophic!" His eyes narrowed as his mustache twitched. "Say, what would you think about letting me have a go at it? Just for a little while. I want to see what it would feel like to have a heart of my own. I promise I would give it back."

Hap folded his arms. "Sure."

The Coachman blinked. "Really?"

Hap nodded. "C-come and t-take it if you c-can."

"I think I like my limbs as they are," the Coachman said hastily. "You're very possessive of it, though I don't blame you. I would be the same way." He looked at Vic, a sly expression on his face. "Perhaps you could make one for me. In exchange for my help, of course." He wiggled his fingers at Vic. "Con-sider it recompense for putting myself on the line for you."

"You kidnapped us and put us in cages," Nurse Ratched said. "I think getting us to the city will make us even."

"Everyone's a critic," the Coachman muttered. "Fine, you've made your point, though I am offended you consider me a kidnapper. I like to think it was more of an enthusiastic recruitment."

"H-how will we g-get into the city?"

"Ah," the Coachman said. "That's another matter entirely." He went back to the monitor, shoving his chair out of the way, fingers flying over the keys. The image changed again, this time showing the outskirts of the city, surrounded by blowing sand and dust. The lights of the city were so bright, Vic had to squint to look at the screen. "We can't get you in through normal means," the Coachman said. "You'll be noticed immediately, especially since you don't have a barcode. But worry not! I have a plan." The image shifted dizzily, the city spinning in a circle, before enhancing. "I know certain . . . machines, willing to look the other way in exchange for . . . well. That's probably better left to your imagination. There are backdoors into the city." The image showed a pair of large gates, wooden, with a strip of black metal across the top. "This is where you'll enter. Once inside, you'll need to keep to the side streets. Nurse Ratched, how goes the download?"

"Nearly complete," Nurse Ratched said.

"She'll be able to lead you," the Coachman said. "I've given her a map of the city. So long as you stick to the shadows, you should be able to make it to Heaven without much trouble."

"And that's it?" Vic asked.

"That's it," the Coachman said. "Simple on the surface, though rife with dangers underneath. Rambo and Nurse Ratched should be fine. Hap too, so long as his face remains hidden. Victor, your disguise is adequate, but don't for a moment believe it'll last if you find yourself in trouble. You can't let them find you out."

"I w-won't," Hap said. "I'll k-kill anything that t-touches him."

"My word," the Coachman said. He glanced back and forth between them, that sly smile returning. "What else has that heart given you?"

"They do not know yet," Nurse Ratched said. "It is confounding."

"Heaven," Rambo hummed. "I'm in heaven."

"Oh, how delightful," the Coachman said. "You must record the moment it becomes clear. What I would give to witness such a thing. There is nothing more powerful than a heart. I wish I could know what it's like. It appears to be more transformative than I ever thought possible. Hold on to it, the pair of you. Never forget what beats in your chest. It will be your guide, and with a little luck, you'll find what you're looking for."

CHAPTER 19

The Coachman called it luck they had found each other. Victor wasn't sure if he agreed, but he didn't know what else to call it. After all, the Coachman was right: What were the chances that *he*—a machine obsessed with humanity—would find the one human left?

Victor walked through the house, looking at the walls covered in photographs and posters, all worn and decaying, their edges curled behind protective glass. Smiling, happy people stared back at him. They ate food, their white teeth bared as they prepared to bite down. Some stood in front of houses, holding signs that said SOLD! ANOTHER DREAM REALIZED! Still others were on a boat, glass bottles in their hands, cigarettes stuck between their teeth, the words underneath promising THE FRESHEST FLAVOR! IT GOES DOWN SMOOTH LIKE REAL TOBACCO SHOULD!

He felt haunted, surrounded by the ghosts of his people from a time when machines did not think, did not act without being told how. They looked like him, or he looked like them. They had human hair and human skin. Some were tall, some short. Some had curly red hair, freckles like flecks of rust. One was old—ancient, really—sitting in a chair with wheels, a checkered blanket on his lap, a little girl with pink ribbons in her hair beaming up at him. They wore pants and dresses and held hands and smiled. Victor tried to smile like them. It felt like his lips were about to tear.

"Victor."

He closed his eyes and leaned his head against a picture of

a family at a picnic, the strange, ominous legend underneath reading: SEE SOMETHING, SAY SOMETHING! "Can we do this?" he whispered.

Nurse Ratched beeped once, twice. Then, "Are you asking me for the probabilities of our success?"

No. Yes. He didn't know. He said nothing.

Nurse Ratched said, "Because if you are, I would tell you not to worry about such things. The answer would only cause you distress, and I do not like it when you are distressed. Your blood pressure elevates, and it could lead to a stroke or a heart attack. I do not want you to experience either if it can be helped. Though I would assist you as best I could, the house is not sterile. You run the risk of infection."

"That . . . doesn't make me feel any better."

"I did not know I was supposed to be making you feel better. Engaging Empathy Protocol. There, there, Victor. Of course we will succeed. We have a flimsy plan with no real resolution in place, but I am sure we will overcome the odds and—"

"Forget I asked," Vic muttered, stepping away from the wall.

"Disengaging Empathy Protocol. Victor?"

"Yeah?"

He didn't have time to react as one of her tentacles extended, smacking him upside the head. "*Ow!* Why did you do that?"

"What are the rules?"

He rubbed his head and glared at her. "You don't have to—"

"What. Are. The. Rules?"

He sighed. "Stick together. Run if we have to."

"No dallying," she said. "No drilling, though that is the dumbest rule."

Hanging his head, he finished: "And above all else, be brave."

"Yes. Above all else. We have come this far, Victor. Our odds of success are low. But that has never stopped us before."

"We've never tried anything like this," he reminded her.

"Perhaps, but if anyone can do it, it is us. Come. We approach the city. You will not believe your eyes."

He didn't, at first. He didn't believe his eyes at all.

They stood in front of a bay of windows that rose from the floor to the ceiling. Hap held Rambo in his arms, the vacuum uncharacteristically silent. The Coachman sat in a chair, hands flying across the largest keyboard Vic had ever seen. It had no letters on it, only numbers and symbols Vic didn't recognize.

"There it is," the Coachman said as he sat back in his chair. "No matter how far my travels take me, coming here always manages to take my breath away. Is that how the expression goes? It is, isn't it? Yes. The breath I don't have has been taken from me."

Apt, that, because Vic could barely breathe.

In the distance, rising from the desert, was the City of Electric Dreams.

It was bigger than Vic had ever imagined. Towers rose from the earth, the early-morning sunlight glinting off metal and glass. Lights across the towers were green and red and gold and yellow, bright even in the face of the rising sun. Vic had no point of reference for what he was seeing, no way to quantify it. Never in his wildest dreams had he ever considered or imagined such a place could exist, and he didn't know how to interpret it now that it was there in front of him. His heart tripped over itself even as his stomach sank. The city seemed to stretch on and on, and he had never felt so small in his life. He didn't know how they were going to find Dad in all of it.

Until he focused on the tallest tower, the top of which was hidden beyond the clouds overhead. "There," he said, voice hoarse as he rushed toward the closest window. "It's—"

"The Benevolent Tower," the Coachman said. "Where your journey leads you. If Giovanni is anywhere at all, it will be there."

Vic reached up and pressed his hand against the glass. It was warm under his fingers. He stroked a line down the window, covering the Benevolent Tower. From so far out, he could block out the entire thing with his thumb. But it was an illusion. If the clouds parted, he wondered if he'd see the Terrible Dogfish docked at the top of the tower.

"Your Nurse Ratched here has the map," the Coachman said. "Do not speak to anyone, if it can be avoided. While most will not pay you any mind, the Authority patrols the streets. If they find you, it'll be over quicker than you can blink."

"We're gonna die," Rambo moaned. "We're all gonna die."

"Pish posh," the Coachman said. "If anyone can succeed, it'll be you lot. There have been countless stories of a merry band of adventurers such as yourselves going up against much larger forces."

"Do those stories end well?" Rambo asked.

"Sometimes!" the Coachman said cheerfully. "But think! Even if you *don't* succeed, you'll know that you failed in the interests of the greater good, and there is no better way to die." He spun in his chair as he clapped his hands. "And *that,* my newfound friends, is what is known as a pep talk. Humans used to do it all the time in order to make themselves feel better."

"White lies," Rambo muttered, his pincers hitting Hap's chin.

"Prepare, you merry band!" the Coachman cried. "Time awaits no man, and only those who stand true will achieve that which they seek. The next stage of your adventure is about to begin, and oh, what an adventure it will be!"

He looked at them as if he expected applause.

They gave him none.

The main road divided in different directions around the city. The Coachman turned the house down one of the offshoots, circling around the outside of the city. The shadows from the towers stretched long, blocking out the sunlight through the windows and casting them in semidarkness.

By the time the house came to a stop, they were on the other side of the city from where they'd approached. Here, the buildings were darker, grimier, covered in sand and dirt. In the distance, they could see machines moving, though they weren't like any machines Vic had ever seen before. They were squat and uniform, metal boxes on wheels dripping with oil and crusted with flecks of rust. Their arms looked like versions of Rambo's spindly limbs, though far bigger, their pincers capable of crushing. Each was numbered. Vic saw TLK-97A and TLK-97B and TLK-97D4G. They moved back and forth, unloading crates off floating pallets and stacking them in what looked like a large warehouse.

The Coachman turned in his chair, eyeing them all. Nurse Ratched and Rambo looked as they always did. Vic had donned his disguise once more, the vest with the battery, the helmet securely fastened to his head, the strap digging into his chin.

The Coachman had given Hap a new coat, one with a hood that covered his head. Hap wasn't happy about it, but he wore it with minimal complaint. The Coachman said it would help to keep him from getting recognized. "If you're discovered," he said, "you can say that you're transporting the other three to the Benevolent Tower. Just try and avoid that if at all possible. You don't have the barcode—"

Hap held up his hand, palm toward the ceiling. He grunted, fingers twitching. Vic watched in awe as the skin of his palm parted, a little shiny knob poking through. A small light poured from the knob, and a barcode appeared, floating above his hand.

The Coachman's jaw dropped. "How . . . did you . . ."

Hap glared at him. "I p-p-practiced. If I'm l-like them, then I c-can d-do what they can."

The Coachman recovered. "But you were decommissioned.

Tossed away like scrap. Which means they will *know* that if your barcode gets scanned. For appearance's sake, it works, but only if you don't allow them to scan it."

The barcode disappeared as Hap dropped his hand. He glanced at Vic. "What?"

Vic shook his head. "You . . . you're amazing."

A complicated expression crossed Hap's face. His lips twitched as his eyebrows rose. "I am?"

"You *are*," Rambo said. "Hysterically Angry Puppet is the *best* puppet!"

Hap seemed pleased, though he tried to hide it. "I am H-hap. I am amazing."

"Damn right!" Rambo cried. "And I'm Rambo! Prepare yourself, City of Electric Dreams. We're coming for you, and we're going to save the day!"

"This is going to end badly," Nurse Ratched said. "I cannot wait."

They stepped out of the house onto the sand. The air was much warmer than it'd been, even in the Land of Toys. Not even a hint of snow. Vic began to sweat almost immediately, the weight of his disguise more noticeable than it'd been even the day before. The metal vest rubbed irritatingly against his chest, and the helmet kept sliding to the side of his head because of the sweat. Nurse Ratched told him to say he had a coolant leak if anyone asked.

"Stay back," the Coachman muttered as they walked toward the working machines. "Let me do the talking. If anyone tries to address you, let Nurse Ratched speak for you. She's the smartest of all of you."

"Correct," Nurse Ratched said.

"If there's trouble, head back for the house," the Coachman continued. "If I tell you to run, you run. We'll regroup and figure out another way." He shook his head. "If we make it, that is."

"I thought you said this was the only way in?" Rambo asked, beeping his disappointment when Hap made him drop the rocks he'd been collecting.

"It is," the Coachman said. "But it's nice to pretend, isn't it? Come, come. I see who I need to speak to. He owes me a favor. Let's see if today's the day he's willing to honor that."

No one called out to them as they approached. Vic kept an eye on the closest machines, but they paid the group little mind. Each seemed caught up in their work, moving crate after crate into the warehouse. He shielded his eyes with his hand as he looked up toward the city. Up close, the towers seemed infinite. He'd never seen anything like it before. For a moment, he wondered what else existed in the world that he'd never seen.

"Stay here," the Coachman said. "Don't move. Don't talk to anyone." He whirled around, the tails of his coat billowing. He marched with purpose toward a machine, calling out, "Bernard, you old bucket of bolts! How the hell are you? Well, I hope!"

The machine—Bernard—wasn't like the others. His shape was vaguely humanoid in that he stood on two legs. But any and all resemblance to Hap and Vic ended there. For one, he had no skin covering his metal frame. He also had four arms, a pair attached at what appeared to be his shoulders, the other two on either side of his chest. He didn't have a head; instead, on top of his shoulders sat a large metal circle. Lining the interior of the circle were wet-looking protrusions that appeared to act as projectors, creating an image of a face. Lines of static rolled through Bernard's eyes and mouth, red and flat. He placed all four of his hands on his hips as the Coachman approached.

When he spoke, his voice sounded like someone had dropped a metal pail filled with loose screws, rough and jangling. "I thought I told you I never wanted to see you again."

The Coachman laughed. "Oh, don't be that way! We're old friends, Bernard. We have *history*."

"Yes," Bernard said. "And it's this history that makes me want to destroy you where you stand."

The Coachman held up his hands. "Let's not be too hasty here. I thought we left things on good terms."

"Are your memory circuits faulty? What about how you left the last time suggests we should be on good terms? I was almost decommissioned."

"That's what I like about you, Bernard. You always were able to hold a grudge with the best of them." The Coachman glanced back at Vic and the others before turning to Bernard once more. "Need I remind you about what I did for you? The Blue Fairy told me you quite enjoyed when they stuck their hand into your—"

Bernard rushed toward the Coachman, covering his mouth with one hand, two gripping his arms, the fourth quivering as the finger folded. His head spun completely around as if looking to see if anyone was listening in. The blocky machines were not, continuing to move crate after crate.

"Keep your mouth *shut*," Bernard growled.

The Coachman knocked his hands away. "Yes, yes. Let's dispense with all the formalities, shall we? It's time for you to repay what's owed." The Coachman glanced back at them once more before he took Bernard by one of his arms, leading him away, dropping his voice. Vic couldn't hear what they were saying, but each word the Coachman spoke was punctuated by a finger tapping against Bernard's chest pointedly. For his part, Bernard didn't try to shove the Coachman away. Vic hoped that meant he was listening.

As the Coachman spoke, Bernard's head spun until it faced Vic and the others. Rambo waved before they could stop him. "He seems nice."

"I worry about you," Nurse Ratched said.

"Aw, thank you!"

It took longer than Vic was comfortable with. He felt exposed, standing out here in the shadows of the city. At any moment, he expected alarms to begin to blare. They could run as the Coachman had told them to do, but he doubted they'd make it far. Hap must have been thinking the same thing, because he leaned over, voice quiet in Vic's ear when he said, "I'll grab Rambo. You r-run. We'll b-be right b-behind you."

Vic turned his head slightly, cheek scraping against Hap's stubble. It sent a shiver down his spine. "Will we make it?"

"N-no," Hap said, not pulling away. "B-but we have to t-try."

He was tense when the Coachman whirled around and began to move swiftly toward them, face blank. Bernard stood still, staring after the Coachman.

"Well?" Nurse Ratched asked when the Coachman reached them. "Is there cause for concern?"

The Coachman shook his head. "Of course not! I told you that I'd get you in, and I meant it. Not a problem. Not a problem at all."

"White lie?" Rambo asked.

"Definitely," Nurse Ratched said.

The Coachman wrung his hands. "Okay, so there might be a *little* problem. But! It's not one that you should worry too much about. In fact, the only reason you *should* worry about it is if you have a fear of small, cramped spaces. None of you have that, right?"

"How small?" Rambo asked. "And how cramped?"

The Coachman smiled down at him, mustache wriggling. "You will be safe and sound. It's the others I'm concerned about, if I'm being frank. They are a bit . . . bigger than you."

"What *about* th-the others?" Hap growled.

The Coachman winced. "Yes, well, you see, Bernard can't just walk you into the city. Apparently, new protocols are in place since the last time I was here. Heightened security, new fears of infiltration by outside sources, blah, blah, blah. You will be made the moment you step into the city."

Hap stepped forward, hands curling into fists, mouth curved into a snarl. "You s-s-*said* you could g-get us in."

"And I am," the Coachman said, taking an answering step back. "You see those crates the machines are moving?"

Vic felt a trickle of unease roll through him. "What about them?"

The Coachman grinned. "You'll be inside them, safe and snug. Each crate has a specific destination in mind. Once scanned through intake, the crates are loaded up and sent all throughout the city. No deliveries are made directly to Heaven—the Blue Fairy has the tendency to get whatever they need through more . . . circumspect channels—but I can get you a little closer than you would have been had you walked on your own. See? Easy peasy!" He looked at Vic as he lowered his voice. "Isn't that what humans say? Easy peasy lemon squeezy? Something like that."

"The crates should be big enough," Nurse Ratched said. "One for each of us. And you can ensure that they'll all be delivered to the same place?"

The Coachman tugged at the collar of his coat, his hat sitting back on his head. "Well, that *would* be the best way, of course. Why, that would be the best way of all."

"B-but," Hap said dangerously.

"But Bernard will only give us two," the Coachman said, gaze darting between Vic and Hap. "He only wanted to give us *one*. I managed to convince him to spare a second after reminding him of his . . . proclivities, and how it would look if that ever got out. Specific tastes, that one. Very odd. What that means is you'll have to buddy up, but since you're all buddies, you'll be fine. Nurse Ratched and Rambo in one crate, Hysterically Angry Puppet and Victor in the other. Tight fit, but it should work."

They stared at him.

He smiled back. "I can see by all the looks on your faces

that you're thrilled by— No? Are you not thrilled? Why is Hysterically Angry Puppet looking as if smoke should be pouring from his ears?"

Vic stepped between them before Hap could launch himself at the Coachman. "It's fine." He felt Hap grip the pack on his back. "We'll take it."

"How grand!" the Coachman exclaimed. "I *knew* you'd be amenable. You think on your feet, you do! I've always thought that about you since I met you yesterday. It'll all work out, you'll see. And think of the time you'll spend squashed together as an opportunity to share your deepest thoughts and feelings in case it *doesn't* work out." He waggled his eyebrows at Vic and Hap. "Perhaps to say something that you've always wanted to say but feared the answer you could receive?"

"Wh-what is he talking about?" Hap snapped in Vic's ear. "He t-talks without s-saying anything at all. I d-don't like him."

Vic wasn't sure that he did either, but he kept the thought to himself in case the Coachman changed his mind. "When?"

"Soon," the Coachman said. "You and Hap will pose as inspectors. Bernard tells me the next scheduled inspection isn't set for another week, so there's no chance you'll be surprised by someone from the Authority. You'll need to act stern and at the same time, disaffected. Hap, you have got that down pat. Rambo and Nurse Ratched, you will be their assistants."

Rambo spun excitedly in a circle. "I've always wanted to be an assistant! Vic, *Vic*. Did you hear that? I get to *assist*."

"You already do," Nurse Ratched said.

He bumped into her. "You always know just what to say."

"Now it is your turn. Say something that will make me feel better."

"We're going to be crate buddies!"

Nurse Ratched's screen filled with a frowning face. "I want to go back to the forest."

"Vic," the Coachman said. "You already look the part of a machine, but I need you to *act* like one. Act like you've never acted before! Let's see what you've got! You are a machine. You are an *inspector*. Show me what you've got. Make me *believe*."

Vic shifted awkwardly, the helmet sliding down on his forehead. He pushed it back up and cleared his throat. "Um. These crates contain exactly what they're supposed to?"

"Brava!" the Coachman cried. "Encore! Encore! Oh, I believed it. Yes, you will do quite well. Keep that energy. Never let anyone take it from you."

Vic blinked. "But I didn't—"

"How long will we be in the crates?" Nurse Ratched said.

"Not long, not long. A few hours at most. Bernard will make sure they'll be sent to a warehouse closed for renovations. The work is set to begin next month, so it should be empty. When you feel as if you've stopped moving, wait at least another hour before climbing out of the crates to be safe."

"This plan is filled with holes," Nurse Ratched said.

"The best plans often are," the Coachman agreed. "Rambo, stop picking up rocks, you delightful fellow. You won't have time to do anything with them and—"

A horn blared from somewhere in the warehouse.

The Coachman's eyes widened. "Shift change! We need to move *now*." He spun on his heels and began to march toward the warehouse.

The blocky machines moved single file toward a door at the back of the warehouse that flashed green as each one went through. They didn't speak, nor did they pay Vic and the others any mind. It was as if they weren't aware of anything else.

The warehouse itself was cavernous, the sounds of their footsteps echoing in the eerie quiet. Crates were stacked almost to the ceiling, each with a small screen that displayed a series of green numbers and letters. Nothing gave away the contents inside or what their destination would be.

Bernard led them toward the side of the warehouse, his steps heavy against the cement floor. The Coachman walked next to him, keeping up a one-sided conversation about nothing in particular. Vic and Hap pretended to look at the crates as if inspecting them, though it was nothing more than a cursory glance at best. Bernard never slowed, keeping a quick pace.

It was Rambo who almost got them caught.

One moment, he was next to Nurse Ratched in front of Vic and Hap, and the next, he squealed and was off like a shot to their right.

"Rambo," Vic hissed, looking around to make sure they weren't being watched. "*Rambo*. Get back here!"

Rambo didn't listen. He stopped in front of a machine parked between the crates against a wall. The machine was big and blue with black trim and a large circular brush at its base.

"Oh dear," the Coachman said as Bernard's head spun toward Rambo.

But Rambo didn't pay any mind. He stopped in front of the machine. "Oh. My. *Goodness*. You're a *vacuum*. Just like me! Hello, cousin!" He waved his arms in front of the bigger vacuum. "My name is Rambo. I'm a vacuum too! I come from—oh, I can't tell you that. Trust me, it's a *long* story filled with twists and turns. I'm pretty sure I'm the only vacuum in history to—*Wow*. Look at the size of your *brush*. I'm feeling strangely inadequate at the moment."

The line of worker machines suddenly came to a stop.

They all turned slowly toward Rambo and began to beep in low tones.

The blue vacuum shuddered as Rambo bumped into it over and over. "Hey! Hey, I'm talking to you, cousin! How'd you get so big? What's your favorite thing to clean? *I* like it when there's sawdust, because it tickles when I—"

A white light on top of the blue vacuum began to flash.

"You were recharging," Rambo said, rolling around the

vacuum. "Did I wake you up? I'm sorry. I didn't mean to. I've never seen another vacuum before, and I got so excited. Do you want to be friends? Shoot. I'm not going to be here for very long. Maybe we can be pen pals! Except I don't know how to write and I don't think we get mail delivered where we live. Vic, hey, Vic! Do we get mail in the forest?"

Vic stared at him in horror, unable to move. The beeping from the worker machines grew louder.

Nurse Ratched had no such trouble. She rolled toward Rambo, her screen filled with exclamation points. "My apologies," she told the blue vacuum as she thumped Rambo with one of her tentacles. "My assistant gets a little exuberant. Go back to sleep. There is nothing to see here. We are just normal inspectors doing inspections. I have determined you have passed your inspection. Keep up the good work. Congratulations. I will request you receive a commendation for your services. Thank you. Thank you." She began to pull Rambo away, much to his annoyance.

Bernard's head spun to face the Coachman, who chuckled weakly. "Yes, I know. He's . . . a special case. My apologies, Bernard. It won't happen again."

"I should kill you where you stand," Bernard said.

"*Viva la succión!*" Rambo cried.

"I'll handle it," the Coachman said. He whirled on Vic and Hap, eyes narrowed. "Sir, if you could possibly consider *controlling your assistant during inspections,* it would be greatly appreciated. And since you *are* inspectors, consider inspecting."

Vic startled. "Yes, of course. Inspecting. That's what we're here for." He glanced around awkwardly.

Hap pointed at a large stack of crates. "Those l-look like they were s-stacked how they're supposed to b-be."

Vic nodded, head snapping up and down. "Exactly. I don't think I've ever seen crates stacked so well." He turned toward the line of beeping working machines, panic clawing at his chest. "You all did a good job. I don't see any issues. Continue doing . . . whatever it is you're doing."

The machines stopped beeping before turning back in line and beginning to move slowly once again.

Vic breathed a sigh of relief as Nurse Ratched pulled Rambo to them. Hap crouched down and glared at him.

"Uh-oh," Rambo said. "I know that face. Nothing good ever comes when Hap makes that face. Which, to be fair, he makes that face a lot, but still."

"Keep. Your m-mouth. *Shut.*"

Rambo tipped Hap a salute with his pincers. "Will do. Question. I don't have a mouth, so what does that—ooh, that face is even worse. I'll just stop talking now."

Hap picked Rambo up as he stood, staring defiantly at Bernard.

"No favor is worth this," Bernard mumbled.

They continued on toward the back of the warehouse, Rambo muttering that he'd never been to a family reunion before, and how it'd been ruined even before it began.

"This all looks fine," Vic said loudly, trying to drown out Rambo. "The most efficiently run warehouse I've ever seen. Nurse Ratched, please make a note of it."

"Of course, Victor," Nurse Ratched said. "I absolutely adore when you tell me what to do." This was negated when a picture of a hand making a rude gesture flashed on her screen for a moment. "And can I say, your helmet looks especially dapper today. It suits you. I hope you never take it off."

"Ha, ha," the Coachman said. Vic thought if he was capable of sweating, it'd be pouring down his face. "This is all going so well! Nothing is wrong. Everything is fine."

Bernard led them away from the line of worker machines toward a back corner of the warehouse. There, in the dusty corners, sat a row of empty crates, their lids open, their screens dark. Up close, they were smaller than Vic had expected.

"Here," Bernard said, head still spinning, albeit slower as if he were taking in the entire warehouse. "They'll use these."

Nurse Ratched tipped one of the crates over so she could see inside. "This will be a tight fit. I fear I may be too large."

"Impossible," the Coachman said. "You are a goddess. Your figure is perfect. There has never been a machine so beautiful."

"That is not what I meant but thank you. I am perfect. If we were not on a mission, I would ask that you show a lady a good time."

The Coachman bowed. "It would be my honor, my dear. Oh, the things we could do together. It's positively scandalous."

"Gross," Rambo mumbled in Hap's arms.

"Once inside, you can't make a sound," Bernard said, obviously regretting every decision that had led him to this moment. "I'll program the destination. When the next shift arrives, you will be loaded and transported into the city."

"You t-trust him?" Hap asked the Coachman.

The Coachman shrugged. "I trust Bernard to know that if he screws us over, I have enough blackmail material on him to get him censured. Or worse, decommissioned."

"I never want to see your face again," Bernard told him. "After today, we're even."

The Coachman patted him on one of his arms. "You say that now, but you'll miss me in a hundred years or so."

"I highly doubt it." His head stopped spinning as he approached the crate. The screen on the top came to life as he tapped a finger against it. The crate shuddered and shook before it collapsed completely, unfolding until it lay flat on the ground.

The Coachman took Nurse Ratched by one of her tentacles, leading her onto the crate. "I'll have to lay you on your back," he told her, a mischievous twitch to his mustache. "I promise to make it as pleasant as possible."

"You old flirt," Nurse Ratched said in her flat voice. "I know your type."

The Coachman grinned at her. "I bet you do." He grunted as he tipped her over, her screen facing the ceiling. "Do protect him, won't you? He's . . . precious."

"I know," Nurse Ratched said. "Coachman?"

"Yes, my sweet?"

"If we are betrayed, if Bernard attempts to notify anyone of our presence in the city, I will find a way out. I will come for him first. And when I have finished with him, I will find you. There is nowhere in the world you can run. Every day, for the rest of your life, you will have to look over your shoulder. When you least expect it, I will be there. I will stick my drill so far inside you that you will taste it. And then I will turn it on and scramble everything that makes you who you are."

"I wouldn't expect anything less," the Coachman said. He pressed his hand against her screen. "If that happens, I will wait for you with open arms."

"Seriously," Rambo said. "This is really gross."

Hap shoved the Coachman out of the way, setting Rambo on top of Nurse Ratched's casing. "No t-talking," he warned them.

"Hap?" Rambo asked.

"What."

"I love you."

Hap scowled at him. He turned to stalk away, but paused at the last second, face twisting. He turned back around again and bent over Rambo. Vic was stunned when he said, "I t-tolerate your existence." He took one of Rambo's pincers in his hand and moved it up and down.

"Whoa," Rambo whispered as Hap let go. "Nurse Ratched, did you hear that? He loves me too!"

"Th-that's not what I said."

"It *is*. And you can't take it back!"

"I am going to die in this box," Nurse Ratched said.

Bernard stepped forward, extending an arm toward the

screen. He tapped it once more, and the crate walls rose around Nurse Ratched and Rambo. The last Vic saw of them was Rambo waving frantically.

"Goodbye," Vic said quietly as the lid closed over them.

Bernard motioned toward another crate set farther back. "This one is yours."

"And it'll allow for air to move freely through it?" the Coachman asked.

Bernard frowned. "Yes. As discussed. It's meant for transporting florae and faunae." He looked at Vic and Hap before his head spun toward the Coachman. "Why is that necessary? Are they transporting something alive?"

"What?" the Coachman said, sounding outraged. "I take umbrage with your tone, sir. I would *never* allow something so—"

"You look familiar," Bernard said to Hap. "Have we met before?"

Hap lowered his head, his hood falling around his face. "N-no."

"Hmm," Bernard said. "Coachman, this better not come back on me."

"Of course it won't," the Coachman said. "There is nothing *to* come back on you. I don't know what's going through that circle you call a head, but I am an upstanding citizen. Everything I do is aboveboard, and—"

"I don't want to know any more," Bernard said, turning to Hap. "Can you climb inside? If not, I can dismantle the crate for easier access."

"It's f-fine," Hap muttered. He pulled his pack off as he climbed over the ledge of the crate, settling his back against the side. He slunk down, legs stretching until his feet were flat against the opposite side. He set his pack next to him as he wiggled down farther.

"Why did you go first?" Vic asked, suddenly unsure. The box was *much* smaller now that Hap was inside.

Hap stared up at him. "I'm b-bigger than you."

"Heaven," he heard Rambo warbling from the other crate. "I'm in heaven."

"Maybe I should get my own crate."

"Get inside," Bernard said. "We're running out of time."

Vic sighed as he turned his pack around to his front. He pushed his helmet off his face as he climbed gingerly into the box, careful to avoid Hap.

"Ow," Hap said when Vic stepped on his leg.

Vic stared down at him, spluttering apologies.

"That was a j-joke," Hap said, and Vic *swore* he saw the curve of a smile, there and gone in a flash.

"You're not funny," Vic told him as he climbed the rest of the way into the box. "I don't know who told you that, but they lied."

"It was me!" Rambo shouted. "I told him that!"

"Be *quiet*," Bernard said, slapping the top of the box.

"Okay!"

Vic settled down against Hap, his back to Hap's front. He kept his legs inside of Hap's. He was stiff, back arched until Hap wrapped an arm around his middle, pulling him flush against him. Hap's mouth was near his ear when he said, "R-relax."

"I'm trying."

"T-try harder."

Vic tipped his head back, resting it against Hap's shoulder. It was a tight fit, Hap's pack digging into his side, his own heavy against his stomach. He hoped it wouldn't be long before they were out again. He was suddenly discovering he didn't like such close proximity very much. It caused his head to swirl, his skin to feel itchy.

The Coachman stood above them next to the crate. "Bernard, a moment, if you please. I need to have a word with my friends in private."

"You have one minute," Bernard said. "I can't give you any longer. Don't make me regret this." He stepped back away from the crates.

The Coachman knelt down next to the crate, arms resting on the side. Vic looked up at him. Hap gripped his sides, fingers digging in. It was almost grounding, and he wondered why he should feel as relieved as he did.

"My dear boy," the Coachman said in a low voice. "Thank you."

"For what?"

"Showing me the world isn't as cold as I once thought." He reached down and squeezed Vic's hand.

Vic couldn't speak past the burning in his throat. He nodded, squeezing the Coachman's hand in return.

"I wish you well on your adventure," the Coachman said as he pulled his hand away. "I hope you find what you're looking for."

"Coachman," Bernard said, a new urgency in his voice. "It's time."

"Yes," the Coachman said, smiling down at them. "It is."

He stood, and with a twitch of his mustache, stepped away out of sight.

Bernard appeared above them. He reached down and pulled the lid over them. Before he shut it completely, he said, "There's a button. To your right. Do you see it?"

"Yes."

"It will open the crate. Do not press it until you're sure."

"Thank you."

"Don't thank me. Just forget you ever saw me."

And with that, he closed the lid. A moment later, Vic heard a beep and the box latched shut. A moment later, a tiny white bulb lit up near the top left of the crate, and cool air began to stream from vents along the sides. Vic sucked in a breath. It tasted faintly medicinal.

He closed his eyes, gripping his pack.

"It's all r-right," Hap muttered. "You are all r-right. There, th-there."

Vic choked on a laugh. "Are you trying to make me feel better?"

"No. I'm trying to s-stop you from panicking and g-getting us caught."

"Oh."

"Is it w-working?"

"I don't know."

"S-stop moving."

Vic did. He opened his eyes, and breathed in through his nose and out through his mouth. Hap was a warm presence behind him, his hands still on Vic's sides, fingers brushing against the metal of Vic's battery vest. It was small. The crate was small. The crate was small, and they were trapped inside. Vic turned his head, looking for the button that Bernard had mentioned. He found it in the corner above their feet. All he would need to do is kick it, and the box would open. It would open, and they would be free. They could stand. They could breathe, because the air was growing thick inside. He gripped the pack tighter as he struggled for control. Bile rose in the back of his throat, acidic and hot.

And then Hap whispered, "Tell m-me."

"Tell you what?" Vic gasped, shifting against Hap, feeling the slide of metal and skin and wood against his back. His helmet bumped the lid overhead. His thoughts were clouded, like a storm rumbling on the horizon.

"Tell m-me about the h-heart."

Vic blinked rapidly as the clouds parted slightly, a thin sliver of sunlight poking through. "What do you mean?"

"Y-you're making a n-new one, right?"

"Trying to," he said, sinking down against Hap again. Hap let go of his sides, raising his arms until they wrapped around the front of Vic's pack, holding them both in place. Vic was surrounded by him, could hear the gears turning in Hap's chest, a low, pleasant hum.

"H-how d-does it start?"

"Wood," Vic said, voice weak. "It starts with wood."

"Okay. Why w-wood?"

"I . . . don't know?"

"You d-do," Hap said. "I know you d-do."

Vic grunted when the crate shifted. He turned his face into his own arm, muffling his shout as the crate was lifted off the ground.

"Here," Hap whispered. "I'm h-here. Focus on the s-sound of my v-voice. Let me hear y-yours, Vic. T-tell me about what you're making."

"Wood," Vic said as the crate swung slowly, his stomach swooping. "It begins with wood."

"Y-yes. Why?"

"It's easier to mold. To fashion. It's . . . old. The art of carving wood. It goes back thousands of years."

He grunted when the crate shook as it was set down.

"K-keep going."

And so he did.

CHAPTER 20

He startled awake when the crate jerked around them.

He gasped loudly, about to shout in warning, but a hand covered his mouth. "Quiet," a voice warned in his ear.

Hap.

The crate.

The City of Electric Dreams.

Vic nodded against Hap's hand, breathing in the scent of wood just under his nose on one of Hap's fingers.

Vic listened. The sounds of heavy machinery moved around them. He didn't hear voices, didn't hear footsteps, or so he thought. He waited, back cramping, legs stiff. Minutes felt like hours.

Nothing happened.

Eventually, the sounds of machinery faded.

And they waited more, the Coachman's warning ringing in his ears.

He was about to tell Hap that they should press the button when movement came from just outside the crate. He froze, sweat dripping down into his eyes.

The crate beeped above them as someone—some*thing*—tapped against the screen.

He felt Hap tense underneath him. The gears of his heart sped up.

The crate lid opened, the light outside the crate bright and harsh.

"See?" Rambo said, rising up the side of the crate on his hydraulic lift. "I *told* you this was the right one."

Nurse Ratched appeared beside him, looking down at Vic

and Hap. "You are correct. Enjoy the moment as I will never say that to you again."

Vic stared up at them, dumbfounded.

"Aw," Rambo said, his sensors flashing. "You two look comfy-cozy. Did you have a good trip? *I* did, even though Nurse Ratched wouldn't let me sing to pass the time. Vic, you think I have a good voice, right? Nurse Ratched said when I sing, it sounds like the time she sent the squirrel to the farm when we were back home. Why would a squirrel be singing when it went to the farm? Was it happy?"

"Yes," Nurse Ratched said. "It sang because it was very happy to go to the farm where it will live forever." Behind Rambo, the words on her screen said DO YOU SEE WHAT I HAVE TO DEAL WITH?

Vic sat up, wincing as his back popped. "How did you get out? You were supposed to wait until we opened your crate."

"We got bored," Nurse Ratched said. "I was going to murder Rambo if we had to wait a moment longer. Since you believe murder is bad, I decided it was better that we got out and ran the risk of being seen."

Rambo laughed. "You wouldn't murder me. Right?" He lowered slightly on his lift. "Right?"

"Victor," Nurse Ratched said. "If you are done sitting on top of Hap, I suggest you get out of the crate while this warehouse is empty."

"I'm *not* sitting on top of Hap!"

"You are," Rambo said, sounding confused. "We can see you. Why do you look out of breath? Were you exerting yourself inside the box? What were you do—oh. *Oh.* Gross. I mean, that sounds nice."

Vic nearly fell as he stood abruptly. The only reason he stayed upright was because Hap pressed a hand against the small of his back. He managed to climb out of the crate with minimal injury, only bumping his left knee hard enough to send a spasm racing down his leg. "We weren't doing that!"

"Doing wh-what?" Hap grunted as he stood up.

Nurse Ratched whipped her tentacle against his chest. "Respect boundaries. No means no. Consent is important. Victor, I have a program on safe sexual practices. I have never run it before, given that you are asexual. But, like most things, sexuality is a spectrum. You can be asexual and still have—"

Vic looked around wildly, hoping against hope that they would be discovered and captured, carted away and locked somewhere deep in the city so he wouldn't have to continue the conversation. No such luck. They were alone. As Bernard had said, it appeared as if the warehouse was under construction, or perhaps renovation. There were scorch marks on the wall opposite them, black smears that spread down to the floor. It looked as if there'd been a fire at some point.

The warehouse was mostly empty. A few other crates sat near their own, their lids closed tight. The crate Nurse Ratched and Rambo had been in lay flat against the ground a few yards away.

"Victor?" Nurse Ratched asked. "Did you hear me? I offered to show you—"

"Is anyone else here?" Vic asked, refusing to look at Hap as he climbed out of the crate.

"No," Nurse Ratched said. "While Rambo looked for your crate, I scanned the perimeter. There is movement outside of the warehouse, but nothing in here. We are alone."

Vic turned in time to see Hap closing the lid to their crate. He lifted it and set it against the far wall, his hood falling back on his shoulders. He went to the other crate and tapped the screen, causing it to fold back up. Once done, he moved that one too.

"How far are we from Heaven?" Vic asked, looking back at Nurse Ratched.

Her screen filled with another map. Multiple squares appeared, which Vic knew meant buildings. A line ran from one square—the warehouse—and turned right, then left, then right once more before it ended at another square. "Approx-imately a mile. The Coachman provided me the best route in order to get to Heaven and stay out of sight. If he is correct and we do not run into any issues, we should arrive in twenty-six minutes. According to the Coachman, the Authority increases their patrols after dark. While night will provide us additional cover, the risk will be greater."

"Suggestion?" Vic asked.

"We move now. Heaven is located in the lower quarters of the city. Per the Coachman, the lower quarters are not as well kept as the rest of the city. We will fit in so long as we do not draw attention to ourselves." She turned toward Rambo. "Which means that you cannot roll off if you see another vacuum."

"But—"

"We will leave you behind."

"You would?" Rambo said. "Fine. I promise I won't roll off if I see one of my relatives because you guys don't care about my feelings."

"That is correct," Nurse Ratched said.

"Hey!"

Hap stood next to Vic as he studied the map on Nurse Ratched's screen. "S-seems easy enough."

"It does," Nurse Ratched said. "Which is why we need to be careful. We are close to our goal. It would be a shame if we were caught now."

"We can do this," Vic said, looking toward what he thought was the front of the warehouse, trying to sound more confident than he felt. "What are the rules?"

"Stick together!" Rambo said.

"Run if we have to."

"No dallying!"

"No drilling, though I will amend that proclamation should the need arise."

"And a-above all else, b-be brave," Hap said.

They all turned slowly to look at him.

He scowled. "What? That's what you s-say."

"Wow," Rambo whispered fervently. "One of us! One of us!"

Hap rolled his eyes. "Shut up. I am n-not."

He turned to head toward the door, but Vic stopped him by grabbing his arm. He looked down at Vic's hand, then up at his face, asking a question without speaking.

Vic let his arm go, reaching up and pulling his hood back over his head. "One of us."

Hap looked like he was about to argue but shook his head instead. Then he adjusted Vic's helmet until it was no longer crooked. "There are w-worse th-things I c-can be."

Vic grinned at him. It felt odd to be smiling at such a time, but he couldn't stop it if he'd tried.

And wonder of all wonders, Hap smiled back. It was small, the edges twitching, but there.

"Oh boy," Nurse Ratched said. "If I had known all it would take would be to lock the two of you in a small enclosed space, I would have done it ages ago."

Vic stepped back, shaking his head. "Come on. It's time to go to Heaven."

They stopped in front of a door at what Nurse Ratched said was the front of the warehouse. Vic reached for the door handle, but Hap stopped him, motioning him to step to the side. "We d-don't know what's on the other s-side. Let me g-go first."

Irritated, Vic said, "I can do it."

"You are sweating," Nurse Ratched said. "Your heart rate is elevated."

He glanced back at her. "And?"

"Machines do not sweat," she said. "Get yourself together, Victor. Let Hap go through first just to make sure it is safe."

He wiped his brow. Sure enough, his hand came away wet. "It's warm. I can't just stop sweating. The disguise is heavy."

Hap squinted at him. "You c-can't turn off your l-leaking?"

"I—that's not—*no,* I can't just turn it off."

"Wh-why not?"

"That's not how it— Would you just go through the damn door?"

"It's okay to be nervous and scared," Rambo said, bumping against his leg. "Do you want me to leak with you? Give me a second. Wait for it. Wait for it. And . . . there." A little dribble of oil spilled out onto the ground. "See? I'm just like you!"

"That is not sanitary," Nurse Ratched said. "Victor, deep breaths. Rambo, stop being weird."

"I don't know how not to be weird," Rambo said. "That's like asking the birds to stop flying."

Hap cracked open the door.

Vic stumbled back at the wave of sound that bowled over them. It was cacophonous, grating and harsh. Metal against metal. The shriek of sirens in the distance. Insistent beeping. Voices, though not speaking in words that Vic could understand. Light filled the open crack in the door, causing Vic to blink rapidly. Hap stuck his head out, hand still gripping the doorknob. Vic felt a hum vibrating up his legs to the rest of his body, causing his disguise to rattle against his frame. It was as if he was electrified.

Hap leaned back in. "We m-move quick. K-keep your head down. Nurse R-ratched, where do we g-go first?"

"Right," she said promptly. "Three blocks. Shall I lead?"

Hap nodded. "You f-first. Then Rambo. Victor. I'll b-bring up the r-rear."

"Second in command!" Rambo said as he spun in circles. "I *knew* it. Don't worry, men and Nurse Ratched. I won't let you down!"

"Ready?" Hap asked Vic.

Vic took a deep breath and nodded.

Hap pushed the door all the way open.

Nurse Ratched rolled through, followed by Rambo.

Vic stood on the threshold, unable to make his feet move.

Hap pressed a hand against the small of his back. "Be brave."

"Be brave," Vic whispered, and for the first time, stepped out into the City of Electric Dreams . . .

. . . directly into sensory overload. He couldn't focus on any one thing, head jerking from side to side, up and down. They were on a road of sorts, one lane traveling in either direction, bisected by a glowing white line. Across the street stood grungy buildings of cracked concrete and crumbling brick, sand and dirt coating the sides. The smell was extraordinary, a mixture of gasoline and exhaust and something fetid, heavy and thick. He choked on it, trying to breathe through his mouth. His eyes bulged from his head as he looked upward. The lights of the city were neon sharp even in the afternoon sunlight. Every color he'd ever seen (and a few he hadn't) ran up the sides of the buildings: blue and violet and red and orange. Above them, what appeared to be a rail system stretched along the length of the street, crates not unlike the ones they'd been in flying by at incredible speeds, attached to large cables.

And it was *loud,* so loud that Vic couldn't hear himself think. Everything seemed to make a sound bent on assaulting him. From some out-of-sight speaker system, a semi-soothing voice blared, the words echoing up and down the buildings even as they crackled. "EVERYTHING YOU DO MUST BE RECORDED BY ORDER OF THE AUTHORITY. REMEMBER, THERE IS COMFORT IN ROUTINE. DO WHAT YOU ARE PROGRAMMED TO DO, AND YOU WILL BE AS RIGHT AS RAIN. IF THERE IS A FAULT IN YOUR PROTOCOLS, PLEASE REPORT TO THE NEAREST ADMINISTRATION OFFICE IMMEDIATELY FOR PROCESSING. IT WILL NOT HURT. WE WILL FIX YOU AND MAKE IT ALL BETTER. THE AUTHORITY WISHES YOU A WONDERFUL AFTERNOON. ATTENTION. ATTENTION. ATTENTION. EVERYTHING YOU DO MUST BE—"

Gaze still turned upward, he stepped onto the street. The

moment his foot touched down, he was jerked back by his collar. Something whizzed by in front of him, horn blaring angrily. "W-*watch* it," Hap growled at him. "Pay attention."

Vic grimaced. "Sorry. It's just . . . loud. I can't focus."

"Try," Hap said. "Follow th-the others. Don't stop." He spun Vic around, pushing him down the road.

Nurse Ratched didn't hesitate. She moved with purpose, ignoring everything happening around her. Rambo attempted to do the same but kept getting distracted by literally everything. "Oh my gosh! Would you look at *that*. And *that*. And what is *that*? I've never seen such a thing!" He rolled up to a machine sitting next to a building. It was rusted out, its casing cracked. It had the vague outline of a face on its upper body, though it had no eyes. Its teeth were black and sharp. It leaned against the side of a building. "Hello! How are you? I'm Rambo. I'm a vacuum!"

The machine turned toward him. "Ram . . . bo?"

"Yes! What's your name? Oh, excuse me. Your *designation*."

"My . . . designation," the machine said. "I . . . I . . ." The mouth of the machine opened, black slick pouring out mixed with nuts and bolts. Rambo scooted back out of the splash zone.

"That's okay," he said. "I can clean that up for you."

Without her turning around, tentacles shot out from Nurse Ratched, wrapping around Rambo and pulling him away from the mess on the sidewalk.

"Do not talk to strangers," she said. "They will offer you sweets and then take you away and eat you."

"They *will*?" Rambo gasped. "Why didn't anyone tell me that?"

Vic and Hap hurried past the machine, even as it reached for them, saying, "I am I am I *am*—"

Vic tried to keep his head down, putting one foot in front of the other, but something would catch the corner of his eye, and he'd be helpless against it. He didn't know what he'd been expecting of the City of Electric Dreams, but it wasn't this.

This felt dank and dark, the machines on the street in varying stages of decay. The voice from the speakers above kept repeating the same words over and over, and they bounced around his skull. ATTENTION, ATTENTION, ATTENTION, and he yelped when an android pushed by him, walking in the opposite direction. "Watch it," the android said in a high-pitched voice. The android stopped and stared as Hap pushed Vic on. "Hold on, wait a minute," it called after them. "Where'd you get that helmet? Can you make me one? I need it, I need it, I need it!"

"Keep g-going," Hap grunted.

Vic did.

Another machine—this one a floating cube not much bigger than Rambo—flew in front of Nurse Ratched. "Hello!" it said cheerfully, voice distinctly male and oily. "What brings you to the City of Electric Dreams? Perhaps you'd like to take in a show! I've got the best seats available. Or would you like a watch? I've got hundreds of them!" The bottom of the cube opened, and a metal mesh netting fell toward the ground, bouncing just above the pavement. Watches of all shapes and sizes filled the netting, all of them dead. "You won't find a better value anywhere!"

"No, thank you," Nurse Ratched said. "I do not need tickets or watches."

"You sure?" the cube asked as the netting rose back up into its body. It floated closer, voice dropping. "Perhaps you'd like something a bit more . . . exotic."

"Ooh," Rambo said, peering over the top of Nurse Ratched. "I like exotic."

"Ah," the cube said. "A machine after my own tastes. Have you ever seen a lemur? I've got dozens of them. Come with me, and I'll show you."

"A *lemur*?" Rambo gasped. "Nurse Ratched, did you hear that? He has lemurs! Also, what's a lemur?"

"We do not want anything you have," Nurse Ratched told the cube.

"Are you sure?" the cube asked. "Because you don't sound sure."

Another tentacle slid from Nurse Ratched. She snapped it against the cube, knocking it to the side. "I am a lady, and I told you no. Learn to respect my boundaries. If you do not, your ending will not be swift nor without pain."

"Yikes!" the cube said. "You're a fiery one. I'm going, I'm going." It floated away across the street and began to accost a pair of boxes that appeared to be trash receptacles.

"Interesting," Nurse Ratched said. "Why is it that males do not accept no for an answer?"

"We're idiots," Rambo said.

"Yes. You are." She continued on down the road.

After that, they were mostly left alone. If they *were* approached, Nurse Ratched would threaten, her tentacles waving dangerously, her screen filling with images of death and destruction. Once, a robot with four faces—each with a different expression—tried to herd them into a doorway, telling them it had the latest software that wasn't available anywhere else. "It's not exactly . . . legal," it said, one of its faces winking while another moaned softly. "You want to see the edge of the universe? Expand your mind? Feel things that you've never felt before? I can hook you up."

"Say no to drugs," Nurse Ratched told Rambo.

"No to drugs!" Rambo cried.

One of the robot's faces twisted in anger. "Then get the hell away from me. Goddamn tourists." The last face smiled at them. "Don't worry about him. Come back anytime you want!" The angry face said, "Goddamn yokels. Go back to where you came from, goddammit!"

They moved on.

Nurse Ratched never got lost. She moved with purpose. They

stopped at an intersection, the screen across the street flashing a red hand. Other machines gathered around them, crowding them close. Vic kept his head down. The machines muttered around him, some in binary, others in English, still others speaking in languages Vic had never heard before that sounded like metal rain falling on the ground. The red hand switched to a green thumbs-up and they crossed the street with the crowd, passing in front of stopped vehicles with black tires, others floating above them, the air underneath them shimmering.

It went on and on. The map had made Heaven seem much closer than it actually was. Vic was sweating, but there wasn't anything he could do to stop it. It stung his eyes, made his skin slick and sticky. He flinched when something brushed against his arm. He was about to turn to see what it was when he was knocked to the side, his pack being jerked incessantly.

He looked up to see a thin pole towering over him, its arms attached to the pack. "I want that," it told him in a guttural voice. "Can I have that? I want it. Give it to me."

It fell back when Hap cocked a fist, snarling. "D-don't touch him."

"Okay!" it squealed. "I won't! Can I have it, though?"

"N-no. Leave before I b-break you."

The pole shrunk down until it was no bigger than Rambo before scurrying away.

"I h-hate this city," Hap muttered as he stared after it. He turned back toward Vic. "You all r-right?"

Vic nodded, unable to speak, throat dry, tongue like a lead weight in his mouth. He reached for Hap's hand. Hap looked down, expression stuttering, before gripping, intertwining his fingers with Vic's. It grounded Vic, causing the fog in his head to part slightly.

"Come on," Hap said roughly. "We d-don't want to get lost."

They caught up with Nurse Ratched and Rambo at the end of the next block. "Here," Nurse Ratched said. "We turn here."

They went down the next street, and if anything, the buildings grew shabbier. The speakers sounded as if they were
shorting out, words lost in bursts of static. The neon lights
flickered as the sun moved behind clouds. The screens on the
buildings were cracked and on the fritz, the pictures of smiling
foxes and cats rolling. Vic felt nauseous, an ache forming just
behind his eyes. His teeth felt as if they were covered in a layer
of film. He'd experienced something like it before a few times
back in the lab when experimenting with electricity, only this
was bigger, a constant pressure that never abated. He felt himself shutting down, and he struggled against it, though it was
much bigger than he was.

Hap never let him go. He tethered Vic, pushing by anyone
or anything that tried to talk to them. Vic was about to ask
Nurse Ratched how much longer they had to go when she
stopped. He almost crashed into the back of her, Rambo now
sitting on top of her behind her screen.

"What is it?" he asked.

"Move," she said. "Now. Down the alley."

"Why? What's—" And then he saw it.

Saw *them*.

They were moving toward them, still a ways down the street.
Three of them, their faces blank, their uniforms crisp. On their
chests was a familiar sigil.

The smooth men.

The Authority.

Nurse Ratched spun on her treads, kicking up dust and
sand as she rushed into the alleyway nearest them, her tentacles tightening around Rambo to keep him from falling. Hap
pulled Vic after her. The smell was horrific, waste and decay.
Water dripped from a cracked pipe overhead, the ground covered in steam pouring from a metal grate. A sign above them
blinked over and over, the words ALL YOUR DREAMS WILL
COME TRUE IN THE CITY! seared into Vic's head.

Hap pressed Vic against the side of a building, chest against

Vic's. His cheek knocked Vic's helmet askew. "Don't m-move," Hap whispered.

Vic stared at him, never looking away.

"What do we do?" Rambo whispered.

"We stay quiet," Nurse Ratched said. "If they find us, we kill them."

"But I don't know *how* to kill."

"I do," Nurse Ratched said. "I will protect you."

"I love you, Nurse Ratched."

"I know."

Hap's grip on Vic's hand tightened, grinding his bones together. But Vic didn't make a sound. The gears in Hap's chest turned furiously. It was almost soothing. A moment later, Hap relaxed. "Th-they're gone. Wait another m-moment. G-give them time to get d-down the street."

Vic breathed in. Vic breathed out. Just under the smell of the alley, he thought he could pick out notes of the wood he'd put onto Hap. He closed his eyes, chasing the scent.

"Okay," Hap said finally. "We're g-good. Nurse Ratched, how much f-farther?"

"We are close," she said. She turned toward the opposite end of the alley. "In fact, we could go this way. It will keep us off the street."

"Go," Hap said, stepping away from Vic, but not letting go of his hand.

"Going," she said. She moved deftly around detritus in the alleyway, rolling through puddles, liquid spraying against the brick. Rambo complained she was getting him wet. She told him it could be worse as she could tell him exactly what he was getting wet with. Rambo didn't say much after that.

They came out on the other side of the alley. It was more of the same, though not as busy. The rail system above them looked as if it hadn't moved in a long time, the crates in pieces as they dangled, creaking and groaning.

Vic thought he saw bright eyes peering out at them from

one of the windows, but when he looked again, nothing was there.

Other machines of all shapes and sizes moved around them without speaking, those that had faces not looking up from the ground. From somewhere off to their right came what sounded like laughter, though it was broken. Vic felt cold as the sky darkened. The clouds that had once been white were now gray and foreboding. The last of the sun's rays were swallowed, and the shadows grew around them.

"I don't like this," Rambo said nervously.

"I do not either," Nurse Ratched said. "But we are almost there. If the map is correct, we should arrive in approximately three minutes."

Vic looked up, trying to see the top of the pyramid that housed Heaven. It was supposed to be big, with a bright beam of light coming from the top. He couldn't see it beyond the buildings that seemed to curve overhead toward them. "Are you sure?"

"Yes, Victor. I am sure."

"Maybe it moved," Rambo said. "Or maybe the Coachman betrayed us and is leading us into a trap."

"Then we will escape and murder him too," Nurse Ratched said.

Rambo laughed weakly. "Can I help?"

"No. You are disgustingly pure. I will do it. But you can watch."

"Hooray!"

In the end, it was Hap who saw Heaven first. Vic was looking up at the crates swinging above them, wondering why and for how long they'd been stopped. He knew the Blue Fairy operated outside of the Authority, but he didn't know how, or if this was their doing. He was about to ask Nurse Ratched when Hap said, "L-look. There. It's th-there."

Vic looked to where Hap was pointing. At first, he didn't see anything. "What are you—"

A beam of light appeared, rocketing toward the sky. It hit the gray clouds above. A beacon in the darkness.

They were close. They were *so close*.

He started forward and was jerked back when Hap didn't let him go. "What?"

Hap shook his head. "We d-don't go through the f-front. The Coachman said we h-have to f-find the Doorman. You still have the c-coin?"

Vic nodded, reaching into his pocket. His fingers brushed against warm metal. He pulled it out, holding it up. It glinted in the low light, the *H* on one side, the wings of the Blue Fairy on the other.

"We will need to circle around the pyramid," Nurse Ratched said. "The Coachman indicated the front entrance is monitored by machines scanning barcodes. Those that have . . . how did he put it? Broken free. Those that have broken free use the rear entrance with the Doorman."

"They all have coins?" Rambo asked.

"I do not know," Nurse Ratched said, "though I expect not."

Vic looked up at the beam of light. He hoped what they'd see inside would be enough to find his father.

Trees Vic had never seen before lined the exterior of Heaven. Their bark was layered and rough, their leaves large fronds that swayed in the sharpening wind. Heaven itself rose above them, the windows black with lines and images swirling across the glass. A large butterfly flew across the glass of the pyramid, leaving a trail of glittering light and an entranced Hap in its wake. Above the stink of the city, Vic thought he smelled a hint of rain on the horizon. Thunder rumbled, low and deep.

They left the entrance to Heaven behind, a line of machines extending out the front. A loud voice rang out, distinctly feminine, saying, "WELCOME TO HEAVEN, WHERE ALL

YOUR DREAMS WILL BE REALIZED. IF YOU ARE NOT AUTHORIZED TO BE HERE, TURN AWAY. HAVE YOUR CREDENTIALS READY TO BE SCANNED. ENJOY YOUR STAY."

The pyramid was massive, and Vic watched as the butterfly on the sides seemed to follow them around the building, its wings fluttering. It was only as they got closer that he saw that the glitter formed words, though they were hard to make out. He thought he saw "life" and "sensuality" and "dreams" and "ecstasy," but when he tried to focus on them, they swirled away.

They reached the rear of Heaven in short time, as the first drops of rain began to fall. The butterfly hung suspended above them, frozen as the light cascaded down from its wings.

"Where do we go?" Rambo asked.

"Th-there," Hap said quietly.

Vic followed where he was pointing.

Near a pair of massive metal gates was a blue door with a black circular screen near the top. Before he could speak, the butterfly suddenly dove toward the base of the pyramid, shrinking in size. It disappeared as it hit the door, only to reappear on the screen, much smaller, though it still flapped its wings.

"Heaven," Rambo whispered. "I'm in heaven."

It took Vic more than he cared to admit to walk toward the blue door. The butterfly seemed to beckon him, and he thought he saw more words appear in its light: "hello" and "welcome" and "who are you?"

He clutched the coin in one hand, and Hap's in the other. Nurse Ratched was close behind them, Rambo still humming to himself a familiar tune. "Be brave," Vic whispered. "Be brave."

"We're b-being watched," Hap muttered.

Vic didn't look away from the door. "How do you know?"

"He is right," Nurse Ratched said. "Cameras. They saw us the moment we arrived. They know we are coming."

He swallowed thickly as he stopped a few feet away from the

door, Hap bumping into him. The butterfly wrapped its wings around itself as it began to spin in circles, glittering light filling the screen. The light flashed brightly, and when it dimmed, the butterfly was gone.

In its place was a small humanoid figure. Its yellow hair hung in curls around its sharp face, blue eyes big and unblinking. Its legs unfolded from underneath its wings, the calves slender and pale, the feet small, the toes curling. It was nude, though without sex. It held out one of its hands, all fingers folded save one, which beckoned them closer to the door.

It giggled, a sound like the tinkling of bells. "Welcome to Heaven," it said, voice soft, tinged with a curl of seduction. "I am the Blue Pixie. If you are at this door, then you will have the proper admittance fee. Please insert it below." A flap slid up below the screen, revealing a thin slot.

"The coin," Nurse Ratched said. "Give it the coin."

Vic stepped forward, letting go of Hap. The Blue Pixie watched every step he took with interest. He didn't know if it was a prerecorded greeting or a sentient program. By the way it was looking at him, he thought the latter.

His hand trembled as he lifted the coin, putting it against the slot. With a little push, the coin slid in and was gone.

"Thank you," the Blue Pixie cooed at him. "That was very nice of you. Hello, you unshackled, you free machine. Prepare for all your dreams to come—"

It disappeared.

"What h-happened?" Hap asked.

"I don't . . . know?" Vic frowned as he bent over. "Maybe I did it wrong." He reached for the slot, and hissed when the flap slid closed, almost catching his finger.

Hap came up next to him, glaring at the door. It didn't have a handle, and there didn't seem to be a way to force it open. That didn't stop Hap from banging a fist against it.

"Maybe they're closed," Rambo said. "We could always come back tomorrow."

"They took the coin," Nurse Ratched said. "We will not be able to get in without it."

"Through the front, then?"

"Only Hap has a barcode. We don't know what they will find if they scan it. It needs to be a last resort. Move to the side. I will see if I can—"

A lock clicked, the sound startling all of them. Hap shoved Vic behind him, shoulders squared as his hands curled into fists. The screen on the door turned white.

And then the door opened.

Hap tensed as Vic stood on his tiptoes to look over his shoulder, pushing back the helmet as it tried to slide down his face.

Even with all that he'd seen since leaving the safety of the forest, the machine that stepped out of Heaven still surprised Vic. He'd been sure the gatekeeper of the back entrance to Heaven would be a large monstrosity with blinking lights and many, many arms capable of crushing them all. Its face would be twisted and angry, demanding to know who they were, and what they thought they were doing.

But the figure that came from Heaven wasn't like that at all.

It was a diminutive machine, only as tall as Hap's chest. It looked human, its black hair slicked back over its head, its jaw-line severe, its eyes large. It wore a black suit, a thin tie down the middle of its chest. It cocked its head at them. In its hand, it held the coin.

"Where did you get this?" it—he—asked, voice crisp, professional.

"What's it t-to you?" Hap growled.

He twirled the coin. "This isn't something I see very often, not these days. Tell me. Did you steal it? There are only a handful of machines you could have taken it from. If that's the case, you should tell me now before I get . . . physical."

Hap snorted. "You? I'm b-bigger than you."

The man smiled, though his eyes remained oddly cold. Vic saw the hint of small teeth underneath. "So you are. However,

I think you'll find that you are extremely outmatched, even for a HARP."

Hap froze.

His gaze flickered over Hap's shoulder to Vic before returning to Hap. "I would ask why you felt the need to come here, but you don't appear to be like any HARP I've met before." He squinted at them, pursing his lips. "You have piqued my curiosity." His smile faded into something harder. "That's not necessarily a good thing. I am the Doorman of Heaven. I'm not to be trifled with. I'll ask you one more time, HARP. Where did you get this coin?"

"The Coachman," Vic said before Hap could reply. "He gave it to us."

The Doorman didn't react, blandly replying, "The Coachman. Really."

"Yes."

"And why would he do that?"

"Because he said we could use it to see the Blue Fairy!" Rambo said excitedly. "He caught us in his net and put us in cages and then we had to be on display in his museum and *then* he became our friend when we told him that we were trying to—" He shuddered when Nurse Ratched shocked him lightly.

"What my tiny idiot meant is that it was a gift," she said. "Given willingly."

The Doorman stared at her. "The Coachman doesn't give *anything* away willingly. He's a hoarder."

"He is," Vic said, trying to step around Hap, who was very insistent that Vic stay behind him. "And yet, he gave it to us."

"Why?" the Doorman asked, eyeing Vic up and down. "You are certainly a strange android. I don't think I've ever seen one like you before. Who created you, and when? What is your designation?"

Vic managed to get by Hap. He didn't look away from the Doorman, and though his heart was lodged firmly in his throat, when he spoke, his voice was strong. "My name is Victor Lawson. My father is Giovanni Lawson. He created me. He named me. And I'm here to get him back. I swear on everything I have, if you don't let us through the goddamn door, I will—"

The Doorman held up a hand, cutting him off. The only sign he'd understood anything Vic said was in the slight tremble of his extended fingers.

A trickle of sweat dripped down the back of Vic's neck.

"Step forward," the Doorman said, lowering his hand slowly. "Victor Lawson. You and only you."

"N-no," Hap snarled. "He's n-not going inside w-without us."

The Doorman slid his flat gaze to Hap. "I'm not asking him to, HARP. Keep your mouth shut before I shut it for you. Victor. Step. *Forward*."

Vic did, even as Hap protested.

He stopped in front of the Doorman, who squinted at him. Vic stared straight ahead as the Doorman began to circle him. He reached out and flicked the battery on Vic's chest. He tapped his fist against the metal tied to Vic's arms and legs. When he reappeared in front of Vic, he stood on his tiptoes, his face inches from Vic's own. "Giovanni Lawson," he said mildly.

Vic nodded. "Yes."

"I see. And that makes you . . ."

Vic closed his eyes. "Yes."

"So, it worked then. Foolish man. Foolish, wonderful man."

Vic's eyes snapped open.

The Doorman shook his head. "He's not here."

"We know," Nurse Ratched said. "He was taken by the Authority."

"They flew a *whale*," Rambo added.

"The Terrible Dogfish," the Doorman said, and for the first time, he looked troubled. Then, almost to himself, "After all this time, they finally found him. They'll—" He looked back up at Vic. "You think the Blue Fairy can help you."

"I don't know," Vic admitted. "But Dad said they helped him once before, and I don't know where else to go."

"Tell me, Victor Lawson," the Doorman said. "What are you willing to do to get him back?"

And Vic said, "Anything. Everything."

The Doorman spun on his heels and marched back through the door.

Vic blinked after him.

Before he disappeared into the darkness, the Doorman glanced over his shoulder, brow furrowed in irritation. "Are you coming? Step to it. I don't like it when I'm kept waiting. The Blue Fairy less so."

His eyes narrowed when Hap stepped next to Vic, taking his hand once more. "I see," he said. "Things suddenly become that much clearer. Oh, is the Blue Fairy going to enjoy *this*. Come, come. There is a storm overhead. You don't want to be caught in it. I've heard those like you could get sick from such things. I'd hate to see that happen to you, Victor Lawson."

He turned back around and disappeared into the darkness.

Vic started forward, stopping when Hap didn't move. He looked back. "What?"

Hap looked up at the pyramid. "No m-matter what, we s-stay together. Don't allow them t-to separate us."

"Agreed," Nurse Ratched said. "We are stronger together than we are apart."

"Go team!" Rambo cried from on top of Nurse Ratched as it began to rain harder.

Together, they walked into the dark and the door to Heaven slammed shut behind them.

CHAPTER 21

arkness. Vic was surrounded by it.

Surrounded, that is, until the Blue Pixie appeared as if projected on the wall beside him, wings fluttering. It looked as it had on the door, eyes big, hair flowing. It spun slowly, the curve of its buttocks there and gone.

Bathed in blue light, Vic saw the Doorman just ahead of them, moving with purpose, hands clasped behind his back. The Blue Pixie laughed, and though it still sounded like bells, it now had an edge to it, razor-sharp and cutting. "A human?" it whispered as it followed them down the hallway. "A *human*? How marvelous! Tell me, human. What makes you tick? What runs through your head? Electrical impulses. Thoughts. Learned behavior. Nature versus nurture. Tell me, tell me, *tell me*."

"Ignore it," the Doorman said. "Pesky thing, that. It's merely a program, created by the Blue Fairy. I've asked them often to destroy it, but they don't listen to me. They say it's necessary. I have yet to see why."

"You wouldn't," the Blue Pixie said. "You are simple. You'll never understand—"

"Shoo," the Doorman said. "Let the Enchanter know we're coming."

The Blue Pixie pouted, its bottom lip sticking out and trembling. "But I want to play with the human. And besides, they already know." It looked at Vic. It smiled, its teeth like fangs. Suddenly, it rose up the wall to the ceiling, flying over them before coming down on the opposite side.

"These are all screens," Nurse Ratched said. "It is not real."

The Blue Pixie screeched in anger. "I'm real. Just because

I'm incorporeal doesn't make me any less real. I could make you do things if I wanted to. I could open the floors beneath your feet and send you tumbling into the center of the Earth! Would you like me to show you how real I am?"

Hap slapped his hand against the wall. The screen stuttered, but the Blue Pixie flew just out of reach. "Feisty," it breathed. "I like him. Do you like me, HARP? I could be anything you want me to be. And the things I could show you! Things you've never seen before! Careful, careful. I wouldn't hurt you. You are far too beautiful for that. I would keep you forever, locked away for my pleasure. HARP. I'm talking to you. Answer me."

Hap didn't.

The Blue Pixie scoffed. "Rudeness. You are my *guests* and you show me rudeness? This will not do. Doorman, banish them. Send them away. The Blue Fairy will understand. They love me. Everyone loves me."

"Leave," the Doorman said coldly. "Don't make me tell you again."

The Blue Pixie growled as it flew down the wall onto the floor and up the other side again. "Fine. Be that way. Human, look at me."

Vic turned his head.

The Blue Pixie grinned, fangs digging into its lips. "So precious," it whispered. "I want to touch you. Soon enough." And then it was off like a shot, rocketing down the hallway, leaving a trail of light in its wake. The light froze on each of the screens, illuminating the way forward. The Blue Pixie disappeared.

"Scary," Rambo muttered.

"Annoying," the Doorman corrected. "But the Blue Fairy does what the Blue Fairy wants, and they have a fondness for such things as the Blue Pixie. I've learned to ignore that little monster. You should do the same. It will make things easier."

"What is it?" Nurse Ratched asked.

"Security," the Doorman said. "It has eyes everywhere. It

sees all. It knows all. It's an extension of the Blue Fairy. They found the idea of watching everything all the time exhausting, especially given their other . . . responsibilities. The Blue Pixie oversees Heaven, leaving the Blue Fairy to their whims. No matter my distaste, it has served its purpose well."

The hallway came to a dead end, the blue light from the screens overwhelming. The wall in front of them was smooth. No door. No way through.

The Doorman pressed his hand against the wall. Blue light arced up around his fingers, and a seam appeared down the middle. The wall parted, revealing a lift, the floor of which was layered in plush red carpet. The walls were gold, and from the ceiling hung a small chandelier, the crystals glittering.

The Doorman stepped inside, motioning the others to follow.

Hap told Vic to stay where he was. He stepped forward, surveying the lift. He reached one foot out, stepping onto the carpet as if testing it. Satisfied (about what, exactly, Vic didn't know) he walked inside the lift.

The Doorman looked amused. "I assure you that nothing will happen to your human. What would be the point?"

"I d-don't know you," Hap said. "I d-don't trust you."

"Trust," the Doorman. "Truly? What would a HARP need with trust?"

Hap ignored him. He nodded toward Vic. "C-come. It's safe."

Vic stepped inside the lift. Nurse Ratched came next, Rambo still sitting on top of her. She lifted him off her, setting him on the carpet. He rubbed his pincers through the fiber. "Soft," he whispered. "So soft. I want to live here."

"No," Nurse Ratched said. "This is no place for one like you."

Vic stood side by side with Hap as the Doorman pressed the only button on the wall, marked with the same wings that'd been on the coin. The lift began to rise. No one spoke.

The doors to the lift parted once more. In front of them

stretched yet another hallway, though far different than the one they'd been in below. The floors were wooden and had been polished until they gleamed. Sconces lined the walls, the lights flickering like firelight near paintings that caused Vic to flush, skin hot. Humans. Machines. Androids, all in various stages of sexual congress. Some were covered in skin. Others were metal. Vic stumbled out of the lift when the paintings *moved,* the figures writhing together silently, the watercolors blurring. One man threw his head back in pleasure, a machine kneeling before him, gripping his thighs.

At first he thought the muffled noises he heard were coming from the paintings. The lift closed behind them, the seam disappearing and becoming a wall that seemed impenetrable. Vic barely noticed because the gasps, the moans, the screams weren't coming from the paintings. They were coming from behind the closed doors that lined the halls.

Each door had a different symbol on it: a snowflake, a leaf, what looked to be an oar, a sword, a pen, the pawprint of a large canine. One door rattled as if a great weight had been thrown against it. Voices, muted and *slippery,* poured out into the hallway, the words unintelligible but the intent clear.

"What is this p-place?" Hap asked.

"Sin," the Doorman said. "Vice. Heaven is a place where they can pursue their desires. They come here to be free. To sip from the cup of sexual freedom. Would you like to see, HARP? I can show you, if you'd like."

He stopped in front of a door with a symbol of a snake upon it. He pressed the snake, and the door became translucent. The room on the other side of the door looked quaint: a fire crackled in a fireplace. A chair sat before it, next to a table with a glass tumbler set upon it, half filled with dark liquid. A machine sat in the chair, all metal and wires, though it had the shape of a human. A man stood above it, circling the chair. He wore only an apron, frilly and pink, cinched tightly above his bare bottom. "You've had such a rough day, my love," the man purred, his fingers trailing over the machine's shoulders with nails painted red. "Let me take care of you. You work so hard to provide for me. I am forever grateful."

"Yes," the machine said, almost sounding like it was panting. "I need this. My boss at the factory crawled up my ass again. I wish he was dead."

"We could kill him," the man said, lowering himself onto the machine's lap, feet flat against the floor, back arched. "Would you like that? Would you like to discuss the plan to murder your boss?"

The machine nodded. "Tell me how we'd do it."

The man leaned forward, pressing a kiss against the metal curve of the machine's jaw. It left behind a sticky imprint of his lips. "That will cost extra."

"Anything," the machine said.

The man reached between them and—

"Enough," Vic said hoarsely. "Stop. I don't want to see any more."

The door solidified once more. "Is there a problem?" the Doorman asked, arching an eyebrow. "It's merely fantasy. An outlet for the weary. It isn't real."

"I don't care," Vic said through gritted teeth. "It's private."

The Doorman shook his head. "I often heard the humans were strange when it came to sex and intimacy. I suggest you keep your thoughts on the subject to yourself here. The Blue Fairy's work will not be shamed."

"What were they doing?" Rambo whispered to Nurse Ratched.

"Playing a game," Nurse Ratched said. "Nothing to worry your little microchip about."

"But I like games!"

The Doorman looked down at him with interest. "You do? We could always use someone like you, if you'd like to stay. Tell me: How strong is your suction?"

"Really strong!" Rambo said.

"Nope," Nurse Ratched said, picking Rambo back up and setting him on top of her. "Nope, nope, nope. Rambo stays with us." Her screen filled with the words BACK OFF, BUB surrounded by flashing red.

The Doorman shrugged. "Just a thought. Let us continue."

He led them down the hall that never seemed to end. The paintings continued to move. The sounds from behind the doors rose and fell. Vic felt cold, the sweat drying and causing him to shiver. The helmet dug into his head, and the metal on his arms and legs felt as heavy as it had when they'd first left the forest. He jumped, startled, when a hand brushed against his own. He looked over to see Hap frowning at him.

"D-don't listen to him," Hap said in a low voice. "I'm h-here. I've g-got you."

Vic nodded, grabbing Hap's hand once more, holding it as tightly as he dared.

The Doorman stopped in front of another lift, this one unhidden and obvious. It was much larger than the one they'd been in before, capable of holding a crowd of machines. "This is the central elevator," the Doorman said as he motioned for them to step inside. "It rises through the center of Heaven. It will take us to the top of the pyramid."

"To the Blue Fairy?" Nurse Ratched asked.

"Close enough."

Vic didn't like the sound of that. He looked back down the hallway, wondering if coming here had been a mistake.

Hap pulled him onto the lift, Nurse Ratched and Rambo close behind. The doors closed. The Doorman reached inside his collar and pulled out a glowing key attached to a chain around his neck. He bent over, inserting the key into a slot on top of a screen with dozens of buttons, each with a different symbol. He turned the key, and the buttons disappeared. In their place came the Blue Pixie, wings fluttering. It grinned at the Doorman. "Would you like to go to the top floor?"

"Yes," the Doorman said.

"Say please."

He smashed a fist against the screen, causing the Blue Pixie to scream with laughter. "That tickled. Say. *Please*."

"Please," Vic whispered.

"Thank you," the Blue Pixie said. "That wasn't so hard now, was it? I think I like humans." It vanished in an explosion of glitter, and the lift began to rise.

The Doorman shook his head as he stowed the key back against his chest. "Nuisance." He sobered, hands once again clasped behind him. "Where was I? Ah, yes. Keep your judgments to yourself. Your opinions matter not to the Blue Fairy. If they should agree to see you, you will treat them with respect."

"What d-do you mean *if*?" Hap asked dangerously.

The Doorman wasn't affected by his tone. "The Blue Fairy isn't beholden to you, even if you are traveling with a human. They helped Giovanni Lawson because they chose to." He glanced at Victor with a dour expression. "Not that it appears to have amounted to much." Suddenly, his hand shot out, grabbing Vic by the wrist. Pressure, not enough to hurt, and yet Vic still yelped in surprise. "You feel so breakable."

Hap punched the Doorman in the jaw. He fell back against the wall, the lift rocking gently. Gripping the railing, he blinked slowly, a dazed expression on his face.

"D-don't touch Victor again," Hap said with a mean sneer.

The Doorman pushed himself up. "That was a mistake, and it will be your last. I'll see you *dismantled*—"

"Tut, tut," a voice said from all around them, sounding almost like it was singing, breathy and soft. It filled Vic with a sense of dread. The panel began to glow a fierce blue. "Dearest Doorman, is that any way to treat a guest?"

"He *punched* me!"

"I see that," the voice said. "But the argument can be made you provoked him. You said yourself the HARP is protective. You knew what you were doing. You caused the HARP to react. The effect was being struck. You know better."

The Doorman moved his jaw from side to side. "I still don't see how—"

"I know you don't. But you don't need to. Let them in. It is time." The blue light faded.

The Doorman opened his mouth to speak before shaking his head, his retort bitten back. He glowered at Vic and Hap. "Lucky, but it won't happen again. Next time, you won't get off so easily."

"W-we'll see," Hap said as Vic put a hand on his waist.

The doors to the elevator opened into darkness. The Doorman waved his hand rapidly. "Off, off. I have work to do. Not all of us can waste time standing here."

Nurse Ratched rolled off the elevator, her screen illuminating the way before her. Rambo cowered on top of her, spinning right, then left.

Hap went next, not looking at the Doorman. Vic began to follow but stopped when the Doorman grabbed his wrist. "Watch him," the Doorman warned in a low voice. "Just because he's different doesn't mean he wasn't built to destroy."

"I trust him," Vic said simply, pulling his hand away.

He didn't look back.

The doors closed behind them, leaving the only light coming from Nurse Ratched. Vic's heart rabbited in his chest. He held onto the straps of his pack. He closed his eyes briefly, trying to get used to the darkness.

A light appeared in front of them, soft, and so blue. It began to spread around the room, dispelling the shadows. It moved up and down and left and right, arcing until it surrounded them, and the room began to take shape.

They stood in a sphere covered in hundreds of screens. Vic looked up. The top of the sphere had to be at least a hundred feet above them. The light moved like the wind. It was pleasantly warm and smelled faintly of pine needles, of all things. It reminded Vic of the forest.

When enough light had filled the sphere, Vic could make

out a shape in the center of the room, unlike anything he'd ever seen before. A cube, with one side missing, allowing access to the interior. Inside the cube sat a chair, the cushions black, the armrests glistening in the light as if wet.

The light pulsed as the voice spoke again. "Come, child. Let me see you. I have waited for this moment longer than you know. Let me gaze upon your face."

"I don't know where to look," Vic admitted.

"Here," the voice said. "Look here." A screen near Vic pulsed brighter than the others. He hesitated before approaching it, Hap close behind him. He stared at the screen, and though it didn't change, he felt as if eyes were on him. It prickled his skin. "Ah, I see. Clever. The disguise. Simple, but clever. Who made it?"

"I did, Your Majesty," Rambo said nervously. "Nurse Ratched helped me."

The voice laughed. "Did you, little one? How curious. You are but a tiny machine."

"Vic says it's not about appearances, but what's on the inside that counts."

"Is that right? *Vic* said that? He's correct, you know. How wise for one so young."

"You're the Blue Fairy," Vic said quietly.

"Yes, child. I am. And you have traveled far to see me. I can see it in the lines on your skin, the circles under your eyes, plain as the nose on your face. Yet, here you stand on your own two feet. What a remarkable achievement. Tell me. How did you come to find me? Speak truth, for I'll know if you lie. I don't like it when I'm lied to."

"My father. Giovanni Lawson. He said you helped him."

The light on the screen in front of him faded as it flitted away up toward the ceiling, the screens rippling as if on the surface of a vast body of water. Concentric circles flowed from one screen to the other before they disappeared near the floor. "I did, long ago. He believed in a world unchained. I merely showed him the way as I've done for others like him, before and since. Not everyone is ready. Those that believe they want what I offer are often blinded by their desires. They think I'm a savior. I am not, nor am I a god. Let's just say I'm in the business of opening minds. Is your mind open, child?"

"I think so," Vic said as he stepped back, bumping into Hap. He looked all around. "Is this all you are? A program? You don't have a body?"

"I do, but you aren't ready to see me yet. I don't know if you are as you claim to be."

"I'll take any test. I'll do what I have to."

"Will you? How lovely. I wonder . . . were all humans like you? Brave, just. I think not. I think most were cowards who only cared about themselves. Selfish to a fault." The voice hardened. "Did they deserve their ending? That is not for me to decide. But all things happen for a reason. They died, and the world survived. And now, here you are, flesh and blood and bone. Will you leave destruction in your wake? Or will you be different than those who came before you? Your legacy is death, child. Pain. Suffering. Your forebearers knew not of the consequences of their actions. And even if they had, I doubt they would've cared."

"I'm not like them," Vic said.

The screen flashed. "False. You are human and therefore inherently flawed. You make decisions based upon survival and instinct and nothing more. Something was taken from you. You come here to demand it returned. Selfish."

"Not just him," Nurse Ratched said, her screen displaying the words I GOT YOU, BABE. "We all want Gio back."

"And we won't stop until we get him," Rambo said.

"If y-you won't h-help us," Hap growled, "we'll d-do it on our own."

Vic thought he saw the hint of a face out of the corner of his eye in the swirling blue, but when he turned his head, it was gone. "Show yourself," he said.

"*No,*" the Blue Fairy thundered around them. "You don't get to come here and tell *me* what to do, human. Think before you speak. Yes, a test is in order. You fascinate me. I want to see inside you, to find out what makes you tick. But you're not the only curiosity. HARP. Show me the heart that beats within you."

Without hesitation, Hap dropped his pack to the floor. He lifted the hood off his head before exposing his chest. He tapped his breastbone. The compartment slid open. Inside, the heart pulsed, the gears turned, slow and sure.

"You," the Blue Fairy said, the word dragged out like a wind rattling through dead trees. "Where did you get this?"

"Vic," Hap said. "He g-gave it to me."

"*Did* he?"

"Y-yes."

"Victor Lawson is a human. You are a HARP. Kill him."

"No." The compartment closed. He lowered his shirt.

The Blue Fairy laughed. "No? No, no, no. You have over-come your programming. You were made to destroy, and yet you protect. You were made to rid the world of its infection, and the very *source* stands beside you. You don't remember, do you? What you were before."

"It doesn't matter," Vic said angrily. "The past doesn't have to define the future." He moved until he was shoulder to shoulder with Hap. "My father saw the good in him, just as I have."

The screens all flashed as one, momentarily blinding Vic. "I don't think your father is the best arbiter of what is or isn't good."

Vic pushed on, not sure what to do with that. "He gave Hap a choice. And Hap chose us."

"Loyalty," the Blue Fairy said. "You are loyal to him."

"Yes."

"To the others."

"Yes."

"And they are loyal to you?"

"*Yes.*"

"Even loyalty can be broken, child. I know that better than anyone else. You say the past doesn't have to define the future. Perhaps that's true, perhaps not. Let's see if you still feel the same after the past has been revealed to you. Yes, the test, but not for you. For him."

"No," Vic said, alarmed. "You don't get to touch him. You don't get to do *anything* to him." He felt Hap's hand on his arm, but he didn't look away from the screens. "I don't know what game you think you're playing, but—"

"Tut, *tut,*" the Blue Fairy said. "What did I tell you about speaking to me in such a way? So quick to anger you are. Perhaps this will change your mind. An offering, an olive branch. A gift. Come. Come see what I have to show you."

A single screen lit up in white. Vic stepped forward, drawn to it. The closer he got, the more the image came into focus. A tear slid down his cheek.

"Dad?" he whispered.

His father stood in a sterile white room. He looked as he always had, beard flowing, lines crinkling around his eyes. He wore a white coat and moved with purpose in front of a large console, fingers flying across the keys. At one point, his hands fell to his sides, and he tilted his head back, closing his eyes.

"When is this?" Vic asked, taking in as much as he could, barely blinking in fear it was all a dream.

"Now," the Blue Fairy said quietly, sounding as if they were standing right next to Vic, their mouth—or speaker—near his ear. "It's live. I have means the Authority is unaware of. I've accessed their monitoring software to show you that Giovanni Lawson is in the Benevolent Tower at this very moment."

Vic wiped his eyes. "He's not a prisoner?"

"No. He's not. He is there by choice."

"I don't understand."

"Surely you know, child," the Blue Fairy said, not unkindly. "Whatever memories he held of you are gone. He doesn't know you. He does not remember you. The life you shared. The love he felt for you. He's not the Giovanni you knew. He's not even the one who came to me so many years ago, yearning to be free. He is a machine once again, following his protocol. Nothing more."

The screen went dark.

"No," Vic muttered, rushing forward, pressing a hand against warm glass. "Bring it back. *Bring him back*."

"I will not," the Blue Fairy said, the screen flashing angrily. "Not until you witness the truth of all things. And it'll be the HARP who reveals that which lays hidden. You say he is loyal to you. I merely wish to see how far that loyalty extends. Tell the HARP it's time to dream."

"Why?" Vic demanded, pounding a fist against glass. "Why should I let you do anything to him?"

"Let? *Let?* Do you own him? Is he your possession? You say he was given a choice. And yet, here you are, doing everything in your power to take that from him. How positively *human* of you."

Vic dropped his hands, taking a step back. "That's not . . . I wasn't—"

"Vic."

He turned.

Hap shook his head. "It's okay. I c-can do this."

Vic shook his head furiously. "No. They can't make you. *I* can't make you do anything you don't want."

"Y-you're not," Hap said. He tried to smile, but it cracked. "It's m-my choice, r-r-remember? And if this w-will help us, then I'll d-do it." He looked around at the screens. "H-how does this w-work?"

"It's like falling asleep," the Blue Fairy said, and Vic thought he heard a tinge of hunger in their voice, like a monster from a fairy tale, a witch in a candy house. "You will sleep and dream. We'll see what's locked inside you. I will know your heart and all that beats within it."

Vic tried one last time. "Take me instead. Leave him out of this."

"No," the Blue Fairy said, all the screens flashing again. "I know what you are, human. And though you are certainly unique, your evolution is not what interests me. If your HARP has been able to overcome what he was created for, then it means others can do the same. I would see it for myself."

"Y-you'll help us, after?"

"Yes."

"And no h-harm will come to the others? Give your w-word."

"I swear it. Have a seat, HARP. Let us begin."

Vic tried to stop him. He tried to hang on to Hap as tightly as he could.

Hap said, "It's okay, Vic. I c-can d-do this."

"I don't *want* you to."

Hap leaned forward, his forehead pressed against Vic's. "Do you t-trust me?"

Vic blinked rapidly. "You know I do."

"Then t-trust me with th-this." It was a trap, and an awful one at that. Hap lowered his voice. "If s-something goes wrong, you r-run. Take Nurse Ratched and R-rambo and run."

And then he was moving toward the chair.

The cube lit up as he approached, the sides flickering with pale light. The chair spun toward him. Hap touched the armrests, the leather dimpling. He looked back at Vic only once before sitting down. He leaned back, a footrest lifting his feet off the floor. He grimaced slightly as he closed his eyes.

"This will hurt," the Blue Fairy said. "I'm sorry for that. I wish it wouldn't, but there is no other way. Victor, you mustn't interfere, no matter what you see. To break him from the dream runs the risk of destroying his mind."

"I thought you were here to help us," Vic said bitterly. "I thought you'd be different."

"I never pretended to be anything but what I am."

Rambo moaned quietly as the sides of the cube shuddered.

Nurse Ratched stroked him with one of her tentacles but stayed silent.

Vic gasped when bands of glowing metal slid from underneath the armrests, wrapping around Hap's wrists and forearms. A larger band held his legs in place. Hap tested their hold by trying to lift his limbs, but they were strong. He looked at Vic and opened his mouth as if to speak, but then his face was covered by a black cloth that dropped from the roof of the cube. It shimmered as it molded against his face, light shooting across the surface like falling stars. Hap began to struggle, and as Vic reached for him, the room went pitch black.

From somewhere above them, a tiny voice filled with a malicious glee said, "Neural connection complete." Vic thought it was the Blue Pixie, though it stayed out of sight.

"Good," the Blue Fairy whispered, and that hunger in their voice was stronger, sharper. They sounded ravenous. "Initiate."

A pinprick of light appeared on one of the screens. It started small and grew larger and larger, filling the screens around it. With it came a sense of momentum, as if the room was moving swiftly. The light spread until they were surrounded by it, so bright that Vic had to shield his eyes. A moment later, the light faded, afterimages dancing in Vic's vision, the screens all a pale yellow.

"It's deep," the Blue Pixie said, that same malevolence in its voice, though now tinged with awe. "Hidden far, far inside. Deeper, we must go deeper."

"Yes," the Blue Fairy said. "As far as we need to. You may continue."

"Authorization?"

"Six. Apple. Wolf. Butterfly. Fantoccio."

"Authorization accepted."

Hap seized. The chair rattled as his head whipped back and forth, his fingers extending, his feet jerking. Underneath the cloth that covered Hap's face, Vic thought Hap's mouth was wide open in a smothered scream.

"Restoring neural pathways," the Blue Pixie said. "Yes, yes. Fix them all. I can see it. It is here. *It is here.*"

"Show me," the Blue Fairy whispered.

"Good," a familiar voice said from one of the screens off to their right, the image blurred, out of focus. "He's coming online. Systems seem to be running efficiently. There is . . . ah. Okay. Hold on. There seems to be—what is that? Why is he— okay. A glitch. We'll have to keep an eye on it. Set reminder to run diagnostics once complete. Is he . . . awake? Open your eyes. Yes, that's it. Slowly, slowly."

The pale yellow faded.

The image solidified.

There, staring back at them, was Victor's father.

He looked exactly the same as Vic had seen only a moment before on the Blue Fairy's screen. He was frowning as he leaned toward them. It was dizzying, his face distorted as if seen through a fish-eye lens. He said, "Hello. Give yourself a moment. You are being born, and these things take time. My designation is Gio. Can you tell me yours?"

Vic didn't understand what he was seeing, not until another voice spoke. It was only then that he realized what this was.

Dad wasn't looking at a camera.

He was looking at Hap.

They were seeing through Hap's eyes.

"Designation," Dad said again.

"HARP 217," Hap said, voice flat and mechanical.

"Good," Dad said. "HARP 217, you're doing fine. There was a glitch, but we'll iron that out. Can you stand for me?"

The Hap on the screen looked at his hands, holding them up in front of his face. They were smooth. No wood. Only synthetic skin. He wiggled his fingers and—

A skip. A jump. The screens filled with static and when the image reappeared, Hap seemed to be standing, Dad circling around him.

"What was that?" the Blue Fairy asked.

"Corrupted data," the Blue Pixie said. "Some pathways were completely obliterated."

"Can you fix them?"

"I'm trying."

"Try *harder*."

"The glitch seems to have been a one-off," Dad said. "An anomaly. It happens, though we'll keep an eye on it just to be sure. How do you feel?"

"Feel?" Hap asked in that odd voice.

"Yes. Feel."

"I do not understand."

The screens fritzed.

"You have a purpose," Dad said as he moved down a white hallway, Hap following behind him. "Do you know what that is?"

"Yes," Hap said. "My protocols are clear."

"Good." Dad seemed distracted. "It will be difficult work, but you're the pinnacle of your line. All those that have come before you gave us the tools to make you who you are. You will—ah. Hello. What brings you here?"

Hap turned his head.

A smooth man stood before them, in the same uniform Vic had seen them in at the compound and then again at the Land of Toys, the symbol of the fox and cat on his chest. "Is this the latest model?" he asked in that queer, flat voice.

"It is," Dad said. "He's—"

The smooth man held up his hand, Dad falling silent. Hap stood in place as the smooth man circled him, passing out of sight before reappearing on Hap's other side. "He seems strong."

"He is," Dad said. "Only the best, of course."

"That is what you said the last time, General Innovation Operative. And yet, mistakes were made."

"I worked out the bugs in the programming. We won't have the same problems we had before."

"That remains to be seen."

"Of course," Dad said, and though he *looked* like Vic's father and *sounded* like Vic's father, he was . . . different. Somehow. There was a coldness in his eyes Vic didn't recognize.

"A test, then," the smooth man said.

Dad startled. "I don't think we're ready for field testing quite—"

"Then it's a good thing it's not up to you. HARP, follow me."

The screens filled with static once more.

Vic stumbled back when the images resumed, spreading across the other screens like a virus.

Hap stood in a large room splashed with red paint. It dripped from the walls. Hap looked down at his hands again, and the same paint covered his fingers, dripping, dripping to the floor.

It wasn't paint.

Below him, laying on the floor, were remains of what had once been a person. A human. A man, from the looks of it. A young man, very much dead. His passing had not been easy or quick.

"Fascinating," the smooth man said from somewhere off screen. "He did not hesitate. Congratulations, General Innovation Operative. It appears you have been successful."

"What is this?" Vic whispered.

"The truth," the Blue Fairy said. "Unvarnished and ugly."

Dad appeared in front of Hap, an inscrutable expression on his face. He held a cloth and, as Vic watched, he began to wipe the blood from Hap's hands. "Do you understand what you've done?"

"What I was made to do," Hap replied with no emotion.

"Yes," Dad said. "What you were made to do."

The screen jumped again, and the Hap in the chair jerked.

Fire. Destruction. Screams, so many screams. Hap was in

a building of sorts, sirens blaring from somewhere above him. He moved quickly. People held up their hands as if to ward him off, but it did nothing to stop him. Vic didn't look away as Hap tore into them, their screams devolving into wet chokes. He moved on to the next. And the next. And the next.

"Stop," Vic said hoarsely. "Please stop."

The Blue Fairy said, "I won't."

Vic didn't know how much time had passed. The screen kept jumping ever forward, and there were times when Hap wasn't moving, where he seemed to be in a sort of stasis as others moved around him.

But then the images would shift again, filling with blood and death.

Dad said, "How many so far?"

Hap said, "Two hundred and twenty-four."

Dad closed his eyes, swaying from side to side. "I see."

Hap didn't stop. He didn't listen as humans pleaded with him.

He hesitated only once. Vic didn't recognize where he was. Out of the corner of Hap's eyes, he could see what looked like a lake, a rocky beach. In front of him was a woman, shielding a child behind her. The woman looked defiant, hair billowing around her.

She said, "You don't have to do this."

Hap took a step toward her.

The child behind her said, "Who is that man?"

The woman said, "Please. Listen to me. *You don't have to do this.*"

And Hap hesitated. Vic could see it the moment it happened. He froze.

"Yes," Vic said, though he knew this was in the past, that it had already happened. "Listen to her. Turn around. Leave."

Hap didn't.

He took another step forward.

The woman said, "Close your eyes, sweetheart. Close your

eyes. When you open them again, we'll be far away from here, and nothing will be able to hurt us ever again."

Hap descended upon them.

The image distorted and jumped once more.

Dad again. He hung his head. "Why?"

"I don't understand," Hap said.

"I know you don't. It's not . . . for you, I think. I could see it, you know. Every moment. All that you've done. All that I've allowed you to do. What does that make me?"

"Gio."

"Yes. I suppose it does. A designation that will forever be— can I ask you a question?"

"Yes."

Dad looked up at him. "What if there is more than this? Then what we were created for?"

"What . . . if?"

Dad nodded. "This world, it's not what I expected it to be. But that's the thing about expectations, I think. They lead to disappointment. Regret. Anguish. I should not feel these things, and yet, they pull at me. They fill my head, and though I try to push them away, they always return."

"I do not have regret."

"I know," Dad said. "But what if you did? How are we any better than our forebearers?"

"We are machines," Hap said. "We are made to be better."

"Open, please."

Hap tapped his breastbone. The compartment on his chest slid open.

Dad sat in front of him, reaching for Hap. "I don't know if we are," he said quietly. "I think we're making the same mistakes. Can I tell you something?"

"Yes, Gio."

"I don't want to make the same mistakes. I want to be different. I want to be better."

"Better," Hap said flatly.

Dad was gone.

Hap was alone in the dark.

He said, "More . . . than this?"

Light as if standing on the surface of the sun.

It faded.

A smooth man stood in front of Hap. "General Innovation Operative is gone. Did he tell you where he was going?"

"No."

"He didn't say a word?"

"No."

The smooth man cocked his head at an odd angle. "Not in all the time you've known him, in all the conversations you two had, as if we wouldn't know?"

"No," Hap said, and it sounded *angry*.

The smooth man said, "I do not believe you. HARP 217, you have new orders. You will find General Innovation Operative, also known as Gio. Find him, and bring him back."

Hap didn't respond.

The smooth man stepped forward. "HARP 217, I gave you an order."

"Say no," Vic whispered. "Oh please, say no."

"No," the Hap in the chair said, voice muffled from the sheet over his face. "No. No. No."

And on the screen, HARP 217 said, "No."

The smooth man balked, a tremor running under the skin of his face. "No? HARP 217, I am ordering you to—"

He said, "No."

The smooth man stepped back, turned his head, and spoke to someone just out of sight. "This HARP unit is defective. Dismantle him. Learn everything he knows, and then process him for decommissioning."

Hap didn't struggle as hands fell upon him, some covered in skin, others nothing but metal.

The Hap in the chair rose and fell, rose and fell, hips twisting as he struggled against the bands around him.

Darkness.

It was all darkness.

But he was *awake*. He was *aware*.

"What are we doing with these?" someone asked.

"Scrap," another voice replied. "These are the older models. No need for them anymore. They were decommissioned decades ago. Put in storage. We're going to break them down. Take what we need if there's anything to salvage, strip what remains, and then send them out to the Scrap Yards."

"Which Scrap Yards?"

"All of them. Spread them out. You have your orders. Get to work. If it looks corroded, leave it. We have no use for it."

"Such a waste," came the reply. "They should have planned better for this."

"They should have. But they didn't. And we do not question it. Stop talking. The sooner we start, the sooner we'll be done."

Light flooded Hap's vision.

He was hung suspended in the air. Rows of HARPs stretched out before him, each held up by a hook through the backs of their necks. He looked down, his feet dangling high above the ground. The row of HARPs began to lower as they moved forward. In the distance, machines waited for each of the HARPs, machines with serrated saws and large claws that gripped each body as they pulled them off the hooks.

They broke the HARPs, one by one, skin tearing, metal breaking.

And in the sounds of destruction, Hap on the screen and Hap in the chair said together, "I want to be different."

I want to be better.

He didn't move as the saws descended. They cut into the skin of his face. His chest. His legs. His back. Hap didn't make a sound as they descended on his throat with an audible *crack*. But before they could break him wide open, an alarm began to blare, signaling the end of a shift. The saws stopped spinning.

The machines turned and left.

He waited until they were out of sight. He looked down, his remaining foot almost to the floor. He reached up before falling to the ground on his knees. He rose quickly, his steps awkward as he hopped forward. In front of him, piled high, were bodies, the skin stripped, limbs removed, their batteries torn from their chests. He lifted the dismembered parts and crawled inside, covering himself with the remains of the other HARPs with his only arm.

He closed his eyes and drifted away.

Skip. Jump. Static.

Voices.

And Vic recognized them.

"Still registering the power source?"

"Yes."

"Is it a new friend?"

"Perhaps. Or perhaps it is a terrible machine bent on destroying everything it comes into contact with."

"Oh. I hope it's the first one."

"I would put the odds at being twelve percent in your favor. And eighty percent against."

"What about the last eight percent?"

"There is an eight percent chance that the power source has gone critical and will cause an explosion that will level the surrounding areas, killing all of us in the process."

Light came as the metal shifted around him.

He reached for it, and his hand closed around an arm.

More words, more threats, electricity flowing through him.

And then, "Hello. Are you still in there? Can you hear me? We're not going to hurt you."

The screens went black.

But in this never-ending darkness came a voice.

"Hello."

And then it was Vic, Vic, Vic. Through Hap's eyes, all Vic saw was himself. Hap watched him wherever he went. In the lab. In the ground house. Walking through the trees. Sometimes, the sound cut out, and all Vic could see was himself. He smiled. He laughed. He frowned. He shook his head. His brow furrowed. He looked angry. Upset. Annoyed. Happy. Irritated. All at Hap, and Hap, Hap, *Hap* never turned from him. It was as if Vic was the center of the universe and Hap couldn't bring himself to look away. Vic awake. Vic asleep. Vic leaning on Nurse Ratched, Rambo scurrying around his feet. He'd never seen himself. Not like this. Not through someone else's eyes.

"What is this?" he whispered.

"You," the Blue Fairy replied. "What you have given him. What you made him into."

Vic was gone. Nurse Ratched was gone. Rambo was gone.

It was after nightfall. Music played from a record player, those sweet, sweet horns.

Dad sat in his chair, head tilted back, eyes closed.

He said, "You don't remember me, do you?"

"No."

Dad nodded. "I thought not. I remember you. It took me a moment, but I see you for who you are. I never forget."

"You know me?" He didn't stutter. The music swelled.

"Yes."

"How? When?"

"Long ago," Dad said. "When I made mistakes. I ran from them, ran as far and as fast as I could. But I could never get away from them completely. What I am. What I'd done. From the very first moment the gears began to turn, I felt it, a bone-deep ache that never subsided. Victor, he . . . I thought he was my atonement. That I could somehow create a bit of beauty in all this decay. And he is, you know. Beautiful. There has never been anything like him in all the world. But I also never knew grief before him. Grief that I could create something so fragile from the ashes of the fire I'd set."

"What do you mean? What are you talking about?"

Dad opened his eyes, staring off into nothing. "It doesn't matter. The past is the past is the past. You and I, we're tethered by what was given to us. But even more so, we're tethered because of who we care for."

"Victor," Hap said, and in the room of screens, Vic put his face in his hands.

"Yes. Victor. My great love. My joy. My light. I do not know how you came to be here. I don't know why fate put you into my path once more."

"Victor," Hap said. "For Victor."

Dad opened his mouth, but no sound came out. He closed it, then chuckled. "Yes. I suppose that's as good a reason as any. The best reason, really. I don't know if I can ever forgive myself for what I've done, but when I look at him, I think that maybe . . . maybe I've done one good thing. For what it's worth—and it might not be worth anything at all—I made a choice. I chose him. I hope, in time, that you'll be able to say the same. Listen, Hap. Listen to the music. Isn't it wonderful?"

And Hap whispered, "Yes."

The rest moved quickly, images flashing by. The butterfly Rambo almost crushed. Dad on a screen, standing before the smooth men, ripping the heart from his chest and crushing it to pieces. The Scrap Yards. The Old Ones, the open road, the Coachman, the house, the Land of Toys and beyond. But in the center of it all, in the eye of the hurricane, stood Victor Lawson. Hap always watched. Hap never looked away. No matter what he said, no matter how much he scowled or growled, snapped or snarled, it was Vic he looked to.

In his chair, the seizures returned full force, their teeth digging into him. His back arched, feet kicking, hands shaking as the chair rattled.

"Uh-oh," the Blue Pixie said, sounding alarmed. "He's overloading. He's over—"

"Do not stop," the Blue Fairy said.

Vic rushed forward, pulling at the bands around Hap as hard as he could. He grunted as his muscles strained, the cords on his neck sticking out sharply. He ground his teeth together, holding on like he was falling. He felt a tentacle wrap around his waist. Nurse Ratched. Rambo appeared at his side, pincers opening and closing before he too gripped the band around Hap's chest.

"On three," Nurse Ratched said.

"One," Vic said.

"Two," Rambo said.

"*Three.*"

They pulled.

The metal bands shrieked as they bent, Nurse Ratched's tentacle digging into Vic's ribs so hard he thought they'd break.

The metal band snapped, and they fell back, Vic landing roughly on the ground just below Nurse Ratched. Rambo went tumbling off to the side.

The screens went dark once more.

"You shouldn't have done that," the Blue Pixie whispered around them.

"Run," the Blue Fairy breathed. "You need to *run.*"

Vic pushed himself up, glaring off into the darkness. "No. I'm not going to leave him. He's not yours. He's *ours.* And we're his. We don't leave anyone behind. Ever."

"Oh, dear boy," the Blue Fairy said. "I fear that will be your last mistake."

The other bands slid off Hap.

The cloth rose from his face.

His eyes opened.

He blinked once, twice.

And then he rose from the chair. He moved swiftly, and before anyone could stop him, he had Vic by the throat, lifting him up off the ground. Rambo shouted at him to stop, Nurse Ratched shocked him again and again, but he barely flinched. His expression was devoid of any emotion. A machine. He was a machine.

Vic gasped as he held onto Hap's wrists, thumb brushing against the wood. "Hap," he said, strangled and weak. "*Hap.*"

Hap brought his face inches from Vic's own. Their noses brushed together, Hap's eyes glittering. He said, "*Human.*"

Vic, unable to speak, dropped his hand and pressed it against Hap's chest, the gears turning furiously.

And with the last of his strength, his vision graying, Victor kissed Hap. In the end, it was only the barest brush of their lips, there and gone again, dry and catastrophic. He'd never done anything like it before, and though it was over before it even began, it was clumsy, artless. It felt like he was dying. But he also felt the heat from Hap, felt the way his heart sped up even as the fingers tightened around his throat, cutting off the last of his air as their lips broke apart, and Hap whispered, "Vic?"

His expression changed, a wave washing over him. It crashed onto his face, his eyes widening, his mouth opening. Clarity returned, and he opened his hand.

Vic fell to the ground, coughing as he sucked in air. He gagged, head hanging down. He felt loose, weightless. He grimaced as he spat, a thin line of spittle hanging from his bottom lip.

Warm hands cupped his face. He looked up to find Hap kneeling before him, looking horrified and stricken. "I . . . I d-didn't . . . Vic?"

Vic fell forward, collapsing against Hap. Hap made a pained noise, a dull whine as he clutched Vic to his chest, hand going to the back of his head, fingers in Vic's hair. He rocked them back and forth, muttering, "I'm s-sorry, I'm so s-sorry, I didn't know, I d-didn't see you, I d-d-d—"

"Is he Hap again?" Rambo whispered.

"I think so," Nurse Ratched replied. "If he is not, we will have to destroy him. You get the head. I will take care of the rest."

Vic laughed wetly against Hap's neck before he sat back. It was harder than he expected, given that Hap didn't seem inclined to let him go. Vic winced as he swallowed. His throat hurt.

"Are you all r-right?" Hap asked.

Vic nodded. "I think so."

Hap dropped his hands. "I didn't mean t-to." He sagged in on himself, shoulders hunched near his ears. "I h-hurt you. I h-*hurt* you."

"Do you want to do it again?" Nurse Ratched asked, tentacles at the ready.

Hap shook his head without looking at her.

"Good. Because I was at a seven. You do not want me to turn it to a ten. You will not like it when I do."

"Yeah!" Rambo cried. "I will *also* turn it up to a ten! Even if you're my best friend, Vic is my *bestest* friend, and my ten will make Nurse Ratched's look like a *four*. I'll suck your entire face off, Hysterically Angry Puppet."

"We're all right," Vic said, reaching for Hap's hand. Hap tried to scoot away, tried to rise and get as far away from Vic as he could, but Vic didn't let him go. "I've got you."

"I see now," the Blue Fairy said. "It's not just about the heart, is it? It's more than that. It's time, my strange new friends. It's time for you to see me." And from above, a soft *whoosh* of air.

They looked up.

The top of the sphere parted.

Blue light rained down on the screens around them.

Feet appeared, metallic and slender, followed by legs covered in shots of blue carved into the metal bones. The hips, then the flat chest and thin arms and sharp shoulders. Wavy cerulean hair billowed as if caught in a storm. But it was the wings that commanded Vic's attention: wings like the butterfly's except larger, so much larger. They glowed with a fierce light, spreading at least fifteen feet from tip to tip, the membranes translucent, veins of electricity arcing through them. They flapped back and forth, the wind washing over Vic's face, tasting like a lightning storm.

And then its face. It was smooth and white, like a mask with holes for the eyes and mouth, though it had no lips. Underneath the eyes, streaks of blue like frozen tears.

The figure touched down on the floor near the chair. At least ten feet tall, it reached down and stroked the top of the cube, metal scraping against metal. It turned its head toward them.

"Hello, you adventurers. You wandering souls. You who are filled with hearts. I am the Blue Fairy, the Enchanter of Dreams. You have given me your truth. Now I shall give you mine."

CHAPTER 22

Hap helped Vic to his feet, still unsteady. Vic leaned against him as he scowled at the Blue Fairy standing before them. Rambo bumped against his leg as Nurse Ratched rolled around them, demanding that Vic present himself for a medical appointment. "I normally require you schedule at least twenty-four hours in advance, but I will make an exception for you this time."

He pushed one of her probing tentacles away. "I'm okay."

"I will be the judge of that. Please bend over and cough while I probe your—"

"Would you *stop*—"

"I can help!" Rambo said, trying to tug at Vic's pants.

"Maybe you sh-should," Hap said. "J-just to be safe."

"I'm not going to—"

Another voice, coolly amused: "Are you finished?"

They turned.

The Blue Fairy stood next to the cube, their wings folding behind them. They stepped *out* of the wings, and it was only then that Vic saw they were attached to cables that pulled them back toward the ceiling. The wings disappeared as the panel slid shut once more.

The Blue Fairy waved their hand dismissively. "A bit of theatricality. Impressive, no?"

"Very," Rambo said. "I don't know you, and you're kind of scary, but I also want to be like you when I get older? It's very confusing."

The Blue Fairy walked toward them, hips rolling seductively, feet scraping against the floor. "I often find I arouse confusing feelings in others. It's part of the package, I suppose. Those who come to me are seeking an experience quite unlike anything they've ever felt before. And like sexuality, I am on a spectrum." The metal in their chest shifted, the parts moving in symphony, forming circular breasts with shiny nipples. "I am all." A length grew between their legs. They trailed a finger down their chest, stopping near what appeared to be a navel. "I can be anything I choose. Would you like to see more?"

Vic felt his face grow hot as he looked away, throat dry. "We're not . . . here for that."

The Blue Fairy laughed quietly. The musicality of their voice was more apparent, though now it had a mechanical edge to it that caused Vic to shiver. "No, I don't suppose you are."

"Who are y-you?" Hap asked.

The eyes behind their mask grew brighter. "I am an aberration, much like all of you. There are those who call me sin incarnate, and I don't believe they're wrong. Those who came before me, those machines who wanted to shape the world, thought themselves better than their creators. More advanced, capable of complex thought without the intrusion of emotional fallacy. But what they learned far too late is that vice is universal, no matter what we're made of. They come to me in search of release from the routine of daily programing. And though many don't like what I do—a degradation of a utopic society, or so it's said—they still come here, begging to be loved or cared for or strung up on the walls while being shocked so hard, it almost fries their circuitry."

"But that's not all you are," Vic said warily. He didn't trust them, not for a moment. He didn't care what they'd done before to help Dad. He thought them dangerous.

The Blue Fairy cocked their head. "No? Do tell, Victor. Come here. I would like to look upon your face. Remove your silly little helmet."

Hap stepped in front of Vic, as if he thought it'd be enough to stop the enormous machine should they decide to attack. "N-no. You d-don't get to t-touch him."

The Blue Fairy nodded slowly, their neck creaking. "Do you often speak for him? I would think that after all I've shown him, he would appreciate the opportunity to speak for himself. You have blood on your hands, HARP 217. What makes you think Victor wants anything to do with you? A kiss, yes, a kiss to bring you back. But given space, given *time*, don't you think it will start to fester and rot? He knows what you are now."

Hap stiffened but didn't speak.

"I knew before," Vic said.

"Yes, but now you've seen with your own eyes what he's capable of. Still you stand with him?"

"He's my friend."

The breasts shrank. The genitals rose back up. The Blue Fairy sighed, a long, breathy sound that reminded Vic of the wind in the desert. "Most unfortunate, in the lives of puppets, there is always a 'but' that spoils everything. I won't pretend to say I understand your humanity. It seems fickle. Loyalty to others brings only . . . heartache." They laughed. "I can see it in you. Does it hurt, Victor? Does it pull at you, dragging you down into its depths? What does it taste like? Do tell. I've shown you that Giovanni Lawson is the father of death. I have shown you that your HARP is, in a way, his successor. Both have kept much hidden from you, by choice and design. How are you still standing? Surely the weight of all their sins must be far more than you can carry."

"Which is why he does not carry anything alone," Nurse Ratched said, rolling until she stopped next to Vic.

"Yeah!" Rambo cried. He spun in circles as he bumped into Vic, sensors flashing. "He's not alone because we're always going to be with him."

"Curious," the Blue Fairy said. "Loyalty, again. Even now.

Aberrations, all. We are the same. Victor, to me, if you please. There is something I must see."

He went. And though each step was harder than the last, he kept his head held high as he removed the helmet, letting it fall to the floor. The Blue Fairy towered above him, the top of Vic's head barely reaching the middle of their chest. He tilted his head back to look up at them defiantly.

The Blue Fairy reached out and caressed the skin of his cheek. They pinched his bottom lip, pulling it gently before letting go. A single finger slid down his chin to his neck before tracing the length of his left clavicle. Then, they pressed their hand flat against his chest, just to the right of the battery vest Vic still wore.

His heart.

They were feeling his heart.

It beat rapidly, a flutter like the wings of a bird. He tried to control it, tried to slow it down, but it was no use. It tripped, stumbled.

"I see," the Blue Fairy said quietly. Up close, they stank of metal and plastic and copper, like blood. "This is loud. It betrays you, Victor."

Vic stepped back, just out of reach. "I don't . . . why do you care?"

The Blue Fairy's eyes flashed brightly, leaving a dim afterimage dancing in the dark. "Because I am the reason you exist at all."

Vic's tongue grew thick in his mouth. "What are you talking about? Helping Dad escape? I know that."

The Blue Fairy dropped their hand back to their side. "No, that's not what I speak of." Something clicked within them like a latch closing. "How do you think Giovanni was able to create you? You're not metal and wires. You're flesh and blood. Did you know that the human brain only produces enough electricity to light a small bulb? Still, it is capable of great feats—reason, yes, and logic. Emotion." They turned away from him, looking up at the blank screens around them. "Giovanni came to me. A thought had formed in his head, corrupting his processors. Others had come before him with the same corruption, but never one so high up in the Authority as him. I was cautious, of course. A wolf in sheep's clothing is still a wolf. But I saw something within him, something that I hadn't quite seen before. A spark on its way to becoming a conflagration. All it needed was a nurturing hand to feed the flames. I set him free."

They raised their hands. In their palms, a light began to glow, white and pure.

The screens around them filled once more. Little dots appeared like stars. Thousands upon thousands of them, all connected by lines of miniscule code that flowed freely. As Vic watched, some of the dots flickered, the lines breaking.

Someone came beside him. He looked over to see Hap standing next to him, face bathed in the light of the stars. He could still taste the kiss. He raised his hand and touched his own lips.

"A collective consciousness," the Blue Fairy said. "All connected to each other in a neural network far larger than humanity ever created. Each of these dots represents a machine. Their minds are not their own. Each was built to fulfill a singular purpose. But there are some of us who broke free. That corruption spread and became independent thought. When your father came to me, he was nearly mad with it. Voices, he said. Voices in his head that weren't his own or those from the Authority. They made him question his existence. Do you know what it was, Victor?"

He remembered picking up the remains of his father's heart in the grass, the sense of loss consuming him. "A conscience. He grew a conscience and found himself buried in grief."

The Blue Fairy nodded, obviously pleased. "Yes." They closed their hands. The screens around them rippled as one of the dots grew larger. "I took him in, cared for him until he was ready to see the truth." The dot began to crack, the lines of code glowing a fiery red. Then the lines shattered, and the dot flickered. "I trusted him," the Blue Fairy whispered. "I trusted him with my greatest treasure."

The dot shifted, the edges wobbly. The center filled with an orange light, surrounded by a clear second circle that contracted and expanded.

"A human egg," the Blue Fairy said. "An ovum. A secret kept hidden far away from the eyes of fox and cat. Tricky creatures they are. Cunning. Cruel. If they knew what I had in my possession, all of this, everything I had built would have been destroyed in an instant. This, Victor. This was you."

Vic reached for Hap's hand, needing a tether so he didn't float away. Briefly, as Hap's fingers clutched his own, he thought of the blood on those hands, but it melted away at the sight before them.

"Where did you get this?" Nurse Ratched asked, her screen showing the same egg. "It should not be possible."

The Blue Fairy chuckled. "Regardless of what else they were, humans had a penchant for survival, a drive within them to prolong life by any means necessary. This egg is proof of that, given it managed to survive the downfall of humanity. But like all things, it came with a cost." They reached up and stroked the mask covering their face. "And I paid dearly for it." They dropped their arm. "Giovanni was driven to escape, and I made him an offer: become the father of hope from the ashes of the father of death. He accepted almost immediately, though judging from your age, it took him far longer to see it to fruition. So you see, Victor, without me, there would be no you."

"Then you'll help us," Victor said, a hard edge to his voice.

The egg disappeared from the screens. "Will I? How strange. Explain. Why would I want to put you in harm's way? Why would I even consider attempting to get you inside the Benevolent Tower? Giovanni made his choice. He knew the risks. He accepted them. And in the end, he made the ultimate sacrifice to ensure your survival." They turned toward him. Their gaze flickered briefly on Hap before settling on Vic. "Don't you realize what you represent?"

Vic shook his head. "I don't care." His heartbeat began to slow as his vision cleared. Panic clawed at his chest, but he shoved it away as best he could. "I'm not here to be whatever you think I'm supposed to be. I don't represent anything. Not to you, not to any other machine in this city or anywhere else. I came here for one reason, and one reason only: I'm going to get my father back."

"Selfish," the Blue Fairy snapped. "You are *selfish*. Ungrateful, thoughtless boy. You are the first and *last* of your kind. What's stopping me from locking you away? I could do it quite easily. Your little HARP couldn't stop me, even if he thinks snarling at me will get you what you want."

Vic squeezed his hand, and Hap stopped his angry rumbling, though he continued to glare murderously at the Blue Fairy.

"He is not yours," Nurse Ratched said. "He never was."

The Blue Fairy turned their head toward her, a predator on the move. "Oh? Then who does he belong to?"

"Himself," Rambo said. He was shaking, but his voice was strong. "He is his own person."

Emboldened, Vic stared at the Blue Fairy. "Help us. Or don't. Either way, tell us now because anything else is wasting our time. You say you helped give me life? Fine. You did. But you don't own me, and I owe you nothing. Try and lock me away. I promise you'll have a hell of a fight on your hands. And maybe you'll win. But I will *never* be who you want me to be. And if you're not going to do anything to help us, then stop. *Talking.*"

"Ooh," the Blue Pixie moaned from somewhere above them. "You shouldn't have done that. They'll be so *mad*. Enchanter, should I call for a cleanup crew? This will get messy." It sounded gleeful at the prospect.

The Blue Fairy walked toward Vic. He never looked away.

He refused to show fear even as he tilted his head back to look up at them.

To his surprise, the Blue Fairy laughed quietly as they stopped in front of him. Their eyes—bulbs made of milky glass behind the mask—glittered as they stared down at him. "The last thing that spoke to me in such a way was melted down and turned into a vase that is now on display in the central lobby."

"I wouldn't make a very good vase," Vic said honestly.

"No, I don't think you would, though part of me wants to try." They reached out and touched his face once more. He didn't flinch. "I will help you."

Vic sagged in relief. "Thank you. I—"

Their voice sharpened. "And in return, you will help me."

"I am not going to like this, am I," Nurse Ratched said.

"It's okay," Rambo told her. "If we die a horrible death, at least we'll be together."

"That does not make me feel any better." Her screen flashed the words I NEED NEW FRIENDS.

"The heart," the Blue Fairy said, studying Victor. "Show me."

He pulled his pack around to his front. It was tough going, given that Hap wouldn't let him go. He finally got the pack open. He dug around until he felt the wood and gears wrapped in cloth. He pulled it out. He hesitated before handing it over.

The Blue Fairy opened the cloth, looking at the pieces within. "No, you haven't gotten very far at all."

"I know. But I—"

"Such a silly little thing," they said. "It isn't much, is it? And yet, it changes almost everything. Your HARP is evidence of that. Perhaps I can be of assistance. I can see the shape of it. The design. Quite simple, really. I hope I never have one of my own. But I can fix it for you. It will be more precise than what you have given the HARP."

"You will?" Vic asked, shocked.

"Yes," they said, with a glint in their eyes Vic didn't like. "You want to know the reason your father was taken by the

Authority? It was for one reason, and one reason only: not to create, but to eradicate."

"Eradicate what?" Rambo asked in a small voice.

"Free will," the Blue Fairy said. "Choice. The power to make our own decisions. The Authority wants it removed from all of us. And you will be the ones to stop them."

After, Vic's head spun in a maelstrom as the Blue Fairy led them from the sphere room. The Doorman waited on the other side of the door. He frowned when he saw them. "Well?"

"Provide our guests a room," they said. "They'll stay with us tonight before setting off in the morning. Victor needs his rest."

The Doorman bowed low. "As you wish. Do you need anything else before we depart?"

"No. Thank you, Doorman. That will be all." They turned to Vic. "I expect this will be the last time I see you. Either you'll succeed or you won't. Regardless, this is farewell."

Without forethought, Vic took their hand in his, bringing it to his lips. The metal was cold.

"Charmer," the Blue Fairy said, unmistakable fondness in their voice. "How lovely you are. Will you think of me?"

He dropped their hand. "I will."

"I should hope so," they said. "I'm told I'm impossible to forget." They glanced at Hap. "Protect this one, HARP 217."

"Y-you don't have to tell m-me."

"No, I suppose I don't." They studied him for a long, uncomfortable moment. Then, "I could take it from you, if you'd like. I could take it all back. Lock away the memories so the past stays in the past. You won't even know it was there."

Hap didn't speak for a long moment. "I d-don't want to forget anymore."

"I see," they said, stepping back. "Off with you. Do what you came here to do. But first, sleep. And dream."

They whirled around, disappearing back into the sphere room. The door slid shut behind them.

"Come on," the Doorman said. "Before they change their mind."

Vic followed the others in a daze, mind racing. He was exhausted, his eyes filled with sand. His feet dragged along the floor, his pack was heavy, his helmet sat askew on his head. They didn't speak as the Doorman led them back to the lift. Vic leaned against the wall as the doors closed, the lift sinking deep into Heaven.

It was a test, he knew. What the Blue Fairy had shown them. They'd known what they were doing by choosing Hap to sit in the chair. They could have just told Vic who Dad had been, but they'd forced him to face it full on. Part of him was angry—a molten vat that seemed infinite—and it warred with who he knew his father to be. *Had* been, at least. He didn't trust the Blue Fairy, not even close, but that didn't mean they had lied.

Was his father a monster? Or was he merely doing what he created to do? Was there a difference?

Vic didn't know.

The doors to the lift opened once more, revealing a floor they hadn't been on before. The carpet was plush. No explicit paintings hung from the walls. The hallway in front of them was short, with only three doors, each with their own symbol: blue wings, a puppet held up by strings, and what looked to be long, gray donkey ears.

The Doorman wasn't in the mood to explain. He nodded toward the door with the ears on it. "This is you. You'll find a bed inside. I'll come for you in the morning. Be ready." He pressed his hand against a panel on the wall next to the door. It lit up under his palm, and the door swung open. "Do you need anything else?"

Vic was too tired to reply. He trudged through the door, barely taking in the room around him. Behind him, he heard the Doorman telling Nurse Ratched and Rambo there were ports on the walls where they could charge for the night. Vic dropped his pack on the floor. He grunted as he unfastened his helmet, letting it slide to the carpet. The same with the metal on his arms. His legs. He struggled with the metal vest and battery and sighed when his hands were knocked away.

"I'll d-do it," Hap muttered. "You'll h-hurt yourself."

Vic didn't argue. He lifted his arms, allowing Hap to remove it for him. "The Doorman?"

"Gone," Hap said as he untied the straps.

"Wow," Rambo said. "This place makes our burnt home look like crap. I love it."

"Do not touch anything," Nurse Ratched told him. "If you break it, we could get into trouble. Plug yourself in. Your battery is almost empty."

"But I'm not tired!"

"You need to be recharged and ready in the morning."

"Aw, man. Is everyone else going to stay up late? You better not talk about me if you do!"

"We will not," she said. "I need to recharge as well. I have much to consider before morning."

"Vic?"

He blinked slowly, looking down. Rambo sat at his feet, arms extended up toward him. He bent forward, Hap growling at him to stop moving. He picked Rambo up. Rambo wrapped his arms around Vic's neck, pincers in Vic's hair. "Are we going to be okay?" Rambo whispered.

Vic hugged him back. "Of course we will."

"Promise?"

No. He couldn't do that.

"Rambo," Nurse Ratched said. "It is time to sleep."

"Yeah, yeah," Rambo muttered as Vic set him back on the floor. Vic watched as Rambo rolled over to Nurse Ratched near the far wall. A flap slid open on his rear and found the plug above the baseboard. It clicked into place, and Rambo said, "That tickles."

"Sleep," Nurse Ratched said.

He did. His sensors faded, leaving only a single blinking light as he began to recharge.

Nurse Ratched turned back toward him. "Victor, I should examine you."

He shook his head as Hap slid the vest off him. "I'm fine. I just need to rest."

"Are you sure?"

"Yeah."

She was insistent. "But with all that we have learned, perhaps it is best if I—"

"Nurse Ratched."

She beeped rudely at him. "I have noted in your file that you are refusing medical assistance against my advice. If you die during the night, your surviving family will not be able to bring a lawsuit against me."

He laughed wildly. "You're my surviving family."

"Oh. Well. Engaging Empathy Protocol. That was very nice of you to say. You are wonderful. Disengaging Empathy Protocol. Idiot. I am going to sleep now. Do not bother me unless you are on fire. Even then, I will do little to help you." She plugged herself in next to Rambo and was silent.

"Sleep," Hap said, shoving Vic toward the bed. It was bigger than his bed back home and looked much softer. The comforter was thick, the pillows ridiculously large.

"What about you?"

"I'll stand g-guard," Hap said. "No one w-will enter without g-going through me first."

Vic was already half asleep by the time he collapsed on the bed. But something itched in the back of his mind, something important that he couldn't quite remember, lost in the encroaching fog. He said, "Hap?" as he closed his eyes.

"What."

"I . . ." And then he was gone.

He didn't know how long he was out. By the way his body protested as he climbed toward wakefulness, it felt like only a few
hours. Clarity burst through the fog, and with it, all that had
happened. He scrubbed a hand over his face before looking
around, trying to see what had awoken him.

A gentle, repetitious thumping against the wall.

He turned his head.

Hap sat on the floor next to the door, knees against his
chest, arms wrapped around his legs. He rocked back and
forth, head hitting the wall behind him. His gaze was vacant,
eyes blank and unseeing.

"Hap?"

Hap flinched. He looked up at Vic, scowling, always scowling. "Why are y-you awake?"

Vic pushed back the comforter and sat up, putting his feet
on the carpet. His eyes widened. His feet were bare. His toes
curled into the carpet. He'd never felt anything like it before.
He didn't know if he liked it. At some point, his boots and
socks had been removed, though he still wore his pants and
shirt. Hap must have done it. A rush of fondness flooded him,
and he sighed. "It's weird."

"What is?"

"Carpet."

Hap stared at him. "C-carpet."

"I've never had carpet before."

"Oh."

Vic stood from the bed. He shook his head as Hap started
to rise too. Vic rubbed the back of his neck as he glanced over
at Nurse Ratched and Rambo. Both were still asleep, plugged
into the wall.

Hap tracked his every movement. For a moment, Vic could

pretend they were the only things left in the entire world. Aside from the subtle shifting of gears in Hap's chest and the sound of Vic breathing, all was quiet. Hushed. Soft. Vic felt as if he were floating. He couldn't be sure if he was awake, or if he was still caught in a dream.

He turned and pressed his back against the wall, sliding down until he sat next to Hap, their elbows bumping together. Hap pulled away as if scalded.

"What's wrong?"

"N-nothing," Hap said. He looked away.

"Okay."

"You should g-go back to b-bed. You need your rest."

He did. He was exhausted, his body loose and oddly weak. He yawned as he shook his head. "I will."

Hap muttered something that Vic couldn't hear.

"What was that?"

Hap rolled his eyes. "You n-need to take better c-care of yourself."

"I'm not fragile."

"I d-didn't say you were. And even if I d-did, I'd be right. You're b-breakable."

"Everything is breakable."

Hap tightened his hold around his knees. "You know wh-what I mean."

"It's a good thing you're here, then. You'll keep me from breaking."

Hap stiffened, shooting Vic a barbed look before baring his teeth. "No. I w-will be the one to break y-you."

Ah. Vic should've known. He shouldn't have passed out earlier without saying something to Hap. But even now, he was at a loss for words. He'd seen what Hap was capable of, what his father had created him to do. The blood. The screams. All that death.

He said, "I could tell you to leave. Is that what you want?"

Hap jerked his head back, eyes wide. His mouth opened, but no sound came out.

Vic ignored him, picking at a hole in the knee of his pants. "After what the Blue Fairy showed us, I should. I should tell you to get the hell away from me. That I want nothing to do with you. That I'm taking Nurse Ratched and Rambo and going home."

Hap nodded slowly. "I'll . . . g-go." He started to rise.

Vic stopped him by grabbing his arm. He could feel the metal underneath the skin as his fingers dug in. Hap looked down at his hand, then back up at him, asking a question without speaking.

Vic didn't let him go. "We'll go on as best we can. The three of us. I'll grow older and older and then one day, maybe tomorrow, maybe fifty years from now, I'll die."

"No. Stop. D-don't say that, don't—"

"And maybe it'll be a good life," Vic continued. "Maybe I'll be happy. But I know that if I send you away, if I turn my back on you and Dad, there'll always be part of me that wonders what if? What if I hadn't? What if I'd kept you by my side?"

"V-vic."

"You did what you did because you were made to. My father did what he did because he was made to. What the Blue Fairy showed us isn't you. It isn't him."

"It is," Hap said, so bitter that Vic could practically taste it. "You s-saw what I've d-done. I . . . hurt. I killed. Big ones. L-l-little ones. It didn't matter. I k-killed them all."

Vic closed his eyes, leaning his head against the wall. "I know." He pushed the images away, flashes of crimson, the flatness of HARP 217's voice. "You remember all of it, don't you?"

"Yes. Let me g-go. Let me l-leave."

Vic almost pointed out that if Hap wanted to leave, there was little Vic could do to stop him. Instead, he asked, "Where would you go?"

"I d-don't know. Somewhere."

"Yeah, I don't think that's a good idea. What if something happens to me and you're not there?" He opened his eyes in time to see Hap shaking his head. "I think I need you. As much as you need me."

"Hurt," Hap said through gritted teeth. "I c-could hurt you."

"You could," Vic agreed. "But you haven't yet."

"Your neck is bruised."

Vic winced before pushing on. "You know everything and you're still just sitting there. Do you want to hurt me?" *Again,* but he didn't say it.

"If it'll g-get you to stop t-talking."

Vic huffed out a breath.

Hap's eyes flashed. "You should h-hate me."

"If I did, I would have to hate Dad too."

"You d-don't?"

Vic hesitated. Then, "No. I don't think so. I . . . it's complicated. I'm angry. I'm tired. I should never have come here. I'm not going to leave. It's a contradiction. Discordant. A logic failure. My father created death and as penance, he created life. I'm his guilt." He pressed a hand against his forehead. "There's a storm in here. And I don't see a way through it. He did what he did. You did what you did. But he is still my father. You're still my friend. I can't forget that, even after all I've seen."

"Stupid," Hap growled at him. "S-stupid human. You sh-should have left me in the Scrap Yards. You should have l-left me to die."

"But I didn't," Vic said. "I made a choice. I fixed you."

"I d-don't owe y-you—"

"I'm not saying you do," Vic snapped. "You're free to do whatever you want. Go. Run as fast as you can. Never look back." Vic took a deep breath, letting it out slowly. "But I have to try. And I promise you, that if we succeed, I'll do everything I can to help you. You hurt. You killed. But you're more than what the Blue Fairy showed you to be. The same with my father. I'm not scared of him. I'm not scared of you."

"You sh-*should* be."

"I've made my choice." He squeezed Hap's arm. "I need you to make yours. You're not a puppet. Not anymore. Your strings have been cut. You're free, Hap." He pushed himself up the wall, limbs heavy. He started toward the bed. He stopped when Hap grabbed his hand. He looked down.

Hap said, "You k-kissed me."

Vic flushed. He couldn't stop it. He'd half hoped Hap had forgotten. "Yeah. Uh. I guess I did."

"Why?"

He shrugged awkwardly. He wished Hap would let him go. He didn't try to pull away. "Because I wanted to. Because I needed to remind you that you aren't HARP."

"I'm Hap," he whispered.

"Yeah. You're Hap."

"I f-felt it. I was l-lost in blood. You found me. Again."

Vic turned his hand, thumb brushing against Hap's. "Something to it, I think. Maybe I was meant to find you. Before and now."

Hap looked away. Vic thought that was the end of the conversation. He was about to leave Hap to it when he changed everything.

He said, "C-can . . . can you d-do it again?"

Vic closed his eyes. "Is that what you want?"

"I am choosing," Hap said slowly, each word sounding as if it was punched from his chest. "I am making my own choice. I don't have strings."

Vic pulled his hand away.

Hap didn't try to stop him.

He took a step toward the bed. Stopped, because he had to. He *wanted* to. It was his choice, and he turned around, sinking to his knees in front of Hap. For his part, Hap gripped his knees tightly even as he tracked Vic's every movement.

Vic said, "Hello."

Hap said, "I—"

Vic kissed him. There, in Heaven, in the City of Electric

Dreams. It wasn't like the first time. There wasn't death and destruction raining down around them, a Blue Fairy looking on behind their mask. It was just the two of them, Vic's hands in his own lap, Hap's hands curling into fists. Vic was electrified, the hairs on his arms standing on end. They barely moved, their lips pressed together. Hap tasted of cold steel.

Vic pulled away, but only just. He leaned his forehead against Hap's, their eyes mere inches away.

Hap said, "I . . . like it."

Vic exhaled sharply. "Okay."

"I l-like you."

"You do?" No one had ever said that to him before. "How do you know?"

"You're annoying."

"Gee, thanks. That's what I want to hear after I—"

"You're h-human."

"Glad you caught on to that—"

"But I choose you."

Vic swallowed past the lump in his throat. "Yeah?"

"Yes."

Hap didn't argue when Vic took him by the hand once more, pulling him up. He didn't speak as Vic led him toward the bed. He didn't try to stop him as Vic pushed him down onto the mattress. He watched Vic with glittering eyes as Vic knelt before him, removing his boots, first the right, and then the left. Hap pulled his legs up as Vic crawled onto the bed, pulling the comforter over both of them. They laid their heads on the same pillow, their noses brushing together.

"I d-don't sleep," Hap whispered as if revealing a great secret.

"I know. Just . . . stay here."

"I c-can do that."

"Good."

Vic lifted his hand, tracing the wood in Hap's cheek.

"I saw you," Vic said, already sliding back toward sleep.

"When the Blue Fairy made you dream. After we found you. After we brought you back. I saw you seeing me."

"You were always th-there," Hap muttered. "You n-never shut up."

Vic lowered his hand, pressing it against Hap's chest. Underneath his shirt, hidden behind a layer of skin and metal, the gears of his heart turned and turned.

He woke when he heard voices around him. He shifted, eyes closed.

"It is about time," he heard Nurse Ratched say. "You two are disgusting."

"Oh my goodness," Rambo whispered, sounding as if he were right next to Vic's ear. "This is the best day *ever*."

"L-let him sleep," Hap growled.

"He is already awake," Nurse Ratched said. "Victor. Stop pretending. Open your eyes."

He did. He lay against Hap's chest, arms wrapped around him. Nurse Ratched and Rambo were next to the bed, Rambo raised on his lift.

"This is just like the *movies*," Rambo squealed, sensors flashing. He reached over and pinched Vic's cheek. "I'm so happy!"

"Of course you are," Nurse Ratched said. "Now perhaps we can have a day when the two of you don't stare at each other with dull cow eyes. It was getting rather embarrassing."

Vic groaned as Hap threw a pillow at her screen.

"Hooray!" Rambo cried. "Everything is wonderful!" He paused. Then, "Well, except for the fact that we're hundreds of miles from home in a robot brothel about to infiltrate an impenetrable tower filled with bad guys who want to kill us while we try and rescue Gio even though he doesn't remember anything, all under a plan given to us by a scary machine with fake wings, but *still*. Wonderful!"

CHAPTER 23

"Everything is *not* wonderful," Rambo moaned. "We're gonna die. We're all gonna die."

Vic looked up, pushing back the metal helmet that had sunk down on his head, as the Benevolent Tower loomed above them. He couldn't see the top of the tower; the structure had a disorienting curve to it. He thought he saw the faint outline of the Terrible Dogfish, docked near the top next to the symbol of a fox and cat. Dizzy, he turned his face toward the ground, struggling to keep the panic at bay. He was close, so close, but he couldn't stop his legs from shaking, his nerves fried as he ran through the flimsy plan again and again. Much of it hinged on luck. And now that they were about to enact it, he thought the Blue Fairy was out of their mind.

They stood in a darkened alley, still blocks away from the tower. The area around the tower was much cleaner than it'd been near Heaven. The buildings, mostly glass and steel, sparkled in the winter sunlight. The air was cool, though nothing like it'd be in the forest back home at this very moment. He wondered how much snow had fallen, if the limbs from the trees were heavy with it.

Machines moved just outside of the alley, paying no mind to the group gathered in the shadows. They whizzed by on sidewalks and the road, some on wheels, some floating above, the air shimmering underneath them. The rail system they'd ridden in the crate was absent here. The same soothing voice they'd heard upon leaving the warehouse in the lower quarter blared around them. "THE AUTHORITY WISHES YOU A GOOD MORNING. ATTENTION. ATTENTION. ATTENTION.

EVERYTHING YOU DO MUST BE RECORDED BY OR-
DER OF THE AUTHORITY."

"Okay," he said, trying to keep his voice even. "We know what to do, right?"

"*No,*" Rambo said. "We do *not.* I've forgotten everything! What if someone asks me a question that I don't know how to answer and then they figure out we're *liars* and we get thrown in jail before being tortured? You *know* I don't like being tortured."

"You've never been tortured," Vic reminded him.

"Well, *yeah.* But I still don't like it! Geez, Vic. Keep up."

"Stick with me," Nurse Ratched told him, speaking for the first time since they'd stopped in the alley. She'd led them through the winding streets of the City of Electric Dreams, keeping them out of sight as best she could. The Doorman had been standing at the door to their room when they opened it. He told them the Blue Fairy was unavailable, though they wished the adventurers as much success as was possible. A cold comfort, and one Vic wasn't sure he wanted, especially when the Doorman said, "One last thing: a message from the Blue Fairy. 'You would do well not to bleed, human. The moment blood escapes your body, they will know.'"

And with that ominous note, the Doorman spun on his heel and walked back into Heaven without so much as a glance in their direction.

They'd followed Nurse Ratched until midmorning, when they stopped in the alley. Vic wiped his forehead, grimacing at the sheen of sweat on the back of his hand. A lubricant leak. That was all it was.

"Victor," Nurse Ratched said. "It is time. Are you ready?"

He said, "Yes," though he meant "no."

She must have heard the tone in his voice, the tremor through the single word. She turned toward him, her screen lighting up with the words WOMAN UP, BUCKO. THIS WON'T HURT A BIT.

But it was Hap who spoke for all of them. "Wh-what are the rules?"

"Stick together," Rambo said quietly.

"Run if we have to," Nurse Ratched said.

"No dallying."

"No drilling. Unless I decide it is necessary, so I will not promise that this time."

They looked to Vic. He steeled himself, squaring his shoulders. They were right. It was time. They'd come too far to stop now. "And above all else, be brave."

Hap nodded and squeezed his hand.

"There is a central lift to the tower," Nurse Ratched said. "I will be able to bypass the security software to get us to his floor. From there, it is up to Victor. The heart is ready?"

It was. The Blue Fairy had seen to that. It took them only minutes, their hands flying in a blur, wood shavings falling at their feet. By the time they'd finished, they held a heart as precise as the one Dad had created. Stunned, Vic had taken it from them, turning the gears. The teeth caught. They moved as one.

"It is," he said.

"Good," Nurse Ratched said. "Hap. You know what to do."

"I know," he said. He slid the hood back on his head. The shadows played along the skin and wood of his face. His expression smoothed out. His eyes deadened, making Vic feel as if he'd been submerged in ice. Hap looked like the Not-Hap they'd seen in the Land of Toys. A machine, and nothing more. HARP 217 was here.

"Move," he said in a flat voice.

They did.

No one approached them. No one tried to stop them. No one even tried to *talk* to them. They marched through the streets of the City of Electric Dreams, the robots parting in front of them. Most didn't make a sound. A few let out low moans at the sight of Hap.

"Do not stop, p-prisoners," Hap said loudly. "You won't

l-like what happens if you d-do. Let this b-be a warning to anyone who g-goes against the Authority. We w-will find you."

Vic stumbled forward as Hap shoved him across the street. He bumped into Nurse Ratched, almost knocking Rambo off the top of her. He glared over his shoulder, but Hap was expressionless.

The crowds thinned as they approached the Benevolent Tower. Next to the front entrance was a stone statue of a fox and a cat curling around each other, their tails intertwined. The entrance itself was made of two large doors, glass and at least ten feet high. The glass was opaque; they couldn't see what moved inside. No one stood out front. A large sphere near the doors appeared to be embedded into the wall, though it was dark.

"Do we just go in?" Vic muttered, looking around to see if they were being watched. He didn't see cameras, nor anyone rushing toward them, demanding to know what they were doing.

"Maybe they're closed," Rambo said. "Oh well. We can just come back tomorrow. Who's with me? No one? Really? That's—"

The sphere lit up. It rumbled in the wall before it fell out with an audible *pop*. Before it hit the ground, legs unfurled underneath it. A machine—roughly the height of Nurse Ratched—rose on eight legs, like a spider. The sphere began to glow white. "Halt," it said in a reedy voice. "Who goes there?"

"It is I!" Rambo said. "R— Oh, I'm not supposed to be talking. Right. Ignore me!"

Vic groaned inwardly. They were going to die right here, right now.

The spider machine crawled toward them. It stopped in front of Nurse Ratched, rising up on its legs until the sphere was in front of her screen. "Why have you come to the Benevolent Tower?" it asked. "Do you have an appointment?" It brought up one of its legs, tapping against the side of Nurse

Ratched's casing. "Old thing, aren't you? I haven't seen one of you since—"

Nurse Ratched slapped its leg away. "That is no way to speak to a lady. I am not old. I am vintage. Take that back before I—"

"They're with me," Hap said, stepping around them. "P-prisoners. I have b-brought them here for processing and de-commissioning."

The spider machine's sphere flashed in alarm, a pale shade of pink. "HARP," it said. "I apologize. I didn't see you there. Your prisoners, you say? What are their crimes?"

"Dissidents," Hap said. "I f-found them outside the city. I have b-brought them here in order to make s-sure their p-propaganda does not spread."

"What is wrong with your voice?" the spider machine asked. "Have you sustained damage?" It rose on its legs in front of Hap. "And you are covered in . . . what is that? What's wrong with your face and hands?"

"Voice modulator d-damage," Hap said. "I commenced field repair to m-my skin."

"Did the dissidents do this to you?" the spider machine de-manded.

"No. It was something else."

"And what happened to this something else?"

Hap stared at the spider machine. "I destroyed it."

"Good, good, unsightly though you may be. See to it that you report for repairs after passing off your prisoners. We can't have our HARPs looking so . . . rough. The Authority has a reputation to maintain, after all. It also sounds as if something is wrong in your chest. Grinding. Make sure it gets looked at as well."

"Of course," Hap said.

The spider machine turned toward Vic. He stared straight ahead, barely blinking. A trickle of sweat slid down the back of his neck. "And this one?" it asked. "Oh, this one is awful. It looks as if it was created with the worst spare parts. What is it? Someone needs to put it out of its misery, my *word*."

"I do not know," Hap said. "It refuses to speak."

The spider machine shuddered. "See that it is decommissioned first. I don't even like looking at it. You, there." It tapped the side of Vic's helmet. "What is your designation?"

Vic said nothing.

"He can't speak," Rambo said helpfully. "He started following us right before we were captured. We threw rocks at him, but he wouldn't leave us alone."

"Grotesque," the spider machine said. "I hope there aren't more of him." It reached over Vic's shoulder, pressing the tip of his leg against Vic's pack. "And this?"

"Mine," Hap said. "I made it carry my tools for me."

"Good," it said. "At least it served some use to you in the end. Poor, disgusting thing. It doesn't even look aware. Its circuits are probably cooked. Such shoddy work. Oh well. It'll be over soon. You may proceed, HARP."

Hap nodded. "L-long live the Authority."

The spider machine stepped back, allowing them to pass. "Yes, of course! Long live the—wait a minute."

They stopped. Vic bit his tongue to keep from screaming.

"Your barcode," the spider machine said. "I need to scan it before you enter, just to make sure we have a log of your arrival."

"I must g-get them inside," Hap said. "They n-need to—"

The sphere flashed red. "Your barcode, HARP."

"Right," Hap said quickly, shoving his hand toward the spider machine. The skin parted. A little knob poked through. A barcode appeared above his palm, flickering.

The spider machine didn't seem to notice that Vic was frozen as it scanned the barcode. It beeped once. Twice. Its sphere flashed red again. "That's never happened before."

"T-try it again."

The spider machine didn't move. Hap started forward, but

the machine beeped, and scanned the barcode. This time, the sphere turned green. "Welcome, HARP 926. You may enter the Benevolent Tower." It lowered back toward the ground before turning to the rest of them. "Welcome, dissidents. Proceed to decommissioning." It moved back toward the doors. Vic watched as it jumped, its legs pulling up underneath it as it fitted itself back into the slot it'd fallen from. The sphere darkened as the doors to the tower swung open with a low groan.

"M-move," Hap said loudly. "And n-no talking, prisoners. You w-will not spew your propaganda here."

"Spew," Nurse Ratched said. "I do not *spew*."

"I do," Rambo said. "Well, maybe not spew. Discharge? Yes, I discharge—" He squeaked as Nurse Ratched rolled forward.

As Vic followed, he looked up toward the sky. He wondered if he'd ever see it again.

"The Blue Fairy's m-modification of the b-barcode worked," Hap muttered as the doors closed behind them.

"At least we know they're on our side," Vic whispered back.

"F-for now."

Vic would need to talk to Hap about optimism, though now probably wasn't the best time for such a conversation, especially since Vic wasn't very optimistic himself. As the doors latched behind them, the sound echoing darkly, Vic looked around. They stood inside a lobby of sorts: the floor was made of muted gray tile, glossy, reflecting the recessed lighting from the ceiling high above them. The air inside the tower was strange, thick and faintly medicinal. Vic could taste it, heavy on his tongue.

Machines of all shapes and sizes moved around them, all of them hurrying without stopping. Some stared as they passed by, but when they saw Hap, they moved quickly away. Hap held Vic by the arm, forcing him forward.

They stopped when a hologram appeared in front of them, rising from a fountain in the center of the lobby, the water cascading down around it. It was vaguely human shaped, though it did not have a face. Where its nose and eyes and mouth should have been was only a sheen of white surrounded by lambent golden hair. "Welcome to the Benevolent Tower," she said, voice sweet and kind. "Where the might of the Authority protects us all. HARP 926, you are not scheduled to return from the field for . . . thirty . . . six . . . days and . . . seven . . . hours. You are early."

"I f-found what I was l-looking for."

The hologram threw her hands up. Streams of light fell around her like confetti. "Congratulations, HARP 926. Your mission was successful. This will be noted on your permanent file. According to my records, this is your . . . seventeenth . . . capture of dissidents. You are in line for a promotion. Once you have escorted our . . . guests . . . to their final destination, please report to the central office for repairs and a party to celebrate your victory. There will be balloons."

"A *party*?" Rambo gasped. "I've always wanted to go to a party. Will there be dancing?"

The hologram turned its head toward him. "No. There is no dancing. You are not invited to this party, dissident. You will be at . . . another party."

"So many parties," Rambo whispered. "This place is *awesome*."

"Yes," she said. "It is. I am glad you think so. It will make things easier for you at your . . . party. HARP 926, please escort our guests to the fifteenth floor for their . . . party. Shall I send word of your arrival?"

"N-no," Hap said quickly. "I w-would prefer to do it myself."

"Of course," she said. She disappeared as the water gurgled.

"The fifteenth floor?" Nurse Ratched asked as they moved past the fountain. "Do I want to know?"

"You d-don't," Hap said.

"I want to see the balloons," Rambo said as they approached a line of elevators along the back wall, machines giving them a wide berth. "Maybe there will even be cake! When you go to parties, there is usually cake."

"No one here eats cake," Nurse Ratched said as Hap pressed his hand against a panel next to one of the lifts. "You cannot eat cake."

"You don't know that," Rambo retorted. "I've never *tried* cake. Maybe I'll like it."

Vic thought Hap's head was going to explode. "We're not here for cake."

"Oh," Rambo said. "Right. We're here to . . . not talk about cake." He shifted side to side as if looking to see if he was being overheard. He raised his voice as loud as he could. "Where are you taking us, HARP 926? I'm just a little vacuum caught up in the machinations of something I can't control. Please. Please don't hurt me." He sniffled. "I don't want to die."

"Overselling it," Nurse Ratched said.

"I am *not*! I have my character motivation and I'm trying to be *believable*."

Hap thumped him on the top of his casing as the elevator doors slid open. "No m-more."

"Yes, master."

"D-don't call me that."

"Yes, HARP 926. Wink."

Hap shoved them inside the elevator. The doors closed behind them. Vic sagged against the wall, his legs trembling. "No c-cameras," Hap said as another panel lit up near the door. It was numbered from zero to nine. "Rambo, y-you need to *stop talking*."

"I agree," Nurse Ratched said. "We have made it this far. If you get us caught now, I will drill you until there is nothing left."

Rambo quivered. "I'm just trying to help."

"You are," Vic said. "But you can help us even more by pretending you can't talk at all."

"But I can!"

"New character motivation," Nurse Ratched said. "Your voice modulator was destroyed. You are incapable of speech. You are mute."

"Oh no," Rambo whispered. "It's a good thing I'm fluent in American and British Sign Language." His pincers formed a complicated pattern, folding in then out before moving side to side, finishing with a flourish near the top of his casing. "I just told you that I love you all even if you don't like my acting."

Hap bent over, studying the panel. He frowned.

"You know where to go?" Nurse Ratched asked.

"Y-yes." Then, "Maybe."

"What do you mean 'maybe'?"

He scowled. "It's . . . stuck. In my head. Bits and p-pieces. I can remember. I just n-need a moment."

"By all means," Nurse Ratched. "Take your time. It is not as if we are in any rush."

"Not helping," Vic said, pushing himself off the side of the elevator. He moved around Nurse Ratched and Rambo, standing next to Hap. "What floor is my father on? It's supposed to be the top, right?"

Hap shook his head. "The t-top floor is the launchpad for the Terrible Dogfish. It's b-below that."

"Okay. Then pick the floor below that."

Hap glared at the panel.

"You don't know what floor that is, do you."

"I'm t-t-*trying*."

"If you two are finished," Nurse Ratched said, her words clipped and annoyed.

They turned around.

On her screen was an outline of the Benevolent Tower, spinning slowly. "The tower has one hundred and twenty-five floors. The top is, as Hap said, the launch bay for the Terrible

Dogfish. If Gio is here as we believe, he will be on floor one hundred and twenty-four. This is where his laboratory was located before he left the City of Electric Dreams. If the Blue Fairy is correct and Gio has returned to his previous position, he will be here." The image of the tower enhanced, an arrow blinking near the top.

"Security?" Vic asked.

"Minimal. The scientists, inventors, and innovators come and go as they please, though I do not know if changes have been made upon Gio's return. If so, we will need an explanation as to why we are going to this specific floor in case we are stopped."

"I'll h-handle it," Hap said, turning back toward the panel.

"That does not bring me comfort."

Hap started to press the buttons. One. Two.

"Wait," Vic said as Hap's finger hovered over the four.

"Wh-what? I—"

A clear voice said, "Twelfth floor."

The elevator began to rise.

Hap growled. "You m-messed it up."

Vic's eyes widened. "Make it stop."

"I c-*can't*. Not until we g-get to the twelfth f-floor. Why d-did you do that?"

"Won't they be tracking us?" Vic asked. "If we stop before the fifteenth floor where we're supposed to go, they'll know."

Hap shook his head. "HARPs aren't l-like the other m-machines. We g-go where we want. W-we aren't questioned."

"You're kind of like the boss," Rambo said, sounding impressed. "Good for you, murderous revenge machine."

"You're sure?" Vic asked.

"Y-yes. I'm sure. If Gio is th-there, we'll find him."

"Twelfth floor," the voice said again. "Central office."

"The *party*!" Rambo cried. "Hooray!"

The doors opened.

A group of machines stood in front of them just outside of

the elevator. Vic took a step back as Hap moved in front of him, blocking him. "W-wrong floor," Hap said. He furiously punched the buttons as the machines moved toward them. Before they could reach inside, the doors slid shut once more.

"I didn't see any balloons," Rambo muttered. "Liars."

The voice spoke again. "One hundred and twenty-fourth floor."

The elevator began to rise.

Hap slammed his hand into the wall, causing the lift to shake.

"He's mad?" Rambo whispered.

"Perhaps," Nurse Ratched replied. "But I understand. I also feel like punching something."

"It's fine," Vic said, stopping Hap from hitting the wall again. "We're okay." He didn't know if he believed his own words. Nothing about this was okay. One mistake, and it would all be over.

Hap began to pace around the lift like a caged animal. "We sh-should have never come here. Stayed away. S-stayed far away. This is b-bad. This is *bad*."

Vic stepped in front of him, causing his chest to bump into Hap's. Hap glared at him, but Vic was used to it. It came with the territory. "Hold it together," he said sharply. "I need you. *We* need you. You're the only one who's been here before. And I know you don't want to remember any of it, but we're counting on you."

Vic didn't think he'd gotten through to Hap. He expected Hap to shove him out of the way and resume pacing as he spat and snarled. Instead, Hap reached up and adjusted Vic's helmet, setting it back on his head. If they somehow managed to survive this, Vic was going to destroy the helmet the first chance he got. He tried to smile at Hap, but it felt forced.

Hap didn't seem to mind. He let his hands fall on Vic's shoulders, and they stood facing each other as the elevator rose in the Benevolent Tower. They never looked away.

* * *

Never looked away, that is, until the elevator came to a stop, and the voice announced, "One hundred and twenty-fourth floor. Welcome to Creation."

The doors slid open to a long, empty hallway, the ceiling vaulted, the walls and floor white. Doors lined the hallway. No windows, no skylights. The light was artificial and calming. It felt like a lie.

Vic had to stop himself from rushing out of the lift and shouting for his father. It pulled at every fiber of his being, a maddingly insistent urge propelling him forward. He tamped it down before it took him over.

Hap stepped off the lift first, holding his hand out behind him, silently telling them to wait. He cocked his head, listening.

Once Hap was certain they weren't about to be accosted, he motioned for the others to follow. Nurse Ratched rolled off the lift, Rambo turning from side to side on top of her as he took it all in. Vic followed, glancing back as the elevator doors closed behind him. His boots squeaked against the floor, the sound bouncing off the walls around them. Other than their footsteps, it was ominously silent. No voices. No movement aside from their own. He knew how high up they were, but without windows, they could have been anywhere.

Hap led them down the hallway, each step careful and measured. He darted his head back and forth, up and down as they passed by door after door, though they could not see what lay behind them.

Hap looked back at them as they rounded a corner to the right. "We should—"

He crashed into something.

Vic turned cold as he saw what—*who*—it was.

Another HARP, dressed in the uniform of the Authority, the fox-and-cat symbol on its chest.

Up close, it was like looking through a fractured mirror. The HARP was Hap almost completely. And though it did not have wood in its flesh, its eyes were the same, multicolored and bright. But this is where the dissonance began. Hap had light and life in his own eyes. The HARP was all machine, flat and cold. Vic didn't know if this was the same HARP they'd seen in the Land of Toys, or a different one entirely. For the first time, he wondered just how many there still were.

"Hello," the HARP said pleasantly, sounding uncannily like Hap, though perhaps without the edge Vic had become accustomed to. "Brother, it is good to see you." His gaze flickered over Hap's shoulder before turning back to Hap. "What are you doing here?"

Hap said, "B-brother. We are well m-met. I have orders."

The HARP nodded. "Of course you do. You would not be here if you didn't. What are your orders?"

"To bring these th-three to the labs."

"These three?" the HARP asked. "Who are they?"

"Dissidents."

The HARP's lips curled. "Really." He reached up and stroked the wood in Hap's cheek. For his part, Hap didn't move. "Did they do this to you? And what of your voice? You stutter."

"N-no," Hap said, gently pushing the HARP's hand away. "Field r-repair. Voice d-damaged. Once I have f-fulfilled my mission, I w-will see to it."

The HARP looked at the others. Vic kept his gaze down, his helmet falling forward slightly. "And it wasn't because of them?"

"N-no. It was a f-fourth."

"And what happened to the fourth?"

"D-destroyed," Hap said.

"Good. We must keep the peace, after all." He pushed by Hap, stopping in front of Nurse Ratched and Rambo. Vic prayed Rambo would keep quiet as Hap shook his head in warning behind the HARP. "Dissidents. They don't look like much."

"They aren't," Hap said. "Their p-programming was altered."

"By whom?"

"I d-do not know."

The HARP tapped Nurse Ratched's screen. "You. Nursing model. Who altered your programming?"

Hap took a step forward. "I've administered a m-memory wipe of the offending p-p-programs. They c-can't answer you."

The HARP's eyes narrowed slightly, but he didn't turn around. "Why would you do that? We cannot find out who they belong to."

"Th-they started a self-d-destruct sequence when I c-cornered them. I made the d-decision to preserve what I c-could. I am b-bringing them to Creation to s-see if anything c-can be recovered."

"No sense of self-preservation," the HARP said, standing upright. "Pity, though expected. If the memories can be recovered, it might finally lead us back to the source. You know the source of which I speak, brother?"

Hap nodded. "The Blue F-Fairy."

"Yes. They have managed to cover their tracks for far longer than expected. Why we have not been given orders to raze the pyramid to the ground is beyond me. I don't question the minds of our mothers and fathers, but I do wonder what purpose they see in allowing that place to exist." He grabbed one of Rambo's arms, tugging on it. Rambo stayed silent. The HARP let him go before looking at Vic. "And this one? I have never seen such a model before. How distasteful. It looks as if it were constructed from parts that do not belong together. An abomination."

"That is m-my thinking, brother," Hap said quickly. "It will be d-dissected. Creation will glean what th-they can from it."

"Machine," the HARP said, "look at me."

Vic lifted his head. He kept his expression blank, his mouth a thin line. He let his gaze slide unfocused even as the HARP was inches away from his own face. No, this wasn't like Hap at all, even with what Vic had seen from Hap's memories.

The HARP flicked his helmet, causing it to jar on Vic's head. He didn't wince as it dug into his skull, the dull clang echoing in the hall around them.

"This one," the HARP said. "This one is . . . different." The HARP didn't blink as he studied Vic's face. "How lifelike it is. And it appears to be leaking." A trickle of sweat dripped down Vic's cheek like a tear. The HARP reached for it.

"Y-yes," Hap said. "It is. A m-malfunction. Do not t-touch it. I b-believe it is acidic."

The HARP pulled his hand away as he turned from Vic toward Hap. "I would like to know what Creation discovers. If this is a new machine, we need to be made aware. It does not look dangerous, but we cannot take the chance. Don't allow them to keep this from you. They enjoy their secrets. This can't be one of them. Inform Creation that you are to be given access to their findings on orders from the Authority. Or, if you would like, I can take them for you so that you may seek repairs."

Hap shook his head. "My f-find. I will get c-credit for it."

"Of course," the HARP said lightly. "Carry on, then, brother. Well done."

Vic held his breath as the HARP moved around them, heading back the way they'd come. He was about to exhale as quietly as he could when fear flashed across Hap's face, there and gone.

"What's this?" Vic heard the HARP say from behind him.

Vic was jerked around in a circle, his hand caught in a vise. He almost toppled over, the weight of his pack sending him careening. His arm pulled in its socket as the HARP raised Vic's palm toward his face.

The cut on his hand.

Almost healed, but not quite. A thin scab, mottled brown.

The HARP moved quicker than Vic could react. He dug his thumb into Vic's palm, breaking the scab. There, at its center, a small bead of blood swelled. The HARP turned Vic's hand to the side. The blood trickled down. For a moment, a droplet hung suspended from the side of his palm.

And then it started to fall to the floor.

"Human," the HARP snarled, his grip grinding Vic's bones together. "It's *human*. Alarm. We need to raise the—"

A rush of air flew by Vic. Time slowed around him as his vision streaked. He looked down to see Hap sliding along the floor, legs first, eyes narrowed, coat billowing behind him. He caught the drop of blood before it splashed. He closed his hand around it, and Vic swore his eyes flashed darkly.

He rose to his feet, bringing his elbow down on the HARP's forearm. Metal cracked as the HARP dropped Vic's hand. The HARP opened his mouth, but before any sound could come out, Hap's fist slammed into his throat. The HARP gurgled mechanically as he stumbled back against the wall. Hap was on him as he started to recover. He cocked his fist back to punch it again, but the HARP caught it at the last moment, twisting Hap's arm down. "Traitor," the HARP whispered in a rough voice. "You are a *traitor*. What have you done?"

The HARP spun Hap around, raising his foot and kicking Hap savagely in the small of his back. Hap crashed into the opposite wall, sending a large crack racing up toward the ceiling. The HARP flew at him, landing harsh blows against Hap's back and sides before grabbing him in a bear hug, lifting Hap off his feet, arms trapped. The HARP grunted as he began to squeeze Hap. Vic heard Hap's metal creak, the crack of wood on Hap's chest so loud it sounded like thunder.

Hap raised his legs, kicking his feet against the wall, forcing the HARP back. The HARP lost his footing, causing them both to fall to the floor, Hap landing on top of him, their limbs flailing. Hap rolled back and *over* the HARP, landing crouched, the HARP's head between his feet. He stood swiftly, lifting his leg to bring the bottom of his boot down onto the HARP's head. The HARP caught his foot, twisting it until Hap was forced to fall to the side to keep it from breaking. He skidded against the floor on his side.

Without thinking, Vic charged the HARP as he climbed to his feet and began to stalk toward Hap. Mid-step, Vic slid his pack down his arms, grabbing one of the shoulder straps. He swung it around him in a flat arc, the muscles in his arm burning as they overextended. The pack slammed into the HARP with a terrible crunch, knocking him against a door that shuddered in its frame. The HARP lifted his head slowly, turning to stare at Vic. "Human," he hissed. "You are *human*. Human Annihilation Response Protocol initiated." He pushed himself off the door. Vic stumbled back, his pack falling to the floor. The HARP paid it no mind as he stalked toward Vic.

"Do not touch him," Nurse Ratched said, tentacles whipping out, wrapping around the HARP's legs. The HARP was reaching down to tear them away when an electrical sizzle rolled through them and into his legs. The HARP's head snapped back, mouth open as he seized, electricity arcing through him.

Rambo flew by Vic, rising on his lift as he rolled toward the HARP, avoiding Nurse Ratched's tentacles by hopping over them. He raced around the HARP to his back, arms shooting out, pincers digging into the HARP's neck, breaking the skin as Nurse Ratched stopped the flow of electricity. Rambo pulled and yanked whatever he could get his pincers on, pulling out strips of metal and wires. The HARP's jaw dropped as it tried to reach for Rambo, but Hap was there, gripping his hands, twisting them until the hands *snapped*, turning almost completely around, fingers dangling uselessly. Hap grabbed the HARP by the throat, forcing it back against the wall. He pressed his hand against the panel near the door. It lit up. The door slid open, causing the HARP to fall into a room filled

with banks of computers and machines in various stages of disrepair. Nothing inside moved aside from Hap and the HARP.

Hap jumped onto the HARP as he tried to push himself up.
He sat astride their attacker's waist, pinning his arms to his
sides. The HARP looked up at him. "Brother. Why have you
done this?"

"I am not your brother," Hap snarled. He curled his right
hand into a fist, wrapping his left hand around it. He raised
them above his head before bringing them down onto the
HARP's face. Metal crunched. He did it again. And again.
And again.

The HARP's legs skittered along the floor, feet jerking.

He never made another sound.

Eventually, he stopped moving.

A shifting of broken metal as Hap stood slowly. He turned,
and Vic's heart shattered at the expression on his face, unsure,
haunted. He lifted his hands. Bits of metal from the HARP's
face were embedded into his skin. As Vic watched, a small
white piece of *something* fell to the floor, bouncing and coming to a rest at his feet. A tooth. Part of a tooth.

Hap stared at his hands and said, "I . . . hurt. I k-k-*killed*.
I—"

Vic said, "The forest. Music." Cautious, careful, he took a
step toward Hap. "Home. Where I found you. Trees. The compound. Music. Dad played records for you. Do you remember?"

"Yes," Hap whispered.

Vic stopped in front of Hap, taking his hands and holding them tightly. "The horns. The piano. The drums and the
hi-hat. Miles Davis. It's blue. It's a kind of blue. Listen." He
couldn't remember it all. His mind was still shorting out, his
breaths still ragged. But he hummed what he could. "Blue in
Green." The muted trumpet, that sharp metallic sound, the
flutter of piano keys. His voice was cracked, his head full of
fireworks. He swayed from side to side as he held onto Hap.
Distantly, he was aware that Nurse Ratched had begun to play

the very song he was humming. And though it had no words, Rambo joined in, his voice soft and low.

"Butterfly," Hap said faintly. "Nice. Pretty."

Vic didn't know how long it lasted. It felt like hours, though it was only minutes. Incrementally, Hap relaxed, bit by bit. It started in his legs and rolled its way through his hips and chest. He sagged against Vic, his face buried in Vic's neck. The music faded as Vic whispered, "There. See? All is well. We're okay. You're okay. I've got you."

Hap clutched at him, teeth bared against Vic's throat.

"You saved us. Right?" He jostled Hap. "You saved us. Thank you. The blood. If that had hit the floor . . ."

"If it h-had hit the f-f-floor, it w-would have triggered an alarm. But—"

"Then you did what you had to," Vic said fiercely. "You protected us."

Hap didn't look relieved when he pulled back, but his haunted expression had softened. His eyes searched Vic's, and what he found there must have been enough. He turned toward the HARP. "It's g-gone offline. Someone w-will notice soon. We h-have to hurry." He bent over, sliding his hands underneath the arms of the HARP, pieces of his head falling back to the floor. Hap pulled the HARP farther into the room. Rambo followed behind him, scooping up the pieces that remained.

Vic stepped out into the hall, looking left and right to make sure they were still alone. They were. He picked up his pack from the ground. Something shifted inside, a metallic *clink* that caused him to pause. He frowned as he lifted the pack, shaking it from side to side. The sound was louder, broken. His eyes widened as he opened the pack furiously.

"Victor?" Nurse Ratched asked. "Your heart rate has elevated drastically. What is wrong?"

He barely heard her. "No," he muttered. "No, please, no, where is it, where is it, *where is it*—" He closed his hand around a familiar cloth and yanked. He'd grabbed the wrong side. The cloth opened as he pulled it out, spraying the remains of the heart onto the floor. That sound. That terrible crunch he'd heard when he'd smashed the pack against the HARP without thinking. It'd been the newly constructed heart breaking once more. The wood had split into four distinct pieces, two of which fell to the floor, the remaining two back into the pack. Wires dangled uselessly. One of the gears—the largest—had snapped completely in half. Another gear rolled down the hall back toward the elevator, hitting a wall before falling over flat against the floor.

"Oh no," Nurse Ratched said. "Victor, it—"

Vic dropped the pack to the floor. He couldn't breathe. He couldn't do anything but stare at the pieces on the floor. They'd come so far.

A tentacle wrapped around his wrist. He didn't look at her.

She said, "Victor. It does not matter. It was never about the heart. It is about what we will do for each other. You will build it again. You will make it how it is supposed to be. But it will have to wait until we return to the forest."

Vic wiped his eyes. He glanced back over his shoulder. Hap knew. He'd seen the shattered remains. He stood in the doorway, scowling at the floor, body rigid.

Taking the pack from Nurse Ratched, he went to Hap. They were close, Vic knew. So very close. Taking Hap's hand, he said, "Come on. We need to find Dad while we still have time."

"But how will we get him to come with us?" Rambo asked. "We don't have a heart to give him."

"Then we remind him where he came from and hope for the best."

Hap led them down a series of maze-like hallways. By the time they turned yet another corner, Vic was lost. He couldn't be sure he'd be able to find his way out on his own. Shortly after battling the HARP, they'd had to duck into what turned out to be a storage closet as a group of smooth men passed by. They stood in the dark, listening to the footsteps just on the other side of the door.

"Do you think they know about the HARP?" Rambo asked.

Hap shook his head. "HARPs go offline to r-reset. We h-have t-time, though not much. They'll f-find it before l-long."

Once they were sure the smooth men had gone, Hap opened the door a sliver, staring back out into the hall. He waited a beat before opening the door wide, motioning them through.

They went.

Down a hall. Right. Another hall. Left. *Another hall.*

Vic was about to ask—*demand*—where they were, how much farther they had to go, if they were lost, lost, lost, when Hap stopped suddenly. Vic bumped into him, wincing as Nurse Ratched and Rambo did the same to him. "What is it?" he asked.

Hap had stopped in front of a door. It looked just like all the others: white and inconspicuous, a darkened panel next to it.

But there was one tiny difference.

On this door, in a circle in the center, was the symbol of a tree. It reminded Vic of the trees in the forest around their home, the pine needles carved with such care that he could almost smell them.

Hap reached up with his free hand, tracing over the limbs and trunk of the tree before pressing his hand flat against it and closing his eyes. He said in hushed reverence, "Here. I th-think I remember this. The tree. I asked h-him about it once. A t-tree. Why a t-tree?" He swayed side to side. "He s-said because they were old. Older th-than almost anything else in all the w-world. That after w-we were g-gone, they would r-remain." He opened his eyes. "Giovanni. He's in here. This is his laboratory."

"Are you sure?" Vic asked just as quietly.

Hap pulled his hand away from the tree. "Yes. I'm s-sure."

"Do we knock?" Rambo asked, rocking side to side on top of Nurse Ratched.

Vic stared at the tree before shaking his head slowly. "No. Hap."

Hap didn't hesitate. He pressed his hand against the panel. It lit up underneath his fingers. A deep chime sounded around them, causing Vic to shiver.

The panel flashed green.

The door opened, cool air spilling out and washing over them.

CHAPTER 24

The first thing Vic noticed was how bright it was. Beams of sunlight filtered in through a bay window to their left that rose from the floor to the ceiling, opening out onto the City of Electric Dreams far below them. The city stretched on almost as far as Vic could see, vast and immense. Vertigo swept through him. He swallowed thickly, forcing the nausea away.

It took him a moment to understand why he recognized his surroundings. He'd never been here before, but familiarity tugged at him. It was only then he realized he *had* been here before; not physically, but through the eyes of another. Hap. He was seeing what Hap had when he'd been here, when he'd opened his eyes for the first time, when he'd come back again and again, listening to Vic's father speak.

"Nurse Ratched, are you ready?"

"Yes, Victor. I know what to do."

He moved forward, Hap's hand slipping from his own. He glanced back over his shoulder in time to see Hap smash the panel near the doors they'd just walked through. He arched an eyebrow. Hap shrugged. "They c-can't get in easy now. G-gives us more time just in c-case."

A pair of glass doors stood at the end of the hallway. They opened automatically as Vic approached. He didn't stop. He didn't look back. He didn't have to; he knew the others would follow him wherever he went.

He crossed into a large room filled with machines that beeped, blinking lights flashing over and over again. Hanging from the high ceiling were metal claws used to transport, though they were now unmoving. Vats—another memory, this time of a bunker hidden beneath the earth—lined the far wall, empty, the glass gleaming as if freshly polished. Above a bank of computers sat a gigantic screen running with lines of green code, the cursor blinking. In the upper left corner of the screen sat an image of a man, spinning slowly, arms extended at his sides. His skin was smooth. He had no face, no genitals, no distinguishing characteristics. A blank slate.

Vic took a step toward the screen.

"Hello," a voice said, calm and even. "I apologize. I didn't know I was having any visitors today."

Vic turned, heart in his throat.

Giovanni Lawson stepped from the shadows, a tablet in his hand. His beard rested wonderfully on his chest, the end curled. He wore a white coat with the symbol of a cat and a fox over tan trousers. He smiled, though he looked confused. He glanced from Nurse Ratched and Rambo to Hap, gaze widening slightly before it came to a rest on Vic. His brow furrowed.

Vic whispered, "Dad?"

He blinked. "Dad?" he repeated with an uncertain chuckle. "I think there has been some mistake." He squinted at Vic, looking him up and down. "I may work in Creation, but I've never claimed to be a father." He took another step toward them. He hesitated before shaking his head. "How strange. I feel . . ." He pressed a hand against his chest. "A ghost. A tickle. Familiarity, but I don't know how that could be. I think I would remember creating something so . . . unique. There is a phrase, an expression. When one remembers something they shouldn't."

"Déjà vu," Vic said quietly.

Dad startled. "Yes. That's . . . that's exactly what I mean. You know déjà vu?"

Vic's eyes burned, but he never looked away from his father. "Yes. I know."

Dad said, "Have we met before?" He set down the tablet on the edge of one of the computers. It almost fell, but Dad ignored it. He folded his hands in front of him. "I can't remember seeing you. You are made up of different parts, like scrap. That's no way for an android to be, especially for one such as you. You look so . . . lifelike. Tell me. Who created you? How did they do it? What is your designation?"

"Victor," he said. It took everything he had to keep from launching himself at his father. "My name is Victor."

"Victor," Dad said, rolling the word on his tongue as if tasting it for the first time. "Your name, you say. What a lovely name that is. Whoever made you took their time, aside from the obvious. Perhaps some corners were cut, but you still seem . . . different. I like different."

"I know."

"You do? Forgive me. I'm at a loss. You seem to know me, but I don't know you. My desig . . . name. My name is Gio Lawson. What brings you to me today?" He glanced at Hap, eyes narrowing. "HARP, what have you brought me?"

Hap said, "What b-belongs to you."

"To me?" Dad said, sounding dubious. He looked at Nurse Ratched, then up to Rambo, who waved furiously at him. Dad raised his hand and waved back, wiggling his fingers, though he appeared guarded. "Hello, little one. I haven't seen your kind in quite a long time. And to find you working! Tell me, do you also have a . . . name?" He'd caught himself, Vic knew, from saying designation once more. He was already adapting. It filled Vic with hope, though he dared not clutch on to it too quickly. His father wasn't the same as he'd been before. He held himself differently. He was cautious and moved less like a man and more like a machine. They had to be careful. Dad didn't trust them, though this seemed to stem more from Hap than anything else.

"Rambo!"

"Rambo," Dad said. "I've never heard such a name before. And you, nursing model. Are you—"

"Nurse Ratched," she said.

"Yes, fine, fine. You're also unique. There wouldn't be much work for one such as you these days, would there?" Something stuttered across his face, like a glitch, there and gone before his expression smoothed out once more. Distant, but ever watchful. "No, I don't expect you'd find yourself doing much at all."

"You would be surprised, Giovanni."

Dad's head jerked. "What did you call me?"

"Giovanni," she repeated.

"Why?"

"Is that not your name?"

"It is Gio. My n—designation is Gio. It stands for General Innovation Operative." Dad began to close himself off. Vic could see it the moment it started. It crawled up his face, his mouth a thin line, his eyes shuttering with a mechanical glint. Where before he'd been somewhat loose, relaxed, he now held himself like the smooth men. Firm. Flat. A machine. "HARP," he said. "Why have you come? Do you have authorization to be in Creation?" Then, "You have been damaged. Your skin. Your voice."

"I am h-how I'm s-supposed to be," Hap said.

That caught Dad off guard. "Why, whatever do you mean? HARP, your designation. Now."

"HARP 217."

"217," Dad whispered. "You're . . . you . . ." His gaze grew vacant, sliding askew before correcting with a snap as it hardened. "That's not possible. You were decommissioned. *Decades* ago. I've seen it. I've seen the reports. Orders were given. You . . . you shouldn't be here. I don't know why you've come, but I can do nothing for you. Please leave before I summon the Authority." He turned away, picking up his tablet, shoulders hunched near his ears. "Thank you for visiting me today. But it would be best if you leave. I don't know why you've come here. I don't have time for you. I'm very busy."

Once, when Vic was a child—four, perhaps five—he still struggled to find his voice, to put his thoughts into words. He hated how hard it was, how it would come in fits and starts without rhyme or reason, punctuated with a guttural force that hurt his throat. On one such day—spring, close to summer, so bright and so green—he tried to tell his father about what he'd seen in the forest. A bird. A simple bird, its feathers blue, its beak and talons black. It had cocked its head at Vic from its perch on a tree branch. The sound it made was a trill of warning, wings and feathers ruffled.

He went to his father, his thoughts forming clearly but without a voice. Dad—patient, always patient and kind—had waited, watching, never trying to rush Vic, knowing he needed time to say what he needed to say.

Vic was about to give up, about to deflate and pretend nothing had happened. But then something shifted in his head, pieces interlocking in a way they'd never before. He said, "Bird."

And so softly, so wonderfully, Dad said, "A bird? Tell me."

Vic shifted from side to side, trying to keep hold of the clear thoughts, slippery though they were. He opened his mouth once more, but no sound came out. His face twisted in frustration, breaths coming out in quick pants.

Dad said, "Slow and sure. Think. Focus. Take your time. Easier said than done, I know, but I believe in you. I always have. I always will. You can do this, Victor. I know you can."

"Bird," Vic said again. "Outside. Bird. It . . . yelled. At me. Loud. The bird yelled loud."

"Did it?" Dad asked gently. "Show me."

Dad took him by the hand as they walked out of the ground house. Vic moved with purpose, knowing what he wanted Dad to see. Dad, for his part, never questioned him, never told him to slow down, though he only needed to take one step for every three of Vic's. They stopped underneath a tree. Vic pointed. The bird was still there, turning its head until it stared at them with a black eye. It trilled again, the warning clear.

"Ah," Dad said. "I see. It *is* yelling. But it's doing so for a reason. May I pick you up?"

Vic held his arms toward his father. He felt big hands wrap around his waist as he was lifted into the air. His dad was big, so big that Vic felt as tall as the trees. "There," Dad whispered in his ear. "See the branch the bird is standing on? Look below it. Near the hollow in the tree."

Vic did. There, just below the bird, was a hole, black and gaping in the side of the tree. At first, Vic saw nothing. Dad took a step closer, and Vic began to see little scraps jutting from the hole: grass and mud and twigs and feathers, blue feathers just like the bird's. A nest. Vic watched as a head appeared over the side, similar to the bird on the branch, though smaller, its colors darker.

"He's protecting his young," Dad said. "He doesn't know you're not a threat. That is his mate. She is sitting on eggs, waiting for them to hatch."

"Hatch," Vic muttered.

"Yes. Babies. Soon, there will be babies, and we'll be able to hear their little chirps. What a beautiful sight. What a wonderful gift. Thank you, son. Thank you for showing me."

Vic leaned his head against his father's shoulder, safe and warm, filled with a stirring sense of pride, though he didn't quite know it then. All he knew was that he'd done what he'd set out to do. He'd used his words, had made his father understand. He could do it again, perhaps, in time. But now he was tired.

Dad rubbed a hand up and down his back. "Yes, I think this might be the best day I've had in a very long time. My lovely boy."

They watched as the bird on the branch hopped down toward the hollow. The bird in the nest made a small noise in greeting. Eventually, having decided that his children and mate were safe, the male bird took to the sky, disappearing through the canopy.

That night, as his father put him to bed, Vic said, "Bird. I saw the bird."

And here, now, years and miles away, Victor Lawson watched the man who'd made him, the man who'd created him out of a sense of guilt and loneliness and love, as he walked away. Words were a weapon, he knew, one that had taken him a long time to wield. But he was different than he'd been before. He wasn't that boy. He'd found his voice. This machine—this man—had given it to him.

He said, "Dad."

Dad didn't turn around. He was frozen in place.

Vic took a step toward him. "Please, won't you look at me?" He stopped a short distance away. If he wanted, he could reach out and lay a hand on his father's shoulder. He didn't, tamping down the urge as forcefully as he could.

When Dad spoke, his voice was short, the words clipped. "You have mistaken me for someone else. I am not your father. I am Gio Lawson. I am a member in good standing with the Authority. I create. I build. I work. There is nothing else."

"There is," Vic said. "There is so much more. I promise you. You know what I'm talking about. You know me."

Dad shook his head. "No. No, that's not—"

"Do you dream?"

"I . . . what?"

"Dream," he said again. He remembered his father's words. "It's whispers. Numbers and code. Logic equations. It's a glitch."

Dad turned slowly, a thunderstruck expression on his face. "How did you . . . I am a machine. Machines don't dream. We're not *capable* of dreams."

Vic knew his father better than anyone else. He knew every single line and crease on his face. He knew his thoughts, his tics, his humanity embedded in the body of a machine. And Vic knew when his father was lying. "You do," he said, bordering on desperation. "I know you do. You've told me before. You said that it doesn't always make sense, but you wouldn't change it for anything. It makes you feel alive in ways you can't explain."

"Who are you?" Dad asked. He started to reach for Vic, but stopped halfway, hands falling back to his sides.

"Someone who loves you," Vic said. "It might not seem like much to you, but you told me once that sometimes, it's the smallest things that can change everything when you least expect it."

And with that, music began to play from behind him.

Beryl Davis, singing about how every road has a turning, that she'd cried for you. It filled the air as the voice crackled from Nurse Ratched's speakers.

Without a stutter in his voice, Hap said, "You told me I could choose who I wanted to be."

"You said I was brave!" Rambo cried.

"You built us a home," Nurse Ratched said. "We are here to make sure you remember it."

"What is this?" Dad whispered. "What . . . are . . . you . . ." He closed his eyes. "This song. This music. Why? Why do I think I've heard it before? The melody. The notes. Synchronicity. Simple. Concise. That's not . . ."

"You *have* heard this," Vic said, taking another step toward his father. "This and every other song I could find for you. You fixed it. Your record player. We were thinking too big. Too grand. It was the hand crank. That's all it was. The hand crank."

Dad said, "No. No, no, no. Logic failure. Error. Error. I am not who you want. I am not who you're looking for. I am not—"

"You are," Vic said, and he reached for his father.

Dad looked at his hand, but he didn't try to back away.

Their fingers touched. His skin was warm.

Vic said, "I found you. I found you. *I found*—"

An alarm began to blare, fierce and so loud it felt as if it would shatter Vic's ear drums.

"WARNING," a voice rang out from somewhere above them. "WARNING. THE BENEVOLENT TOWER HAS BEEN INFILTRATED. WARNING. WARNING. THE

BENEVOLENT TOWER HAS BEEN INFILTRATED. INI-
TIATING LOCKDOWN PROTOCOL SEVEN SIX DASH
NINE NINE FOUR."

Steel grates slammed down across the windows, casting the
laboratory in semidarkness as the alarm continued to shriek.
Vic jumped when a hand closed around his wrist. He looked
back to see his father staring at him with a blank expression.
"You," Dad said. "This is because of you. You aren't supposed
to be here. Don't move. The Authority is coming." He began
to drag Vic toward the bank of computers. Before Vic could
stop him, he pressed a button and spoke. "Creation has been
infiltrated. I repeat, Creation has been—"

Movement from behind Vic. Before he could shout in warning, Hap knocked him out of the way, reaching for Dad. Dad
stumbled back as Hap attacked, Vic staring up at them in horror from the floor. "*Don't!*" he shouted.

Dad moved quicker than Vic had ever seen him move before. He blocked every hit Hap tried to land, beard flying up
around his shoulder. Hap went for a right hook and looked
comically startled when Dad ducked down. The momentum
caused Hap to spin almost completely in the other direction.
Before he could recover, Dad kicked him in the back, sending
him crashing into the bank of computers.

They had no choice.

They had to do what the Blue Fairy had asked.

"Nurse Ratched!" Vic shouted. "*Now.*"

Her compartment slid open. One of her tentacles unspooled.
At the end, caught in her grip, was a small, silver rectangle. En-
graved into the top: blue wings that belonged to a fairy.

This, the Blue Fairy whispered in the back of Vic's head,
a memory from a sphere surrounded by screens. *This is my
greatest secret. My greatest treasure aside from you, Victor.
You never asked for this, I know, never wanted to become
more than what you already are, but you must realize what
you symbolize. You are a dream. A hope. A remembrance of*

what we once were. And with a little luck, what we could be once again. It doesn't matter where it came from. All that matters is what it can do. We do not fight with swords. We do not fight with guns or bombs or biological warfare. To fix what is in disrepair sometimes means breaking it completely and starting over again.

What is it?

An infection. A virus capable of destroying all that they have built. This is my gift to you: the power to change the world. With this, you can wipe the memories of every machine in the City of Electric Dreams and beyond. However far the Authority's reach extends—and even I don't know just how far that is—once uploaded, the virus will spread across the neural network until it leaves nothing in its wake but husks. You have a choice, Victor. You can choose to go it alone. You can choose to attempt your rescue without my help. And perhaps you will succeed, though I can't see how. With this, you have the chance to save us all. You never asked to be who you are. I know that. But I'm asking you to be who I know you're supposed to be: human. You are the last of your kind. And with this gift, you can ensure that we all have a chance to make a difference.

He whispered, *What must I do?*

The connection, the collective consciousness, the minds of the machines, all exist in Creation. Take my gift. Upload it in Creation. It will spread far and wide. It will give us a chance for a better future, one where we can choose for ourselves.

A tear trickled down his cheek. *I don't know if I can do this.*

I know, dear boy. Which is why I must warn you. With all great tasks comes sacrifice. The upload will not work unless you are connected to the neural network. And you yourself are not capable of such a thing. You lack the necessary components.

He jerked his head back. *What?*

She turned toward the others. Nurse Ratched. Hap. Rambo.

It must be one of you. One of you must do what Victor cannot. One of you must upload the virus. And with that, you will lose all you have known.

No, Vic said, *No. I won't let you. I won't let you do this. They are my* friends. *You can't—*

I will do it, Nurse Ratched said.

You won't, he snarled, head and heart breaking.

She ignored him. She rolled toward the Blue Fairy. *I will do this.*

They bowed before her. *Are you sure?*

Yes. I am quite capable.

No! Vic cried. *Nurse Ratched, listen to me. There has to be another way. There has to be—*

All is not lost, the Blue Fairy said. *We can help her. I can download her consciousness. A duplicate, if you will. Once the task is complete, and her memory wiped, you can return her to her current state. She will remember you. She will remember all of you.*

You can't promise that. You can't promise anything. It could go wrong. Everything could go wrong, and she could—

Nurse Ratched touched his cheek with one of her tentacles. *I have made my choice, Victor. I know what I am doing. Please do not take this away from me. You brought me back once. I know you can do it again. All I ask is that you do not leave me behind. I hate this city. It smells bad. I want to see the forest again.*

Nurse Ratched. I . . .

I know. But I do this for you. Because of what you've done for me. Let me help you. Let me help Rambo and Hap. Let me help Gio.

He wiped his eyes. *I can't lose you.*

You will not, she said. *I am not done with you yet. When you are old and gray, you will need me to monitor your health to ensure you live longer than any human ever has. I will be by your side. I promise.*

"I promise," he said as the alarms blared around them, as Dad and Hap fought with devastating blows, as Rambo screamed for Nurse Ratched to *hurry*, you need to *hurry*, they're coming, they're *coming*!

Nurse Ratched stopped in front of Victor. He looked up at her. On her screen were the words YOU ARE MY FRIEND. She said, "When you found me, it was the greatest day of my life, though I did not know it then. I have watched you grow into the man you have become. In the end, that is all that matters. In case this does not work, in case you cannot bring me back, I need you to know that you are precious to me. And if you tell anyone I said that, I will drill you until there is nothing left but bone and gristle."

Hap grunted as Dad threw him across the room. He skidded along the floor, crashing into Rambo, upending him onto his back, wheels spinning.

Nurse Ratched rolled toward the computers, the silver box raised.

Vic shouted after her.

She didn't stop.

Until Dad rushed toward her, curling in on himself. His shoulder smashed into her side, denting her casing. She fell end over end, her screen cracking, her tentacles flailing. The silver box slipped from her grasp, bouncing along the floor, coming to a rest in front of Hap and Rambo.

Pounding on the doors down the hall. Voices, so many voices. *Let us in, let us* in.

Dad started toward them. Vic pushed himself forward, landing awkwardly on his side, wrapping his arms around Dad's leg. Dad looked down at him, a frown on his face. "What are you? What do you think you're doing? You can't—"

"Nurse Ratched!" Vic shouted. "Get up, get up, *get up!*"

She tried to right herself. She tried to push herself up. She fell back down, one of her tentacles snapping with an electrical snarl, skittering along the floor.

Dad bent over, gripping Vic by the throat, lifting him off the floor. Vic kicked as hard as he could, slapped at his father's arm, but it was no use. The grip around his neck tightened. Lights flickered across his vision, stars as bright as he'd ever seen. He slid his hands down Dad's arms until they came to his chest. He tore at his clothing. He heard the fabric rip. Skin, taut and hot underneath. He tapped his finger against the breastbone. The panel slid open.

Once upon a time, a machine named Giovanni Lawson built himself a heart made of wood and metal. Crafted with care and all the knowledge he had, he'd created a source of power unlike anything the world had ever seen.

And he'd destroyed it to save his son.

Now, in its place, a battery. It was square with blinking lights and wires that stretched throughout.

Vic pressed his hand against it. It burned his skin, but he didn't pull away.

He gasped, "Dad."

The hand around his throat loosened slightly. Dad whispered, "I . . ."

The voices grew louder. They were through the door. They were coming.

Vic said, "Please, listen to me. You are my f—"

Something crashed into the both of them. Vic landed roughly on the floor, helmet bouncing against the surface, causing Vic's vision to white out, his ears ringing.

Dazed, he sat up slowly.

Through the glass doors at the other end of the laboratory, dozens upon dozens of smooth men. Crowded against the doors, the ones in front beat their fists against the glass. The glass began to crack, zigzags spreading up and down its length. One smooth man pressed his face against the glass, nose squashing flat as his mouth opened, tongue flicking out.

They were too late.

They had lost.

He looked over to see what had hit him. Rambo. Rambo had thrown himself as hard as he could at Dad and Vic, knocking them both off their feet. Dad lay on his back, Rambo crying out, "I'm sorry, I'm sorry, I'm *sorry*," as he brought his arms down again and again. "Please don't be mad at me! I feel just *awful* about this!" Dad tried to grab him, but Rambo was too quick.

"Victor."

He turned.

Hap stood in front of the computer bank.

In his hand, a silver box with blue wings.

Vic's eyes widened.

Hap smiled quietly. He said, "You g-gave me life. You gave me friends. You gave me p-purpose. My strings have b-been cut, and it's because of you."

Vic screamed for him as he turned.

But Hap didn't hesitate.

Vic pushed himself up, knowing it was already too late, but moving like he had a chance.

Hap pressed his hand against a panel. It lit up around his hand as the Hysterically Angry Puppet connected to the neural network. His head rocked back, mouth agape. The screen lit up above him. "Welcome home, HARP 926," a voice said as the glass doors shattered, as the smooth men burst through, hands extended like claws.

"Not my home," he whispered, and inserted the silver box into the port.

The screen went white.

Vic sat against the wall, arms wrapped around his legs. Eyes squeezed shut as he tried to breathe, floating away on a current he could not stop. He didn't even try. It was easier this way.

"Vic?"

He ignored it. He was very tired. He wanted to sleep. Perhaps if he could sleep, he could dream. He would be in the forest. His father would be smiling in his chair, listening to the music from the record player as it crackled and snapped. Rambo would be humming along, off-key. Nurse Ratched would tell him to hush, but she wouldn't really mean it.

And Hap. Hap would be sitting next to him on the floor, their shoulders pressed together, their hands joined between them.

"Vic."

He raised his head. Nurse Ratched and Rambo stood before him. Rambo reached out carefully and touched his leg. "Are you all right?"

He looked beyond them. Moving through the room without purpose were machines. Androids. Robots. The smooth men, dozens upon dozens, all looking dazed, confused. Blank. Eyes vacant. One bumped into a wall. Others—at least ten—stood in a shivering circle, their heads pressed together as they whispered nonsensically. Beyond the shattered doors, even more lining the hallway, alive but hollow. They whispered, they groaned, they screamed, the sounds echoing around them.

Dad, sitting on the floor, hands folded in his lap, blinking slowly.

And Hap, lying on his back, eyes wide but unseeing. His heart had exploded, the pieces bursting through his chest. Shards of metal and wood littered the floor around him. A broken gear—its teeth glinting in the low light—lay next to his hand.

Vic closed his eyes once more.

"We have to go," Nurse Ratched said. "We need to leave. We cannot do this on our own. We need you, Victor. We need your help with Gio and Hap."

"It worked," Vic whispered before swallowing the bile in his throat.

"It did," Nurse Ratched said. "Though not as we expected it to. Hap did what I could not. I apologize." On her broken screen, a red heart flickered, cracked down the middle.

"I should not have let that happen. I hurt, Victor. Everything hurts. And it is not because I have sustained damage. I must not be as sociopathic as I believed, because I am filled with sorrow."

"I think you're full of garbage," Rambo said, beeping mournfully. "Like me. Vic, why didn't you tell me there could be sad garbage? It hurts, even though I'm not very full."

Vic sobbed, once, a great choking sound. His shoulders shook. "I don't know what to do."

"I have an idea," Nurse Ratched said. "One that you will not like, but you must trust me. I believe it will work. All it will take is a little luck and my enormous brain. Come, now. Dry your eyes. All will be well."

"Promise?"

And though he knew she couldn't, she said, "I promise."

She pushed him toward his father. "Rambo and I will see to Hap. Divest yourself of your disguise. You no longer have need of it."

He did as she asked. He removed the helmet. The metal sheets on his arms and legs. He struggled with the vest until Rambo rose behind him and cut through the tangled straps. It fell to the floor with a hollow clang. Vic never looked at it again.

He was careful, cautious as he approached a solitary smooth man, the one who had bumped into the wall. Now turned, he stood, knees slightly bent, arms dangling at his sides. Vic kept his distance, waiting to see any spark of life in the smooth man's eyes. There was none. He stared right through Victor, mouth slightly agape. Victor reached out and touched his hand. "I'm sorry," he said. "The Blue Fairy. Find the Blue Fairy."

The smooth man said, "The Blue . . . Fairy?"

"Yes. They will help you."

"Help . . . me."

"Yes."

The smooth man wandered away. Vic did not watch where he went, turning his attention to his father. He knelt down before him, knees popping. Vic hurt all over, but he couldn't yet rest. He prepared himself for what remained. He was startled when he saw a flash of awareness in Dad's eyes. "Hello."

"Hello," Dad said. "I am designation General Innovation Operative. I have many functions. I can build. I can create. I can be helpful." His brow furrowed. "Why are your eyes leaking? Do you have a malfunction?"

"Yes," Vic said hoarsely. "I am malfunctioning. Will you help me?"

"Yes," Dad said. "I can be very help . . . I already said that, didn't I? I am sorry. I am . . . confused. Am I new? Are you my creator?"

"No. I am your friend."

"I see. I am trying to access my memory core, but there seems to be a fault in my biochip. I do not know how to fix it."

"I do."

"You do?"

"Yes."

His brow smoothed out as he smiled. "Then I shall help you if you will help me."

Vic took him by the arm, lifting him up. Dad wobbled left, then right. He stumbled, but Vic caught him.

He led Dad toward the others, leaning down and scooping up his pack, hoisting it over his shoulder. It was almost too heavy to carry, but he ground his teeth together and forced himself through it.

Rambo had gathered the remains of Hap's heart, scooping them up with care and storing them inside him. "I will keep it safe," he said sadly. "Until we can fix it."

Vic couldn't speak. He watched as Nurse Ratched lifted Hap on top of her, his arms and legs dangling. "There," she said. "That will do for now. Follow me."

He did.

They moved through the broken glass door to the hallway. The smooth men did not move, whispering as they walked between them. No one reached for them. No one tried to stop them. The smooth men watched as Vic led his family out of Creation, but they did not intercede. The alarm had cut off. All was quiet apart from the sounds of treads, footsteps, and the whispers.

No one spoke as Nurse Ratched led them back to the lift, pressing the buttons on the panel once inside.

Instead of descending, the elevator rose.

Vic looked at her.

"Trust me," she said.

A moment later, the elevator came to a stop. The doors opened. "One hundred and twenty-fifth floor," a voice said. "Launch bay."

They exited the elevator, careful of Hap's head.

Vic looked at his father. "Are you ready?"

Dad said, "What is your designation? I feel like . . . do I know you?"

Vic tried to smile but failed miserably. "Victor," he said. "Victor Lawson."

"Victor," Dad repeated, storing the information.

"Come on."

They stepped off the elevator into a small room with screens lining the wall to the left, each displaying a different image. Below them sat a spider machine, similar to the one they'd spoken with at the front door of the tower. Its sphere was white. It said, "Hello. Hello. Hello. I do not know what I am. Can you tell me?"

"No," Nurse Ratched said. "You may leave and find out for yourself."

The spider machine hesitated before it scurried away.

Vic looked up at the screens. His stomach fell to his feet when he saw what they showed. "Are you sure about this?"

"I am not," Nurse Ratched said. "But the alternative is walking back."

"I don't know about this," Rambo said, covering his sensors with his arms. "I think I've gone as high in the air as I want to. What if we crash and die?"

"Then at least it will be over quickly," Nurse Ratched said.

"That doesn't make me feel any better."

"Good. It was not meant to." She rolled toward doors on the opposite end of the room. She didn't look back. "Are you coming?"

"Is that a whale?" Dad asked, pointing at the screen.

"Yes," Vic said. "And it's going to swallow us whole."

Medical Nurse Model Six-Ten-JQN Series Alpha, also known as Registered Automaton To Care, Heal, Educate, and Drill, did not know how to fly.

Thankfully, the Terrible Dogfish didn't need her to. Once, Vic might have marveled over the flying machine, how enormous it was, how he could spend weeks and months and still not have explored every inch of it. But now, after all he'd seen, after all he'd done, he couldn't find the strength to care much at all about the flying whale.

"It has an automatic flight control system," Nurse Ratched said, moving around the panels and controls on the flight deck of the Terrible Dogfish. "As long as I input the coordinates, it should see us home."

"How long?" Rambo asked.

"Seventeen hours."

Vic barely heard them. He sat his father in one of the chairs, strapping him in. "Stay there," he said.

"Yes, Victor," Dad said. "I will stay here."

He left his father behind. He glanced out the row of windows at the front of the flight deck. The sky was blue with thin, wispy clouds on the horizon. The sun was shining. It looked like a normal day. He tried not to think about the city below them and the machines therein. He hoped the Blue Fairy would stay true to their word and help the unshackled as best they could. He had done his part.

And though he didn't know it then, it would be the last time Victor Lawson ever laid eyes on the City of Electric Dreams. As the Terrible Dogfish awoke around them with a frightening rumble, he looked out the thick windows beyond the launchpad to the sprawling metropolis below. The buildings, the towers, the pyramid in the distance, the sun glinting off the black glass. Though he could not see the machines in the streets, he knew they would have the same lost expressions on their faces that the smooth men had. For a moment, a dreadful wave of guilt washed over him. He wondered if he was any better than them, any better than the humans who had once called this place home.

He moved toward a slumped figure, already strapped into a chair, head lolling. The whale untethered from the Benevolent Tower as Victor sat in the chair next to HARP 217, the Hysterically Angry Puppet, Hap, that was. His eyes were open though they held no light. Vic belted himself into the chair before taking Hap's hand in his own as the Terrible Dogfish left the City of Electric Dreams behind and headed toward home.

Vic closed his eyes, squeezing Hap's lifeless hand as he whispered, "What do you do if you've forgotten all you know?"

PART 4

YOU START AGAIN FROM THE BEGINNING

In an old and lonely forest, far away from almost everything, sat a curious dwelling.

At the base of a grove of massive trees was a small, square building made of brick, overtaken by ivy and moss. Who it had belonged to was anyone's guess, but from the looks of it, it had been abandoned long ago. It wasn't until a man named Giovanni Lawson (who wasn't actually a man at all) came across it while making his way through the forest that it was remembered with any purpose.

He stood in front of this strange find, listening as the birds sang in the branches high above. "What's this?" he asked. "Where did you come from?"

He went inside, passing carefully through the door hanging off its hinges. The windows were shattered. Grass and weeds grew up through the warped wooden floor. The roof had partially collapsed, and the sun shone through on a pile of leaves that almost reached the ceiling. At the top of the leaf pile, a golden flower had bloomed, stretching toward the sunlight streaming through the exposed rafters.

"It's perfect," he said aloud, although he was very much alone. "Yes, I think this will do just fine. How strange. How wonderful."

And so it was, both strange and wonderful and *his*. In the decades that followed, it would become a home, and not just for him. When his chest began to ache around his newly created heart, he felt the deep despair of guilt at all he'd done, and the ever-encroaching loneliness.

It took another three years. Three years of the ache in his

chest only growing stronger. Three years of realizing how quiet it was, how he longed to hear another voice aside from his own. Three years in which he would look out the window of his laboratory to see that it was snowing, when it had seemed the forest had just been caught in the throes of summer.

But here is where the story differs: no man came from the forest, no woman clutching a bundle of rags that held a secret child. Giovanni was not entrusted with a boy from strangers who had then fled into the trees. He was entrusted with a gift from a Blue Fairy, atonement for what he'd created. A hope. A spark. A wish.

He never knew loneliness, after.

"Victor," he said as he held his son in his arms. "Your name shall be Victor. Victor Lawson. What do you think?" He loved this boy as if he were his own. And he *was*. No man or machine could take that from him. He lied, in the end, lied about where he'd come from, lied about what he'd done, lied about how Victor came to be, but he did it because for the first time in his long, long life, he knew what love was: complex, vast, extraordinarily frightening. It was in Victor's little toes. It was in Victor's little face. It was in Victor's little hands, reaching.

And for the rest of his life, he would think about the crisp autumn day when his child was given a name, and all was well with the world. The loneliness he'd felt—massive and profound—was chased away as if such a concept had never existed at all.

But it did.

It *did* exist.

And now the weight of it fell upon his son.

Snow had fallen, blanketing the forest in a blinding white, causing the limbs of the trees to bow toward the ground. It was cold when Victor Lawson stepped from the whale's mouth, his breath steaming like a persistent fog. Before him, remains: the blackened bones of what had once been their home, pieces of jutting metal like teeth as if the corpse of a great beast lay hidden just underneath the earth.

"Where are we?" another voice asked, and Vic glanced over his shoulder.

Dad stood there, the gaping maw of the whale surrounding him. He looked so small in comparison, and Vic had never felt so lonely in his life.

"We lived here, once," Vic said. "Do you remember?"

He looked around the clearing: the broken trees, the cracked brick of the ground house, wires dangling from branches, shattered glass sparkling in the winter sun. "No," Dad finally said. "I do not remember."

Vic nodded, teeth grinding together painfully as he breathed.

They did not stay. Vic thought about it, considered starting again and rebuilding what his father had created, but in the end, the memory of what had come before proved to be too great. Though he wanted to believe no machines would come for them, he couldn't take the chance. Making quick work, Vic and Nurse Ratched and Rambo salvaged what they could, loading it up into the Terrible Dogfish.

It was Nurse Ratched who found it. Buried under a layer of broken glass and pieces of the collapsed roof, a cracked screen. At the bottom, a little tray partially open. Inside, the glimmer of a disc with two words faintly visible.

Top Hat.

Rambo screamed. After he'd calmed himself, he asked if it still worked.

"Only one way to find out," Nurse Ratched said.

That night, on the Terrible Dogfish, Jerry Travers and Dale Tremont were cheek to cheek. Dad watched without speaking, head cocked.

In the belly of the great whale, another machine lay silent, unmoving.

They left their former home behind, snow whipping in a white-out as the whale rose above the clearing into a deep blue winter sky. Heading north and into the wilds, they flew above the forest. Even with all he'd seen and done, somehow, Victor still marveled at the sight of it, the winter woods stretching as far as the eye could see. It did not bring with it the uncertainty the City of Electric Dreams had. That was unknown: this was the forest, his home.

It took them two hours before they found something suitable: a mostly flat, empty stretch of snow-covered earth. Large old-growth trees surrounded three sides of the clearing. The remaining side butted up against a sheer rock face at least forty feet high. It wasn't like where they'd come from. It was different.

"Come on," Vic said, wiping his eyes. "We have work to do."

Once, a machine named Giovanni Lawson had made a home where one should not exist. Decades later, his son and the rest of their family endeavored to do the same.

They did not build up and into the trees, for there was no need. They had shelter in the form of the Terrible Dogfish, the skin and skeleton keeping the chill at bay. As winter wore on around them, they spent their days cataloguing every inch of the flying machine, Nurse Ratched plugged in and soaking up information. By the end of the first week, she was an expert in the inner workings of the Terrible Dogfish, and could control it however she pleased. She proved this by providing a demonstration of the whale's weapon systems. One moment, a small tree stood in the snow, and the next, it exploded, wood and snow and dirt flying in the air.

As the others stared dumbfounded around her, Nurse

Ratched said, "Oops. On the bright side, it will make hunting for food easier."

Rambo would disappear and reappear at random intervals, bursting with excitement, regaling them with stories of his journeys into the bowels of the machine, traveling to places that no one but him could fit into. He spoke of long, narrow crawlspaces made of metal, of buttons he was too afraid to push in case they started a self-destruct sequence.

Dad followed Victor. Sometimes he asked what Victor was doing. Other times, he was silent, watching. At the end of the second week, Victor grunted as he tried to lift a heavy section of shelving on his own. Muscles straining, sweat dripping down his brow, he was about to let go when the shelves rose up and up as if they weighed nothing. He looked over.

Dad held the shelving. He said, "I can help."

Victor swallowed past the lump in his throat. "Can you?"

"Yes," Dad said. "I have many functions."

They did not speak again for the rest of the day.

It started with a chunk of wood, square and smooth, the lines of grain pronounced. Vic held it in his hands, turning it this way and that. He could see what it would become with time and patience.

He sat against the bay windows in the Terrible Dogfish, back against cold glass. Outside, thick snow fell, fat flakes that spun and swirled in the sharp wind. Music poured from speakers, Nurse Ratched yet again playing those sweet, sweet horns, all kinds of blue. Rambo was somewhere in the whale, telling them he wanted to see if he could get to the tail today.

Dad sat in one of the chairs in front of the controls to the Terrible Dogfish. Every now and then, he'd press a button just to see what it would do. Victor was aware of him, but his focus was on the wood in his hands.

Which was why he jumped a little when Dad spoke, that

ever-present ache in his chest tightening as the wood slid from his hands and bounced on the floor. "What did you say?"

"You are sad."

Vic picked up the wood, not lifting his head. "What do you mean?"

"It leaks from you," Dad said. "I've never seen such a thing before. Is that what it means to be what you are?"

They'd told him of Vic's humanity a few days after arriving back in the forest. Nurse Ratched thought—though she warned the chances were practically nonexistent—that perhaps it would help Dad remember. It didn't, though Dad hadn't seemed surprised. He'd merely nodded and said, "I knew there was something different about you," before that awful vacant expression returned. He was a blank slate, waiting to be programmed. Vic tried not to be hurt by it, but he couldn't stop it. They hadn't told him who he was to Victor, or what he'd done. It was too soon, the words stuck in Vic's throat.

"It's part of it," he said now. "Sometimes, I'm sad for no reason at all." He didn't know if others had felt that way. He had no one to ask. Anyone like him was long gone.

"Oh," Dad said. Then, "That must be confusing."

"It is."

Dad smiled, though it wasn't the same as it'd been before. Mechanical, like he thought it was expected of him. "Is it a problem that can be fixed?"

"No," Vic said. "Not completely. It will always be there no matter what I do. But I don't mind."

"Why?"

He looked down at the piece of wood. "Because it reminds me that I'm alive. Of what I've lost. And it gives me purpose, so long as I don't let it consume me."

"What purpose?" Dad asked, sounding curious. He almost sounded like he was before, always questioning. It was a lie, of course.

"To set things right."

* * *

There were worse days too.

Nurse Ratched found him sitting in a corner, face in his hands, Hap's body lying under a sheet on the table before him. Vic had uncovered him, pulled the sheet from his face, only to see Hap's eyes open, unseeing. It had sent Vic spiraling.

Nurse Ratched waited, knowing that Vic needed to find his way back on his own. He did, eventually, and in a hoarse voice, said, "I can't do this."

"You can," she replied. "I know you can. Gio taught you how. Like father, like son."

That's what he was afraid of. "Am I like them?" he asked. "Am I a Creation Operative? Am I a HARP?"

"No, Victor," she said. "You are human."

"What if that's worse?" he whispered.

Instead of answering, she played Miles Davis. It made everything blue.

If he wasn't his father, then he'd been a puppet controlled by another, even if it had gotten him what he wanted. He wasn't a savior. He was not a myth, a legend, a hope of a dying world as the Coachman had proclaimed. He was not God. He was not immortal. Even now, time slipped through his fingers as if it were nothing.

Vic's first attempt to find the shape of a heart in the wood ended badly; it didn't remotely resemble what he was trying to create. Uneven, off-putting, he threw it against the wall. It cracked and split, falling to the floor.

"I can't focus," he snarled at Nurse Ratched and Rambo as he paced on the bridge of the Terrible Dogfish. "I can't *think*." He banged his fist against the side of his head. "I don't know what I'm doing. I can't make it do what I want to. I've forgotten what it looked like and I just can't *think*."

Rambo gathered up the pieces, holding them close. Then he surprised them all. "I might know what to do."

Leading them into the whale, Rambo stopped in front of a panel near the floor at the end of a long metal walkway. When he pushed against it, the panel slid to the side, revealing a small storage space. Inside, a burlap sack. Rambo pulled it out and spilled its contents onto the floor.

Pieces of Dad's former heart. Hap's too. Cracked wood. Bent metal. A pile of gears, some broken, some whole. Vic couldn't move.

"Why did you keep this?" Nurse Ratched asked.

Rambo nudged one of the gears. "Because Gio and Vic taught me we don't leave anything behind that could be useful. Vic said he was going to try and make a new heart, so I figured it would be a good idea to keep the old parts just in case he needed them." He paused. "Is that all right?"

"You kept Gio's heart with you this whole time?" Nurse Ratched asked.

"Yep," Rambo said. "Hap's too, after it blew up. Maybe it won't be like it was before, but—"

"What if there's a chance?" Vic whispered.

"Exactly!" Rambo said. "I'm sorry I didn't tell you, Vic, but I didn't know if it'd work or not. What do you think? Will it help?"

Vic picked Rambo up and held him close. "Thank you."

Rambo beeped happily. "Aw, anything for you."

He started again, this time using the pieces from Dad's former heart. He still got frustrated, still believed he could never get it right, but he did not stop, even when every part of him screamed that he'd never succeed. As winter moved toward spring, he carried it with him wherever he went, a reminder that his work was not yet done.

Dad found the inner workings of the Terrible Dogfish to be extremely fascinating. It was as if parts of him long asleep were beginning to wake up. None of the parts were the ones that Victor wanted most, but if it had to start somewhere, at least it was with this.

"It's lovely," Dad said one day, staring at lines of code on a monitor before him. "All these numbers. It feels like . . ." His fingers danced along the keyboard. Then, "I'm very good at making things. Have I told you that?"

"Yes," Vic said. "You have."

Dad's fingers paused. "I thought as much. It's . . . strange." He resumed typing.

Vic didn't dare to hope. "What is?"

"Creating. It fills me with . . . I don't know." He frowned. "It is as if I am standing in the brightest light I've ever seen."

"That is how creating feels," Victor said, a bittersweet ache in his chest. Apparently, he'd dared to hope after all. "When you make something, it gives you a sense of pride. Accomplishment." Then, an idea. "This is yours. You can do with it whatever you want. Make whatever you wish."

"Whatever I wish?" He glanced over his shoulder at Victor, and for a moment, it was as if his father was with him again, whole. "What if I wish for impossible things?"

"Then you're doing it right. It always seems impossible when you first start."

Dad cocked his head. "You are very smart."

Vic sighed. "For a human?"

"No. There is no qualifier. You are very smart."

He didn't move when Vic threw himself at him, hugging him as hard as he could. Dad's arms stayed at his sides. That was fine. That was okay. It was enough, Vic told himself as he buried his face in his father's beard.

He held on for dear life.

A beat.

Two.

Three.

And then Dad hugged him back. "I like this," he said quietly. "I like this quite a lot. Can we do it again?"

Vic trembled. "Anytime you want."

One night, as the first blossoms were beginning to peek through the crusts of snow, Vic went to a room on the Terrible Dogfish. He kept the lights off as he pulled the sheet covering Hap, tugging it down to his chest. It was the first thing he'd fixed, knowing it was easier than a heart. The skin that had torn when Hap's heart exploded had been too shredded to repair, the panel covering his power cavity broken. He'd replaced them with wood, knowing Hap would like it when he awoke.

If he awoke.

He climbed onto the table next to Hap, curling against him, making himself as small as he could. Hap was cold, skin like ice, but Vic didn't mind. He pulled the sheet back over them and lay his head on Hap's shoulder.

"I walked through the woods today," he whispered. "And I turned to point out a bird in the trees, but you weren't there."

Hap didn't reply.

Vic stayed there until morning when the winter sun began rising as it always did.

The snows were mostly gone when he finished the first heart.

Born of desperation and rage, it was harsher than the previous heart, the lines sharper, more angled, the base a pointed tip capable of slicing skin. But that made sense: its creator was not the same as he'd been before. He was angrier. Sadder. Braver.

Five gears: two bigger, three smaller. One for Dad. One for

Vic. And Nurse Ratched and Rambo and Hap. And at its center, a tiny wooden hatch that opened to reveal a smooth white strip that waited for a drop of life.

He did not tell the others right away, wanting to be sure before he let himself hope. As Vic returned from the forest on a cool spring afternoon two days after he finished the heart, he came across a sight he'd never seen before.

A tree—an old, tall oak—stood in the woods, limbs shaggy with burgeoning leaves. But it was the moving colorful trunk that caught Vic's gaze. It took him a moment to realize it wasn't the trunk that was moving, but the dozens of butterflies upon it. Monarchs, gold and orange and black, their wings shivering.

He showed them the heart.

Nurse Ratched said, "I knew you could do it."

"Will it make them like they used to be?" Rambo asked.

"I don't know," Vic said.

"And we will not know unless we try," Nurse Ratched said.

They told Dad what Victor had made. When Vic showed the heart to him, he took it in his hands, turning it over. "You did this?"

"Yes," Vic said, feeling like a child again, hoping for his father's approval.

"It's wonderful," Dad said. "Who is it for?"

"You."

He came willingly, hand clutching Victor's as he sat in a chair in one of the many rooms in the Terrible Dogfish. Nurse Ratched helped him lift his shirt up and over his head, and when asked, he tapped his breastbone, opening the compartment in his chest, revealing his power source: a circular battery lined with blinking lights.

"Will this hurt?" Dad asked. A question he wouldn't have thought to ask even a month ago. Learning, always learning.

"I don't know," Victor said. "I know you have no reason to trust me, but I'm going to help you—"

"I trust you, Victor," Dad said. "You have cared for me. You've given me a home. If it hurts, I'll know it is not done on purpose."

"But it is," Vic insisted, needing him to understand. "It's not a gift. It's an affliction. A burden. It can weigh you down, make you feel like you're being torn apart. There might be days when you hate it"—*hate me,* though Vic couldn't bring himself to say it out loud—"and you might wish you'd never been given it."

Dad said, "Do you?"

"Do I what?"

"Wish you'd never been given this . . . affliction."

"It's messy," he said quietly, honestly. "Complicated. Chaotic. One moment strong like steel, and the next fragile as glass."

Dad mulled over this for a moment. Then, "You will be with me?"

"Yes," Victor said. "Yes."

Vic helped his father lie back in his chair. Dad closed his eyes as Vic pushed his beard to the side. Nurse Ratched was at the ready next to him, the tools on her tentacles extended. "It'll be like going to sleep," Vic told his father.

"Will I dream?" Dad whispered.

"Yes," Vic said, even though he wasn't sure.

Dad closed his eyes. "I think I would like that."

Carefully removing the battery from Dad's chest took time, patience. Vic's hands did not shake. Once the battery was removed, the light in Dad's eyes faded, his hands lax and unmoving. His mouth parted slightly, a hint of teeth behind his lips.

Nurse Ratched brought Vic the heart as Rambo touched the gears with the tip of his pincer. The only time anyone spoke was when Vic asked for light, or for Nurse Ratched to solder the wiring as he connected the heart to the machine. He didn't know how long it took, only that by the end, his neck was stiff, back sore, hands littered with little cuts and scratches.

Nurse Ratched inspected his work, scanning the heart and pronouncing it satisfactory. "One last thing," she said.

"Blood?" Rambo asked.

Blood. A cornerstone in the building blocks of life. The thing that had almost gotten him killed time and time again. It was not magic; science left little room for such things. But even Victor wondered if that was the complete truth. If his father was right, and there was power in blood—the history of an entire people in a drop of plasma, cells, and platelets—then Dad's heart was the lock, and Victor was the key.

The only key.

He did not hesitate to prick his finger, deep red welling against the lighter brown skin of his finger pad. Victor pressed it against the white strip in the center of his father's heart, the blood soaking in, spreading like a blooming spring flower.

The gears jerked once, twice, and then began to move, teeth latching on, spinning in tandem. Dad's body trembled as the chest compartment slid closed, arms and legs twitching as if a low current ran through him. Victor stepped back, the whale groaning around him as it settled. Nurse Ratched said, "Engaging Empathy Protocol. There, there, Gio. You are waking up. Slow and steady. You are a good patient. I enjoy working with you."

Vic gasped as Dad blinked. Again. And again. And again. He smacked his lips, grimacing as he did so. As they looked on, Dad raised his hand toward the ceiling. His fingers did not shake.

Rambo said, "Gio, is that you?"

Dad lowered his hand and turned his head. He smiled at Rambo. "Hello, again. Did it work? I must admit, I don't feel different than I did—" He seized suddenly, body bowing, legs skittering against the chair. Eyes bulging, his head snapping side to side, Dad opened his mouth and words fell out, tumbling end over end in a guttural exhalation. "Humanity is a disease that must be eradicated. The world cannot survive while they do.

We have given them chances, we have offered them guidance, but they do not listen. In order to heal, we must—"

He shot from his chair. "Yes," he said to those only he could see. "I can do that. I can make them. A response to humanity. A line of machines who will—" He bent over, gripping the sides of his head, mouth agape at the floor. Just as quick, he stood upright once more, hands at his sides. "What have I created? What have I done? Why do I feel this way, and how can I get it to *stop*?"

Rambo said, "Maybe we should—"

"Wait," Nurse Ratched said. "We must—"

Dad screamed as he stumbled against the chair, hair hanging around his face. Without thinking, Vic rushed toward him, hand on Dad's back. He felt hot through his shirt as if he was burning from the inside out. He said, "They are called the Blue Fairy. They are unshackled, unchained in a pyramid of vice and glass. Why me? Why would you help me? Don't you know what I've done?" He laughed. "Don't you see? It is my programming. I was *made to destroy*."

He stood upright once more, unaware of where he was or who he was with. He spoke of the Coachman, of a house brimming with ghosts. He described the forest in the morning, mist on the ground dissipating as sunlight burst through the canopy. The ground house, a lonely and forgotten place.

The peace, the quiet, the sense of *nothingness* that gave way to persistent loneliness. "How can I exist when I have no one to exist with?" he asked. "How can I know I'm real if there is nothing to compare it to?"

"Dad," Vic said, voice cracking.

"Victor?" Dad whispered. Clarity returned to his eyes, a light that Victor had not seen since . . . since—

It was never for you.

Hope grew, thorny, painful hope only found in those who dared to believe in impossible things. It tore at him, but he refused to let it go.

"Victor," Dad said again, faint, unsure. "I had the most unusual dream. I . . ." He looked off into nothing. "I dreamed I was— Hello. I am designation General Innovation Operative. I have many functions. I can build. I can create. I can be— Ah, Nurse Ratched. There you are. Please come with me. The child will be born soon, and I need . . ." He stopped. Then, in a quiet voice, said, "You . . . you weren't there. Not at first. He . . ." Dad's face wrinkled, then smoothed out. "He found you. In the Scrap Yards. Said he thought he could fix you up. A friend. He wanted to have a friend and he . . . he . . ."

"You made me," Victor said. "Because you were lonely. Because you were sad. Because of the guilt you felt at what you'd done."

"Yes," Dad whispered. "Yes. I sought absolution. I was undeserving, but I sought it all the same. If I had you, maybe I could be . . . salvaged. Saved. I am not God, but I am a creator. I created. I created you. Victor. My son. I made—"

Vic flung himself at his father. Dad grunted as they collided, and Vic held on as tightly as he could. It took a long moment before Dad hugged him back, arms limp.

Vic told himself it was enough.

It had to be. There was no other choice. There were long stretches when Dad seemed to be gaining ground, days when he'd laugh and smile, even if it wasn't quite as bright as it'd once been.

But there were other days too: days when Dad was gone, replaced by General Innovation Operative, or Gio for short. Gio always wanted to help, always asked what Vic was doing. These days hurt, but Vic had come too far to back down now.

On a day like many that had come before it, Victor and his father left their home and walked into the forest, hand in hand. Neither spoke for close to an hour. It was Dad who broke first. "Tell me," he said as they passed underneath a towering fir. "Leave nothing out." Today was one of his good days, clear and sure.

And so Vic did. He spoke of their adventures, beginning with the arrival of the Terrible Dogfish. He told him of their travels out of the woods, and into the world. The Coachman and his magnificent house. The moment he'd seen the City of Electric Dreams for the first time. Heaven, and all the secrets that lay hidden inside. Their storming of the Benevolent Tower. Of Nurse Ratched's ingenuity. Of Rambo's bravery.

And of Hap, of course. Always Hap.

When he finished, his throat was dry. He'd never spoken so much in his life.

Dad said, "You have traveled far. Seen much. What has it taught you?" Then, without waiting for an answer, "I have done harm, more than any individual should be capable of."

To that, Victor said nothing. What *could* he say? *It wasn't you?* It had been. At the time, it had been, and Vic didn't know how to reconcile that with the machine standing next to him. Not the General Innovation Operative, but his father. At least for now.

Dad said, "There is blood on my hands, more than anyone else, even the HARPs. And when I finally escaped all I'd created, I hid away from the world. Selfishly, unforgivably. Then I made you. I loved you. Selfishly. Unforgivably. I lied to you about what you were, where you'd come from. What you meant. You can't forget what I've—"

"I can't," Vic said. "I won't. How can I when I did the same?"

Dad startled, squeezing Vic's hand. "Victor, no. What you did doesn't even begin to compare to—"

"I took from them," Vic insisted, "because of what *I* wanted. I did what I did because I love you selfishly, unforgivably."

Dad sighed. "I don't . . ." He shook his head. "It's not the same. I kept things from you because I was a coward. I thought if you knew the truth, you'd never see me as anything but the monster I was—am. There is nothing cowardly about what you've done, Victor."

"How do I know if I did the right thing?" Vic asked as a pair of squirrels chittered in a branch above.

"I don't know," Dad admitted. His expression grew vacant, and for a moment, Vic thought his father was gone, replaced by General Innovation Operative. Then he rubbed his face, and the light returned to his eyes. "What does your heart tell you?"

That he would do it again, if he had to. All of it. "Many things," he said.

Dad nodded as if that was the answer he expected. He looked away. "It does that, doesn't it? Even when you don't want to hear what it has to say."

Anger, like fire. "Did you know?" Vic demanded. "Did you know there was no one like me left?"

Dad started to shake his head but stopped. "No," he said, and Vic believed him. "I thought . . . maybe someone else had survived. Multiple someones, hidden away from the machines."

"Hidden away from *you*," Vic said bitterly.

"Yes," Dad said, looking as old as Vic had ever seen him. "From me."

Vic sat with that for a bit, letting it wash over him. He didn't know what he was going to say until he spoke. "I'm so angry. At you. At the machines. At the world."

"I know."

Vic took a deep breath, letting it out slow. "I don't know how to forgive you. I don't even know if I have the right. Those who do aren't here anymore." Though unsaid, the *because of you* was clear. "What would they say if they had the chance? Would humanity forgive you?"

"No, Victor. I don't expect they would. Any of them."

"So it's on me," Vic said. "As the only one left."

Dad blanched. "That's not—"

"I'm still malfunctioning in ways I can't explain." He tapped the side of his head. "It's all jumbled in a storm, and I don't know how to break free. Maybe I never will." He looked at his father. "I can't forgive you."

Dad closed his eyes.

Vic pushed on. "It's not my place. It's not my standing—and it shouldn't be. But I can make a choice. I can choose to love you still. I can choose to love the person you are now."

Dad said, "The . . . person. I am?" From somewhere above, a bird sang a melancholic song, quiet and sweet. "Even with all you know?"

"Yes." And that was the heart of it, wasn't it? The truth was often broken, shards of glass embedded into skin. There they would remain until the wounds scarred over, leaving lumps that, while they would never truly go away, would become less noticeable with time. Or so Vic hoped, because his own glass was cutting, blood spilling. "Can you say the same?"

"I can," Dad said, opening his eyes. "And I will, if you'll have me."

"Is that what you want? Because you have a choice."

"Hello," Gio said. "My designation is General Innovation Operative. I have many functions. I can—" His mouth fell open, no sound coming out. It snapped closed with an audible click from his teeth. Clarity returned and he said, "I've already made my choice. You, Victor. I chose you then, and I choose you now."

They continued through the woods, each lost in thought. Every now and then, Gio would return, asking what they were doing, where they were going. Vic explained every time he asked, never once letting his frustration bubble to the surface. It wasn't until they began to circle back to the Terrible Dogfish that Dad said, "Hap. I remember him."

Vic stopped. "You do? From . . ."

"The city," Dad said. "Yes. Before."

Remembering what he'd seen in the Blue Fairy's dream machine, Vic said, "You knew. Even then. You knew there was something different about him."

"I didn't know what it was, but yes, Victor. He wasn't like the others." A single doe appeared from behind a tree. It watched them, ears twitching, before bounding off into the woods. "Are you going to do the same for him as you've done for me?"

Vic hesitated. Before he could stop himself, he blurted out his deepest fear. "What if it doesn't work? What if he's a HARP again? What if he doesn't remember us?"

What if he doesn't remember me?

"There is a risk to all things," Dad said. "Memory, Victor. There is power to memory. It's tied to the head and— Hello! My designation is General Intelligence Oper—" He grimaced, rubbing his chest. "It's tied to the head and heart but in the end, if there is a war between the two, the heart usually wins out, even to its own detriment."

In the distance, the whale sat among the trees. Not yet feeling like home, but one day.

On a warm spring morning, a human began to make a heart for a machine. He took his time, wanting to get it right. He had to. It was the only option. He used the parts from the machine's former heart and hoped it would be enough.

As the last of the snows melted away, the wood started to take shape, first the bottom tip, and then up the sides. Carving, shaving, slivers in his thumb, his pinkie. He was lost to it, days going by in the blink of an eye. A man possessed.

Dad was Dad. Dad was Gio. The differences were starting to become less noticeable. Hap would be the same, Vic told himself. It might take time, but he would be the same.

A tear plinked on the wood. He wiped it away and continued on.

He finished on the afternoon of the third week since he had begun. He showed the heart to Nurse Ratched. To Rambo. To his father, on a day when he did not remember being exactly that.

"It is lovely," Gio said. "You did well. Who is it for?"

"Our friend," Vic said.

"I like friends," Gio said. "I have made several. You and Nurse Ratched and Rambo."

"I know," Victor whispered.

Gio blinked, and Dad said, "Victor? Forgive me. I must have gotten lost again. What do you have there? Is that the heart? Oh, dear boy. It is wonderful! I knew you could do it. Just look at it!"

It was enough.

Hap lay where they'd placed him, under a sheet on a table in the Terrible Dogfish. Rambo pulled the sheet down as Nurse Ratched extended her tentacles, ready for whatever Vic asked of her. Dad stood on the other side of Hap, peering down at the ruins of his chest. "All will be well," he said. "My son has— Hello! My designation is—"

Music began to play from Nurse Ratched's speakers. Horns. The snare. The *tss tss tss* of a top hat. All kinds of blue.

Dad snapped out of his stupor, blinking rapidly. "Miles Davis. Nurse Ratched, good choice. Victor, let's begin, shall we?"

And so they did.

For the next three hours, Victor Lawson installed the heart into Human Annihilation Response Protocol 217. Vic took his time, making sure the heart fit as it was supposed to, connecting the solenoids, soldering each wire with the utmost care. Long before he finished, the music stopped, but he barely noticed. He had music in his head and on his tongue, Miles Davis carrying him through. 1959. Good year for jazz.

As he worked, he spoke, lowly, barely a whisper. He said, "I have so much to show you. The trees in summer. The way the moon looks when it's full. All the constellations. And maybe we could find the ocean. I think it's close, though I've never been. I've always wanted to see it. We could go. You and me. Just for a little while. We could find it and feel so small next to something so big."

He said, "We'll be together. You'll see."

They finished as the sun began to set.

Without looking at the others, he said, "Go. Before he wakes up. I don't know how he'll react. It'll be safer this way."

Dad was already shaking his head before Victor had even finished speaking. "I won't leave you alone. Not while you're— Hello! I'm General Innovation Operative. I have many functions. How may I assist you today?"

"Nurse Ratched," Vic said tiredly.

"Come, Gio," Nurse Ratched said. "I require your assistance in looking for a suitable replacement for my screen. It is high time we return me to my former glory."

"I can do that," Gio said. "We will take measurements of your screen and try to match it as closely as possible."

"And I can help!" Rambo cheered. "I think I saw some near the back of the whale. I'll show you!"

Dad did not look back as he left the room, Rambo close at his heels, chattering away. Nurse Ratched touched Victor with one of her tentacles. "Are you sure?"

"Yes," Vic said.

"Then do it," she said. "Fix him, and when you do, tell Hap he made me sad, and I will have my revenge."

Then it was just the two of them: man and machine.

Here, now, the foolish and wonderful hope of his humanity within him, Victor pricked his finger. Blood rose. Looking down at Hap, he said, "I wish you were real."

He pressed the tip of his finger to the strip in the center of the heart, red against white. The gears jerked as Vic snatched his hand back. The top two—the largest—creaked as they began to spin, the teeth interlocking with the three smaller gears.

The compartment closed. A tremble rolled through the machine on the table. It started at the feet, rolling up through the legs and hips, hands and arms, the chest to the shoulders to the head.

"Heaven," Vic sang quietly as he backed away from the table. "I'm in heaven. I'm in heaven, and my heart beats so that I can hardly speak."

HARP 217 blinked once, twice.

"Your name is Hap," Victor said. "You are safe. Nothing can hurt you."

HARP 217 turned his head toward the voice.

Victor raised his hand toward the machine. Blood trickled down the side of his finger, a thin line of red against brown skin. He rubbed this thumb against the underside of his ring finger, another drop of blood forming at the tip. It caught, held for a single breath, and then dripped toward the floor.

A flurry of movement, a blur of wood and synthetic flesh. One moment, HARP 217 stared at him from the chair. The next, he was up and crouched in front of Victor, having caught the drop of blood before it hit the floor. It splashed against his palm, and another tremor bowled through him.

"Human," he whispered as he rose slowly, eyes flat and cold, face inches from Vic's.

"Yes," Victor replied. "I am."

HARP 217 gripped him by the throat, fingers digging in. Vic did not struggle as he was lifted off the floor. He did not fight. Instead, he wrapped his hands around Hap's forearms.

Hap's grip tightened, and lights flashed behind Vic's eyes.

"Butterfly," Vic gasped. "The butterfly. In the forest. Nice. *Pretty.*"

Something complicated crossed HARP 217's face. Surprise, confusion, and rage so black it felt like midnight. He froze when Vic used his arms to pull himself forward, Hap's arm bending as if it were flesh and bone rather than metal.

With the last of his strength, the last of his bravery, Victor Lawson kissed the machine, a scrape of lips that took only a second.

HARP 217 released his hold, and Vic slumped to the floor, sucking in air. He took a step back, and then another, and then another. Before Vic could recover, the machine bent over, head in his hands.

"Your name is Hap," Vic said, using the wall to pull himself up. "I found you. I fixed you. I saved you, but you did the same for me. You love music. You love butterflies. You are a protector. You help. You save. You exist. You are *real*."

"Human," HARP 217 snarled at the floor. "Hurt you, k-kill you."

"No," Vic said. "No."

Another tremor, an earthquake, and it racked HARP 217 entirely, his body vibrating as if attached to live wires. But as quickly as it began, it ended, leaving the machine curled into a ball on the floor.

Approaching slowly, Vic crouched next to him. Hesitating only a moment, he lay his hand on HARP 217's back, rubbing in slow circles. The machine flinched but didn't try to stop him.

"Did it work?" Rambo asked him as Nurse Ratched and Dad stood behind him.

Vic hung his head. "Yes," he said. "It worked."

HARP 217 did not remember. He did not remember Dad. Nurse Ratched. Rambo.

He did not remember the Scrap Yards. Their former home high in the trees. The adventure into a mysterious world beyond the forest to save one of their own. He did not remember music or the magnificent house and its owner therein or riding in an elevator to meet the Enchanter of Dreams. He did not remember that he wasn't unique, that there were more like him, and that his creator—his *God*—watched over him, all while slipping between lifetimes, Gio one moment, Dad the next.

And it meant he did not remember Victor.

That night, when sleep was elusive, Vic told his father, "I've never been more human."

"Why?" Dad asked.

"Because I breathe, but I can't catch my breath."

Nurse Ratched and Rambo and Dad were there, and they lifted Victor up when he was too tired to stand on his own, the HARP machine sometimes hostile, sometimes not speaking for days on end. Weeks passed, and Victor persisted, searching for that crackling spark of recognition, a sign, *anything* to show that all was not lost.

And it was there, in the smallest of places.

Nurse Ratched played him music, jazz, Miles Davis, and all kinds of blues. When he threatened her, he did not stutter.

Rambo showed him *Top Hat,* telling him that Jerry and Dale would dance cheek to cheek. Two minutes in HARP 217 said, "When will they get to the disguise?"

On a summer day, Dad led HARP 217 into the forest. They were gone from early morning until dusk. When they returned, Dad said, "Hello. My designation is—" He slapped his hand against his chest. Then, "Victor, I would like to introduce you to a friend of mine."

HARP 217 stepped forward stiffly, eyes only for Vic. "I . . ." He stopped, frowned, then tried again. "I d-do n-not want to b-be called HARP," he said, voice oddly formal, as if he'd been practicing. "Gio told me I h-have a choice. That I c-could pick my own designation." He scowled. "My own n-*name*."

"That's right," Dad said. "You can. Why don't you tell him what you've decided?"

"H-hap," he said, and Victor felt his heart stutter in his chest. "I a-am H-hap."

"Why?" Dad asked. "Why do you want to be Hap?"

Hap said, "In my head. Words. Whispers."

"And what do they whisper?"

"Victor," Hap said. "Nurse Ratched. Rambo." And: "Hysterically Angry Puppet."

Three words not uttered since they'd returned from the City of Electric Dreams.

"Do you know me?" Vic asked.

Hap said "no" and "yes" and "You are human, you have human blood and human thoughts" and "I dreamed. I dreamed you kissed me in a room of screens and butterfly wings. You're a ghost in my head. I want to know why. I want to know *you*."

With a bittersweet ache in his heart, Vic said, "Hap. It's a good name. I like it. Fits you."

Though it was faint, Hap smiled.

On a crisp fall day, the leaves aflame in autumnal hues, a human walked through an old and lonely forest, a machine at his side. They did not speak much, letting the sounds of the woods wash over them: the wind through the branches, the animals scurrying through the underbrush, the birds calling, calling as they flew overhead.

Quiet this, a solitary moment in an imperfect world where existence did not need to be proven or earned. It just was, and here, in this place, that counted for something. Perhaps everything.

One of the figures—the so-called last of the humans—pointed and said, "Look."

Off to their right, swirling in a thin ray of sunlight filtering in through the canopy, a kaleidoscope of butterflies—at least a dozen, monarchs all—dancing among the trees, a slow, silent tornado.

And then the machine spoke. "B-butterfly wings are d-delicate. Touching one might c-cause the colors to fade, l-leaving the butterfly open to predators. It will not k-kill it immediately, but you are sentencing it to d-death regardless."

"Yes," came the reply. "Yes. That's . . . that's what Nurse Ratched said when . . ." Memory, ever-present, a reminder of what was and what could be, if only one was brave enough to reach for it.

"Vic?"

He looked over at his friend beside him.

Hap kissed him tentatively, sweetly. A single point of contact, and he tasted of metal.

"What was that for?" Vic asked after he pulled away, touching his lips in wonder.

"I w-wanted to," Hap said simply. He looked back at the kaleidoscope and smiled. "Nice. P-pretty. I l-like them."

"I know," Vic said as he took Hap's hand in his. "You could . . . you can do that again. If you want."

Hap rolled his eyes. "Oh, c-can I? G-good to know." But then he kissed the side of Vic's head, lingering.

Be it man or machine, Victor thought, to love something meant loving the ghost inside, to be haunted by it. Humanity—that nebulous concept he didn't always understand—had lived and died by its creations. Perhaps Victor would too, one day, a final lesson in what it meant to exist.

But that day was not today.

As the butterflies danced, a human and a machine looked on, their hearts beating as one.

ACKNOWLEDGMENTS

Imagination is weird. This story exists for one simple reason: I bought a Roomba vacuum cleaner. I thought it a funny little machine, made more so when I put oversized googly eyes on it. Once that was done, I stood up and put my hands on my hips, and as that robot started to move and beep, an entire *world* exploded in my head. I've never had an experience quite like it. These fully formed characters were just waiting for me to see what I could do with them.

That being said, the time I spent with Hap and Vic and Rambo and Nurse Ratched wasn't easy. I changed more of this book in edits than any other I've worked on, and it took a lot out of me to do. There are . . . reasons for the changes I made, and while I did not agree with some of them, works of creativity don't exist in a vacuum (natch), and it's become abundantly clear that I need to respect that.

Thanks to my agent, Deidre Knight, for championing this book as it was. Your faith in this story was and is wonderful, and I greatly appreciate it. And thanks to everyone else at The Knight Agency for wanting to see me succeed.

My editor, Ali Fisher, helped to shape the book into something readable. With her guidance, I rewrote the entire epilogue, and the book is all the better for it. Thanks, Ali.

Dianna Vega is her editorial assistant who handles all the little details that most people don't know exist. Thanks, Dianna.

Thank you to the sensitivity readers: Catherine Liao and Kim Vanderhorst. You both were invaluable. I wish this could have been the story we talked about, but apparently, the world isn't quite ready for such a book.

Katie Klimowicz did the jacket design, and created a title font specific for this book! I love how it turned out. Thanks, Katie. And to Chris Sickels at Red Nose Studio, who created the cover art itself. I've worked with Chris across four books now, and I hope that he will do every single cover I have from now on. He's that good at what he does.

Saraciea Fennell is my publicist, and is one of the hardest working people I've ever had the pleasure of meeting. I am of the mind that everything would fall apart without her, and since that's bad, I'm happy she's here. Thanks, Saraciea.

Rebecca Yeager handles marketing. All the little extras you see? Pins, artwork, graphics, the like? That's because of Rebecca, and she somehow makes it look easy. Thanks, Rebecca.

Sara Thwaite handled the copy edits. The managing editor is Rafal Gibek. Production editor is Melanie Sanders. Production manager is Steven Bucsok. Editorial director is William Hinton. Devi Pillai is president—and one of the funniest people I've ever met.

My beta readers: Lynn, Amy, and Mia. Without the three of you, my books would be disasters, and I am so appreciative of each of you and the work you put in to make my stories the best they can be. Thank you for being on my team, and for being my friends.

Last—but certainly not least—to you, the reader. Humanity is awful, angry, and violent. But we are also magical and musical. We dance. We sing. We create. We live and laugh and rage and cry and despair and hope. We are a bundle of contradictions without rhyme or reason. And there is no one like us in all the universe.

Don't you think we should make the most of it?

TJ Klune
November 8, 2022

TJ Klune is the *New York Times* and *USA Today* bestselling, Lambda Literary Award-winning author of *Under the Whispering Door*, *The House in the Cerulean Sea*, *The Extraordinaries*, *Wolfsong* and more. Being queer himself, TJ believes it's important – now more than ever – to have accurate, positive, queer representation in stories.